New Arcadia: Stage One

Printed in the United States of America

ISBN: 978-0-578-84612-5

New Arcadia: Stage One

Eric Jason Martin

Table of Contents

Prologue

From the Journal of Lucas Dekker
Monday, April 23rd

We have finally found our man.

His name is John Chambers, and he is a stubborn fool.

That is to say, he's perfect.

Mr. Chambers is the most bullheaded, tunnel-visioned player I have ever seen. To use the words of the old reality television programs, "He is not here to make friends." No, he pursues his singular goals, regardless of the cost.

In this way, at least, he is a man after my own heart.

However, he is isolated to a fault, refusing to engage with any other players at all. And this stubbornness leads to a serious lack of perspective, a reliance on tactics with almost no strategy. He is completely capable of socializing with others, and he is perfectly able to see the bigger picture; however, in every case, he simply refuses to do so.

Which makes him the perfect candidate to be our very first beta tester for our new game, codenamed Project X.

Although he does not know it yet.

I can say all this with confidence, because Project X has officially passed its internal corporate review today. Just barely, I must admit, but we passed, nonetheless. Our game world has been cleared to receive beta test subjects, effective immediately.

By end of day tomorrow, the chambers will be ready to receive new recruits. We will scale up quickly over the next two weeks to 20% capacity of the test server onsite, with more milestones to follow in the weeks ahead.

The board is far from convinced that Project X is the right path forward for our customer-citizens, but at least now we have a chance to prove ourselves. We can finally onboard real players to test the game mechanics, to gain critical data on how effective this game world truly is in bringing groups together.

John Chambers, our prime beta candidate, will understand our game mechanics intuitively. He will remember the time and setting with no small degree of nostalgia. And his considerable emotional and psychological traumas are the very ones we must work to solve on a societal level.

Tonight is his last night in our other, public-facing game. I still cannot believe how successful this stupid maritime trifle has been in attracting players, in spite of its obvious flaws. Still, the large player base makes it all the better to pick and choose the very best beta testers for Project X.

Our algorithms identified this player's actions as worthy of review two weeks ago. Last week, our team began monitoring his play via video feed, and I myself have been watching him each night for the last few days.

I am shocked to say that this man is on track to actually defeat our endgame as a solo player. He is accomplishing this all within an impossibly-tight timeframe and without any cooperative assistance, and indeed he just might succeed.

We will see how he performs tonight. Then, tomorrow, we will let him rest while we prepare his chamber in the laboratory.

I must admit, I can scarcely believe that this moment is finally here. All we have been working toward, day and night, for these last three years... At long last, all of this considerable toil and hardship is about to pay off, in a most spectacular way.

This is the critical moment. There is so much to do and so precious little time. With so much at stake, I must not lose sight of the main vision, of our one overarching goal.

I know that Project X is the best opportunity we have to bring our people together again. To literally save us all.

So, let the game begin.

Chapter 1

One White Whale

This is it, John.

I painfully rise from the floor of the hull, reaching my feet right as another towering wave crashes over my tiny boat. The wall of water slams into me and I stagger. Yet somehow I remain upright, standing strong and true.

This is your final chance.

The only emotion I have felt over these endless days is constant, grinding panic—not knowing if there will be another meal, another gulp of water, another sunrise.

I gaze down at my gaunt body, clothed only in tattered rags, the exposed skin lashed with jagged scars and bright bruises. These are the traumas of endless battles with man, with beasts, with nature itself.

I am all by myself.

Just like Celine Dion. You know, from the song. Not the *Titanic* one.

It is here, at the far ends of this cruel earth, that I will make my final stand. Even though, at this moment, I can barely stand at all. Blood pours freely from the new slash in my side, staining the floor and bench of my small rowboat a dark, slick red.

Uh... Eric Carmen. That was the guy who sang the song originally, *All by Myself*. Was that in the 70s? It was before I was born, that's for sure.

No matter. I plant my feet wide, holding both myself and my boat as steady as I can against the pounding current. I use all the strength I have left to hoist my harpoon above me. I hold the giant weapon there, even though my chest heaves with exertion, my legs wobble, my arms shake against their will. Just when I feel I cannot fight the vicious pull of gravity any longer, I spy him. My nemesis.

The white whale.

Water jets into the air. There she blows. Oh, that's where that phrase comes from. The massive creature then begins to crest the watery surface of the far horizon, perhaps 200 yards away.

Is that a league? Is he a league away from me?

Forget it, John, you don't know nautical terms. Even after a month of this business, you never bothered to find out. It doesn't matter, anyway.

I cast a glance to my right. Off in the distance, I spy another craft—the large whaling ship Essex. They have been a constant and most unwelcome presence on the sea with me, their crew relentlessly scouring these waters for the same giant prize. These last days have been a race against time, yes, but also a race against that elite team of whalers.

All I would have to do is send them a message right now. One cry of SOS from me, and the giant prow of their ship would turn swiftly around, swoop right in, and save the day. Without their help, I have almost no chance here.

But then they would steal my prize. And I cannot accept that.

Freakin' jerks.

My eyes focus back on the giant white whale. He is closer now, this much is sure. He softened me up and is coming in fast for the killing blow.

Wait, is it a he or a she? You don't say there *he* blows. Let's just keep it a *he* for now, it doesn't matter.

The creature's great upper lip briefly emerges above the waves and our eyes lock. Well, his eyes are pretty much on the sides of his head, but it *feels* like our eyes lock.

In that moment I know: it's me or him.

The world has not been witness to a naval battle like this since Kevin Costner faced off against Dennis Hopper in *Waterworld*. 1995, Director Kevin Reynolds.

The foul beast is now only thirty yards away, or however many leagues that is, or maybe it's knots. Again, it doesn't matter. Focus, John.

I track the whale's progress expertly, using all of my acquired skills to line him up in the sights of my harpoon. The practiced motions I've honed relentlessly on scores of lesser sea creatures are second nature to me now. I hold steady until the exact moment that I feel in my bones is right and true, and then I pull the trigger.

Nothing.

Dammit. My harpoon must have been damaged in the melee. Broken in the previous run when my nemesis took out a chunk of my boat, as well as a chunk of me.

No matter. Let him come, we can do this hand to hand. Or hand to fin. Whatever.

I switch my grip to hold the weapon aloft in both hands, ready to stab down. I'm shaking with exertion, every nerve and muscle is on edge as the giant beast looms closer, closer. Now he is so near that he envelops my entire field of vision, erupting slowly from the water, his top row of gigantic teeth cresting up over the wave.

This is the moment.

"CALL... ME... ISHMAEL!"

I scream these words as I stab my harpoon down with all my might.

Not caring that my actual avatar name is not 'Ishmael' but 'Qu33qu3g,' with 3s wherever the letter E should be. Ishmael was of course already taken long before I got here. Not caring that what I'm yelling is actually the very first line of the novel, and not the thing that you yell when you kill the whale at the very end. Not caring that, spoiler alert, Moby Dick doesn't actually get killed in the book at all.

But this isn't some book, this is my life. And in my life that I'm living right now, this infamous white whale is about to get very dead. And I'm going to yell out this famous line right now completely out of context just because it feels great. I can do what I want. It's what I paid for.

Well, what I paid for in time and not money. Because this life of mine is actually being lived inside the free trial period of *World of Moby*.

World of Moby is a virtual reality video game.

In my actual for-real reality, I'm not named Qu33qu3g but John Chambers. And it's not dusk, it's sometime after two in the morning, most likely. I'm perched not on the prow of my ship but rather at the foot of my bed at home, sitting ramrod straight, wearing a blackout VR helmet and headphones, squeezing a pair of haptic hand controllers in death grips, grunting and flailing about in the black and quiet night.

Yet here on this twilit ocean, I'm a bad-ass lone wolf sea captain, thinking and speaking exactly like a 19th century guy would do...mostly. I have a crew of zero, and only my starter rowboat to keep me afloat.

So yeah, I may have not taken on any teammates or vehicle upgrades as I've played. But I have worked so hard on my own, and leveled up my avatar so thoroughly over these last thirty days, that when the tip of my harpoon stabs down and pierces the literal wall of flash before me, the entire whale actually *explodes.*

The blast shoots out gigantic gouts of blubber and fins and teeth all around me. It's ridiculous and not at all realistic and it's also kind of gross, but it's *awesome.* My god, the beauty and the horror of it. And of course, the sweet, sweet profits.

I can make so many freaking artisanal candles from this haul.

All I have to do is scoop out the whale goo and craft it until my inventory is stuffed to the maximum. And then I can open a shop in the village and sell the whale blubber candles and become a Cape Cod millionaire and live in a remote cabin and never have to see another person again.

I'll never have to be back in the real world again, I'll just live in beautiful nature and spend my days staring out at the sea from my porch.

That's all I want. And now, I finally have it.

Long moments later, the bloody blubber rainstorm finally ends, the whale viscera piling up in a wide arc of red-and-white scum on the ocean surface. The lingering showers of gore continue to mist and swirl and dissipate, and as the whale showers clear, I can now see an incredible golden chest before me.

The box is beautiful, ornate and incredibly detailed. It's perched on the splintered bow of my little ship, waist-high and gleaming brilliantly in the final embers of daylight.

My arms collapse to my sides, my hands now empty. The broken harpoon literally disintegrated in the melee. I sink to my knees in bone-deep exhaustion and gratitude. This is the moment I've been playing for. I reach out to this giant chest before me, more than ready to unlock my hard-earned reward.

I press the button, and the moment I do, the world shifts before my eyes. A great screen is erected in front of me. After a moment, I realize it's a pop-up parchment window that appears prominently in my field of vision. Text begins hastily scrawling on it before my eyes, as though emerging from the nib of an invisible quill pen.

YOU HAVE REACHED THE END OF YOUR FREE TRIAL.

"What the—" I exclaim, in shock.

The parchment floats up and away from me, allowing me to see more of the game world again. The treasure chest is still before me, still glowing.

"No, no, no..." I mumble, feeling my way around the clasp, looking for a latch or something I can use.

I knew this moment would come, but I thought I had more time.

I press hard on the clasp a few times, then smack it with my palm, but it does not give at all. A new parchment appears in front of my eyes, blocking everything else, and a most unwelcome message scrawls onto the sheet.

SUBSCRIBE NOW FOR JUST 100 CREDITS A MONTH.

OR GET A PLATINUM WORLD OF MOBY MEMBERSHIP FOR 200 CREDITS.

I have a choice right now.

I could press the button and subscribe to *World of Moby*.

Or I could pay next month's rent.

I know exactly how this will play out. I've read enough news stories to know. If I choose the path of glory and decide to stay in this game, I will get exactly eight more days of said glory—until the first of the month. At midnight on the first, with no more credits in my account, the power to my house—my real house in the real world—will be cut, and I'll be promptly kicked out of the game world. At dawn the next day, people in hazmat suits will knock my front door down and kick me out of my house.

And with the virus still raging unchecked in every town that's still left, it's a pretty decent bet that I will be kicked out of my actual life in short order, too.

WOULD YOU LIKE TO PURCHASE CREDITS?

I sigh deeply, and the sigh turns into a long, angry scream of frustration. Finally, I press the *CANCEL* prompt floating in front of me.

ARE YOU SURE?

"No, I'm not sure! I want to play!" I yell, imploring the open seas, the gods above, the game designers.

"I WANT MY REWARD! GIVE ME MY WHALE FAT!!"

But I have no choice, no choice at all. Defeated and deflated, I punch the *YES* button, and all light fades away.

One moment, I'm looking at a deep red-and-blue dusk on the horizon, and the next, it's all blacker than midnight. I hear the crash of a giant wave, the splintering of wood, and then I feel myself lifted bodily on a great wind. I'm sailing now, but this time, it's through the air. I'm hurtling forward through the darkness, spinning end over end, sick with vertigo.

Suddenly I stop, hard, and I'm sprawled out over wet sand. I was flying fast through the sky but now I've just stopped. Ow.

I pat myself gingerly; I'm okay, no injuries. I still hear the waves, but they're more distant now, and the light fades back up slowly. It's no longer pitch-black, now bright stars and a crescent moon are faintly illuminating this new scene before me. I'm back on the sandy shore, deposited mere yards from the very point on the beach where I had started my final voyage.

And then, one more quill-penned prompt appears on a new parchment overlay before me.

THANK YOU FOR PLAYING WORLD OF MOBY.

COPYRIGHT 2023 NATTAGAME LLC.

The cruel message fades away into the twilight, and I fall asleep right there on the shore.

✪✪✪

I awaken to the soothing sound of those same ocean waves.

Actually, no, not the same. It's white noise; my virtual reality headset has switched to night mode. You're not supposed to sleep in these VR rigs, but if you do, they try to make it as comfortable as possible. Gentle noise, a subtle night light effect, even the hand controllers switch to a slow, steady pulse, a kind of gentle massage mode.

I'm soaked in sweat, sticking to the bedsheets beneath me. I had passed out above the covers, and I'm only wearing a pair of shorts, but it's still sweltering in here.

I shake off the attached hand controllers, wiping my palms on the bedsheets, then wiggle out of my VR helmet, leaving the pieces all on the bed where I lay. God, it's bright in here. I squint so that my eyes adjust to the sudden light, and slowly the real world comes back into focus.

It's morning in America, or whatever they call this place now. The Federation of Western States. Whatever.

I reach out blindly, and after a few tries, I successfully grab my computer tablet off my nightstand and perch it upright on my chest before me. This is my one electronic device for work, home management, and personal use. Not that I have a personal life, but if I did, I could theoretically employ it for personal use. I swipe broadly across the touchscreen surface, opening the home screen, and I start to read it. It's still piercingly bright, so I have to squint at it through one eye. Eventually, I can make out the following:

8:07 AM, WEDNESDAY, APRIL 12TH

PROPERTY OF CHUM, INCORPORATED

"I don't have much time," I say out loud, my voice cracking and tentative from the dryness in my throat.

I have to log in for work at 8:30am, sharp. I can tell I have a serious VR hangover, so I'm going to be struggling all morning, at least. I take a long drink of water from the glass on the nightstand. Good lord, I'm thirsty.

"Ah... Man, I've got to take a shower," I say in a normal and more hydrated voice. Then I swipe over to the home app on the tablet screen.

CURRENT OUTSIDE TEMPERATURE: 104 DEGREES

CURRENT INSIDE TEMPERATURE: 95 DEGREES

Oh. That explains why I still feel like I'm on the open ocean, only it's an ocean of my own sweat this time. It's an absolute sauna in here. And because the virus is airborne now, opening the windows to get a nice breeze is not a possibility. These days, somebody thirty feet away could kill you; it's that transmissible now.

People thought the first virus was bad—and it

was—but then it figured out a way to get a lot worse. The mutation happened in Kazakhstan or Uzbekistan or one of those 'stans, and it made its way around the world real quick.

This time, lockdown wasn't enough. This new virus emptied all the cities, spreading the survivors out to the hinterlands. Out here in the desert, they keep us sheltered, clothed, and fed. But there are others, tribes of rebels who still survive out there on their own, and they could all be carriers. So our windows and doors all stay shut. Nobody goes in; nobody goes out.

I press my tablet screen to bring the temperature down in here. It starts to drop fast, past 93 degrees, 90 degrees. It stops suddenly at 88 degrees, and then it won't let me go any further. I frown, thinking it's got to be an error, so I press down harder. Nothing. After a few more presses, a new prompt appears.

INSUFFICIENT CREDITS

Good god, I don't get new credits until the first of the month. Is this how I'll have to live for the next week? And it's only April, how much worse is it going to get this summer?

Then, I get some good news, for a change.

YOUR SUPPLIES ARE BEING DELIVERED TODAY

NORTH FONTANA - HOME DELIVERY

ESTIMATED TIME OF ARRIVAL: 4 MINUTES

Excellent, this week's shipment is arriving just in time. I honestly forgot when it was supposed to be coming. I've kind of been spending a lot of time in VR lately. Here in the real world, I have no ReadyMeals left, and only a couple of ChumBars.

Next, I swipe over to my personal email. I check it out of habit, even though I almost never get anything. I certainly never write anyone, haven't for years now. But this time, I do have a message in my inbox. It's from my employer.

SUBJECT: HAPPY BIRTHDAY FROM CHUM!

Oh my god, I forgot.

In permanent quarantine like this, one day feels like the next. And it doesn't help that for the last month, I've spent every minute I'm not working, eating, or sleeping, grinding away in *World of Moby*.

I'm forty years old today.

"Hello, John Chambers:

Your partners at Chum want to wish you a very happy birthday!

You were born in 1983, a totally tubular year! Americans were watching Flashdance and WarGames, listening to Men at Work and Bonnie Tyler, and playing games like Punch-Out and Elevator Action in the arcade!"

What do I care? I mean, those are all great pop culture references, but I found about them years later. What does anybody remember from when they were none years old? I have absolutely zero nostalgia for my own birth. And why rub it in that we all used to be Americans? Now I'm just sad.

The misguided missive continues:

"We know that times in 2023 are challenging, but we want you to know that Chum cares. Look for a special

cupcake treat in your next Personal Supply Shipment!"

The moment my eyes scan over the final word, digital confetti pops and floats down the screen, and the sound of party favors goes off, which I immediately mute. Okay, fine. I will look for a special cupcake treat, thank you very much. Thanks for the stupid email.

With a great effort, I heave myself off the bed, wincing as my feet hit the ground, getting a sharp pain in my right lower back. Now I'm feeling every minute of my forty years on this planet. That's what you get for sleeping in VR again.

"Ow! You're a middle-aged man now, John, you can't do that stuff anymore," I chide myself. I pretty much talk to myself all the time. Who else am I going to talk to?

I limp over to the small bedroom window and squint through the blinds to greet the morning. It's an obscenely bright and cloudless day here in the new company town of North Fontana. We're about fifty miles east of Los Angeles, past the edge of the far suburbs, a neighborhood half-full of frightened worker bees cooped up in the unforgiving desert. I have never seen my neighbors but I assume they must be there, locked up in their homes, just like me.

When it all went down three years ago, when the Relocation happened, this is where I was assigned: a partially-built residential development on the far edge of civilization. In the chaotic rush out of the virus-ravaged cities, they had to put us wherever they could.

Thankfully, this house was pretty much finished when they put me in it. Other homes on the street are in a similar state to mine, while others are just wood frames that are rotting away. There are garages but they're all sealed up tight, and there are no cars on the street, only a couple of now-heavily-rusted abandoned construction vehicles at the end of the block.

Nobody comes in or out of their little home quarantine situations. There's only a small door-within-a-door on the bottom of each front entrance, like you would have for a pet, but it's for drone deliveries only.

Which reminds me. I automatically gaze up toward the sky. Traffic is already busy, at least a dozen drones are buzzing to and fro in their invisible shipping lanes overhead. Some are carrying in their payloads of supplies, others are heading back empty, returning to their home base about fifteen miles to the north.

There are no stores, no restaurants here. Everything we need to survive comes in a remotely-delivered package every seven days from one of a system of warehouses spread across the old United States. Across most of the continent now, really. Lots of people were wiped out, but there are still plenty of us left on this planet. That's a whole lot of mouths to feed, and Chum was the only corporation that figured out how to do it here. Yay us.

My eyes are drawn to a sudden flash in the sky, followed a second later by an echoing crack. Moments later, I hear a corresponding crash. It sounds like it's just outside of town. The houses across the street are blocking my view, but I know who's responsible even before I hear the drone hit the ground.

The Scummers. Desert dwellers, living off the grid, taking down our supplies with guns or bolos or even boomerangs to scrounge out a living. They're not just here in the West, bands of them survive like parasites everywhere that Chum has a delivery center. Which means that they're all over the continent. I've never actually seen one of them, but the news reports say they're usually covered from head to toe in rags, at least out here in the desert.

I have a sinking feeling I know where that particular drone was heading. I glance down at my tablet.

NORTH FONTANA - HOME DELIVERY

ESTIMATED TIME OF ARRIVAL: RECALCULATING

The word RECALCULATING is blinking. I watch it intently. After a full minute, the word disappears entirely, and new text appears.

ESTIMATED TIME OF ARRIVAL: UNKNOWN

Yeah. The Scummers just nabbed all my food for the week. And my birthday cupcake.

"Great. Just great," I exhale.

✪✪✪

At 6:00pm, I finish my very long, very hungry day of work, sitting at my kitchen table.

I'm a drone coordinator for the Chum Corporation, which means my job is to prevent the very thing that just happened to me. I'm not a drone *pilot*, mind you, I'm a drone *coordinator*, which means I'm basically playing a glorified arcade puzzle game all day, every day.

I have a bird's eye view on my tablet of the new company town of West Diamond Bar, about thirty miles east of here, closer to the old city of Los Angeles. I spend every workday watching all the drones go back and forth across the grid, trying to stop them from being shot down

New Arcadia: Stage One

by Scummers.

Sometimes, I succeed. Today, I wasn't so great.

Finally, I log out of my tablet, rubbing my eyes, and at that moment, I hear the familiar whirr of a quadcopter outside. Less than a minute later, a most welcome cardboard box slides in through my little dog door, where I'm waiting to pounce like a Pavlov experiment, and I do. First, I immediately wipe the package down with sanitizer. I'm supposed to wait ten minutes to let the sanitizer sink in fully to all the fibers or whatever, but forget it, I'm too damn hungry.

I rip the box open like a madman, and the meager contents spill out onto the ground. These fourteen plastic-wrapped ReadyMeals and ten ChumBars (Assorted Flavors) are supposed to last me for the next seven days. There's also a travel size tube of toothpaste, not that I'm traveling anymore, and two rolls of toilet paper. I riffle through the slim pickings, looking for the least-awful dinner option.

After several swipes through the slim pile, it quickly becomes clear that there is no special birthday cupcake treat in this replacement shipment.

It stings. Very badly. I don't think I realized how much I wanted a stupid cupcake.

My eyes are...irritated somehow. I feel choked up, not sure what that's all about. Curious sensations. I guess it's been a very long time since I've felt anything other than dull frustration in the real world.

Then a song appears in my head. Distant memories of restaurants, other people, going through their dumb old rituals.

I sing out softly, "Thiiiiis is your birthday song, it isn't very long...." The words echo hollowly off the walls of my sad little house.

What am I supposed to play now?

What am I supposed to *do* now?

✪ ✪ ✪

The 'Salisbury steak' dinner was not completely inedible. So that's nice.

I guess I didn't realize quite how tired I've really been all day. I don't even make it up the stairs to my bedroom after I finish eating. Instead, I just sort of slide down from my chair, spill onto the kitchen floor, and lay on the tiles.

Ah, that's better. It's a little cooler here on the ground.

"So this is how I celebrate my fortieth birthday," I tell the ceiling above me, arms crossed over my chest, fingers laced over my heart. "Not sailing the high seas in search of adventure, slaying monsters and amassing great treasures. There's no candle shop, and no cabin by the sea."

My stomach grumbles, and I clutch it to try to squeeze it into silence, but it doesn't work. Guess I'm still hungry. Nothing to be done about it now.

"No, instead I'm locked up here in my half-finished house, sweltering in the desert, all alone, entering the fourth year of a dire pandemic with no end in sight, passing out on my kitchen floor at 6:57pm."

And with that, I fall dead asleep right there on the

linoleum. And I don't wake up until the morning.

That's when all hell breaks loose.

Chapter 2

Wakey Wakey

The first thing I hear is the screaming of a dying planet. Or it sure as hell sounds like it.

The moment I register the noise, my eyes automatically pop open, and then immediately squeeze shut again. It's way too bright in here. The scream continues, long past the point of any human's breath. Oh my god.

After a few moments of pure panic and dread, my brain begins to understand that the sound is an alarm.

My alarm is blaring. I am alarmed.

I open my eyes again, certain now that my house is on fire.

It's still too bright, but I force myself to look anyway. I can make out an ugly popcorn pattern in front of me. I look down a little bit, and I see a wooden cabinet.

That's right. I'm still in the kitchen, lying on the

ground, looking up at my stupid ceiling. I pull my head up to look down at my body before me on the floor, grunting with the effort.

The good news: I'm still in one piece.

The bad news: There's a sudden pounding noise now, terrifying and immediate. It's so loud I can hear it over the alarm. I can feel it in my body too. My heart skips a beat.

All of this feels like it's stretching into eternity, but it's actually been maybe...five seconds? Maybe less? The pounding stops, then I hear a muffled but distinct voice.

"CHUM PERSONNEL. OPEN UP, PLEASE."

Wait a minute. That's not my fire alarm.

It's the doorbell. I have visitors.

When Chum moved its workers here to North Fontana, it never finished building the houses, but it sure figured out how to keep you inside them. And they *really* wanted to let you know when someone was at your front door.

But that's not right—it can't be Chum personnel, they always let you know in advance when they're coming. No, it's got to be the Scummers, posing as Chum personnel. I know this scam; I've read stories about this on ChumNews. They come inside and take all your stuff and then you get the virus and die.

I crunch myself up into a sitting position so I can see what's on the kitchen table in front of me. Perched on the edge is my tablet. The screen is on, and the time is 7:00am on the dot. I squint a bit more and can read a large glowing notification underneath.

CHUM PERSONNEL AT FRONT DOOR.

Huh, it really is them. Well, that's a relief. Sort of.

I have to say, all things considered, this day has been off to a pretty rough start. In the space of about ten seconds, I went from thinking I was going to be burned to death by a house fire, then raided and killed by a Scummer murder party masquerading as my corporate overlords, but now it's a comparative relief to know that I'm merely being raided by my corporate overlords at dawn for entirely unknown reasons.

"CHUM PERSONNEL. OPEN UP PLEASE," the unknown representative of my corporate overlord bellows, starting to pound on the door again.

"Just a minute!" I scream, even louder than I intended to, and scramble unsteadily to my feet. I have no idea if they hear me, but I hope they do. I need to buy some time, any time I can.

I search for my old cloth facemask on the counter. It's not there.

Where did I put it? I guess I moved it months ago, I haven't used it in so long. I start opening kitchen drawers and riffling through them, searching for the damn thing. Silverware, spatulas, placemats, twenty-four D batteries that I'll never use, and why do I have all these matches? And no mask, dammit!

The pounding on my front door stops again, and then, blessedly, my doorbell alarm finally stops.

I stop, too. I slowly pull my hands out of the open drawer before me and slide them down to my sides. I don't move. I barely breathe. Maybe they'll go away if they can't hear me. Maybe they didn't hear me scream over the pounding on the door. Maybe I'm not home... Maybe I've gone out to run some errands? Yeah, that's the ticket.

I become as still as I can, a living statue, vigilant, every nerve on edge. Listening for any sound, although I don't know how I could hear anything over the hammering of my heart.

It turns out that I can hear the pounding on the door just fine when it restarts a moment later, thank you very much. I jump and wince at the sudden noise, backing up against the kitchen counter, squeezing my eyes shut.

"CHUM PERSONNEL, OPEN THE FRONT DOOR. YOU HAVE THIRTY SECONDS TO COMPLY," the muffled voice yells from behind the door.

Left unsaid is the rest of the sentence, *or we will break down your little door and let ourselves in, and we won't be particularly happy about having to do that, or maybe we will be because it will make what we have to do next a lot more fun, which is murdering. So much murdering of you to death by us. All of the murdering.*

Stop it, John, you're thinking crazy thoughts.

The screen on my tablet flashes, catching my eye. It doesn't switch over to a video feed of the front door, so I can't see who's out there, but it does show a new message.

Chum Personnel Requiring Entry. You have been authorized to open your front door for official company representatives. Please put on your protective facemask. Open your door, step back six feet, and await further instructions.

Dammit.

I'm yanking drawers out of the kitchen cabinet now, turning them over and spilling the contents out onto the ground, looking for that mask. Nothing. Where did I put the mask? Come on, John, you have guests! You can't be a disease vector for a deadly airborne pathogen now! You're being a very bad host!

Finally, panting, exhausted, stressed to my breaking point, standing in the middle of a gigantic pile of kitchen utensils and discarded drawers where twenty seconds before I was soundly sleeping off a heat-exhaustion-and-virtual-reality-game-related hangover, my eyes settle at a spot on the kitchen counter.

I see a roll of paper towels, still standing upright because I didn't bother to put the spool into the little holder screwed in under the top cabinet because I'm a dude and I live alone.

It gives me a crazy idea, which is good because I don't have any other ideas right now. I'll have to make it work.

✪✪✪

It's bright outside. So bright.

I'm standing at my now-open front door facing blinding white light, and a shadowy dark blob before me quickly resolves into two separate silhouettes—human figures.

I've got half a roll of paper towels wrapped around the lower half of my face like a bandanna, and I'm holding it closed with my right hand. I made it to the door just in time. I'm very proud of myself.

"BACK UP, PLEASE," the figure on the right says. The door is open, but the voice is still muffled yet weirdly amplified. I can't see his face at all, but it sounds like a man's voice.

These guys must be wearing protective hazmat suits. Like in *E.T. The Extra-Terrestrial*, 1982, Director Steven Spielberg.

Startled, I instantly comply, moving back while facing them, moving fast, so fast I forget there's a couch behind me and I flip over it backward, somehow landing in a sitting position facing the other way. Good enough.

I feel them come into the room behind me, and now they're standing in front of me, only a few feet away, staring down at me on the couch.

Wow, it really has been a while since I've seen other people. I have just definitively decided that I don't like them. People, I mean. I don't like people.

"STAY SEATED, PLEASE," the amplified voice calls out.

I can't see their faces at all. Opaque visors cover their eyes, and big respirators cover their noses and mouths, all connected to the hazmat suits. Their voices must be amplified through the respirators so that I can hear them. I get the sudden wild thought that they sound like when I was a kid and would talk into a spinning room fan, trying to make myself sound like a Transformer robot.

One of the hazmat bros, the taller one, holds up a thermometer to my head. The other little dude holds up what looks like a smartphone. I see both of their screens light up bright green.

For a moment, the house is eerily quiet, except for my own fast, panicked breathing through the paper towels, and their steady robots-in-disguise respirating from their hazmat suits.

Then, Tallboy with the thermometer says, "CLEAR."

"YOU MAY REMOVE YOUR MASK," the little guy, let's call him Short Round, says as he pockets his smartphone device.

"Oh, this old thing?" I say, pointing to my mummified face, hoping to break the ice, but I can barely read their faces through the reflections on their shiny face shields. I can't tell if they think I'm hilarious and engaging. Probably not.

I carefully unroll the paper towels from around my face and fold it all up gently next to me on the couch. Can't let it go to waste, I'll probably re-roll it after they leave. I'll probably survive to use it again.

The moment I set the paper towels down and look back up at them, Tallboy comes forward with a briefcase in his other hand. I flinch, then realize he's setting it on the coffee table in front of me. He opens it, and I see that the briefcase is itself a laptop. The screen is blank, and it's pointed towards me on the couch.

Tallboy backs up, and he and Short Round now stand behind the laptop, forming a perfect triangle. From farther away, and with my eyes now adjusted to the light, I can more clearly see their bright yellow hazmat suits, covering them from head to toe.

"Hey, uh, the movie *Outbreak* called, guys. They said you're late to set."

They don't say anything. I swear I used to be funny at some point. I might be a little rusty. My references might be a little out of date.

I keep talking. "Yeah, director Wolfgang Petersen was on the line, said something about Dustin Hoffman running through the jungle after a monkey. He seemed upset that you weren't there, back in 1995. If you, uh... catch my drift..." I trail off. If they catch my drift, they do not indicate it with words or behavior.

I'm joking with them, but it's only because I'm completely terrified.

"Have a seat, gents, you're making me nervous. Can I get you something to drink?" I offer, starting to rise from the couch.

"STAY SEATED," Tallboy bellows.

"Okay, okay." I raise my hands in surrender as I sit back down as fast as I can.

Careful, John. One false move and these guys could finish you.

Short Round presses the screen of his smartphone, and then the screen on the laptop in front of me powers on, revealing a ChumNet logo. After a moment, the logo dissolves into a video feed.

Online video has gotten a little better over the last few years, but not by a lot. It still skips and slows down and pixelates. This is a perfect connection, though. It's a crystal-clear image, 4K—hell, maybe 8K—and no compression that I can see at all.

A man's face is framed dead center in the screen. The first thing I notice about him is his pure white, shoulder-length hair. Then his relatively youthful features. He's a handsome guy, clean-shaven, well-dressed—at least from the chest up, for all I know he's not wearing any pants. Piercing blue eyes. Looking at me. Clearly, he's looking at me.

"John Chambers," he says by way of greeting.

"That's me," I confirm. "Can you hear me?"

"I can hear you just fine. Thank you for allowing me inside."

"You're very welcome. I, uh... I did not get the impression that I had a choice."

"There's always a choice. My name is Luke Dekker."

"It's a pleasure, Mr. Dekker," I say evenly.

"Please, just Dekker."

"Not Luke?" I clarify.

He frowns. I decide to try pushing him a little further, just to see what happens. This could backfire spectacularly. Only one way to find out.

"Also, is Dekker spelled with a CK or with two Ks? I'm a visual learner," I inquire innocently.

A slight pause, then he confirms, "It's Dekker with two Ks."

"Ah, much cooler that way. Dekker's a cool name." And I mean it. That's probably the reason I haven't gotten vaporized yet: my sincerity. "It's been a long time since I've had guests, Dekker. Can I get you something to drink?"

He laughs, and then sips from a very fancy thermos sitting offscreen. He's being a very good sport. So far.

"I'm good, thank you, Mr. Chambers," he says.

"Please, call me John. So..." I continue, unsure of what to say next. It feels so strange to actually be talking to somebody other than myself. "To what do I owe the pleasure? I should note I'm due to start work in just a few minutes, so we'll have to make this quick," I explain.

"I have good news, John. You have the day off." Dekker pauses and waits for my reaction. I don't want to give him the pleasure.

"Oh, that's an interesting turn of events," I say, forcing my voice to sound as nonchalant as possible. "What will I do today? Maybe I'll start a new *World of Moby* trial account."

"I have another game in mind. More than a game, really. It's an opportunity. I'd like to talk to you in more detail about it."

Wait, more than a game? "I'm listening," I tell him.

"This is something you should hear in person."

"Well, come on over, Dekker. It turns out I have the day off. What time is good for you?"

"Right now. And these men will escort you to me," he says, indicating both sides behind him by turning his head, as though he were actually in the room with me and looking at my guests.

I peer up at the two hazmat bros looming past the table. "Oh, it's like that?" I ask.

"It's like that, John," I hear Dekker say.

I shift my gaze from the bros back down to his face on the computer screen. "You guys went to all this trouble just to invite me over to your...house? Office building? Why?"

No answer from Dekker.

I look back up to the men. "Anything from you guys? Tallboy? Short Round? Jump in any time." The men don't say anything. They don't even move. I figured as much, but still, worth a try. "Those are my names for you guys," I clarify, extraneously. "On account of your heights, which are the only distinguishing features I can make out. At this point in time."

"This is something you should hear in person," Dekker repeats.

I shift in my seat. "Is it...you know, dangerous?"

I know full well it's dangerous as hell out there.

Dekker smiles a smile that doesn't reach his eyes. "I know what you're thinking, John. You're worried about the virus catching up with you outside of your door. I am happy to inform you that we follow very strict protocols, and that I can guarantee your safety in the real world."

What does that even mean? What is he offering? I really, really don't want to leave this house, but I must admit this is an intriguing sales pitch. I mean, they really went all out.

I slowly exhale and take another gander at the hazmat bros facing me. Then I make a careful examination of Dekker's unlined face, with his visibly clenching jawline. I feel like I'm wasting these people's time by drawing this out. I decide that I'm alright with that.

I take a deep breath in, then exhale again. "Okay," I finally acquiesce.

The moment I accept, Tallboy immediately pulls out a square-shaped object, twice the size of a Rubik's Cube, from a side pouch on his hazmat suit. He then starts walking directly towards me.

"Ah! Whatwhatwhat?" I scream suddenly as he advances, recoiling and skittering up the couch into a protective ball, certain that I'm about to be probed or knocked out or something else that's awful.

Tallboy doesn't slow down. He comes right into my personal space. His face remains an unseen enigma behind his visor as he sets this new box down on the table, next to the laptop in front of me, and smoothly steps back into formation behind the coffee table. I slowly sink back down on the couch and unclench, staring at the item. It's blue, cardboard. It has a little red bow on top of it.

Suspicious, I gingerly pick up the box, put it to my ear, listen to it. Is it a bomb? There's no sound. I shake it—gently. I'm still alive. I open the box in a single savage rip and hurriedly dump its contents onto the table.

It's a frosted cupcake. Vacu-sealed for my safety. Rainbow sprinkles.

I pick it up and see the number "40" etched in brown dust in a sugary white coin on top.

I peer up over the cupcake in my hands to the laptop screen. Dekker is right there, smirking.

"Happy birthday, John. Please follow these men. I'll see you in a bit."

Chapter 3

The Offer

I'm terrified. But I'm here. In the back of the van.

We still haven't moved out of the driveway.

"This is a very good cupcake!" I call out, with a mouthful of said cupcake.

I'm very hungry. I guess I didn't realize how hungry I was. I mean, I didn't have breakfast yet, but even if I had, I'd still be hungry. Last night's sad little dinner just wasn't cutting it. And I'm sure waking up in a dead panic and thinking I was going to die screaming in flames followed by a home invasion probably, you know, burned some calories too.

Hence, I'm terrified. So I'm currently stress eating and trying to improve the mood with some light banter.

I swallow the bite and exclaim, "Mm! This is a bona fide treat."

No response from the hazmat bros up front. Tallboy

is in the driver's seat, fiddling with the touchscreen in the middle of the dashboard. He's been doing this for five minutes, like he's an airline pilot about to take off. Meanwhile, Short Round is sitting shotgun and fiddling with his smartphone.

"So, guys...when you do you think we're going to..."

"BUCKLE UP, PLEASE." Tallboy interrupts. Startled, I do. The moment I fumble the seatbelt on, we start to reverse. I feel a sick thrill in my stomach as we start moving.

We back up onto my street and start driving through the neighborhood. I haven't seen any of this in over three years, not since I first got transported here. Back then, I was a solo passenger in a new driverless car, and I was much more concerned about not dying than enjoying the scenery.

Not that I really missed anything, these houses all look the same. Well, except for the ones here on the periphery. Some of them are just bare wooden beams, unfinished, falling apart in the unforgiving desert sun. At least my house was mostly complete when they put me in it. Mostly. Only the best for the loyal Chum workers.

Then, I have an unsettling thought. I'm inside this van, but I'm outside of my house. Definitely outside the safety zone for the virus.

"Hey, guys, do I need a hazmat suit, too?"

Silence. My question sits there heavily for a moment, then I reply. "No? Okay, great. That is a relief."

We continue to head north, passing a sign that I've never seen before as we leave my subdivision. I read it to myself quietly, "Whispering Pines? I live in Whispering Pines? In all my time here, I have never once heard a pine whispering."

Now, we pass the border of North Fontana, and the wide residential road narrows to a two-lane highway. I peer over to my right through the far window, where the large freeway should be a couple of miles to the west. Only two cars are going by on the far horizon, the only way I know the road is still there.

But up in the sky above, it's rush hour. There's an absolute legion of flying drones, all going to and fro, dropping off supplies or heading back to pick up more. As a certified Chum drone coordinator, I know this world very well—at least from the point of view of my kitchen table, staring down at my tablet screen.

I watch their patterns for a while, alternating between the van's side window and its tinted sunroof, and realize the drones are pretty much all following the same path we are—due north. I turn my gaze down, and through the windshield up front, I can spy our likely destination.

We're heading to the warehouse.

The warehouse is officially called the Chum Distribution Center. It's a gigantic complex in the middle of nowhere. It's the staging ground for Chum's physical goods, where the great drone delivery fleets are based.

I've seen it rendered as an icon on my tablet screen every day for years, but I've never seen it in person. Now, it's straight ahead.

"We're going to the warehouse?" I call up to the front.

Silence. The only sounds are the hum of the tires on the road below us, and the roar of the air conditioning system. It's about one million degrees outside, but it feels nice and cool in here. I could get used to this.

"While I'm here, will I be doing my performance review in person?" I have my annual job review scheduled this week. Maybe I'll actually meet my boss in person today. Boy, I can't think of anything less exciting.

More silence. I look back out my window. We're now speeding through some rocky hills, going at least eighty miles-per-hour. I look up at the crest of a nearby hill and see...something. And then something on the next hill, too. A glint of light, a rustle of movement. A helmet, goggles.

We're being watched. By the Scummers.

The bane of our society, as well as the bane of my job. Always stealing supplies from Chum drones.

But also from the occasional Chum delivery van.

"Uh, guys, I think we've got Scummers on our left!" I yell up to the front.

No response. I peer out the far-right window. I spot more rags on outcrops on our other flank. The Scummers are blending in pretty effectively with their camouflage, but now that I know what I'm looking for, it's easier to see them. They've got to be all around us.

"Uh...and on our right!"

Not a peep from these stiffs up front. We're driving right into an ambush and these idiots aren't doing a thing.

"Hey. Guys. Should we be worried?" I say in a voice that quite clearly communicates that I'm very worried.

"NO," Short Round says, turning around slightly, his amplified voice bouncing around the van.

Success. They do remember how to speak. "Oh really? How do you know that?"

Tallboy now chimes in, throwing precisely one half-assed glance back at me. "WE'RE PICKING UP, NOT DROPPING OFF. THEY DON'T WANT YOU. THEY WANT DENTAL FLOSS AND FIG NEWTONS."

Well, I can't argue with that. It's nice not to be wanted. Just the way I like it.

Ten more minutes pass in silence, and then we're there. The warehouse has been looming larger and larger as we get closer, but now on the final approach, the scale of the complex grows from gigantic to unbelievable. It's ridiculously large, definitely its own zip code. Maybe its own county.

We stop in front of a large chain-link gate, and Tallboy flashes a badge at an empty kiosk to our left. The gate crawls open, we roll through, and then we're instantly surrounded by insanity.

It is true organized madness here. Trucks are zooming by, fleets of drones are taking off and landing from several launch pads connected to the main building. I can't believe we're not bumping into anything, even crawling forward at five miles an hour.

The warehouse building before us is only ten stories high, I'd guess, but it's got to stretch on for...two miles in either direction? Is that even possible? We're driving up to it now, and I can barely see the edges of this thing. It's just one giant wall before us, and it's crazy to think that behind this wall are every meal and every knick knack needed for every surviving citizen of the former Los Angeles metropolitan area.

We're inching toward what appears to be the main entrance to the warehouse. The opening is like a massive gap in reality itself, reaching almost to the top of the building and stretching out over maybe a football field in length. I don't know, I'm just guessing here. I can't make out much of what's inside the door, due to the glare on the windshield, but what I can see looks like mechanized chaos. Our van finally rolls to a stop a few yards from the warehouse entrance.

"EXIT THE VEHICLE, PLEASE," Tallboy commands.

I do, scrambling over to the van's sliding door, pulling and then yanking at the door handle, then realizing that the bros control it. Short Round hits a button on his armrest, and I spill out of the van's opening door, grunting as my feet hit the ground. I'm squinting and shielding my eyes from the desert sun, as I have no sunglasses. I do have jeans on, however, which is a real change of pace for me. This is the first time I'm wearing something other than sweatpants or shorts for a very long time.

I'm a little unsteady on my feet. It's loud and chaotic, and now I'm outside in the middle of all of it. The van door closes automatically behind me, and then the hazmat bros join me outside. Short Round motions to me with his yellow hazmat hand.

"FOLLOW US, PLEASE."

I comply, walking around the van to see a passenger tram waiting for us at the entrance. That's the best term for it. Four open air cars, nobody sitting inside them, and no driver up front. It looks like something you'd see in a theme park parking lot.

They walk me over to the third tram car, and the door slides open automatically as we approach. I get inside and sit down before they tell me to. They take the last car behind me, surely to keep an eye on me.

"Please keep your hands and arms inside the people-mover at all times!" I call out. A great joke, I think. Nobody cares.

The driverless tram starts gliding forward at a stately pace, and we enter the warehouse. Once we cross the threshold into the building, the roar of noise transitions from very loud to almost deafening.

My eyes finally adjust to the light, and then I'm blown away by the scale of this place all over again. Stacks of goods are piled four huge levels high, like Ikea times ten kajillion. I want to ask if they serve the little Swedish meatballs here, but I'm too stunned to say a word.

I feel so small. I close my eyes for a moment to calm myself, and to use my other senses, a trick I used to use in the before times. The environment is still overwhelming like this, but now I only have to deal with four senses, not five. I inhale deeply and decide that this place smells like they built a gas station inside a Bed Bath and Beyond.

I open my eyes again, and first I see buzzing drones, hundreds of them flying overhead, the familiar quad-copters pulling items off the shelves with their retractable cranes. There are bigger drones, too, ones I've never seen before. These massive vehicles are flying larger items and pallets down to the floor from the top shelves.

This tram makes me feel like I'm at Epcot Center and I'm on a dark ride exploring the wonders of future technology, with an emphasis on *dark*. This is awesome but also pretty terrifying. Sure, there's a machine world dystopia everywhere I look, but at least it sends me my toothpaste. Dental hygiene is very important.

I look down now at the ground level. It's a maelstrom of activity before us, like we're driving into the eye of a tornado. The whole floor is teeming with self-driving carts and bipedal robots, all moving at blazing speeds in insanely-choreographed dances. They all subtly break away from our tram's wake, as if they sense our presence and know to move away due to their programming. No human being could possibly have the reflexes to navigate this tangle.

And yet, some people are. I begin to see a few of them peppered in among the aisles; outnumbered by the robots, for sure, but definitely still a presence. The machines haven't taken over yet, not completely.

We pass a human pushing a cart. He's a young guy wearing gloves, goggles, and a mask. My eyes pass over to his payload—an overstuffed roller cart bulging with giant cardboard boxes. I notice the top box says, "Salisbury Steak," in quotes. I'm glad to see they don't think it's really food, either. As we pass, the young worker suddenly gets clipped by a bigger robot cart speeding by, and he falls right on his ass, hard.

"Whoa, are you okay?!" I yell automatically. I turn back to the hazmat bros in behind me. "Is he okay?"

They don't say anything. I don't know if he's okay. Probably, though. It didn't look too bad. Probably.

We continue farther into this wild tangle of massive activity, farther down the endless aisles. We turn a corner at the end of our aisle, and suddenly there's a building a hundred yards in front of us.

A building within a building.

Actually, there are several of them, a few smaller ones forming a single enclosed campus made of white concrete. Outside the main warehouse it would probably look pretty big, like a healthy-sized corporate center in the suburbs. But inside here, it's simply dwarfed by the massive beast it lives inside.

I can tell right away that that's where we're headed, and I'm not wrong.

Our tram pauses at the gate of this fortified complex-within-a-complex. The gate rolls open, and we drive inside.

We roll up to the front entrance of the main building. The structure is two stories high, windowless except for the main double-doors made of glass. The path is lined with large potted plants leading up to the front door, in an effort to bring in a touch of nature, I suppose.

The tram begins slowing as we reach the front door. I start to say, "Please remain seated until the vehicle comes to a full and complete..." and then trail off. Tough crowd, here.

We stop, and my little door slides open, so I exit. Tallboy and Short Round fall in behind me as I approach the main doors of the building. The doors slide open as I approach. I glance behind me, and the hazmat bros both nod in the affirmative, so I walk inside.

I enter an empty, gleaming, spanking-new corporate lobby. Not that it's used for spanking, as far as I can tell, it's probably just for waiting for your appointment. Blinding white walls and furniture. A front desk with nobody at it. Behind the desk, a sleek gray logo: "Nattagame LLC."

I stop, considering. Something gets tickled in the back of my mind. I know this name. Why?

Ohhhh, of course, that's the company that made *World of Moby*.

Hold on, Chum is behind *World of Moby*?

I turn back to the guys, "Hey, Chum owns Nattagame?"

Saying it out loud for the first time, I get the joke. How did I miss that? "Not a game." Immersive virtual interactive experiences and whatnot. Har har.

The bros say nothing, as expected, only nod toward the single glass door to the left of the front desk. It slides open as I approach.

I enter a large corporate conference room. It's more comfortable in here, this room has a more muted look with off-white walls, potted plants in each corner. There's a large squarish table in the center of the room with twelve chairs arranged around it, and more overflow chairs lining the four walls. At the corner diagonal from our entrance, there's another single sliding door. This one is opaque, and it must lead deeper into the complex.

«*Please place your head in the headrest and face the machine*," a robotic but pleasant voice suddenly says behind me.

I turn around and see a stand-alone med station right next to the door I just entered. It looks like a bathroom vending machine, but there's a head-sized opening in the middle of the box, with a dark pane of glass inside the hole. One last check to see if I have the virus.

I position myself in front of the machine, place my chin on the rest, and stare at a light green laser inside, like something you'd see at the eye doctor. Wow, remember going to the doctor? It's all just telehealth now. I hear a metallic beep, and I'm surrounded by a green halo all around my peripheral vision.

«*Scan complete. Thank you,*" the machine says, and I back away. I'm good. No virus.

I shake my head and hands to loosen them up. I was gripping pretty tight to the sides of that med station. I then walk further into the conference room, getting a bit of swagger back in my step, remembering in my bones what it's like to be a businessman doing business again.

Tallboy and Short Round hang back at the entrance. I sweep my gaze expansively over the conference room, run my finger along the table as I walk by, then stop when I notice a nice spread on the table. Bottles of water arranged in a big triangle. A basket full of granola bars.

"Can I have one of these?" I ask the bros behind me. "Okay, thanks," I say before they have a chance to not-reply, then I grab a bottle of water and one, two, oh hell why not three granola bars. I sit down there at the table and begin to munch.

Halfway into my third granola bar, the far door slides open, and Dekker enters the room.

He's medium-tall, probably a couple of inches taller than me, slender, and very focused. He moves like a shark. Thinking of that gives a whole new meaning to the word Chum. Not the friendly meaning, but the blood in the water kind of meaning. How stupid am I that I've been working for them for three years and never once thought of the more sinister definition of the word? You don't get to the top of your industry, practically *all* industries at this point, by being a nice buddy.

I stand up instinctively, feeling heat rise to my face. "Dekker! Hello, it's me, John. Should we shake hands or... bump elbows? I'm not sure how people greet each other anymore..."

But it's too late, he's already stalked in and sat down directly across from me at the large table. Smooth, John, way to make a first impression. Do you think he forgot what you look like?

I sit down, uncertain if I should be sitting down. I don't know what I'm supposed to do here.

"Thank you for coming here today," Dekker begins.

He's sitting about ten feet away, but he doesn't have to project much in this space. He's calm, relaxed. Meanwhile, I'm about to run out of here screaming. But I play it cool.

"Thanks for having me. It's much cooler in here than in my house," I say. "Both the temperature and, uh... in terms of...cool furniture. Like, this is a very nice table," I finish lamely. God, have I forgotten how to speak?

"Thank you, that's very kind," he says, then he opens a beige file folder he brought in with him. He begins reading from the top sheet of paper inside. "John Chambers, forty years of age, never married," he begins.

"Um, are you my boss now?" I ask.

He looks at me blankly for a moment, then laughs

in surprise. "Ah yes, I see. We both work for the Chum Corporation, this is true, but while you work as a drone coordinator in our shipping division, I am the vice president of master planning for our civic affairs division. It's an entirely separate reporting structure, although our team does interface with all the other divisions on integrative strategy."

It's my turn to look at him blankly. "I don't know what any of that means."

He smoothly changes gears. "I also have an additional role as President of Nattagame, a fully-owned subsidiary of Chum. As you can see by our facility here, we are part of the greater Chum family, but we are also our own self-contained operation."

"Well, it's an honor," I say in all sincerity. "It really is. I mean, I didn't know I would be meeting with the makers of my new favorite game."

His face registers a hint of confusion, and also distaste. "Oh, you mean *World of Moby*? That stupid piece of shovelware?"

Shovelware? I'm stunned by his reaction. I love that game. I feel heat rising to my cheeks. I spent every moment I could in that world for a long time, worked my fingers to the virtual bone.

"Uh... I kind of enjoyed it," is all I can manage.

"We assembled that game as quickly and cheaply as possible, you know. We found an IP that was in the public domain, and then we applied a simple cookie cutter design and rather lazy scripting, just enough to get it out the door. The dev team derisively called it 'DickWorld' internally until that became an HR issue, as you might imagine. It's a mindless credits-grab for an imprisoned and entertainment-starved customer base. I'm very surprised you got any satisfaction out of it at all besides the lizard brain rewards of checking boxes and gaining levels. But the project did accomplish two very important things for us."

I'm too shocked to say anything. He presses on.

"First, a source of capital. Nattagame is a fully-owned subsidiary of Chum, but we don't have much of an operating budget. We're a bit of a skunkworks op, which has its advantages, but money is not one of them. We don't receive nearly enough funds for the scope of what we need. *World of Moby* was a way to make some fast money through micro-transactions from a sub-class of addicted players, so that we could pour almost all of our resources into our *real* game."

"Which is what?" I ask.

"Secondly," he continues, ignoring me, "our new project, our real game as I say, requires a cadre of skilled players. And we need to identify and then recruit these special players, these future beta testers, who would be particularly suited for what we have created—who might *need* our game."

I get it. It comes to me all in a flash. What they're doing. Why I'm here. "So you *Last Starfighter*-ed me?"

He doesn't say anything but smiles sweetly from across the conference table.

"As in, small-town kid plays an arcade shooter, gets the high score, gets recruited to pilot an alien spaceship in a real-life intergalactic war? Movie released in 1984? Directed by Nick Castle, the guy who played Michael

Myers in the original Halloween? Starring Robert Preston, the guy from the *Music Man*, but old?"

Dekker reflects for a moment. "I'd say that's fairly accurate, and by the way, that's fascinating trivia. I had no idea about the director. Except we are not aliens, John, we are a business."

"Same difference."

"Have you even read *Moby Dick*, John?" He can tell by my silence that I have not. "Have you even seen the movie?"

"I don't... I don't watch movies anymore," I say, staring down at the desk in front of me, feeling heat rising back to my cheeks.

I sense Dekker staring at me, but I don't look up. After a long moment, he says, "We are recruiting you to play our new game, but not because you're the best player. I'd say you're slightly above average, at most."

Suddenly, I feel a tightness in my chest, a pressure on the back of my neck. It takes me a long moment to realize what I'm feeling is hurt. "I'm...pretty good," I say feebly.

"Do you want to punch me in the face, John?" he asks suddenly.

My stomach drops, and my heart begins to race. I'm stung by his words, but I never would consider doing anything like that. No way. I'm a peaceful guy.

"W-what?" I stammer, dumbfounded.

"Or what if I stood up, walked around this table, and came over and punched *you* in the face? What would you do?" he asks calmly, curiously.

"I... I..." What would I do? That's such a crazy thing to ask. I'd kick his ass. I'd hide under the table. I'd ask if we could work something out. I'd start flipping over chairs and acting crazy. Wait, what *would* I do?

"I don't know," I finally admit.

He stares off into space, his index finger perched under his bottom lip, considering.

"Hm. Interesting," he says quietly.

After a moment, he collects himself, then continues back on his original line of thought as if nothing had happened.

"It took you two years to save enough credits to purchase your new Chum Virtual Reality headset, stashing away what must have been all of your spare income for all that time, which admittedly at your level is not that much. And to help get you over that final hump, it looks like you also reduced your food deliveries by twenty-five percent for these last three months."

I stare down at my hands, which are locked together in front of me, my elbows perched on the table, my legs crossed under the desk. I'm tense. Hearing the details of my sad life repeated back to me isn't helping. "I wanted to get out of the house, so to speak," I offer weakly.

"When you finally acquired the VR headset, you did not have enough credits to purchase a game, so you played the thirty-day free trial as much as you possibly could," Dekker continues. "Many other *World of Moby* teams finished much faster, cooperated well together, spent lots of credits on helpful micro-transactions, and came up with wildly clever ways to exploit the game mechanics and solve group challenges. Note I said the word *teams*."

He pauses, forcing me to finally say, "Yeah?"

«*You*, however, stubbornly plowed forward on your own. You didn't spend a dime to get ahead. You rejected all friend requests in the game. You spent every available minute of your life that you were not working, eating, or sleeping during the thirty-day trial period immersed in this world. And through sheer tenacity and grit, you actually defeated the legendary white whale, and in your ramshackle starter rowboat, no less. No cooperation, no friends at all, using the barest amount of strategy, just grit and passion and guts."

He had been leaning forward with great interest as he spoke these words to me, but now he relaxes back in his chair and smiles.

"And that's exactly what we're looking for, John."

I don't know what to say. This guy has me down cold. Hearing it all out loud like this, it's hard to take.

Finally, I mumble, "I thought *World of Moby* was a pretty good game."

"Well, if you enjoyed that little trifle, you're simply going to love what we have cooked up for you now, John. We have a brand-new game, completely original. Nothing off-the-shelf, no stale IP from the public domain. That means intellectual property."

"I know what it means."

He continues smoothly, "New areas to explore, new challenging enemies to conquer. And the technology, John, the technology is like nothing you've ever experienced before. You will feel like you are actually present inside a virtual world. It is not hyperbole when I say that it will feel like you really are right there."

Something finally clicks. I think I realize now what he's hinting at. And it's big, if true.

"Wait," I say. "Are we talking total immersion? Not just the VR headset and the hand triggers, but complete full-body immersion? Is that even possible right now?"

Dekker does not respond directly to my questions. He smiles tightly and continues, "In fact, you don't have to stop the game to go to work. You don't have to stop for anything at all. We'll place you on paid leave, and your job will still be waiting for you when the beta period is over. You'll leave your home and go inside the game world as a brand-new twenty-two-year-old player. No flabby midsection. No back pain. You'll be a warrior in the prime of your life."

I instinctively grab at my paunch under the table. It's not so flabby. Is it? I consider his words. If this is true, it sounds incredible. You hear about the next leap forward, of course, but can't imagine it will actually come. Is this for real? If this tech actually existed, I suppose Chum would be the ones to figure it out, and this fortified complex would be the perfect place to keep it all.

"Are you an arcade fan, John?" Dekker continues.

"Uh..." I begin, thinking of what to say. "Sure. I used to love those games when I was a kid. Although, I have to say, it's been a while since I've been to one. Since I've been...anywhere, really."

Dekker smiles. "I'm a fan of them too, John. We

both grew up with the arcades. They shaped the way we experience games up to the present day. And they still have much to teach us," he says cryptically.

"So," he continues, clearly coming to the end of his big pitch. "This new experience will bring back the beloved arcade thrills of yesterday, married with the technology of tomorrow. I regret I cannot tell you any more at this exact moment, but believe me when I say without hyperbole that this is *not* just a game, and it's not just a fun little trip down memory lane. It is supremely important for the future of our civilization."

I reflect on his words for a long moment. That sounds a little overblown, but then again, I haven't seen it yet. I don't understand what he means about the future, but there's nothing more I'd like to do than to go back in time. Before this virus, before this blazing heat, before this dead-end job. Before this endless isolation.

"In that case, Dekker," I begin, clearing my throat. "I'd like to share a quote with you that I learned from the romantic poet Eddie Money. 'I want to go back and do it all over.'"

Dekker smiles at the reference to the 80s pop song, then says, "There is a catch, of course."

"'...but I can't go back, I know,'" I sigh as I finish the song lyric, disappointed. There's always a catch.

Dekker laughs. "Oh no, you certainly can go back. We've made sure of it. There's just a small added condition to your core play experience. It's nothing you can't handle. You see, our game is structured at the root level to be a cooperative experience."

Oh, great. I think I know where this is going. And I

don't like it one bit.

"You can't play this game like you played the other one, John, it's simply not possible. You can start off solo, of course, but at a certain point, in order to progress, and even to survive, you will ultimately need to team up and form a group—a gang, if you will—with other real human players in the world. No single-rider rowboat here, no quiet life of solitude. This is a community game, in every sense of the word."

I say nothing, setting my jaw and grinding my teeth while I finish hearing him out.

"But it's a small price to pay when you consider the wonders, the true wonders, that await you just beyond this room." Dekker pauses, smiling broadly, convinced he's hooked me. Made the sale. "So, John. Would you like to see it? It's all right behind this door. A new world, a new challenge, a new life of adventure. And you'd be the very first person outside of this building to experience it. Our prime beta tester."

He ends his spiel, rests his hands on the table in front of him, and looks at me evenly, expectantly. I say nothing. The room gets very quiet. I only hear the soft hum of the med station behind me, a tiny squeak as one of the waiting hazmat bros shifts his position near the door. I'm looking down at my hands, considering my place, considering this opportunity.

I lift my head up and look him squarely in the eyes.

"No."

Chapter 4

The Revenge

There is silence at the table for a long time. A classic boardroom showdown, someone has to break it. It's not going to be me.

Dekker begins, "Did I understand you..."

I immediately cut him off, satisfied that I won. A small victory.

"You know what would work for me, Dekker? A lifetime platinum subscription to *World of Moby*. That's what I really want."

Dekker arches an eyebrow at this. I can't believe I'm saying this out loud. My stomach drops, my face is flushed, but I press forward anyway.

"A top of the line ship. Maybe my own yacht, a cruise ship, something where I don't have to see anybody else again. I want to spend all my days on the open seas, not another person in sight. Put electrodes on me, monitor my heartbeat and even my innermost thoughts, I don't care. Just don't bother me."

Dekker says nothing, he continues to watch me. Listening.

I'm terrified, completely out of my comfort zone saying all this. I almost shut down right here, almost lose my train of thought and drop out of my chair and hide under the desk. But I'm angry, and so instead I ignore all that and keep talking.

"I mean, look, this new game you've created sounds awesome. An incredible leap forward and all that. Congratulations to you and your team. And thank you for thinking of me for it, even if you were kind of a dick about it. But this is not the experience for me. I don't work with other people and I like it like that."

"Do you," he says, halfway between a question and a statement, which infuriates me somehow.

"Look, I used to be a team player, okay? I used to trust people and look where it got me. On the edge of a desert hellscape, stuck inside a half-finished house. I'm just one more expendable drone jockey slinging vacuum-sealed beef entrees and toothpaste to the good people of West Diamond Bar, California. But you know what, I'll take that option any day of the week over giving up one bit, one iota of control. I don't need anybody. Ever again."

I can't believe I just said all that to him. I don't feel good.

Dekker considers for a long moment, then finally speaks. "Well, I certainly hear what you're saying, John. And again, you wouldn't immediately have to work with people, perhaps you would consider a trial period before the difficulty scales up to the point where—«

"You don't get it!" I suddenly yell, slamming the table with an open palm. Come on, John, keep it together.

Dekker sighs, changes his tone from persuading to matter-of-fact. "I do get it, John. That's why you're going back home. We're not forcing you to do anything, I said there was always a choice and I meant it."

"Well..." I begin, looking at him and working my jaw, no more sounds coming out. "Great," I finally finish, surprised I don't have to fight him anymore.

"But I do ask you to consider my offer, John," he says. The salesman is back, but he's brusque now, and even more formal. "You have twenty-four hours to think it over. I'd offer you more time, but please understand that we have a rather large operation here, and a rather strict timetable for accomplishing our objectives."

He looks down at his watch. It's a very fancy watch, it has to be the new ChumWatch Series 7. Calls and music go directly to your eardrums via skin conduction, no earbuds required. I could certainly never afford one. But he's just checking the time.

"Tomorrow at ten a.m.," he confirms. He looks up and behind me to Tallboy and Short Round, who have been quietly perched at the entrance to the room, two giant yellow canaries in the coal mine that is Nattagame, Inc. "You can follow these gentlemen out the way you came in. Think it over. Please take as many snacks as you'd like before you leave."

Good. I get to go home. "Thank you, Dekker. I'm fine."

He purses his lips in another approximation of a smile, then stands smoothly and glides out through the far door he came in from. I watch him go, then stand up, turn around and nod to the two hazmat bros. They make no move to leave.

I have to go first, apparently. Which means the bros get to watch me scoop up all the remaining granola bars from the basket and stuff them into my pockets like a hoarder. But I don't care. I'm not coming back here.

✪✪✪

"Good-bye, guys, thanks for the ride!"

I'm waving from my front door to the hazmat bros parked in my driveway.

"CLOSE THE DOOR," Tallboy barks.

"Okay, I will!" I keep up the smiling facade. "You boys take care now!" I'm fumbling for the door handle. "Drive safe now!"

I enter the house and shut the front door behind me. It immediately locks with a loud click. The moment I'm out of sight, my smile evaporates, and I drop my head heavily onto the door frame.

I listen as the van doors close outside, and then the vehicle backs up onto the street and drives away. They're gone.

"aaaaaaaAAAAAAAAAGGH!!" I yell, stepping away from the door and letting the scream of frustration build. I've been holding it together all morning. But I can't stand it anymore.

"AAAAAAAAAHHHH" I continue to yell.

I walk over to the couch, target a throw pillow, and start beating the hell out of it with my fist.

"AHHH! AHHH! AAAAHHHHH!"

✪✪✪

"Okay, I feel better now," I tell myself.

Ten minutes have passed. I went three rounds with my throw pillow and then got tired and laid down on it. Now, I swing my legs over the side of the couch and slowly stand back up, looking around at my house.

It's good to be back. I was gone for only a couple of hours, but the place feels different, somehow. Nothing has changed that I can see, but it feels smaller. Emptier.

It smells stuffy, too. Not terrible, but you know, I have a little perspective now, like, "Oh, did I live like this? All the time?" Junk is piled up in different places, dishes, stacks of paper, work stuff. Plus there's all the stuff I dumped in the kitchen. It's not filthy, by bachelor pad standards, but I'm thinking I could probably stand to do a little spring cleaning, a little tidying up around here.

I had spent the return van ride in mortal terror, certain that we were going to be ambushed at any moment and I was going to be captured by a Scummer gang and forced to join their tribe and scavenge in the wastelands for a brief, desperate interval before succumbing to the omnipresent mega-virus, but nothing ever happened.

I wash my hands thoroughly in the bathroom, then head into the bedroom to grab my tablet. I've got the day off, might as well see if I can somehow create a new trial account for *World of Moby*, maybe with a new email address. But I'm surprised to see a flashing notification on the screen. Which means work.

I swipe at the tablet, and it unlocks to reveal a calendar request. "ANNUAL PERFORMANCE REVIEW - TODAY." Huh.

The appointment is scheduled for 1pm. That's in less than half an hour. Stunned, I swipe to get a full day calendar view. The morning is still blocked out for paid time off, but now the afternoon is scheduled for work.

Well, I guess that's the way he's gonna play it. Dekker may not be my boss, but he sure does "interface with all the other divisions at Chum," and this is clearly part of his damned "integrative strategy" to get under my skin and mess with my day.

Which means I have just enough time to put on some nice clothes, comb my hair, wolf down some food, and log in at the kitchen table.

Which means I definitely *shouldn't* waste time going through my personal email, but I can't help it. I press the app icon. There's only one message.

Subject: Offer

John -

Great to meet you today. Thank you for considering our offer, which expires tomorrow at 10am. If you would like to discuss further, I am reachable via chat at this <u>*link*</u>.

All My Best,

LD

Lucas Dekker

VP, Master Planning

Chum

I delete the email and toss the tablet on the bed. Time's a-wasting.

✪✪✪

"...and your operational excellence score is Does Not Meet Expectations," the voice on the tablet drones on.

I nod, then run my fingers through my hair again, to fix it as surreptitiously as possible. I can see myself in a little video box on the right of my tablet, but the text of my job performance review takes up the bulk of the screen's real estate.

I have to admit, it's not going very well.

My tablet is set up on the kitchen table, attached to its keyboard and stand. I am sitting on the literal edge of my seat. I did not have enough time to comb my hair. Is my hairline receding? Is there that much gray? Do I really look like this now? I mean, I look at myself in the bathroom mirror every day, but I guess I don't notice any of it. Being seen like this really makes you see yourself in a new light.

"Which means your overall rating is Does Not Meet Expectations," concludes the droning voice of my boss, Jim. I've only talked with him two other times, for each of my annual performance reviews. The rest of the time he's just a stupid name on a dumb email.

The screen now shows the document scrolling down to the bottom, revealing a giant letter D. I'm not sure if that stands for Does Not Meet, the letter grade D, or the word Dumb. It doesn't matter.

The main screen image cuts away abruptly from

the doc, revealing a tight video shot of my boss. Jim is balding, with a mustache, and although I've never met him in person, I can tell he's on the shorter side. He reminds me, and I realize this is a deep cut, of an old New Yorker cartoon by Roz Chast. In the cartoon, there's an illustration of what she calls "an angry, florid little man," who's part of the "Make Work For Jerks" program. That's what this all is, after all. Make Work for Jerks.

Yeah, I used to read the New Yorker when I was in high school, so what? I wanted to be a writer, maybe a screenwriter, write some of the movies that Steve and I used to love growing up.

Now all I want to do is play mindless video games. And sit on a deck chair on a boat. Or play a mindless video game about sitting on a virtual deck chair on a virtual boat.

But what I'm actually doing with my life is coordinating a bunch of shipping drones. And apparently, I'm doing it very badly.

Mustache Jim blathers on, "What this means is that you will be placed on a performance program. For the next three months, you and I will check in for a video call at the end of each work week. We'll go over your work and we will expect to see immediate and sustained improvement in these areas. If you incur any additional infractions, it will be grounds for termination."

No more job means no more games. Because I won't have a tablet. Because I won't have a house. Because I won't have a life, because the virus and/or the Scummers will take it from me, real quick.

"Not to put too fine a point on this, John, but this is

your last chance. We do not want to see you go, as you do provide a valuable service, albeit intermittently, but we will not hesitate to terminate if your performance is not up to standard."

I don't say anything. I just stare straight ahead and keep my jaw tight, and my face neutral.

Mustache Jim takes a deep breath, and I can see he's trying to be sensitive, trying to relate on a human level. It's hard to do that when he's clearly such a florid little man. A very punchable little man.

Whoa, that's not fair, John. Violence is never the answer.

And here it comes: "This is not irreversible, John. I had one of these reviews myself earlier in my career. I worked hard to overcome it and look at me now."

Yeah, a dumb idiot in a slightly-less terrible house, remotely bossing around even dumber idiots like me. But I don't say that.

His balding, mustachioed face fades away on my screen, replaced by a new document marked "PERFORMANCE PLAN FOR DRONE COORDINATOR."

"Please review and sign," he says.

I don't review. I swipe down immediately to the bottom of the doc and smear my finger over the signature bar, then smack the "SIGN AND DATE" button.

Mustache Jim fades back in, his eyes focused on what must be the now-signed document on his screen, then countersigning himself. His eyes then shift to me, or to my image on his screen, and he says, "Well, it's one-thirty now, so you've got the rest of the afternoon to get a good start on turning over a new leaf. You're a smart, capable worker, and you can do this, John. It's all up to you."

I nod my head as slightly as possible. Just enough to let him know he should sign off. He does, without another word. My screen returns to the desktop.

I let out a long sigh, then I tab over to my delivery screen and get back to work, slinging more frozen dinners over to the surely-fine people of West Diamond Bar, California.

✪✪✪

"Man, this is crazy! I haven't done this in thirty years."

I'm still at my kitchen table, talking to myself. But it's after dinner, and work is over.

It turns out I couldn't make a new trial account for *World of Moby*; they locked me out based on my location. I had to come up with something else to do tonight.

So now I am playing *Street Fury*, an old arcade game from the 1990s.

Maybe it was what Dekker said earlier about punching him, or maybe it was thinking about punching my stupid boss through the tablet screen. I'm not a violent person, I would never actually do either of those things, of course, but I guess I just had the old arcade games on my brain.

The internet is pretty locked down these days. We're actually surfing on a company-branded ChumNet, even during personal time, but I started poking around, and eventually I found a ROM file for the original *Street Fury* arcade game.

This game was at the Safeway grocery store by our house growing up, and my older brother Steve and I would run there after middle school every day and spend all our quarters playing it.

It was one of our favorite things to go and do together. Until we got the home version a couple of years later for Christmas.

They call it a "beat 'em up" game because that's exactly what you're doing. You're just walking from left to right through gritty city streets, punching a bunch of punks who want to punch you. And when they punch you enough times, you lose your life and have to put in another quarter.

But when you punch them enough times, you eventually save the city.

There's no coin slot or arcade stick on this tablet, but there are virtual screen controls and a virtual quarter interface on the bottom of the screen. It's not an ideal way to play, but I can swipe and smash at the tablet screen and it's close enough.

Street Fury was made in 1990, one of the earlier games in the beat 'em up genre. It's fairly primitive, showing a little pixelated guy with a mullet and cutoff jean jacket moving from the left side of the screen to the right, punching pixelated gang members in a little back alley.

But it's still very fun. And it's bringing me back to my childhood, big time. I remember the music, the satisfying thrill of your character's fist making contact with a jerk trying to beat you with a crowbar. It's brutal but kind of cartoony. Very fun.

"Dammit! That was a cheap shot." I'm sandwiched in between three punks and just got caught in a damage loop between them until I died. Insert another coin. The game switches to a continue screen, where you're inexplicably tied up and rolling down a conveyor belt towards a table saw. I insert a virtual quarter before the countdown ends, and I'm back in the game.

I'm four stages into this now, and I have to admit, it's starting to wear a little thin. It's all pretty one-note.

I mean, sure, you're still beating fools up, and you can jump-kick them as well as punch them, and there's a special attack, and one stage has you fighting through a restaurant that's on fire, which is pretty cool. But there's not a whole lot of depth to it. The music and constant sound effects of dudes getting slammed in the gut is starting to grate on my ears. So for maximum nostalgia, I start streaming the ChumMusic app's Calm Retro Mix for Gamers playlist.

Ahhh, this feels good, getting back to my youth, before all of this. Although I've read that these games were primarily made for adults. These games were manufactured in Japan, and now I'm picturing some anxious middle-aged salarymen in rolled-up dress shirt sleeves and their ties wrapped around their foreheads like sweatbands, taking out their frustrations at the end of a long day.

After a day like today, I can definitely relate.

"Dammit!" I just lost half of my health bar in a single combo attack. This is a lot harder than I remember.

I knock open a crate and try to pick up the health power-up that spills out of it, but a jump-kick from the annoying tall guy enemy knocks me to the ground. Then my limp body blinks out of existence. I swipe the screen and add another virtual quarter to get me back in the game.

This game lets two other people play with you cooperatively, which can help a lot, but it's a real quarter-muncher solo. The sheer numbers just overwhelm you, especially in this final stage. I mean, I have unlimited virtual quarters, but this is still relentless. I'm dying every twenty seconds now, doing this boss rush of all the stage bosses together at the end. I'm getting fed up with this stupid thing now.

It doesn't help that I'm still exhausted. I mean, today was the craziest day I've had in a long time. No sense trying to power through this last level right now. Maybe I can just...rest on the ground here next to my chair.

No! You can't crash on your damn kitchen floor two nights in a row! Get your ass to bed, you monster. You need a good night's sleep. You don't want to get fired, do you?

So, I exhale deeply, and I close the arcade webpage. I can't save my progress. I'm going to have to start over when I want to play again, just like the real arcades. I stand up and bring the tablet with me into the bedroom.

I hit the sheets like a bag of rocks, and I don't even turn off the ChumMusic playlist before I close my eyes. I'm using the free version, of course, so an ad plays after this song. I'm fast asleep before it ends.

"Here at Chum, in these challenging times, we take care of you. Chum Delivery, for all of your essential grocery and supply needs, now with more reliable shipments.

Chum Health, featuring new diagnostic and telehealth tools to make sure you live your best life. Chum Choice, your favorite entertainment, including classic TV, films, and now virtual reality games..."

✪✪✪

I'm back on my rowboat. Back on the sea. But I'm not alone.

Michael Caine is here; he's sitting right next to me. We're each holding on to a paddle.

We're on the hunt for the white whale. Or is it the great white shark? I'm not sure. Are they the same? I turn my head, taking in our surroundings.

The ocean that's surrounding us is not an ocean at all. It's actually a giant pool.

Behind us, the beautiful blue sky is really just a long billboard, a massive set painting that runs along one entire side of the huge pool. The real sky above us is an ominous black. It's still daytime, but it's like the moments before a powerful storm.

I recognize this place. I was here when I was a little kid. We're on the Universal Studios backlot in Hollywood.

This is the outdoor movie set for the notoriously terrible 3rd sequel to *Jaws*, *Jaws: The Revenge*. 1987, directed by Joseph Sargent, who before that directed *Nightmares*, a horror anthology from 1983, featuring a young Emilio Estevez battling creatures that pop out of an arcade machine.

"What are you doing here?" I ask Michael Caine.

He looks at me and says brightly, in his charming

accent, "I'm here for the money, guv'na." He famously did the film for the large paycheck he was offered. I remember this fact very clearly from my brother Steve's movie trivia book.

"I don't have any money," I admit.

"Pip-pip," he merrily replies, and then we start rowing together. Rowing toward the shore, in perfect synchrony, an asphalt road and trees obscuring the skyline beyond. We're a pretty good team, Michael Caine and I.

If he's Michael Caine, then who am I? I must be Lance Guest. Lance Guest, the main actor in *Jaws the Revenge*, the handsome leading man. But wait, before this, Lance Guest played the main guy in *The Last Starfighter*. The one who got recruited from playing an arcade game to fight a real battle in space.

I must be Lance Guest, the last starfighter, slayer of the great white whale-slash-shark. Is he/am I still alive? I've got to look that up on ChumNet.

As we near the shore, our oars cutting steadily through the calm waters, a tram drives up on the asphalt path toward us. But it's not a Universal tram from the tour. It's the tram I rode earlier today from the Chum warehouse, driverless. Each of the four open-air cars is now jam-packed with tourists wearing masks, taking pictures. I can't make out their faces.

Back in the days when we went to theme parks, I used to see the Asian tourists wearing masks, and I would chuckle to myself knowingly and assume it was because their air pollution was so bad. Now I realize it's because they lived through the SARS virus in 2003;

that's why they wore the masks. Turns out to have been a pretty good idea. One we adopted a bit too late in the old America, and look at us now.

As we finally reach the shore, the clouds darken further, and the skies finally open on us. The steady rain quickly worsens to a violent downpour by the time our boat slams onto the shore.

There's something else. Drums, humming. Music is starting to come in, so low over the din of the rainfall that at first I think I'm imagining it.

You are *imagining this, John. You're imagining all of this.*

The tram is parked directly in front of me. The tourists have their cameras out. They're ready for the show.

I turn around and Michael Caine is gone. I'm in the boat alone; it's filled to the brim with rainwater. I get out, and as I do, the music swells. It is clearly music, I'm not crazy. And I realize this music is from *Free Willy*, the 1993 hit movie about the kid who became friends with the whale. Who's the director? I don't remember now. Michael Madsen played his dad. It's hard to watch that movie after watching *Reservoir Dogs*, I can't look at him the same way. Scary.

I stand at the water's edge, in the pouring rain, everyone in the tram is looking at me.

Michael Caine is in the tram now, too; his happy smile is gone, replaced by a look of profound worry. Michael Caine is sitting next to my brother, Steve. How could he be here? Steve looks worried, too.

Suddenly, water from the theme park ocean erupts into the sky, and a giant creature emerges from the sea.

It's the whale. It's the shark. It's Leviathan.

I can only see glimpses of the gigantic beast from the flashes of the cameras on the tram, barely enough to comprehend its immense size and terrifying speed. It leaps into the air and as it does, the world slides into very slow motion, gouts of water exploding from the sea and into the skies. I watch the spray slowly swell upward.

I saw *Free Willy* in the theater, and I remember that the iconic shot from the movie is the kid on the horizon, pumping his fist into the air in triumph as the happy whale jumps from the water and crests over him.

But now this music darkens, and the arc of the creature becomes clear as it begins its descent.

It's heading right toward me.

It's bearing down fast. It's going to smother me under its weight, and I know that I must fight back. I must raise my fist like the kid from *Free Willy*, but not in triumph this time.

I must raise my fist to punch the creature in the face.

Its massive form roars towards me, inescapable and total, and the music fades under its horrifying cry. It is a train engine barreling towards me, the end of all things.

I twist and launch my whole body into the blow, screaming all the way.

I punch the whale in the face.

I'm up. Bedsheets soaked with sweat. The room is dark.

I'm gasping for air.

I look to my right. Tablet on the dresser. 5:39AM. It wasn't real. It wasn't even virtually real. But it feels like more than a dream.

I grab blindly for my tablet, finally swipe it from the nightstand, and prop myself up to a sitting position as I dive into my email. I rummage quickly through the trash folder, and then click the link I find.

Almost immediately, Dekker is there, peering at me through his wristwatch like Dick Tracy, very close on my screen. Hair pulled back in a ponytail, dressed in a track suit. Off to the gym, no doubt.

He stares at me without saying a word. I say nothing at first, catching my breath.

Finally, I speak.

"I'm in."

He smiles.

"I am very pleased to hear that, John."

Chapter 5

Terms and Conditions

I have no appetite and yet I've somehow eaten two more granola bars.

I'm back in the conference room inside the Chum warehouse, having gone through the exact same pickup routine again with Tallboy and Short Round, driving through my quarantined desert subdivision and past the fleets of warehouse drones and the aisles and aisles of Salisbury steaks and other assorted rations, and then back into the inner sanctum of Nattagame, LLC.

I'm alone in here. I had started out pacing the length of the table, but after a few laps around it, I forced myself to sit down. Don't let 'em see you sweat. Under the table, my legs are throttling with nervous energy. I never do that, am always pissed when I see somebody else doing it, back in the days when I saw other people, but now I can't help it. I try to focus all my energy on the far blackout glass door, waiting for Dekker to come in.

But there's no Dekker. I reflexively check the wall clock again. It's been...ten minutes. Is that all?

A loud beeping begins, and it makes me jump in my seat. It sounds like a truck backing up. I stiffen and look around, ready for anything—security officers, a ninja attack, a PowerPoint presentation. Red alarm lights start spinning on the far wall next to Dekker's door, moving in time with the beeps, and then the wall begins to...open. This whole side of the room slowly and smoothly slides back, revealing another room beyond it.

I stay right where I am. The beeping stops but the lights continue flashing.

"Hello?" I call out.

Nothing. The new room is completely empty. I realize instinctively that I'm supposed to go inside there, but I don't want to. I don't trust it. It's cold in this conference room, but I'm sweating now.

So I sit and I wait, idly checking the wall clock every few moments, pretending that nothing has changed.

Finally, I hear a familiar voice through speakers I don't see.

"John, we're all waiting for you." It's Dekker, of course.

"Dekker, I'm actually waiting for you."

"I'm downstairs, John. Please take the elevator. I'll meet you here."

"Where's the elevator?"

It's a stupid question, clearly that new room contains the elevator, probably behind another secret wall. But I don't want to give him the pleasure. When it's clear he's not going to say anything more, I sigh, finish my third granola bar, and step into the newly-revealed room.

The same off-white color scheme and carpeting extends to this anteroom. I step in carefully, and the moment I'm inside, the beeping resumes.

«*Please move to the center of the elevator and stand away from the closing door,*" an automated voice intones.

I comply and watch the door, or wall, glide smoothly shut, trapping me inside.

Then, I'm moving. Oh, this whole room is an elevator. Got it. I have no idea how fast I'm going, but the descent seems to go on for a long, long time.

The journey lasts long enough for me to start thinking about all of this. They're going to be bringing more players in here soon. Maybe they'll bring them all into the conference room, make them watch a video or something, and then send them all down together on this elevator. The game space must be absolutely huge if they had to build it underneath this warehouse.

But there aren't other players down here, not yet. I'm the first. And I'm all alone.

Just the way I like it.

"*Please stand clear of the opening door,*" the automated voice warns, pleasantly.

We have finally come to a smooth but definite stop. I watch as the opposite wall slides open to reveal a small entrance antechamber, dimly lit and metallic.

Standing in the center of the room is Dekker, smiling broadly. He's sharply dressed, wearing slim black pants and an open-collared white shirt with a vest. Who the hell wears a vest these days? Who wears anything but sweatpants these days? He's standing inside a warm spotlight overhead, so it presents a cool tableau. He certainly knows how to make an impression.

"Welcome, John," he calls out.

I step out carefully and hear the wall begin to slide closed behind me.

"Nice place you got here," I say.

The wall closes and the beeping finally stops. Thank God, that was annoying.

"You haven't seen anything yet. Follow me, please." Dekker turns on his heel and strides down the hallway behind him.

I follow him down this hall and into another hallway, and another. The walls are bare concrete, with fiber optic cables and metal boxes lining the walls and ceiling, like we're entering the lair of a master supercomputer. I'm almost immediately lost and struggling to keep up with Dekker, with both the speed of his walking and of his talking.

"So this is our test facility. Please forgive the clutter, it's all still a bit in flux down here. We're leading you to the game world entrance. Once inside, you'll have quite a bit of time on your own at first, as I promised. You will be the very first player to experience the world other than the folks on our internal team. Exciting, right?"

"I... Yes. It's very exciting. What is this we're doing?"

He ignores the question. "It will be overwhelming at first, we know that much."

"I'm already a wee bit overwhelmed."

"The city of New Arcadia is a very immersive and kinetic environment."

I laugh out loud. "New Arcadia? Is this game set in the LA suburbs? Why not call it New Irwindale? Neo West Covina? Uh... Nuevo El Toro Y?"

"When you arrive," Dekker deflects, "there will be a tutorial stage to start, and I will walk you through it personally."

"So what's the name of this game, anyway?"

Dekker replies, glancing back at me, "We don't have one. Still figuring that out, actually. Internally, we call it Project X."

"Oh, like the Matthew Broderick movie with the monkeys that they used to show on HBO all the time? 1987, Director Jonathan Kaplan?"

"Like that," he agrees.

"Is that what this is about? Am I going to be a lab monkey?"

"In a manner of speaking," he says, not dismissively but with excitement, a hint of the showman.

"Well, what kind of game is this? Am I going to be fighting dragons? Racing cars? Finding the hidden object?"

Silence. Only the sound of our quick footsteps echoing in the hallways.

"Dekker, did you create an immersive virtual world based on the Junior Jumble?"

"The *what*?" I finally said something weird enough to get a rise out of him.

"You know, from the old funny papers. The Junior Jumble. Unscramble the letters to form words and then take certain letters from each new word to form a new mega-word. Will I be spending all of my waking hours unscrambling and reassembling words in a virtual newspaper world, Dekker? Is that what you all built down here? Seriously, what am I going to be doing down here?"

"Ah." More footfalls echo while he says nothing. Then, finally, "Let me just say that the genre will be very familiar to you."

At this moment, we round a corner, Dekker opens a door, and we come to a stop.

"Oh, this is insane," I breathe.

We've stepped into a medium sized room, but with a very high ceiling, maybe thirty feet tall. We're not alone anymore. There are almost a dozen people in here, far more than I've seen in a long time. They're all honest-to-god white-coated scientists, checking computer terminals, making notes on clipboards, and hustling to and fro. The walls of the room are covered with computer equipment, giant monitors and workstations. Some of the long cables running down the hallways seem to run into these computer workstations and end here, while many continue to rooms just beyond this one.

I take in all this activity in an instant, and then my eyes are drawn to the middle of the room.

In the center, there is a giant clear tank, about ten feet tall, perched on a large base and ringed with more computer screens and flashing panels.

I understand the moment I see it what this all means. I'm not walking into the game world. I'm entering it virtually, suspended inside this vat.

It's an aquarium. And I'm the big catch.

"This is insane," I repeat, swallowing to get some moisture back in my suddenly-parched mouth. "This is like the *Empire Strikes Back*. 1980, director Irvin Kirschner. On Hoth. The tube that Luke goes into."

I feel Dekker's presence to my right, sensing that he's watching me intently as I take it all in. "Congratulations on your second 80s film reference in thirty seconds."

"Thank you, it's my special talent," I reply without looking at him, still in shock. I'm really supposed to get inside that tube?

Dekker senses my apprehension. "This is the best way to keep you immersed and engaged in the game, John. We've tried having our players sitting down, then laying back in a deck chair style bed, even lying prone, but in every case, they started getting sores and circulatory problems. The clear gel compound inside this chamber is engineered to have you feeling like you're being suspended on a fluffy cloud. Some of our staff have even said it's like being in the womb. And when you enter the game world, you won't notice it at all. You'll be completely immersed in the appropriate sensations. We'll keep you continuously fed and sustained, comfortable even, while your mind is fully in the game space."

"Will I be able to breathe?" I ask, finally turning to

Dekker.

He looks evenly at me, "Yes, John, I promise you we've figured that important part out."

"No need to be a jerk about it," I retort.

I break from his gaze and slowly approach the vat before me. So this is going to be my new home? I guess it's better than my current one.

I touch the glass gingerly and peer through it, my face almost pressed up to the edge. I can make out the clear gel that's inside, filled almost to the top but low enough that it won't overflow when I get inside.

Dekker watches me inspect the chamber and says, "The gel solution inside will keep you fed, irrigated, and generally at ease, supporting all your autonomic functions. This will allow your mind to focus on the game. We have made it easier for you to do that by creating a very familiar progression structure, very similar to other games you've played in the real world. There will be levels, persistent characters, all the standard things you know from traditional games. But this game will feel very real, or perhaps hyper-real. We expect you will adjust to it all very quickly. If not, we can modify the gel composition on this end to accommodate. Everything is meticulously designed to ease you into the game, so that your body doesn't reject it."

Suddenly I'm alarmed. I pull back from the vat like it's made of lava, turning to Dekker and wincing. "That can happen?"

Dekker grimaces slightly. "It's certainly not fatal, but it is not pleasant. It's quite a large biological and psychological adjustment. Especially for a subject that's been cooped up in a house for years sitting in front of a computer tablet and not exercising."

"Hey, that's not nice," I warn.

He looks at me with surprise. "Is it untrue?"

"...no. It's not...not true." I offer weakly.

He continues to look at me impassively.

"It's true," I state plainly. Jerk.

Dekker begins absently brushing dust off his fancy vest.

Changing the subject, I ask, "Do I need to do some medical tests first? Get on a treadmill with some electrodes attached to me? Turn and cough?"

"It's all already been taken care of. When you used the med station upstairs in the conference room yesterday, it registered your vitals, and even generated your medication profile. The remaining relevant data was simply pulled from your Chum Health records."

"Oh, well, that all seems very ethical," I say sarcastically.

He replies straightforwardly, "Well, it saves a lot of time, I think you'll agree."

"Sure, I'll give you that." I take a deep breath and exhale. "Okay, I'm ready."

"No, you're not. Not yet. Please review and sign this user agreement," Dekker says, and he hands me a computer tablet.

On the screen is a contract for participating in Project X. Unlike my stupid performance plan at work, I do try to read or skim through this one, but it's clear right away that there's a whole lot here. The indicator on the right side of the screen when I start to scroll down barely travels. Around us, the low hum of commotion continues, with computers beeping, and scientists science-ing. I start scrolling faster, and Dekker starts to explain.

"Basically, this is a ninety-day contract. We'll be monitoring your vitals and responses throughout that time. At thirty-day intervals, we will pull you out for a day of recovery and debriefing. At the end of the ninety-day period, there will be the option to extend, if both parties agree."

I'm still scrolling to the bottom. This thing is huge. "That sounds reasonable."

"I should note that you have but one life to live, so to speak. In that sense, it's quite similar to the real world. Unless you have means acquired within the game world, once you lose your life, you will forfeit the game. This action will return you to your current living situation, meaning back to your desert home and your present occupation. So play carefully."

"That sounds pretty strict," I say.

"Are there any friends or relatives you want to list as contacts in case of an emergency?" he asks.

I pause for a moment. "No," I finally say, then continue scrolling through the document.

Dekker nods, then continues, "Also, this includes a standard non-disclosure agreement. Perhaps beyond standard, actually. In fact, let's call it an aggressive NDA. Nobody else outside of this room and the highest levels of this organization knows we have achieved anywhere near this level of technology, and frankly, nobody else needs to know."

I nod in understanding as I continue to swipe down. Finally, I reach the end of the contract, position my finger above the signature line, and hesitate.

Dekker senses my question before I even ask it. "You of course have the ability to exit the game world yourself at any time. Just vocalize your desire to leave the game. The algorithms will hear and will notify us."

"And you'll all be watching me too, won't you?" I ask. "Your first guinea pig in your big new expensive experiment."

He peers over my shoulder at the tablet, indicating a dotted line. "Just sign right there."

I swipe a little squiggle that approximates my actual signature and wait. Nothing happens.

Dekker peers back over my shoulder and frowns. "Oh, I think you need to scribble another line. It's reading that line as a single name and not a full signature."

I look at him sharply. "I certainly hope the game interface is smoother than this."

He returns my gaze evenly. "This is a beta test, and the team will be reviewing and incorporating your feedback into future versions of the game experience."

I smile at him, hoping he reads the sarcasm on my face, and quickly smear a second squiggle on the signature line. I press the "AGREE" button firmly, then hand it to him. He looks at it carefully, then counter-signs quickly. He brings his right arm up, bent at the elbow, presenting his forearm to me.

I stare at him for a moment in confusion before I realize what this is. An agreement. For modern times.

I mirror his gesture, and then we reach forward and bump elbows, mostly non-awkwardly.

"Welcome to the game," he says with a smile.

We stand there for a long moment, facing each other. My heart is racing.

Finally, I break the silence. "So, do I get to watch the intro video? Create a username? What's next?"

He nods over to the tank. "Get in."

Chapter 6

Another Bad Creation

I do feel like I'm floating on a fluffy cloud. Dekker was right.

It's dark here. I can't see a damn thing.

Then, small patterns of light begin to break through the darkness. Tiny spots of color dance lazily in front of my eyes.

When I was a little kid, laying in my bed before I would drift off to sleep, I would see these same lights with my eyes closed, these little rainbows in the blackness. I used to rub my eyelids with my hands to make the color patterns change and dance. That probably wasn't a very good idea, I'm sure it's right up there with crossing your eyes on purpose, but we didn't have smartphones back then. There wasn't a lot else to do.

Anyway, that's what these lights remind me of. After a few leisurely moments of dancing color spots, everything shifts, and the world around me brightens.

The fluffy cloud sensation is gone. My feet are now on solid ground.

I appear to be standing in an endless gray room. It looks like I should be falling through the world, because it's all the same color—there's no horizon that I can see—but I'm not.

The space appears infinite. There are no ends. Something tells me if I think about this too hard, I'll get completely disoriented and start screaming in horror. So, I don't think about it. For now.

In the real world, of course, I'm suspended in gel inside that tube-shaped aquarium, or chamber, as they call it. I'm stripped down to a pair of Nattagame-branded boxer briefs and wearing a blackout helmet on my head, connected to a tangle of wires overhead.

But it's not a VR helmet, there are no goggles. No, this is all happening inside my brain. My brain thinks this is real, and my body is acting accordingly.

I inhale deeply. It smells like I've just opened an old comic book, pressed my nose to the spine, and sniffed. It immediately puts me at ease; it's a very comfortable feeling.

When I first got into the chamber, I was thrashing about in terror, but only for a moment. I was lowered into the vat by robotic limbs under my arms, submerged into the gel solution, and it promptly felt like I was blind and drowning for one terrifying beat. Then the oxygen kicked in, the fluffy cloud fluffed up around me, and I suddenly felt serenely calm and supported.

But that all feels years ago now. Because now there is only the endless gray of this new space.

"Hello?" I call out. Nothing. At least my voice works here.

"ECHO!" I yell, expecting to hear my voice bounce back, but there's no echo in this space. It actually sounds muffled, almost like I'm yelling into a pile of clothes.

"HELLO?" I yell out, even louder. No answer.

This grayness is legitimately going on forever. Like, for infinity.

"Uh..." I begin, my voice trembling. I'm standing still but now I feel like I'm slipping, first slowly and then all at once. Like I'm hurtling a million miles through space. My mind feels like it's separating from my body. I'm freaking out, man.

Almost as if the world understands, gridlines of bright light begin to be drawn in around me, defining the space. Immediately, I feel relief, a sense of grounding, like I'm in a real place again.

These gridlines fill in with solid colors, then with texture. The world is literally being drawn around me. Bright pastel colors, very sharp and clean. Was the game world calibrating? Figuring out what I could handle?

I suddenly think to look down at my body, and thankfully, it appears that I have one.

It's me, but it's not me, not quite. I'm wearing a basic outfit: white T-shirt, blue jeans, boots. The outlines of everything seem slightly cel-shaded. It's both a cartoon and incredibly realistic. It's not like *World of Moby*, that was a standard VR game, although primitive by comparison to this, bulky and awkward.

I bring my hands up and wave them around in front

of my face. This feels real, like I'm actually here. These are my hands. My hands are small, I know, but they're not yours. They are my own. That is so deep. Oh god, Alaskan songstress/poet Jewel was actually a genius. How did I not realize that before?

Uh oh, I might be going crazy in here. Let's file that away as evidence I might be crazy.

Then I reach my hands down—*they're not yours, they are my own*—and lift the bottom of my shirt. I poke at what appears to be a perfectly-chiseled six-pack. That's crazy. I haven't had abs since I was, what, 22? Even then it was tenuous. But these are perfect.

I look back up to witness the last bits of the world being drawn in. I'm now standing on a patch of bright green grass, a lush forest right behind me. Ahead is a narrow strip of beach, beautiful blue waves reflecting the sunlight.

Across this body of water is a giant modern city. It reminds me of New York very much, but it's not quite. There are similar landmarks, but the skyline is slightly different. It's like a dream version.

"This is New Arcadia, I take it?" I call out, assuming Dekker and the scientists are all monitoring me and listening to my every word. "It's okay. You don't have to say anything."

I slowly do a complete 360-degree turn, taking in every detail of this world, my new home. It's surprisingly alive and full and present. I remember the first time I finally got my VR helmet at home and hooked it up to my tablet. I thought I knew what to expect, but I still had my jaw open in wonder for the first hour I had it. This is a million times more impressive because it feels so real, and my jaw is even wider now.

I breathe out "Wow...wow..." as I notice birds flying by through the trees, squirrels on the ground rubbing their tiny little hands together, sunlight peeking through the gently-swaying leaves, as I slowly spin in place.

When I finally complete my turn back around toward the city, a table is standing ten feet in front of me. It's an outdoor folding table, with what looks to be a computer tablet sitting on top. That definitely wasn't there before.

"Hey, guys! Who put the table there?" I call out. No answer.

I walk toward the table. I move slowly at first, feeling my way, half-thinking I'll trip on some VR wire. But it all feels totally normal, like I'm in the real world, so I take the last few steps quickly and confidently to the table. I examine the tablet sitting there, and it looks a lot like the one I have for work. On a white screen, there are black letters that say "PROJECT X - CHARACTER CREATION" in a simple font. I pick up the tablet.

I reach forward to swipe the screen, but things change. I don't know how else to say this, once I focus on the screen, it zooms in so that I'm *inside* the screen.

I now see myself in a handy full-length mirror, positioned to my left. The man standing there looks like me, but he's not quite. He's much younger.

My mouth is wide open in shock. I close it, and I see my mirror image's mouth close, too—which makes our mouths open wide in shock all over again.

My character stats are printed out in text floating to my right. It looks like I can change some of them.

"What kind of game is this? How should I build my character? What's my goal?" I call out, hoping to get some guidance. "What do I want to be when I grow up?"

Silence. I guess this must be part of the process, maybe they want to see what I do. Maybe it doesn't matter what kind of character I create, as long as it feels good to me.

But first, I spend a good solid minute making faces at myself in the mirror. Actually, I have no idea how much time is passing. It's crazy; this avatar moves exactly like me, but it's more animated, somehow? But still real? It's very uncanny and weird, but I'm already getting used to it. I like it.

I look to my right at the text box, next to my hairline, which by the way is now healthy and full and no gray at all, thank you very much. The first row of text displays a name, already filled in. The word END is blinking at the end of the text, like an arcade name entry.

The name says "BLAZE."

I kind of dig it. And I can't think of anything better at the moment. I reach out and press the "END" button, and the name stops flashing.

"Hi, I'm Blaze," I say to no one. "How do you do? Just Blaze, actually. Yeah, like the fire." I shake an invisible hand in front of me, laugh at my hilarious antics, then return my attention to my stats. Back to business.

Age: 22

Height: 5'10"

Weight: 165

I can't seem to change any of those. Aside from the weight and the age and maybe the height by a couple of inches, that's pretty much what I am in real life.

Next is a field for upper body, and next to that is a slider. I grab at the slider icon, but my fingers go right through it. Frowning, I will it to move with the powers of my mind, still nada. I then make a swiping movement with my arm, imagining at the same time that I'm moving it. That seems to do the trick.

The moment the slider moves, I feel a sudden tightening and a bulging through my chest and arms. I just made myself bigger, by moving the embiggening slider, which I believe is the technical term for it.

"Ow!" I cry, but it's not too painful. It's more surprising than anything. I call out to Dekker and the gang, sure that they are observing. "That hurt! Not a fan of that. I hope you're taking notes for the next game patch."

I look back at my mirror image. My arms are visibly bigger, a small but noticeable swelling, as is my chest. I glance to the right, and notice my weight is now at 170 pounds.

I slide the notch up and down the scale some more, experimenting a bit with my look. Each click of the notch causes change I can viscerally feel in my body. It's painful, but cool.

"Ow! Ow! Ow. OW!"

I'm now at the max setting, looking like a 'roided-up monster.

"Check me out, I'm all swole!"

I strike a classic muscleman pose. The figure staring back at me is a puffed-up buffoon. I look kind of ridiculous. Not my style. Let's dial this back down.

"OW! Ow! Ow."

I wind up pretty much back where I started, 170 pounds and a bit beefy, but still lean and agile. Damn, I look good.

Lower body looks great, no changes needed. Same with the next: Hair - Brown (no gray streaks, thank you very much). Eyes - Blue.

There's one final choice to be made. On the bottom right of my field of vision, there's a selection box for Fighting Style.

I swipe at it with intention, and it reveals a drop-down menu. There are eight different fighting styles, including two that are locked, their names obscured. No indication how to access them. I guess you've got to play the game first.

Fist of the Pissed - PUNCH

Foot Smasher - KICK

Brawler Mawler - AGGRO

Zen Crusher - BALANCE

Sneaky Leopard - STEALTH

Hot Mess Master - DRUNK

LOCKED

LOCKED

Since it seems you'll be able to change up your play style at some point, I decide to go with the default first choice. Let's see what the game makers intended. A prompt appears.

ARE YOU SURE YOU WANT TO SELECT "FIST OF THE PISSED"?

"Yes," I say. Nothing happens. "Come on," I mutter.

Then, underneath, a new message appears, with two buttons marked "YES / NO."

I swipe. Nothing. I focus all my energy.

"Dekker, this UI sucks!" I call out. "That means User Interface. I'm telling you this because I'm not sure you know what those words mean."

The buttons begin glowing. Taunting me.

"Yes! Yes, I accept!" Nothing.

In my frustration, I picture punching the YES button very, very hard. Then I scream out and punch at it as fiercely as I can.

That does it. Cool.

I am now an official follower of the path of Fist of the Pissed, whatever that means. Everything fades to a neutral gray again. It makes me dizzy.

Chapter 7

El Solo Hobo

Now I'm flying through the gray infinity again. It's not my favorite feeling.

But I'm holding it together, barely. It helps that it doesn't feel like I'm out of control, hurtling willy-nilly through space. It feels like there's a gentle guiding force pushing me forward to a set destination.

After a few moments, I feel myself slowing, then solid ground touches my feet. White grid lines quickly appear around me, then fill in with color and texture, resolving into a new scene.

It's dark in this new place, shadowy and enclosed, but high overhead, blue sky peeks through. It takes my eyes a few moments to adjust. I look around and see that I'm in a narrow urban alleyway, sandwiched between two tall rows of buildings. I must be inside that city I saw from earlier, inside New Arcadia.

My body feels...different now.

I feel incredible physical power surging through me, my muscles rippling and flexing with it. There's knowledge, too; my brain pulses with energy, bursting with newfound wisdom.

"I know Kung Fu," I say in awe.

"No, you don't."

Dekker. I hear his voice everywhere, in my head and all around me, all at once.

"Ah! Christ that scared me!" I yell.

And also, frankly, it hurt and disappointed me. What do you mean I don't know kung fu? I distinctly feel that I have the battle-tested knowledge of the ancients now coursing through my powerful veins.

"What you know is the basic Level 1 version of our custom-created fighting style, Fist of the Pissed, which is only very loosely related to some specific aspects of Kung Fu, and is in fact a proprietary and trademarked Nattagame LLC battle system."

Is this what I sound like to him when I call him on his fancy watch? Vibrating through his eardrums and into his brain? I gotta say, the effect is a little much.

"Well, it still feels cool, Dekker. So bravo to you and the team. Credit where it's due."

I can see a little more clearly now, the dark shapes before me are resolving into objects. Trash cans, trash bags, wooden boxes, bottles. This alley is a mess.

"Where am I? What is this place?"

There's no reply from Dekker. However, in my field of vision, a floating text box appears. The new message hovers a few feet in front of me.

Place: New Arcadia

Time: 199X

And then:

Tutorial Stage - Alley

Underneath that, the following appears in urgent, blinking letters:

GET READY TO FIGHT.

Oh my God. This is what I think this is.

I break into a slow, wide smile as I finally put together all the pieces. A crime-ridden East Coast city. An alleyway full of enemies. Fisticuffs and flying kicks. The 90s.

I'm in a virtual beat 'em up arcade world.

It's like *Street Fury*, back at the Safeway, that's what all this is. They've spent a fortune and developed generation-leaping cutting-edge technology to build a new *old* video game world for me to live in.

This is...exactly what I wanted.

Isn't it?

I break into a huge smile. "Dekker, you sly dog! You've created a..." I search for the right words to classify this place. "...retro arcade...brawler world, haven't you?"

New Item Unlocked: Personal Storage Device

I absorb this new notification, and then I feel a weight begin to pull slightly on my groin. It's like a sudden presence, where nothing was there before, I don't how else to describe it. I look down and see a black bulge peeking out under my very flat abs; it covers nearly the whole front. This definitely was not there a moment ago.

"Is this a codpiece?" I ask myself out loud.

But no, it's wider than one of those would be, and it seems to be sitting around my waist. I grab it and pull at it. This mystery object is lashed tightly around me like a belt. I tilt it up to face me, and I see two zippers in front. It's a large pouch, with a small iron-on patch in the center—an icon of a single red flame.

Oh my god. I look up from my groin and up toward the sky.

"Am I wearing a fanny pack now?"

"Welcome to the 90s, John, or should I say Blaze?" is Dekker's omnipotent reply, emanating from above and echoing off the walls of the alley. "You are correct. This is a living, breathing urban space that shares certain temporal and activity-based characteristics consistent with a classic fighting game experience. A...beat 'em up, if you will."

"Yeah, I will," I reply, smirking and nodding with barely-contained excitement. "I most definitely will."

"By the way, we don't call it a fanny pack, John. It is a personal storage device for your inventory. A convenient place where you'll keep your critical items for the game world."

"Yeah, okay, sure. We can both pretend it's not a fanny pack."

"Why don't you have a look around, Blaze? Explore your surroundings a bit."

I walk a few steps over to the side of the building to my left. It's a brick building. I press my hand against it. It's absolutely like you'd expect it to feel, solid. Even the coarse and chipped textures of the bricks and mortar are exactly right.

Next to my hand is a dumpster. It stinks, just like you'd expect it to. They totally nailed the stench. So cool.

An empty tin can rests on the lid of the dumpster. I swat at it like a cat. It clatters to the ground and rolls to a stop. Wow. The physics are incredible. This is basically the real world, but cooler. I start laughing with excitement. I feel like a kid again.

"This place is awesome, Dekker! I can't believe they gave you all this money to make it."

I can sense the tension in his voice without seeing his face. "If I'm right, Blaze, this game is in fact perfectly made for these times. I believe it's exactly what our world needs right now."

I shake my head, still grinning. "I can't imagine how that could possibly be true, but I think this is really cool anyway. I gotta say, I'm looking forward to punching some street jerks!" I say, genuinely excited now.

"Soon enough," Dekker reassures me. "Blaze, you won't normally hear me in the game world, but since you're the first actual player to go through this experience, we decided it would be easier for me to walk you through the basics before we spend a lot of time and money automating this acclimation process for future players. After all, what if we went through all the time and expense of designing the tutorial and the player was too stupid to figure out what we had created for them?

We don't have any time to waste."

I narrow my eyes and peer into the dark alley before me. "I'm ready," I say, all tough, like a cool guy.

"You say that. We shall see, grasshopper," he says, with a hint of a *Kung Fu* impression. I've never seen the old TV show, but somehow, I still know the reference. Through cultural osmosis, I guess.

And then, an actual grasshopper blinks into view in front of me, next to a filthy puddle at my feet. It's huge, though, many times the size of a regular grasshopper. It comes up to just above my ankle. The giant insect stands there calmly, doing its insect thing, being gross.

"This is a little on the nose," I call out to the ether.

"Speaking of on the nose..." Dekker begins.

A new text box appears in my field of vision.

Punch the grasshopper.

Okay, my first task in the game world. Stand in an alleyway and punch a bug in the face. Kinda cool, I guess. I shrug, bend down, and examine the giant creature carefully. It's not scared of me, and it's not drawn to me, either. It just continues to stand there.

"How do I do it?" I call up to the sky, "Do I just...do it? It's pretty small. What if I hit the asphalt by accident?"

"That's where physical control comes in, a skill you will need to develop and master."

Okay, I'll show him. I used to watch my mom's Tae Bo VHS tapes, so I know how to throw a punch. And I'm not at all squeamish, either. I kneel with one leg behind me for balance, focus my energy, and tap out an underhanded little punch at the creature.

Although it's literally just a gentle little rap of my fist, the creature instantly explodes in a tangle of limbs and thorax, or whatever the hell that part of the body is called. Just like that. The grasshopper pieces rain down to the ground, blink a few times in and out of existence, then disappear entirely. A green check appears next to the *Punch the grasshopper* text, then it all fades away.

I stand back up, grunting as I straighten, but only out of habit. It's surprisingly easy to rise to my feet now. Because, I realize, I'm not a middle-aged man anymore. In fact, I'm totally ripped, bro.

"Ha! No sweat!" I call out. This isn't bad. This basically feels like playing the old *Street Fury* game, but this time, it's really happening right in front of my face. I'm not just mashing buttons, but really smashing my fists. I think I could get used to this.

"So you know how to toss a punch. That's a good start," I hear Dekker reply. Was that a hint of sarcasm? Hard to tell. Probably.

Now, two large rats blink into existence in front of me. These creatures are also comparatively huge, much larger in scale than normal rodents, coming up to mid-shin. Both creatures stand there, darting their heads from side to side, compulsively sniffing the air. But they're chill. Not skittering around.

I mentioned I wasn't squeamish earlier, but now I'm frankly starting to get some squeam. I mean, these rats are gross. I'm not punching these things.

As if on cue, a new prompt appears in a text box in front of me.

Kick the rats.

Okay, *kicking* these things I can do. I take a deep breath to steady my nerves, step forward, and shoot a foot out and up in my best approximation of an NFL punter.

I hit the rat on my left square on its little rat jaw, and it bloodlessly explodes into furry limbs and, weirdly, a lot of teeth and also an entire ribcage—like this is the original *Mortal Kombat* or something.

The moment I do this, his buddy suddenly snaps to attention and lets out a terrifying hiss, locking eyes with me. Then this other rat immediately lunges straight at me.

"Aaaaahhhh! Get away! Get away!"

I start kicking at the little creature, but I'm panicking, and my efforts are not having much effect. It's dodging around my kicks, hissing, baring its teeth, and biting at me like a crazed Muppet. I'm screaming and shuffling around, trying to keep this thing's teeth away from me. It's crazy aggro, super vicious. I don't like any part of this.

After a few moments, though, I actually start getting bored of being terrified. I take a huge breath to center myself, and then jump up in the air as high as I can, which it turns out is quite high because I'm in great shape, and land directly on the beast's head.

I hear an audible pop as I land and stumble forward. I catch myself before tripping and falling, and I turn around just in time to see the rat blink out of existence. He's gone.

A green checkbox now appears next to the second prompt. Apparently stomping counts as kicking for the purposes of this task, good to know.

Okay, punch, kick. I got it. Easy.

A new text prompt appears.

Move forward and exit the alleyway.

So I do. It's about fifty yards ahead. The path is littered with trash. Even though it's daylight, it's very dark in the shadows of these tall buildings, and I can't see all the way to the end. I cautiously make my way forward.

I inch forward for a while, then I start striding a bit faster, with more confidence. Soon, I'm practically sauntering down the lane, already planning what I'll do when I get out on the street. First pass the tutorial with flying colors, then start wailing on some bad guys until I get to the boss. Yeah, this is going to be awesome.

I'm swaggering down the alley now, imagining the world beyond, and when I reach the halfway point, I start to hear what sounds like mumbling. It's just barely audible over the ambient city sounds, the roar of traffic and distant car horns, but it gets louder the closer I get to the exit.

As I approach the end of the alley, a warm light suddenly illuminates the darkness. I can see why it was so dark here—the alley is blocked off entirely at the entrance to the street. Large wooden boxes are stacked ten feet high from end to end; it's a crude and very video-gamey indication that I can progress no further at the moment.

But before I can get past these crates, first I have to get past this guy in front of me, standing over a newly-lit fire.

He's an older man, his face eerily lit by the flames dancing above a large red barrel in the middle of the alleyway. He's dressed in layers of filthy rags, and he's warming his hands, clad in fingerless gloves, over the fire.

I stop in my tracks, startled at the sight. I watch him from a short distance, maybe fifteen feet away. I remain in the darkness, controlling my breathing. He doesn't seem to notice me; he just continues to warm his hands. There's something especially unsettling about this tableau, and I don't quite know what it is.

Then it hits me. It's about 70 degrees out here. There's a slight city breeze, probably from the nearby river. It's a perfectly lovely day all around, no reason to be warming your hands around a fire. This man is not well. Another text box now fades up in my vision.

Jump-kick the hobo.

"Uh...no," I say, more quietly this time, so as not to disturb the man in front of me. "This is all a bit much. No, thank you."

Now the man is reaching down, gingerly picking up a hubcap from the ground, then holding it over the fire. I can see dark liquid rolling around inside its curvature, beginning to steam.

He is literally about to drink coffee from a hubcap.

"Again, a bit too on the nose vis a vis the hobo coffee, Dekker," I whisper, trying to control the tremble in my voice. "This scenario is relying on stereotypical and outdated archetypes, and I frankly won't stand for it. So I'll just...ah...go back down the alley and exit the other way."

The coffee drinker suddenly stops, pulling his head away from the fire to sniff the air around him. Oh, I don't like that at all. Then he looks up in my direction, although I can't tell if he sees me in the darkness. He bares his teeth as he wrinkles his nose. Or rather, he bares his *tooth*. His eyes narrow, and he points in my direction.

Okay, he sees me.

"I'm s-sorry, sir," I call out. My heart begins to hammer in my chest. I feel slightly faint, and my mouth gets dry. "I didn't mean to disturb you. I'll let you get back to your barrel fire."

He's still pointing at me silently, trembling with rage. Every moment he stands there makes me more and more convinced his next step is to open his mouth and scream at me like Donald Sutherland in the remake of the *Invasion of the Body Snatchers*. 1978, director Philip Kaufman. I never saw the movie, but I have absolutely seen short clips on the internet, and I don't like it one bit.

But he doesn't unleash a sudden, inhuman shriek. Instead, he smoothly pulls back his makeshift coffee cup from the flames and steps suddenly around the barrel toward me, his face now shrouded in darkness.

"What'd you say to me?" he slurs menacingly.

"I... I..."

He advances, shambling toward me. I thought he was a feeble old man, but now he looks younger and stronger. Now he's five feet away.

"I... I..." he repeats my words in a mocking yell that makes me flinch. I haven't felt this helpless since I was ten years old and a kid named Jock Peters was threatening to stuff me in a garbage can. I escaped with only a "dead arm" that time, a punch that made it numb for a while, but I don't think I'm going to get off so easily this time.

He violently smashes the hubcap to the ground. The horrible sound it makes as it clatters and bounces off the narrow brick walls overloads my brain. I let out a little scream.

"You made me spill my delicious java!" the man screams in rage.

"I'm sorry! I'll buy you another one!" I'm backing up now. This feels too real. Now I'm having very unpleasant flashbacks to the first days of the virus, when another person on the street was an enemy just by being near you, by breathing on you. That's ridiculous here in the game world—after all, we're all the way back in 199X, over twenty years before—but my body doesn't know that, and it cringes uncontrollably.

Now he's right up in my face, and I can smell his terrible breath. He's bigger than I thought, a few inches taller than me, and although he's skinny, he's still a serious threat. He's running on crazy, and I'm scared out of my mind.

I can defuse this. I have skills. Granted, I'm a little rusty, but I still know how to calm down a situation.

"Hey, there," I soothe. "Let's walk down the street together and I'll buy you a new cup of whatever..."

I don't get to say the words "you like" to finish the sentence, because suddenly, my mouth is full of fist.

Everyone has a plan until they get punched in the mouth. Somebody said that once, I remember at the time that I thought it was so wise. Though it turns out I didn't know the half of it. All I feel is shock. Everything just stops.

Then the pain comes. And then the anger.

I lash out with my fist, but it's ineffective. It's more of a push to his left chest. He staggers a bit, yelps with surprise, then goes deadly silent, rears back, and *really* punches me.

This time, the pain comes right away.

I've never been in a real fistfight before. I've punched thousands of people virtually, scrolling side-to-side on a CRT monitor, but never up close and intimate like this. I'm not pressing buttons anymore. This is (virtual) reality. Life and death.

I don't like it at all. I want to go home.

But I can't go home because now I'm in a headlock, being yanked around the alleyway by this raging maniac. I flail with my fists and try to make contact with his body, but he's in control, pulling me around like a ragdoll. I'm just along for the ride.

I can only see the ground, which allows me to focus on my peripheral vision. Up top, I notice an overlay of my health bar, just like I would have expected on an arcade screen. And the health bar is way, way down, also just like I would have expected.

We spin to a stop, and then, from out of nowhere, I see his fist again. The uppercut sends me staggering away from him. My health bar gets lower, down to maybe 30% now, an accurate visual representation of how physically painful this is.

I'm in serious trouble. And if I die here, I know I'm not coming back.

"Eye of the tiger, Blaze. Eye of the tiger!" Dekker encourages from everywhere around me, his voice reverberating in my brain.

I steady myself and launch forward, socking my aggressor in the face as I scream out in reply to Dekker with each punch to the hobo's jaw.

"You're...not...helping!"

The man staggers but doesn't go down, and the prompt reappears: *Jump-kick the hobo.* So, I take a deep breath and run forward, kicking out and screaming like a floppy maniac. I have no idea how to do this.

My kick goes wide. In fact, my foot goes right into the flaming barrel, which tips over and knocks into the man, promptly setting him on fire.

"Oh my god, he's on fire," I say to myself.

He starts screaming as flames race up his jacket. God, that was fast. He must be soaked in whiskey.

Hey, don't just assume that, John, that's very stereotypical.

The hobo is screaming now and flailing around in raw panic. I'm panicking now, too. This was really not supposed to go this way.

"Stop, drop, and roll! Stop, drop, and roll!!" I yell out, wanting to help.

He takes the direction and collapses to the ground, rubbing himself fiercely into the filthy asphalt and eventually coming to a stop, motionless in a smoking heap.

I walk over to him and peer down. I watch his filthy rags heave up and down slowly. He's still breathing. Good lord, this isn't over yet.

The new text box before me is bigger, and the words are now flashing red.

Jump-kick the hobo.

"Good god, still?" I sigh heavily, then follow the letter of the law, doing a tiny perfunctory hop up in the air and letting my right foot lash out, catching him gently in the midsection. That's apparently enough for him to start blinking out of existence.

As his prone body appears and disappears, flashing in and out of this world, he looks me dead in the eye and says, "I can't feel my feet no more."

And then, my tormentor is finally gone, he's completely disappeared. I barely notice this, because I'm hunched over, gasping for breath, trying to focus through the pain.

Then Dekker's voice returns to my ear. "Congratulations, you've almost passed the tutorial."

"Dekker, that was *horrifying*. I have trauma."

"Yes, you've been injured. You need to recover your health," Dekker agrees.

"I need to recover my *mental* health. Are there counseling services here in the city of New Arcadia? A free clinic I can go to?"

"You're about to find out," Dekker says. "There's only one more thing to do, Blaze, and that's to get through this stack of crates and out into the city proper."

A new prompt appears.

Use your special move to escape.

Dekker continues, "However, utilizing your special move requires a small expenditure of health, and you are not in great shape at the moment. I strongly suggest you eat something right now to regain some of your health. Take a look at the barrel."

I move my eyes away from the puddle where the hobo was laying only a moment before, over to the broken pieces of the barrel, which are still on the ground. The fire is now completely out, and in the epicenter, where the barrel once stood, sits a steaming turkey. Like, a full-on dinner plate with a big turkey leg on it, sitting on a nice bed of lettuce.

Ah, yes. The classic beat 'em up game trope, recover your health with food from a broken barrel. It makes sense on an arcade monitor, sort of, but here, it feels truly weird.

Still, I'm hungry. I pick it up and eat the whole thing. Once I start, I can't stop, it's so delicious. I feel restored and confirm it by watching my health bar creep back up just above the halfway point.

Dekker's voice returns as I'm finishing the last bite, "You've got fifty percent of your health back now. You're out of the danger zone, at least. You'll probably want to stop at a restaurant or food stand to get the rest of it back."

"Great, want to meet me for lunch?" I quip.

"You won't hear from me again in the game world

unless it's very important. You'll be able to explore this neighborhood now. It will be your home base, probably for a while."

"Okay."

"Well, what are you waiting for?" he asks, and then is silent. If he's still there, he's not saying anything.

"Yeah, what am I waiting for?" I ask myself.

I focus on the wall of crates before me. I breathe slowly, conjuring an image of the bright, shining city behind them. Then I picture myself smashing through the wall to reach my new home, a spray of two-by-fours and splinters exploding all around me. That's how it's going to go. I mean, I'm a special guy, I can do a special move.

I stand several feet away, then step forward with focus and intention, unleashing my perfectly-pissed fists.

POW.

Chapter 8

Burger Time

T he POW turns into a POW-POW-POW-POW-POW. I'm
spinning and I can't stop.

I smash easily through the wall of crates, and
wooden beams and splinters rain down around me as I
burst out of the alley and spiral out onto the sidewalk.
My fists are still flying in circles, I can't stop them, and
my head faces in the direction I'm traveling, like a dancer.
I am not normally this coordinated.

"Watch out, buddy!" a man yells.

I can barely hear the guy's voice above my own
scream, and in my peripheral vision, I see a young dude
leap back on the sidewalk, bringing his arms protectively
to his face. I barely missed knocking him out.

"Sorry!" I yell back at him between spins. "I don't
know...how this...works!"

I feel so powerful, but also profoundly out of
control. This special attack seems to have a programmed
animation, which means my body won't stop executing it
until it's finished.

I look down to admire my fancy footwork, watching helplessly as my legs continue to dance, and then my head automatically rears up to the sky. I unleash a primal bellow of rage and exhilaration, one final burst of energy.

Finally, I begin to slow down, my steps decreasing and arms lowering. Now I'm staggering to a halt, doubling over with my hands on my knees, breathing heavily, staring at the sidewalk.

"Hey, man, you almost punched me in the face!" the same voice cries out.

I look up, still doubled over, to see the young guy I almost clipped with my special move. He's standing in front of me, wearing blue jeans, a blue sport coat, and a chunky necklace over a white turtleneck. His hair is blond and perfectly coiffed, one side is buzzed with little horizontal lines shaved into it. He looks like Zack Morris from *Saved by the Bell* and he's puffing out his chest, looking for a confrontation. I decide to give him one.

I push up to my full height and raise a fist, yelling, "It was unintentional, but I'd be happy to try it again if you'd like!"

My retort was dumb—too stilted and formal. I'll have to work on it. But it does the trick.

"EEP!" he actually, literally yells, and then Saved by the Bell turns and runs away.

I watch him haul ass down the sidewalk for a bit, smirking, then shift my gaze to take in a vibrant urban scene. I'm standing on a wide avenue packed with rushing pedestrians, cars and bicycles rolling down the street, all framed by three-story buildings showcasing bustling storefronts. As my eyes sweep across the scene, a giant title card appears in my entire field of vision. It reads, in an appropriately retro font:

STAGE 1: THE STREETS

Whoa. This is awesome. I can't stop grinning. Then, another phrase fades in underneath the title in the box.

Defeat the stage boss to proceed.

Okay, I can do this. Let's start punching a straight line right up to the main bad guy.

The title card fades away, and I focus back on the scene before me, ready to fight. But there are no hordes of bad guys with brass knuckles, no epic brawls waiting for me.

It's just...a normal East Coast city street. Busy, but peaceful.

Wow, I haven't been in a city in years. Plus, L.A. doesn't really count, so it's actually been even longer since I last took a trip to see a real city. And that was for a conference in Boston, and I didn't really leave the airport hotel. When did I last visit New York? I guess it's been six years.

People are walking past, and I can see their whole faces! Nobody's wearing a mask. A business lady clops past in her high heels, giving me a wide berth. Not because she's afraid of some virus. She's not, because there is no virus. No, I realize that everybody is choosing to ignore the person who moments ago was a flailing, shrieking madman busting out of the alleyway with his spinning fists. I suppose that's just as well.

I look around some more, taking in what I missed on first glance. I scan over to the intersection, and I can easily read the street signs there. Wow, my vision hasn't been this good in years.

174th Avenue, it reads. I must be uptown. And the wide avenue, the one I'm standing on, is Fuller Avenue. Got it.

I do a quick check of my stats and see that my health has gone back down a bit below 50%. That's the price of the special attack. I scan the shop windows and signs on both sides of the avenue, looking for something to eat. There's a donut shop straight ahead. Mmmm, donuts. There's also a shoe store, a bodega...all sorts of places. It's a little rundown here, this is obviously not the best neighborhood, but it's alive, thriving even.

Yeah, still no endless hordes of enemies to beat up. There was only that lone scaredy-cat preppie that ran off. Part of me thought I'd be halfway through Stage 1 by now.

My eyes are now drawn to another place entirely, away from the storefront enticements. Across the street, I spot a beautiful green place—a simple neighborhood park.

And that's where my feet start taking me. I feel compelled to check it out right now, even though my stomach is grumbling fiercely. I move slowly, in a trance, making my way through this rushing, bustling city street. A young blond woman rollerblades past me, rocking a neon pink helmet and matching kneepads. This used to be the height of fashion, as I vaguely recall from the Sears catalog.

I have to step to the side to avoid a hard-charging man in a business suit, bellowing into a giant brick of a mobile phone as he stalks down the street. Super-rude behavior, but I don't knock him out cold, like I know I could. I'm really not feeling violent at all right now, just quietly awed at the city life, the traffic noise, the smells from the hotdog stand across the street. I guess I never thought I would experience anything like this again.

I cross the street and enter the park. It's small, but cozy here. With the taller buildings farther away, the midday sun shines down brightly, casting a warm, inviting glow on the trees, the green grass, the rainbow sprinkle of flowers everywhere. I follow a quaint cobblestone path and make my way to an empty park bench.

I sit down, lean back, and rest my arms on the back of this wooden bench, gazing up at the sky through the trees. The city sounds have faded to a low ebb behind me, and I focus on the gentle birdsong, the call-and-response from all corners of this peaceful oasis.

It's a genuine comfort to be back among people again. I'm surprised by how familiar and good it feels. I figured when I busted out of that tutorial, I would be ready for action, ready to knock out some jerks, but I really need this quiet space right now. This warm sun-kissed bench, this green verdant space, this brilliant blue sky above me. It may not be strictly real, but it sure feels like the real thing, and I never thought I would feel this again. I didn't know until I sat down how much I missed it.

I turn my head gently from side to side, up and down, soaking it all in with wide eyes and an open mouth, and then I close my eyes. I breathe, slowly taking in the sounds, the smells, the sensation of the bench beneath me, the cool breeze and warm sun. I am not ready, player one. Not yet.

✪✪✪

Some time later, it's impossible to say because I don't have a watch, I slowly stand and stretch. It has increasingly dawned on me over these last few minutes that I can do anything, absolutely anything at all in this place. Go anywhere, see anything, set my own schedule.

I am finally and truly free again.

I should grab some lunch.

I start walking back down the cobblestone path and make my way back to the busy avenue. Man, I am really hungry now. I need to find a place to get a bite. Sure, I could bust up a few barrels and probably find another turkey leg or something, but it's been so long since I've been to a sit-down restaurant. I suppose I'd settle for just about anything right now.

The initial shock of the freedom of the city is fading, so my ingrained habits are returning, and I'm now finding it harder to walk near people again. I'm recoiling from everybody that gets closer than a few feet away, earning me some suspicious looks from my fellow citizens. I still have a fear of getting a virus; it's a perfectly reasonable one, considering all that I've been through. None of these people have any idea what's coming for them one day.

Wait, hold on, this isn't actually real life, John.

Excuse me, that is to say, this isn't actually real life, *Blaze*.

And I don't think these are *people*, exactly. I think they're, like, computer programs, or algorithms, or artificial intelligence, or whatever. They may look real, and feel real, but it's all part of the simulation. I could get directions to the subway from them, but if I started talking to someone about, say, philosophy... I bet things would get real weird, real quick.

They're not real people, and they're not full of a deadly virus, Blaze. It's the 90s, and everything's still great. Peace and prosperity. No more cold war. Rock and roll music.

With that in mind, I force myself to walk confidently down the street and try to unlearn what I have been conditioned to fear, head held high. A young couple passes me, and I barely flinch this time. Okay, I can do this.

I pass the donut shop, exerting all of my willpower to force myself to keep walking. After all, I've got a hot bod to maintain now, have to keep it in shape. I somehow keep strolling down the street without stopping in and emptying their display cases, hoping something else will pop up soon.

Something does pop up, just down the block, and it's a good old-fashioned fast-food place. Wow, talk about a blast from the past. I can tell it's a hamburger joint before I even reach it, because there's a large circular sign that juts out perpendicular to the sidewalk, and it's in the shape of a giant burger, with neon tubing around the buns and meat for when it's nighttime.

I reach the front door of the restaurant and take it all in. On the front door, giant letters over the glass spell out the words BURGER ITEM.

Huh. So, the name of the restaurant is...Burger Item. If this is a franchise, I certainly haven't heard of it before. Maybe they invented it for the game. Maybe the game developers could have done a better job coming up with a name.

The whole storefront is made up of large windows, so I shift my focus to check out the interior, and John aka Blaze's instant restaurant review is that this place is kind of a dump. There are a few single folks sitting in plastic booths in a row underneath the windows inside, and a few more loners at small tables in the center of the restaurant.

I step back and peer farther down the avenue. Nothing else jumps out at me, so I decide to give this place a shot, because I really can't wait any longer.

I step forward and kick the front door open with a sharp bang. Partly to be cool and show off my street fighting moves, and partly because I'm still freaked out to touch any shared surfaces with my hands.

Everybody looks up at the loud sound, and then focus on me with their weary, uncaring eyes. After a moment, they all sink their heads back down to their tables, concentrating on shoveling more precious junk food into their gullets. I take another step inside, and then promptly freeze in place. My legs lock up and my throat gets dry. I squeeze my eyes shut to block out the sight. There may be only a few people inside here, but to someone who's been completely alone for over three years, it's a lot more than I'm used to.

I start breathing slowly and deliberately, a trick to calm myself down. I feel the front door slowly shut behind me, notice the city sounds fade swiftly away when it does, and I use that as a cue to open my eyes again. I can focus much better now, and I start looking more closely at the people sitting to my left. I begin to notice health bars above their heads, and even their names, if I look just right.

There's a businessman just to the left of me. He's sitting alone in the first booth, facing me. Eyes downcast, wearing thick glasses, white shirt and tie with no suit jacket; he's laser-focused on wolfing down a basket of cheese fries. I gotta say, they look gross, and yet also pretty damn good. I glance up over his head and see his life bar, which is steadily increasing, and also a character name. D. Fens. Huh. I wonder what the D stands for.

My eyes drop back down to the man himself, sullen eyes staring into or perhaps right through the tabletop, munching his fries mechanically. Then I look back up to his information. I'm focusing, then refocusing between the man and his floating stats, like I was looking at a Magic Eye print. You know those art books that have the weird color patterns that hide 3D objects on a 2D printed page? If you were alive back in 199X, you'd remember. After a few moments of concentration, I can see both the outline of his head and the blurry lettering above it at the exact same time...

Suddenly, the sounds of the street rush back to my ears. I feel a hard shove on my back, and I stumble forward, tripping over my own feet and almost spilling to the ground before I catch myself. Somebody just pushed me!

"Watch it, loser!" a nasally voice behind me sneers.

I hold a hand up to the store wall on my right, steadying myself, then look wildly around, trying to find my bearings. I see a figure in front of me right as it pushes me back into the wall.

The figure keeps moving past me, and now I can see

he's an honest-to-God punk rocker, sporting denim and leather, large metal screws for earrings, and an actual bright pink mohawk. This person really went to the trouble. I'm too stunned to even remember to fight back, and now he's already walking toward the far counter, surely to order some food.

Should I kick his ass? I could totally kick his ass right now. I do a quick gut check. I'm not hurt, just surprised. I think for a second, and then I realize, oh, I was blocking the front door. It was maybe my fault a little bit. This is probably not worth fighting over. Not yet, anyway. I decide I'm going to give him one more chance before I smack him, secretly wishing he blows his chance so I can indeed smack him in the face.

I step forward calmly and line up a few feet behind the punk, who's now at the counter, ordering some food. As I'm waiting, I notice a metal bar that appears to be on his face. I can't tell what it is from my spot behind him. It looks like it maybe goes through his nose, but he's completely turned away from me, so I can't be sure. Could it be a giant safety pin going through his septum?

I try not to get too distracted. I need to know what garbage food I'm going to be getting, after all. And man, I am really hungry now. So I'm doing the Magic Eye thing again, only this time looking at the menu while trying to simultaneously keep an eye on the punk's pink head, hoping he'll turn around so I can see what weird situation he has going on with the metal rod on his face.

Before I realize it, he's finished with his order, and he turns right around to face me.

"What are you looking at?" he sneers at me.

Sure enough, he's sporting a comically giant safety pin, at least a foot long, jammed right through his nose. A life bar and stats are now visible above his tall pink mohawk. His actual Christian name appears to be Punk.

"Uh...a punk!" I offer.

He stares me down. Hard. This is it. I tense up, every nerve on edge.

In these last moments before the imminent attack, I realize he looks almost exactly like the guy on the bus Spock gave the Vulcan neck pinch to in *Star Trek IV: The Voyage Home*. 1986, director Leonard Nimoy.

But he doesn't throw a punch. Instead, he suddenly throws his head back and laughs.

"Ahahaha... That's right, I am. A real punk! And don't you forget it!" Then he throws the sign of the horns with his hand, closes his eyes, and sticks out his tongue, head-banging with great vigor.

I just stand there. It's a little awkward.

Suddenly, he stops, no expression on his face. He walks straight to the soda machine next to the pickup area at the counter and positions his mouth underneath a spigot named "Ebola Cola - Twice the Viral Load!" Huh, remember when Ebola was all we had to worry about? I realize the drink is supposed to be all edgy and hardcore and super-caffeinated, but really, it's making me kind of feel sweetly nostalgic. These are simpler times.

I barely have time to consider all this before he slams on the lever and drinks a long quaff from the spigot. He takes a little soda shower, too. Then he sticks his mouth back underneath to gargle a final gulp, treats

New Arcadia: Stage One 127

the restaurant to a very impressive belch, then swipes an apple pie off the counter and sits at a table, trailing rivulets of sticky sweet Ebola Cola as he goes.

That was really gross, yet also quintessentially punk. I have to hand it to him there.

"Uhm, sir, how can I help you?" a quivering voice asks me, which pulls my focus back to the counter.

Right, it's time to order.

I step forward, still staying a few feet away from the acne-faced kid behind the register out of habit. I look around for a digital display for a few seconds before I realize I'm supposed to tell this person, an actual human being, sort of, what I want to eat. I've been opening canned food from drones for a very long time, and even before that I was pressing touchscreens and tapping credit cards in fast-food joints for years.

But not here. Back in good old 199X, you still have to talk to be-pimpled young wage earners.

"Uh....yeah..." I begin.

I glance down at his name badge. It says "Skip," and then in smaller lettering beneath that, "Assistant Manager." Above his head floats a full life bar and the character name "Trevor Pants (aka Skip)."

"Trev— Skip," I continue. "I'd like to have..."

An uncomfortable silence. I can see the food menu above me, but I'm not focusing. This is all still a little much.

The kid nervously clears his throat. "Sir, can I interest you in one of our Burger Item Urban Meals?"

"What's in that?" I ask, looking back down at him. "No, you know what? Just give me some...just give me some cheese fries, actually."

"Large or upsettingly large, sir?"

"The second one, thank you," I confirm.

"Okay, one upsettingly large order of our Fries to Power, add cheese. Anything else, sir?" he asks, pushing buttons on his old-school cash register, no LED displays in sight.

"Maybe just a cup for water," I decide.

"Perhaps you'd like to try an iced Cappio? It's the latest in refreshing coffee beverages."

"No, I... Wow, jeez, Cappio? I remember Cappio. A bottle of that tasted like a shoe full of sugar. Wow. Uh...no, just the water, please," I conclude.

Jesus, *Cappio*. Never thought I'd hear that name again. I wonder if they have Squeeze-Its here in the bodegas? It seems like they haven't licensed current brands to use in this game world, but I guess old zombie brands are somehow fair use.

"Alright, that will be a dollar and seventy-nine cents, sir," Skip says.

"Ohhhh..." I drawl. "Like, American money?"

Right. All this time, I had been just sort of ignoring the whole economy element of all this. Hoping that there would be some system in the game I hadn't been trained on yet. That a glowing money pouch would magically appear.

Nope. My pockets are empty. So is my fanny pack.

In a lifetime full of embarrassing and sad moments, it's going to be hard to beat reaching into my fanny pack to pay for fries and realizing that I can't. And yet, it's also kind of comforting to know that there's at least one thing this place has in common with the real world. In both of them, I'm dead broke.

"Hey, um..." I begin, sheepishly, "I don't think I actually have my wallet with me right now...."

But I don't say anything more, because I'm cut off by the sounds of high-pitched shrieks. Something's happening. Danger. What is it? I see the kid's eyes suddenly shift to focus behind me.

"Get it away, get it away! AAaaaaaAAA!!" a voice screams in terror.

I recognize that nasally whine, and I instinctively spin around to size up the threat.

Right behind me, I see a giant rat—just like the ones in the tutorial—standing on a nearby tabletop, yanking a warm apple pie pocket out of its paper sleeve with its disgusting buck teeth. Standing on the chair behind it, gibbering inconsolably and holding up his baggy pantlegs like they were the hem of a skirt, is the pink-haired punker.

"No no noooooooo!" the punker cries, pulling at the denim around his thighs so his pant-legs rise. He dances back and forth on his tippy-toes. I have to say, he's not nearly as intimidating now as he was when he first entered the store. He's clearly scared to death of this rat. To be fair, it is ridiculously large and ghoulish-looking.

"Ah, sir..." I hear the kid behind the counter begin tentatively. I turn from the frightened punk back to Trevor

Pants aka Skip, who is impressively calm, considering the ruckus in his store. "If you could take care of our restaurant issue, I'm sure we can come to an agreement on the fries."

The kid has the beginnings of a mustache, and I realize that kind of puts me at ease. Like he's vaguely an authority figure here, and that's comforting somehow. Also, there's a prompt that appears right next to Skip's doughy face. The text box is translucent and ephemeral, and I'm sure only I can see it.

Quest: Get a Job - deal with Burger Item's rodent infestation.

Rewards: free lunch and offer of gainful employment.

I consider this for a moment. The old beat 'em up games didn't have quests. By this time, I would be halfway through the third stage, and about three dollars in quarters. The designers seem to have blended modern game mechanics into the arcade shell. Okay, I can roll with this.

I turn to Skip and nod gravely, signaling that it's on. He smiles. The text prompt is still there, though. I haven't officially accepted the quest yet.

Confused, I swipe at the pop-up screen near his face. I push at the button, but my hand goes right through it, so I try again and again. The kid looks confused, I'm basically pawing at the air next to him like an idiot. The punk is still screaming behind me.

Then I remember my training: I have to push it *with intent*. I reach out again and imagine pushing the button as I make the same motion with my hand. That does the trick. I see the button push in, both hear and feel a very satisfying click, and the pop-up fades away. I have accepted the quest. Skip's face changes from confusion to delight.

"I gotcha, Skip," I say with a smile, rapping my knuckles reassuringly on the counter.

I take three steps over to the table. The pie-munching rat is still right there, and so is the simpering punk quivering above it on the chair. I rear back and punch the hell out of the rat, just like in the tutorial.

It's a stunning blow that stops the beast in its tracks. For that matter, it stops the shrieking punk, too. They both stand there slack-jawed. The rat is still there—it must be more powerful than the other ones I faced—so I pop it again. That shakes the creature out of his stupor. Suddenly, his terrifying buck teeth are bared, and he rears back to bite me. But before he can, I punch him once more.

The third time's the charm. The rat basically explodes. It's very satisfying. Quite gross, too.

The punk has shielded his eyes and is turned to the side. His face and clothes are covered in exploded rat, but it's already blinking out of existence. He'll be all clean in just a moment. Well, he'll still be filthy in the sense that he doesn't seem to have taken a shower in a while, but at least he'll be rat-free in a few seconds.

Sure enough, the rat parts disappear, and the punk slides slowly down the chair until he's seated again, sobbing with gratitude the whole way.

"Enjoy your pie," I say, casually reaching down and tossing the dropped apple pie remains back up onto the table.

"Thank you," the punk whimpers. Then he starts scooping the remaining pie pieces into his trembling mouth with hands shaking from fear as I slowly walk away.

God, that was cool. I'm such a cool guy right now.

Quest Complete: Get a Job - deal with Burger Item's rodent infestation.

An experience meter appears below my health bar; it's smaller than the health one. The experience bar inches up, showing that I've gotten a little closer to Level 2. It looks like I've still got a long way to go, but it's a start.

I saunter back to the counter, reaching it right as Skip says, "Order up!" in an awed tone of voice. He bows his head and holds out my tray of cheese fries. I accept them gladly.

"Sir, that was awesome!" he gushes. "We actually have a job opportunity available right now. I'm not sure if you're looking currently, but..."

No way. I'm riding high on my first victory. I feel like I could take on the world right now. Become boss of this whole city. I offer him a condescending bark of a laugh.

"Ha! I appreciate the offer, kid, but..."

Then I stop. I start to really think about it. Here I am, in a brand-new world. No money in my pockets. No idea what I'm supposed to be doing. And what was the scope of my big triumphant victory just now? When you really think about it, all I did was punch a rat in the face so I could get some free cheese fries.

But maybe with a job, a little stability, I won't have to sleep in the gutter tonight.

Jeez, you never had to worry about these kinds of problems in *Street Fury*. In the old games, you could solve all your problems with punches. But it's becoming increasingly clear that that approach won't work here.

"Actually...yeah, that sounds great, kid," I admit. "Uh... When can I start?"

"Really?" Skip is so happy, it's quite touching. "Wow! Well, I don't know when... I mean, you can start right away, sir!"

"Oh, that's great! Really, that puts me at ease." I feel my stomach grumble again. "Hey, uh, do you mind if I eat these fries first? I'm actually pretty hungry right now."

"Yes, sir, although I must note that you have just touched an unclean creature, would you like a wet nap before you enjoy your meal?"

I consider for a moment. "You know what, Skip? I would enjoy a wet nap. Also known as a moist towelette." I repeat the horrific phrase for my own amusement, savoring every word. "Yes. A moist. Towelette. Would be very helpful. Thank you."

Chapter 9

Gritty City

For the last three hours, I've been wearing a stupid striped shirt, a paper sailor-style hat, and allowing a barely-mustachioed waif of an assistant manager named Skip to very politely boss me around.

At this point in the game, I figured I'd have my fists slamming into the face of the final boss, then sitting back and watching the credits roll. Instead, my fists are full of frozen fries, and now I'm tossing them into a bubbling fryer in the Burger Item back kitchen.

And...it's kind of awesome.

It's busywork, sure, but it's not so bad. I mean, it's no different than pecking at my tablet screen to make sure my delivery drones don't get shot down. No different from crafting harpoon upgrades in *World of Moby*. Well, actually, this might be better. Because as stupid as this sounds, I'm really working with my hands, truly connected to my labor. Or at least, my brain is sure fooled into thinking I am.

And I like it! It's been too long, and it feels really good. Like what I'm doing matters. You know, for the fake digital people who come in here and want to eat fake digital garbage food.

"Wow, sir, you've really gotten the hang of this quickly! It took me at least a week here before I stopped crying," Skip says, peering over my shoulder, flashing a proud smile.

"Well, Skip, my first job was at a cafe, so I've done food prep before, once upon a time. I guess it's just like riding a bike." With the fries now crisping into a golden brown in the fryer, I start cleaning the counter space around it and arranging the paper sleeves for serving.

"Yeah, I had a bike once. It was stolen," Skip chirps, which makes me glance up at him. He's still smiling. The effect is a little disconcerting.

"I'm sorry to hear that, Skip. This seems like a pretty tough neighborhood. How long have you been here?"

"Well, as long as I can remember, I suppose. Satan's Pantry is a nice place to live, very walkable, which is quite handy if you don't have a bike. On account of it got stolen."

"I'm sure," I agree. "Wait, that's the name of this neighborhood? Satan's Pantry? Seriously? That sounds... both scary and stupid." It takes me a second, but I get the lazy rewrite. Hell's Kitchen, Satan's Pantry. Chum has all the money in the world and they can't hire a decent set of game writers?

Skip considers for a moment. "Hm... I always assumed the name was from the original Dutch settlers.

Something that maybe got lost in translation." He stares blankly into the distance for another long moment, then suddenly shakes his head. "Anyway, how long have you been here? Are you new in town, Mister Blaze? And please forgive me if I'm asking too personal a question."

"You can call me Blaze. And no, not at all. In fact, I am pretty new in town. Anything I need to know about this place?"

Before he can answer, a loud beeping begins, and Skip nods over to the fries. They're ready to go.

I pick the basket up by the handle. The fries inside are sizzling. They look delicious. Skip winces and recoils a bit, signaling for me to be careful as I set them down to cool. He's very sensitive, but a good tutor.

"Very nice," he says, beaming with pride. "Well, Blaze, as I said, overall this is a nice neighborhood to live in, more or less…" A pained expression returns to his face, this time because he seems to be struggling with how to tell me some bad news diplomatically.

"More or less what, Skip?"

"Well, sir, it's all the punkers and the gangs hanging around here."

"Oh! I didn't know there were gangs here." This is what I was hoping to hear. Finally, some enemies to fight.

"Yeah, it's true, you've gotta be careful out there. There are some very mean gangs in this city. They're always fighting, and if it's not with each other, then maybe it's with you or me."

"Tell me more," I encourage.

"Well, the ones in our neighborhood are called the Spankers. It's because they'll whack you good if you cross them."

"That sounds very scary," I say.

"Yeah, it can be. Just keep an eye out, and you should be okay. What you've really got to watch out for is... Oh, maybe I shouldn't say."

"No, what? You can tell me, Skip. I'm sure it would help me be a better Burger Item employee," I say over my shoulder as I start emptying the soft-serve spillover tray.

Suddenly, I feel two quick boosts. Like I've just had two quick tequila shots, but without the burning in my throat. It feels good. In my peripheral vision, I receive the following notifications.

Social - your conversational skills have gone up. More dialogue options are available when speaking with other characters.

Cooking - your food preparation skill has gone up.

Huh. Okay, that's great. I guess that's how the game works. I don't see any numbers, but maybe it's all running under the hood, out of sight. I have to say, those notifications felt pretty good, like I was getting two dopamine hits.

I turn to face Skip, and he's smiling. "Well, sir, since you put it that way, I'll tell you. The word on the street is that the Spankers are pushing a new drug. But not a drug like medicine is a drug. It's an illegal drug, very bad and very powerful." He lowers his voice to almost a whisper. "It's called...Drug X."

"Wow," I say. Hm... Drug X, Project X. Maybe there's a

connection. "Drug X, huh?"

Skip winces and puts his finger over his lips. Apparently, I'm being too cavalier by saying it out loud. He continues, in a quieter voice, "Yeah, sometimes you'll see people come in here, and I'm pretty sure they're on the stuff. They're imagining people that aren't there, making up whole stories in their brains. It seems so real to them, like they're working out some really heavy issues, like psychologically and stuff, but there's, like, nothing there. If you know what I mean," he finishes, eyes downcast.

"I think I get it. Thanks for letting me know," I reassure him.

Skip smiles broadly, the little wisps of his mustache turning up to the sky. "Winners don't use drugs! That's what the mayor says, and I believe him."

Huh, that's the phrase that used to be on the attract screen of every arcade game in the early 90s. "Yeah, it's great advice. You know, where I'm from, Skip, they say G.H.O.S.T."

"What's that?" He laughs nervously. "That sounds scary."

"It's an acronym. It means, Get High On Sleep Tonight."

They don't actually say that where I come from. My brother Steve and I made it up one night. Thinking of Steve makes me suddenly sad.

"Haha, that's very funny! And also great advice!" Skip chortles.

"I know, it's served me well," I say glumly. With a sigh, I try to push Steve out of my mind. "None of that funny stuff for me. I don't even drink anymore, not since the quarantine."

"Not since the *what*?" Skip asks, scrunching his eyes and pursing his lips, not understanding.

"Oh, nothing," I say. Shoot, I forgot where I was. "Just a figure of speech, Skip. Where I come from, we also say the words "hella" and "badical.""

He laughs. "Oh, I've heard of those! You must be from California. Well, speaking of getting high on sleep tonight…" Skip checks his watch. "Yep, it's closing time. I'll take it from here, sir. We can train you on closing another day."

I start taking off my apron, feeling proud of my labor. "Sounds good. I gotta say, Skip, this was a surprisingly fun day. I…really enjoy working here."

He beams with joy. It's very sweet, really. "I'm so glad to hear you say that, Mr. Blaze! I think it's important work that we do here. Providing food for the city."

"Just Blaze, please. So… Do you pay me now or when I clock out or…"

"You're in luck! Payday is actually tomorrow," Skip tells me.

"So…not tonight?" Oh, great.

"Like I said, payday is actually tomorrow! That's very soon, Blaze."

"Thanks, Skip," I mumble over my shoulder, stumbling over to my locker in a daze. I change out of my work shirt to my t-shirt, all the while my mind is playing the same thought over and over again.

Where the hell am I going to sleep tonight?

✪✪✪

I'm back on the street, walking down Fuller Avenue.

The half-moon is rising just over the horizon. It's just past dusk and getting a little chilly. There are only a few people out and about now. Everyone's very quiet. This must be a part of town that shuts down pretty early. Either it's more of a nine-to-five kind of neighborhood, or, more likely, a dangerous place to be after dark.

I spot an ornate four-story building up ahead, past the 171st Street intersection, with beautiful ionic columns in the entranceway. I get a little closer to discover that it's actually a library, the Fuller Avenue branch of the New Arcadia Public Library. Maybe I can find a way to stay here overnight? But no, when I can look past the front columns, I see that the main doors and windows are completely boarded up.

Damn, so much for my brand-new dream of just checking out all the books I want and sleeping in the library basement and staying away from people and reading all day, every day for the rest of my life.

I peer farther down the street and see a homeless shelter. This would be a good option for tonight, but then I discover that this place is boarded up, too. Damn, this really must be a bad part of town.

I amble down the avenue another couple of blocks. I haven't passed a single soul on the street. Finally, I stop next to an overflowing trash can on the sidewalk. I look down, sigh, and grab a discarded newspaper from the top of the heap, then start trudging back where I came from.

Should I just go back to Burger Item and sleep in the alley there? I don't know, they had some pretty sketchy customers in there, even during the daytime. But then I pass by the library again, and I think, what proper street gangs are gonna hang out where books are? This place is probably as safe as I could possibly be tonight. I peer around the back of the building and see that the back alley seems to be quiet and well-shielded from the neighboring structures.

I find a relatively cozy and hidden spot near a short staircase to a rear basement entrance, then make a newspaper pillow and a newspaper blanket, and lay down, snuggling into my surroundings. It's not so bad, I suppose. Not much worse than my little house in North Fontana, and here the weather is much more pleasant. Under the dim fluorescent light from the building, I can make out the day's headlines on the newspaper page laying above my chest.

The New Arcadia Tribune

April 25, 199X

"Drug X Hits Home for New Arcadia Residents"

It's a short article about the new dangerous drug in town, one that messes up the minds of its users and terrifies everyone in its orbit. It seems like it's become a real problem here.

"Mayor Vows Action Against Gang Menace"

This one is a short article about the various gangs in town, including the Spankers of Satan's Pantry. Apparently, they've grown from a simple street gang to a citywide terror in recent weeks, simply by being a prodigious and reliable seller of the hot new wonder drug.

Underneath the article is a picture, or rather, a silhouette—just a black outline of a hulking man's head and chest. He's clad in a leather jacket with spikes on the shoulders, posed in front of a blank gray background. The caption reads: "The head of the Satan's Pantry Spankers gang is believed to be connected to Drug X suppliers. Please contact NAPD if you have any information."

The words start to blur on the page, and it's no wonder. I'm exhausted. It's been quite a day. I lay back and let the newspaper page cover my chest.

Even under these very less-than-ideal circumstances, I drift off rapidly into a deep, dreamless sleep.

Chapter 10

Join the Fun Club Today! Mac.

G ood morning, New Arcadia.

My eyes are still closed, but ambient light is seeping through the thin membrane of my eyelids. My mouth is dry, and my lips are pursed tight. I feel frozen in place, with a dull, pulsing ache in my bones. If I had dreams in the night, I don't remember them.

Slowly, I shake off the sleep, becoming aware of crunching papers as I stir, and I peek one eye open a tiny bit.

There's a bright, beautiful sky above, framed by the roofs of the library and other brick buildings across the alley. Many of the newspaper pages I used for makeshift blankets have blown off or been kicked away in the night. I lift my head up from the ground to peer down at my body. Everything's still there, although all I really have are the clothes on my back. And my dumb fanny pack. The zipper's still zipped, so that's a relief.

I slowly shake the sleep from my head, then stretch my back from side to side on the ground. As a forty-year-old guy with a degenerating disc, this is usually a pretty involved procedure, with plenty of grunting and wincing. But as a twenty-two-year-old totally-shredded martial artist, whose corporeal body is no more than a collection of artfully-arranged ones and zeros, it feels great, like I'm made of tightly coiled new springs.

"Hey."

A raspy male voice calls from down the alley. It's at least ten yards away, but how did this guy get so close without me noticing? I say nothing in reply, deciding to ignore it. I close my eyes and feign sleep, but I'm on guard, listening intently.

"Hey!" the voice calls again. "Hey, buddy, I got something that will wake you up good."

My new alleyway neighbor is now inching a little closer to me. It's still dark down here where I lay, but I can make out his silhouette against the early morning sky. He's a skinny, shambling fellow, wearing a bright yellow parka with the sleeves ripped off. On the chest, there's a circular toxic symbol where there would normally be a sports team logo or something. He's wearing dark sunglasses that make me wonder how it's possible for him to see anything at all, and he's rocking a huge mane of bright and sickly green hair. He grins when I open my eyes, which shows off a set of...let's call them *poor quality* teeth.

I pretend to have just awakened now and prop myself up on my arms, my legs still lying on the ground in front of me.

"Oh! Hi," I begin in a friendly, chipper tone of voice. "Thanks for the offer, friend. I was actually going to head down the street and get an everything bagel toasted with cream cheese and a medium-sized coffee. That should do me fine..." I search the stats floating above his head. "... Pepper," I conclude.

"Man, bagel and coffee?" Pepper spits out with a look of utter disgust. "That's baby food. You need the good stuff, man. You wanna know why they call me Pepper?"

"Don't care."

"Because I bring the SPICE," he smiles, very proud of himself.

"Still don't care."

"You think you don't care *now*, man? You take one hit of this..." Pepper holds up a tiny baggie. Inside is a fine glassy powder, colored the same sickly green as his hair. "You won't have a care in the world."

"Let me guess," I begin. "You're part of the local neighborhood gang the Spankers, and that's a dose of the powerful new street narcotic named Drug X."

"Ding-ding-ding!" He smiles broadly, then shakes the baggie in front of him like it's a ball I'm supposed to fetch. "First one's free."

The powder in the bag catches the first rays of morning light. It looks like elementary school powdered soap, the kind that rips the skin off your hands. It gives me a visceral reaction, and I can't hide my disgust. I can barely look at it. I can't even imagine putting it in my body. Do people really do this stuff? Even fake computer people?

"That's a very generous offer, Pepper," I lie. "I think I'm going to pass. I don't have any money right now."

"Maybe you didn't hear me, man."

"I heard you, man, no charge for the introductory offer. Message received. You know, Pepper, let me tell you what's on my mind right now." My voice takes on an expansive, regaling tone, like I'm a master storyteller. "Let me rap about the issues with you, Peppy. If this were a school classroom, imagine me grabbing the chair, turning it around, and sitting on it backwards to level with you."

He pauses for a long moment. "What?" he finally asks. He had to think long and hard about it, I see.

"In times like this, my old Pepito, I think back on the words of former FBI director William S. Sessions."

I bring up the feds and predictably, that gets him hot. "Are you a narc, man?" he sneers.

"Listen here, Pep-Pep. Mr. Sessions may have been ultimately fired for alleged ethical improprieties, but before he was booted out, he left a treasure trove of wisdom for the good people of America."

Pepper narrows his eyes, flares his nostrils in confusion, and says, "Like what, man?"

I continue, "William S. Sessions' advice, and it was so important that he plastered it on the attract screen of every single arcade machine in the land for several years, was simple, yet powerful. He told us, 'Winners Don't Use Drugs'."

Pepper says nothing. He may still not understand what I'm saying, so I spell it out.

I point to myself. "I'm a winner, Pepper." I point to him. "And you're a damn loser."

I'm expecting anger, rage. Instead, his face sags, his mouth drops open in hurt. Wow, it looks like he's going to cry. Normally I don't want to make people sad, but now I don't care. I'm angry at this gang member, and I'm getting high on my own pop culture references, and I'm not done yet.

"Oh and hey, you know how they say, 'Wouldn't you like to be a Pepper too?' Well, not me. Pepper's stupid and it makes you sneeze. I don't want what you're offering, and I don't want you, Pepper. Get out of my sight."

I would never speak this way in the real world. Mostly because I'd sound like an idiot. But here, I'm dressing down a computer simulation, a guy that doesn't really exist, and to the extent that he does exist, it's to kick his ass to give me enough experience points to level up and kick his friends' asses, too. Who cares what he thinks? *If* he thinks?

Except now his glassy eyes sharpen and narrow, and his open mouth tightens to a grimace. His fists ball up tight. He is very, very angry. I feel it for real, and it scares me.

"I'll teach you to mess with the Spankers," he snarls. "Get ready for a serious paddling. You've been a very bad..."

I'm much faster than I realized, and I'm already up and on my feet. The first punch catches him right in the mouth. It stings my knuckles, but it feels very satisfying.

"Hey!" he sputters, bringing his hand to his teeth to check for breaks.

Pepper then surprises me by swinging out at me with that same hand. Terrified in the moment, I duck back with all my might. It's too much effort, as it turns out. I easily dodge his attack, but it knocks me off balance. He follows up with a low punch to my gut that connects. It knocks the wind out of me and bowls me over. I clutch my stomach and moan. "Owwwwww."

Confident he has the upper hand, I see him smile, compose himself, and put everything he has into a giant haymaker punch. I'm recovered, but I play winded.

The moment he rears all the way back, I slide in with a brutal jab that catches him right in the gut. Now it's his turn to moan, "Owwwww."

Here we are, just a couple of bums doubled over clutching our stomachs, fighting over a bag of street drugs. What am I doing here? This is everything D.A.R.E. warned us about. Officer Jepson would be so disappointed. I can't believe I remember his name from the sixth grade.

I look up at Pepper. He's still stunned and clutching himself in pain. I haven't tried my kick yet. Let's do it.

It turns out, my kick works just fine, connecting solidly with the side of his head. He flies back to the ground, out of commission.

I'm so mad, I don't stop. I mean, the absolute nerve of this drug-pushing punk. I'm a winner. Ergo, I do not use drugs.

I yell the next sentence one word at a time, punctuating each word with a savage kick to his prone midsection. He's now blinking in and out of existence on the ground below me.

"Do. Not. Mess. With me. Before. CoffeeeeeAAAAA"

He blinks completely away as I snarl the last word. My final kick connects with nothing but air, and the momentum sends me flying sideways into the sky, then straight onto my ass in the gutter.

I lay there for a minute, breathing heavily, feeling pain in my jaw, my gut, and now my lower back. This was a very bad way to wake up, all things considered.

As the pain subsides and my breath returns, I'm thinking about why the enemies are blinking out of existence. In the old arcade games, it was literally because the old computer hardware only had so much memory to allocate for all the on-screen action. Once guys were out of commission, the computer had to focus on what was left in action, so it had enough memory to bring new enemies in. So why is it happening here, in a world where every detail is lovingly rendered by what I'm sure is a cluster of the world's most powerful supercomputers?

Maybe it's just nostalgia. Maybe they wanted to continue the trope to connect it to the old games. Or maybe they really don't have enough working memory to manage it. It's most likely not a necessary effect. But I kind of like it. Except when it sends me flat on my ass.

I slowly get to my feet, deciding that I'm definitively not a fan of my current living situation. I'm going to need to find a real place to stay.

Thank god today is payday.

✪✪✪

"Here you are, sir!" Skip says, handing me a stack of bills straight from the cash register.

Eight hours of hard work and dedicated service to the good people of New Arcadia later, my shift at the Burger Item restaurant is over. I leaf through the dirty, sweaty dollars with glee. This is great—no checks to cash, no paperwork to sign. I could get used to this.

"Thank you, Skip. You're a very good boss." I say, folding up the bills and keeping them in my hand.

Skip smiles broadly, and his eyes moisten with emotion. I guess he doesn't normally get a lot of appreciation. "Thank you, sir. Management has been a difficult and lonely road. I appreciate that compliment, sir."

"Mm," I say, not really hearing him. "Hey, do you know if there's a motel around here?" I ask offhandedly, like it's no big deal that I'm desperate and sleeping on the street and getting ambushed by drug-dealing gang members.

Skip sniffs loudly to clear his sinuses, then launches right back into his happy-go-lucky persona. "Yessir, the Plentiful Gardens Motel is just a few blocks down the street. Take a left when you leave the front door," he instructs, helpfully indicating the direction with his open hand.

"Wow, I must have just missed that last night. Sounds like a pretty nice place!"

"It's a real dump, sir!" he says brightly.

"Thanks, Skip. See you tomorrow. Okay if I come in before my shift to have a free breakfast?"

He recites happily, "Store policy is that meals served to employees not currently on the clock can be offered at a twenty-five percent discount!"

I offer him a tight smile. "That's great, Skip. Have a nice night."

"You too!" he says, waving happily.

I exit the Burger Item as the sun is setting. I turn left and walk down Fuller Avenue, passing the library, then the shelter. Both places are still boarded up. I walk a little farther, coming upon a storefront with a mannequin wearing a sweet cutoff denim jacket in the display window.

I look up at the sign, which reads "Pete's Pawn Shop," then back down at the blank-faced mannequin behind the glass. Something about the way the jacket catches the glow of the streetlight, maybe it's the tough-guy pose of the figure or the acid-washed texture of the denim, but it just looks so damn cool.

Awesome. I know what I'm saving up for. I'll be back for you, Pete, and for your cutoff jean jacket.

I still don't see anyone else out here after dark, which isn't to say they're not around somewhere. Some Spankers are probably hanging out in a nearby alley, slinging their nefarious Drug X. Maybe they're waiting in the shadows for dummies who are still outside after sundown, like me, to walk on by. I quicken my step and move out to the middle of the street, just in case there's an ambush.

I continue one block further, and sure enough, I see the buzzing, half-broken neon sign for the Plentiful Gardens Motel, or as it now reads, the Plen Gar Mo.

It's a horseshoe-shaped, two-story complex, crumbling and decrepit. I can already smell the bleach. Skip was right, this is a real dump.

"Well, it's better than sleeping on the street. Possibly." I sigh and head into the little office building to my left.

Ten minutes later, I'm laying on a mattress that probably has digital bedbugs and maybe digital chlamydia, too.

But I now have a place of my own. That's a start.

The good news: it's a cheap room. Rents by the week. My hours at Burger Item should cover it, plus a little bit extra for supplies and savings. For food, I can eat at work during my shifts, and I'm sure I can find my other meals after punching a few barrels.

The bad news: it's profoundly filthy in here. The room is pretty small. And the TV's out, it shows only black-and-white fuzz, no matter how much I adjust the old-school rabbit ears on top. So instead I turn on the small alarm clock radio. It's playing some catchy chiptunes music, like you'd hear in an old school game, and it sounds pretty damn good. Plus it drowns out the noise of people yelling and bottles being thrown, either from across the street or from distant rooms in the motel, I can't tell.

I think about doing some pushups, but I'm too tired. I drift off to sleep without getting under the covers, or even taking off my boots.

✪✪✪

I'm a few days into my stay in New Arcadia, and I finally feel like I've got a nice routine going.

I wake up, do some pushups, make some coffee in the little pot on the dresser, and then head outside to punch the barrels in the alley until I find some food inside one of them. Maybe it's a steaming box of rice, a tin of beans, maybe a can of Ebola Cola. One time I even find half a pepperoni pizza sitting on a paper plate. It was hot, too. That was a good day. Every morning, the barrels outside seem to regenerate and get filled up with new food, and sometimes items. A toaster, a can opener. I save these treasures for Pawn Shop Pete.

Then I walk down the street and work a full shift at the Burger Item. At least once a day, giant rats scramble around on the tables, and I have to punch them. I seem to be getting some experience points for it, plus my cooking skill is getting better, but my character is still stuck on Level 1.

With my player level so low, I'm still terrified whenever I'm out on the street, especially after dark. Every night after work, I'm holed up in my motel room, listening to music, doing a routine of sit-ups, pushups, and what I'm pretty sure are burpees but I can't be certain, and then go to bed.

It takes me three full days of this to awaken to the fact that although I have an entire city to explore, I'm still doing pretty much exactly what I was doing in quarantine in the real world.

But as limited as my life is, this routine is helping me. I'm starting to calm down a little bit, I'm noticing more and more about my little slice of the world each day. I'm slowly gaining confidence that I can roam a little farther afield and check things out safely.

✪✪✪

Before I know it, I've been in New Arcadia for a week and a day, and it's payday at Burger Item again. I get another greasy wad of bills from the cash register, and now it's my day off. Now that I've got some walkin' around money, it's time to do just that. See what's good in the 'hood.

I pop over to the motel office to pay the bored old man behind the counter my next week's rent, then head down the street to Pete's Pawn Shop. I open the door and head inside, hearing a mechanical "ding-dong" bell to indicate that I'm here. It's early, the store just opened, but it already has a few shoppers. I see a customer haggling at the counter, but I can't quite look around the high shelf there to see who's running the place. I walk over to the mannequin in the store front and admire that sweet cutoff denim jacket I've had my eye on.

Man, once again, this is a great jacket. Maybe a few more zippers than are strictly necessary, but that just adds to the style. And it seems to be my size, too, from the looks of it. I notice a tag pinned to the front, so I reach around and lift it up to inspect it: $50. I unzip my fanny pack to check my current funds, which is still just as embarrassing as you'd imagine it would be. After rent, I have exactly $26 left to last me the week.

Damn. That's probably not enough, and I don't trust my haggling skills at this point. I make a solemn vow to myself to come back in after next week's payday and walk out a bad-ass full-denim street warrior.

I step back outside into the bright morning sun, enjoying the warm breeze, and decide to take a little detour off the main drag, turning the corner from Fuller Avenue and walking down 170th Street.

It's quieter here, more residential on this block,

although there are still a few shop fronts here and there. I take it all in at a glance, and now I'm staring down at the sidewalk, playing the game where I try to avoid stepping on a crack, lest I break someone's back, and I don't notice anything in my path until I hear laughter just ahead.

I look up, and three Spankers are right there.

They're sitting around a stoop off the sidewalk, just ahead. They're laughing, probably at a joke one of them told, but the laughter has a menacing edge. I stop in my tracks, and that makes them turn and look at me. Not good. They all rise to their feet, standing there on the stoop. We all stand where we are for a long moment, facing each other. It's very quiet now.

The Spankers slowly walk down the few steps to the sidewalk, facing me, still about fifteen feet away. The tallest one steps forward. He has a shaved head and sunken cheeks. Without a word, he pulls an item out of his pocket and holds his hand out.

I can't tell what it is until he squeezes it, and with a Wolverine-style SNIKT sound, it suddenly doubles in size. Oh, it's a switchblade.

He stands there with the blade for a moment, grinning. The two Spankers behind him start to grin as well. They like the odds.

The only thought that goes through my mind is a crazy one: why did they put a blade inside a switchblade comb? The only switchblades I'd ever actually seen in person were the combs you won if you had enough Skeeball redemption tickets.

Another thought comes now: This is it. This is the game.

This is not a game.

The tall dude starts to move toward me, excuse me, *Switchblade Steve* starts to move toward me. I can now read his stats: he's Level 1, same as me. Okay, I have a shot at this. He moves slowly, his knife held out in front of him, still pointing up to the sky. The other two, Dirty Jack and Crowbar Craig, both also Level 1, fall in right behind Steve, all eyes now fixed on and glaring at yours truly, John Chambers, aka Blaze.

I plant my right foot back and raise my fists in front of me, squaring my stance. I'm ready.

They're closer now. Twelve feet away. Let them come.

Ten feet away. I begin to notice how terrifying they are. Battle-scarred faces, chipped and broken teeth, eyes wide and bloodshot. The leader's right eye is twitching uncontrollably.

Eight feet away. I immediately turn around and run as fast as I can. I may or may not have yelped. Screw this.

I hear one of them yell, "HEY!" and then hear heavy footfalls as the three take off after me. I'm running as fast as I can, but they are too, and they're just as fast as me. Maybe faster.

Up ahead is the main drag, Fuller Avenue. I decide to keep running full-out rather than round the corner and take my chances in the intersection and the other side of the avenue. I lower my head, focus on my breathing, barely notice my arms whipping back and forth in front of me as I sprint, pushing even harder now. I'm tracking the Spankers' approaching footsteps behind me over the sound of my breathing and my heart racing, hearing them narrow the gap. They're right on my heels now.

One chance. Here's the intersection.

BAM. Suddenly, I go sailing, spilling out into the avenue. I intuitively tuck into a semi-graceful tumble, and I keep rolling and rolling with the momentum. Then I hear piercing screams behind me.

I land heavily in a sitting position, clear on the other side of the street on the far sidewalk, now facing behind me, looking back where I just came from. My eyes track the sound of the pained cries. There it is.

An overturned fruit cart. A stunned vendor standing next to it. On the sidewalk and in the street: melons, bananas, apples. Splayed on the curb, two of the Spankers—Jack and Steve—clutching themselves. The third Spanker stands just behind them, having stopped himself just in time.

The vendor must have been pushing his fruit cart around the blind corner. I must have run into it and spilled straight over and tumbled all the way to the other side of the street. Then two of these jerks must have slipped on the spilled fruit.

And now the third Spanker is pointing at me and bellowing a death-metal roar. No words. Just rage.

Good god, that sounds horrifying. I try to scramble backwards and get to my feet, but my limbs aren't moving yet. He's still roaring. This guy should get a record contract. He sidesteps the messy fruit salad and stalks out into the street, smoothly pulling out a large crowbar I hadn't noticed before, strapped behind his back.

I have only one thought in my head: I now know

why they call him Crowbar Craig.

With one hand expertly spinning the metal rod and the other still pointing at me, he takes a loud gulping breath to refill his lungs, then resumes the death metal roar. The whole effect is really very unsettling. He's stalking through the intersection, quickly closing the gap between us while I continue to flop like a fish on the ground, unable to stop him, unable to help myself.

He makes it precisely three-quarters of the way across the street before a checkered cab flies out of nowhere down the avenue, blaring its horn as it slams into the raging Spanker at full speed and doesn't even slow down.

The Spanker sails into the air at what must be hundreds of miles an hour, his roar now transformed into a high-pitched scream. I watch in awe as he continues to sail into the air, higher, higher, my god it's so fast. His tinny squeal fades as he recedes to a distant point in the sky, then disappears.

The taxi knocked him clean out of the game world.

I work my jaw, but no sounds come out. What the hell just happened? There are a few passersby, they've all stopped for the moment, frozen like me, taking in the crazy scene before them. Then they snap back into movement and continue with their day, as though nothing has happened. The street sounds slowly return, and life is normal again. Crowbar Craig doesn't come back down.

I close my eyes, shaking my head vigorously to reboot my brain. Then I find the strength to control my limbs again, lock my arms and press my hands against the sidewalk, pushing myself to my feet. I stagger until I steady myself on the brick wall to my left, then look up to the sky. Still nothing.

I cup my hands to my mouth and yell, "Dekker! Your game physics are seriously jacked up! You guys gotta fix that!"

I double over after delivering my de facto bug report and continue to catch my breath.

My heart rate is finally going down. This is giving me a moment to think, to consider all the crazy things that just happened. Messed-up game physics aside, the real headline here is, Complete Dumbass Screws Things Up But Good.

When it came right down to it, to a do-or-die, fight-or-flight situation, you flew. You flew like a total scaredy-cat, a scaredy-cat that is also somehow a bird that can fly.

This is not how these games are supposed to go. You're supposed to march from left to right, beating up a steady series of punks for half an hour until you beat up their boss and win the game. Instead, eight whole days into this thing, I'm still slinging burgers for minimum wage, living in a flophouse, saving up for a cutoff jean jacket, and squealing and running away from measly street trash because they might give me a boo-boo.

I completely suck at this.

More moans from the other two punks across the street snap me back to the present moment. I look up and see both of them kneeling on the ground now, shaking their heads in confusion. They'll be up and at 'em soon.

Panicked, my eyes dart everywhere, looking for an escape. I step back and realize I'm standing next to a double-door, and one of them is open to the street. Above, a wooden sign with a silhouette of two boxing gloves frames the word GYM.

This could be my chance. Not just to escape these guys right now. But to train, to build my strength and ability. To get confident enough to finally fight back.

✪✪✪

I cross the threshold from the bright city street into a dark, cavernous room.

It's musty in here—dusty, too. Also a little crusty, frankly. The only light in the room comes from a few dim overhead bulbs and a single shaft of sunlight beaming down from a high window onto a boxing ring in the center of the room. Various workout stations are arranged along the four walls. Men and women are at every station— punching their bags, jumping their ropes, kicking their mannequins.

"Hey, kid," a gruff, yet feminine, voice calls out.

I look to my right and spot a dark figure lurking in the shadows. She steps forward and stops under a bare bulb dangling from the ceiling. Her face catches the harsh light, revealing striking features. She's wearing a pink tracksuit and beret over her shapely figure. The picture is complicated somewhat by a nose that's clearly been broken a few times. Then her face violently scrunches, and she suddenly spits a giant wad of tobacco into a spittoon at her feet.

It's a very confusing overall picture. But she seems like the real deal. Powerful.

"Hi, um. I'm here for training," I offer, my words

echoing flatly in the cavernous space, making me sound even weaker and more pathetic than I feel.

She says nothing. I look above her head. Her stats give her name as Big Louise.

"I want to get stronger...uh...Big Louise. Learn how to fight. I'm a student of The Fist of the Pissed..."

"Bahh... I don't know what the hell those words mean," she says, flailing her arms and swatting at the air in front of me like I was an annoying fly.

Her voice is another incongruity. She looks young, but her voice is raspy and more mature. She may be dolled up in the finest athleisure apparel, but she kind of reminds me of Burgess Meredith as Mickey in the Rocky movies. Not *Rocky I* or *Rocky II*, I'd say *Rocky III*, 1983, director Sylvester Stallone.

She continues, "But you've come to the right place, kid. We call it by many names. The Pain Dojo. The Punch Brunch, with Bottomless Fist-mosas. It's Training Men, Hallelujah. I'm particularly fond of that one. But my favorite name for this gym is the Fun Club, because there's nothing more fun than vanquishing your enemies with your bare hands."

Huh. That sounds familiar. Oh, yeah, I remember now. *Mike Tyson's Punch-Out!!*, for the original Nintendo Entertainment System. Your boxing coach would give you advice in between rounds. One of the things he said was, "Join the Nintendo Fun Club! Mac." Your character name was Little Mac, which explains that part. But even as a little kid, I could tell the in-game advertising was a bit much, not to mention the poor punctuation. Is this Dekker's knowing homage to the *Punch-Out!!* series?

"Hello, hey! Hey there, kid." She's trying to get my attention. I guess I drifted off down memory lane. "Hey, Mac!" she cries, snapping her fingers.

'Mac,' eh? Well, Punch-Out!! homage confirmed.

With a smug smile, I reply, "Okay, yes, I'd like a membership to the Fun Club, please."

Suddenly, her face gets serious, and she purses her lips. "Well, I'll tell you what, sonny boy, I haven't decided whether I'm gonna train you just yet."

She steps forward, eyeing me carefully from head to toe, then grunting. Is that a good sound? I don't know. She stares into my eyes, coolly appraising me. She grabs my face, smooshes my cheeks together, then pulls them apart, while my eyes go wide with shock. Then she smacks my cheeks twice, pulling away with a satisfied nod. Apparently, I passed the inspection.

"I train in a very special fighting style. It's very ancient and powerful," she begins. "It's called Kicking Ass."

I stare at her blankly.

She clarifies quickly, "Well, there's punching, too, it's not just all kicking. Punching Ass just sounds different, though. It has a different connotation. I try to be sensitive to the nuance of language. But, yeah, punching and kicking, a jump-kick if you're feeling fancy, that's about it in terms of the moves I teach. Just the basics."

"Ah… Okay…" I stammer.

"You know, I seen you down at the Burger Item, in your stupid paper hat. Your French fries suck, but you punch them rats pretty good."

"I... Thanks?"

"Yeah, I think you got some real potential, kid."

"Th...thank you."

"What's your name, sonny?"

"Uh... Blaze," I say, failing to match the serious badassitude of the name with my extremely halting tone.

"Tell you what, Porkchop—because that's your name now, Porkchop—I'll train you for five dollars a week, plus you sling me a hot fresh apple pie every day I come into the restaurant."

"I... I don't know if I should be taking inventory from the restaurant..." I begin.

"Ah, you don't have to steal 'em," she says, waving dismissively. "You can just buy 'em with your employee discount for me. Look, I don't care about how you do it. All I care about are gettin' them sweet apple pies, you capisce?"

"I understand," I say, nodding vigorously. "Deal."

She smiles, but her eyes are cold and deadly.

"Then drop and give me twenty, Porkchop."

Chapter 11

Movin' On Up

The moment I punch the rat, everything changes.

I've been training with Big Louise for the last four nights. I spent that first night barfing in a bucket in between conditioning exercises, then endured the next day in slow-rolling agony. Every movement brought pain. I would sit at every break during my Burger Item shift with a large fry sleeve full of ice from the soda machine, moving it from ache to ache. My body felt like rubber, but the exercises got a little easier after that.

Now, back at work again, I'm dealing with the third rodent infestation of the day. But this encounter is different than all the others. This time, I've finally punched enough creatures and jumped enough rope to gain a level in this game.

A notification pops up in front of me.

New level acquired.

Blaze: Character Level 2.

My whole body is glowing with a warm light. It's a glorious feeling, like I've just had a full-body massage, and I'm stepping out of the sauna into the cool air.

The rat had taken a bite of me before I struck back, and now I watch my arm completely heal in front of my eyes. Behind my arm, I can see the exploded rat parts blinking out of existence.

The glow finally fades away. I lower my arm and see the old woman sitting across from me at the table. She's looking at me in awe, rat parts covering her face, her shirt, her order of cheese fries. Then it all disappears, and she's clean, like it was never there.

"Oh my," she says. She's completely overwhelmed by my raw power. Totally understandable.

"Uh..." I begin, standing up from the chair and adjusting my paper hat. "Can I take your tray, ma'am? Would you like a refill?"

"Yes, please!" she says, shaking her cup eagerly at me, ice cubes rattling. "Soda water with plenty of ice, please! I want new ice, too! Throw out the old ice!"

I sigh deeply, grabbing her cup and heading to the soda fountain to get it for her.

✪✪✪

That night, Big Louise teaches me my first combo. It's very simple stuff, just a one-two left-right punch attack. But it makes a big difference, both in my fighting prowess and in my confidence. At the end of the session, I let her know it.

"I gotta say, Big Louise. Not only do I feel stronger, but I feel more in control—both of my environment, and of my emotions. I don't know, I feel like I can take on any punks that get in my way. And that's all thanks to you. I really do appreciate it."

I expect her to wave off the compliment and tell me to drop and give her twenty, but instead, she holds up a hand, turns it so her palm faces upward, and balls it into a tight fist. Then she extends an index finger and points it at my face, squinting down the finger's path as she stares dead into my eyes.

"Remember this, Porkchop. You come across some punks that get in your way, you don't hesitate. You've got the tools now to Kick Ass, and you've got to use those tools, which are your feet, which you'll use for the kicking of the asses. They're also an important part of jumping. And also use the tools that are your fists, for the punching. You hear what I'm slinging your way, kid?"

I gulp audibly and take in a halting breath, my mouth is suddenly dry. I nod until my mouth works again. "Yes, Big Louise."

She smiles and nods gruffly. "Good. Now grab this jump rope and do the skippy thing with it. Go real fast. Don't stop until you puke."

I oblige.

✪ ✪ ✪

The days continue to fly by, and the next thing I know, it's my two-week anniversary in New Arcadia.

I wake up the next morning, and it's my day off from Burger Item. Rent is due today for the week, but I've had my eye set on that denim jacket at Pawn Shop Pete's. There's no way I'm not going to get that first. Before I've even had my standard back-alley broken barrel breakfast, though, I receive an interesting surprise.

Punching the newly-generated barrels behind the motel, one of them yields not a roasted chicken leg or a delicious salad bowl, but a tiny glowing light.

Looking closer, I see that it's a small, smooth oval object. It's not a light source of its own, it's reflecting the sun overhead. Picking it up, I see it for what it really is. The translucent text above the object reads, 'Gem.'

Huh. Fancy jewelry, cool. I wonder how much this is worth. I have no idea, but I know who would know.

✪✪✪

The door opens, triggering the familiar DING-dong chime, and I step inside the pawn shop. The denim jacket is still on the mannequin in the shop window, thank god. Otherwise, the inventory has changed quite a bit since I was in here last week. There are now more musical instruments, including a couple of electric guitars and half of a drum set. I spot a few hockey sticks and a badminton set, too.

It's quieter in here today, just a couple of customers milling about. None of them are at the counter, so I walk right up to it. A tiny old woman sits behind the cash register, leafing through a TV Guide, or rather "TV Shows On TV," as it's called here. On the cover is a profile shot of a bespectacled Latino teenager, holding out his suspender straps as he smiles like an idiot at the camera. At chest level, in gigantic cartoon letters, is a single word: "DURKEL." Huh.

"Hello," I begin hesitantly, trying to gently get her attention. "I'm looking for Pawn Shop Pete."

The woman peers up from her digest-sized magazine.

"That's me!" she beams proudly.

"Excuse me?"

"Pawn Shop Pete, that's my name!"

"Oh!" I exclaim, searching for more words.

"Short for Patricia!" she offers.

"Is it! Well, uh, I have a... I have this...item."

I fumble in my pocket and pull out the gem.

"Ahh!" Her eyebrows raise, taking in the new object with fascination, and when they lower, the glasses perched above her face drop down into place on the bridge of her nose. One of the lenses contains an additional powerful magnifying lens on the bottom. It's a neat trick—very practiced, I'm sure—but still quite impressive.

"This is a standard gem," she quickly assesses, in a business-like tone.

"Are there non-standard gems?" I ask.

She casts a withering glare at me, like I'm an absolute idiot. Then she says, "I'll give you three hundred for it."

Three hundred dollars. That's enough for a deposit and first month's rent for a studio apartment at the rundown complex next door to the Plentiful Gardens Motel. It would be a real step up in the world for me. To being slightly less awful.

I'm about to accept the offer, and then I remember

why I came in.

"Uh... Throw in that denim jacket over there and you've got yourself a deal," I counter. 'Bundling,' they used to call it on that show *American Pickers*. I'm bundling.

She casts an appraising eye toward the mannequin up front and starts calculating, looking for all the world like she's grappling with the equation that Russell Crowe did in *A Beautiful Mind*. 2001, Director Ridley Scott. There must be numbers and fractions and exponents flying around her head, but I can't see any of that.

She snaps back to reality with a suddenness that shocks me, and now stares deep into my eyes, probably into my soul. "Two-seventy-five," she states, a strong note of finality in her voice.

Think fast, Blaze. Okay, I don't think I could get a better deal at this point.

"Um...deal," I stammer.

Suddenly, her entire demeanor changes back to before, and she flashes her warm smile at me again. "You drive a hard bargain, mister, but I accept."

Negotiation: increases by 1.

She nods over to the mannequin, imploring me to get the jacket. I walk over, remove it from the mannequin, and try it on immediately, checking myself out in the mirror near the entrance. It fits perfectly. I look so cool.

Style: increases by 2

You're damn right it does. Pete then opens the cash register and hands over a familiar stack of bills. $275 filthy dollars, cash money.

High Roller: Level 1, have over $250 on hand.

I have no idea what these notifications mean or how they impact the world or my character, but it makes me feel happy to get them, and I want to get more of them.

Pete swipes the gem off the counter and into her pocket with a practiced move like a world-class magician, and I head out of the store.

Before the door closes, I hear, "Come back anytime! Pawn Shop Pete is always looking for a deal!"

I've got to say, it feels pretty good, walking down the street with a fistful of cash. It puts a spring in my step. I think back to just a week ago, when I was running away as fast I could from a few measly thugs. Now, a full level higher, with several days of intense training under my belt-slash-fanny-pack, I'm lord of the streets. Styling hard in my new second-hand Canadian tuxedo.

Speaking of which, something on the jacket's front pocket catches the corner of my eye. I stop in my tracks to look down. Ah, it's the sales tag. Suddenly, I'm pushed out of the way from behind, then I'm staggering forward, almost tripping on myself.

"Watch where you're going!" an older businessman with a briefcase calls out as he brushes past.

"Hey, I'm walking here!" I call after him, *Midnight Cowboy*-style. 1969, director John Frankenheimer. No wait, John Scheslinger. I never actually saw the movie.

"No, you weren't. That's why we ran into each other," he replies without looking back.

"That's just semantics!" I call out feebly. "I'm Lord of the Streets!"

"You're a fruitcake!" he yells back, and keeps walking.

I could run right over and beat the hell out of him. I mean, after all, I'm a total bad-ass now. But that would be morally wrong. Not to mention it might attract the attention of the police, who, although infrequent, still drive past every once in a while.

Plus, I really want to get this sales tag off my jacket. It takes me a minute to fiddle the safety pin open while still holding onto my money. There's no way I'm stashing this wad of dough in my fanny pack. I want it safe in my hand until I can sign the new lease. I earn a couple more dirty looks from passersby for hogging the sidewalk, but nobody dares to mess with me.

It must be because I look so cool.

✪✪✪

It's checkout time at the old Paradise Gardens Motel. I'm moving up in the world and setting down new roots.

My worldly possessions now include two plastic bags' worth of essentials. This includes items like hair gel, very important for my brunette pompadour; toothpaste, not sure if brushing your teeth in this world is strictly necessary, but it does give a nice health buff, and offers a pleasant tingling sensation; and a whole bunch of rejuvenating protein bars. I pack them all up and take them with me out the door. I toss the room keys to the startled half-asleep old clerk behind the counter and set out for my new dream home.

Well, my new apartment. And it's more of a *bad* dream. The apartment complex is just around the corner, one street over on 10th Avenue and 169th, exactly parallel to the Gardens. I turn the corner, and straight ahead, I see the big sign.

The Ten E. Ments.

So-named because we're on 10th Avenue, it's the East Side, and...it's run by a family named Ments? Why am I trying to justify this terrible pun from the game developers?

"Hey, Dekker et al, this is a stupid name for this apartment complex. Bad pun, on the nose, not good. A new name and sign should go up for the next game patch, please!" I call out, assuming the developers are listening, surprised at myself for how quickly I'm feeling comfortable in my virtual neighborhood, almost entitled. I get a couple of side-eye glances from other pedestrians for calling out what surely must sound like nonsense to them.

I continue to approach the complex, and the buildings are becoming clearer. They're taller than the motel is, five stories each instead of two, and rather than a horseshoe shape, the complex contains three rows that are each two buildings deep, with narrow driveways between them all. The first floors of each building are a series of garages, side-by-side, running all the way to the back of the complex.

I look at the building before me, Tower 2, front and center. Floating above the rooftop is the familiar translucent explanatory text. I never had Google Glass, but I half-watched an online video about it once, and this is basically the enhanced vision thing from that tech, only you don't have to wear the bulky glasses. The message reads:

TEN E. MENTS. MONTHLY LODGING.

VACANCY: TOWER 5, 1 BEDROOM

$300/MONTH

Perfect. Thanks to my paycheck and my new pawn shop haul, I have just enough for the first month's rent, with a few bucks left over. I may have to live on barrel food for the rest of the week until next payday, but I'm used to that. If it's something that I really want—like for example, a VR headset—I'll do what I have to.

Based on the layout, I'd guess that Tower 5 is in the back, right behind this Tower 2. I take the long driveway to my left, walking into the heart of the complex.

It's a little depressing, the sameness of the place, with its endless rows of garages, tiny windows dotting the levels above. All stamped out in cookie-cutter fashion. Very lazy game design, like the designers just copy/pasted.

Then I realize: yeah, but how is this different from actual real-world urban design? Real people live like this, too. Hell, just think about your own desert subdivision, every house basically stamped out of the same mold. Copy/paste, man.

I'm glad I'm not high right now—one, because winners don't use drugs, and two, because this observation would completely blow my mind. I'd curl up against a building and fold into a fetal ball for an hour, just thinking in an endless loop about design choices and life choices.

Thankfully, I'm a man of action now. And I'm on a mission. A mission to get one of these crummy apartments with my new pawn shop money.

I don't see anyone else outside. It's pretty quiet here, except for a hint of music coming from a nearby open window on an upper floor. It's a little spooky here, actually, a bit like an Old West street at high noon. Although I don't have a watch yet, I'm pretty sure it's about noon right now, so my observation is thematically appropriate.

"High noon. Totes appropes. Totes appropes..." I mumble to myself, filling the eerie quiet with a bit of noise.

A sudden loud roar makes me jump. The sound was close, I could feel it in my body. I quickly zero in on a nearby garage to my left, just behind me. It's one of those roll-up single-car garages, and it's starting to raise from the ground. That's the noise. It's the sound of the automatic garage door opening.

I stop in my tracks to watch it, then decide to run a few steps over to the other side of the driveway, so I'm not out in the open. Now I'm standing behind one of the staircases leading up to the main level on the second floor, effectively hidden from view, unless you're looking for me.

The garage door's gears are really roaring, and then there's an awful shrieking noise—it sounds like something got caught. The door grinds to a halt only about a foot off the ground, the gear still whirring ineffectively. Inside the garage, it's practically pitch-black, but now I can see shadowy feet approach the entrance, and then a single hand appears under the door.

It's a young woman's hand, perfectly manicured,

with bracelets, rings, long red nails. The hand grasps the bottom of the garage door, and with an effort, pushes up. The hand struggles at the bottom, with not much leverage, but it powers through and pushes the garage door higher, moving faster as it goes.

The hand guides the door up to the top, and daylight pours in to reveal a beautiful woman standing inside. I'd guess she's in her early 20s, with perhaps Asian facial features, but it's difficult to say. What's clear is that she's in scary good shape, perfectly toned, and wearing a gray sequined miniskirt, almost blinding in the sunlight. She's also sporting long black high-heeled boots and full-glam makeup. Her hair is permed and teased out in the classic retro style, with especially tall bangs, like I would see in my older brother's yearbooks.

Behind her is a shiny, cherry-red sports car, no license plate. Must be brand-new. Who is this woman, and why is she here in this dump?

I scan the space above her head from my hiding place, about twenty feet away, trying to solve this mystery. Immediately, I can tell something's different about this woman. The translucent words floating above her head are a different color than everyone else I've run into, orange instead of blue. It's even a different font, a blockier pixel style.

Player Name: Jessica

Level: Not Available

I fixate on the level. Why can't I see how powerful she is?

She reaches into her tiny black purse, pulls out a small red disk, and opens it in front of her. It blazes brightly, and I shield my eyes a bit. It's not until I see her drawing on her lips while leaning forward that I realize she's touching up her makeup in a compact mirror.

Hold on a minute. I'm thinking about those words "Player Name" above her head. Every other character I've seen here has the word "Name" only.

Oh my god. It's another player.

Jessica is a real person, for reals.

I bet if she looked over here, she would see a "Player Name" above my head, too. Except we're not real, we're virtual. Whoa. Again, glad I'm not smoking weed right now.

She's running her fingers through her hair now, adding to the poof. There is a considerable amount of poof going on. Next-level poof. If I had to describe her look in a single phrase, I would say "urban action VHS tape cover girl."

She suddenly claps her mirror shut, snapping me out of my reverie, and looks straight up. Not at me, thank god, but down the driveway, from where I came in.

Twenty feet away, three thugs stand in a triangle pattern, facing her.

I was so focused on Jessica, and she seemed to be so focused on her hair, that we didn't see them at all. I don't think the thugs noticed me, either. They've got to be Spankers. Two thugs are in the rear, both wearing denim jackets, although mine is much cooler, and wearing red headbands and black T-shirts, each with a giant telltale wooden spoon logo.

Yeah, they're Spankers, all right.

These guys seem like they mean business. There's *Paco*, short, dark, and powerfully built, then *Beanpole*, tall, pale, and skinny. Both Level 2, they would certainly be a challenge to take on together, though not impossible.

But then there's the big guy in front. He's built like a linebacker, both wide and tall. He's a little older, with slicked-back black hair and a three-day growth of beard. He's wearing a leather jacket with metal spikes at the shoulders. He looks familiar somehow, there's something about his outline...

Yeah, that's it. From the newspaper my first night in town. This has to be the mysterious boss of the Spanker gang. The big guy himself.

I scan above his head, searching for info on the mystery man. He's Level 4. Dammit, that's probably too powerful for me.

And his name is...*Many Boss*? Is that a typo? It's like they wanted to call him Mini Boss, you know, like he's the Stage 1 boss, not the final boss. I can see a crown icon next to his name to indicate that he's in charge. I check the name again, sure enough, it's spelled Many Boss. Or maybe it's pronounced 'Manny'?

I look back to the woman, Jessica. She slips her mirror back into her purse in a practiced motion, all the while staring right back at them, giving as good as she's getting, standing tall. I look back at the men. They're also rooted in place, glowering and growling. The air is charged, tense. Something bad is about to go down.

Meanwhile, I'm completely frozen in fear and dread. The Spankers approach her, slowly. She stands her ground. The two thugs close the gap, stopping right in front of Jessica, while the Many Boss hangs back a few feet. Still no words are spoken. A silent standoff.

In a flash, I realize what this scene reminds me of. My god, this is uncanny. I've seen it a hundred times in the arcades. It's the opening cut scene of the beat 'em up classic *Double Dragon*, the bit that launches the street war that takes place over the course of the game. The gang punches out the girlfriend of one of the heroes, Billy or Jimmy, I don't remember which one, and then they kidnap her. Even with the primitive graphics and tinny sound effect, it's a powerful, upsetting scene in the game.

But seeing it happen for real, in front of my very eyes, and not being able to do anything to stop it? This is a thousand times worse. I feel sick to my stomach. Come on, John. Get it together! Do something!

Before I can will myself to move, one of the thugs sucker punches her, right in the gut. It's the little guy, Paco. I wince and flinch like it's me getting hit. I've been expecting this to happen, but it still shocks me when it connects, still horrifies.

Jessica doubles over with a groan, her health only goes down a bit; he must have pulled his punch, but still. This is awful. Beanpole is right there to catch her. He scoops her up, then squats low and hoists her over his shoulder.

And just like that, the two thugs turn around and face their boss, who nods in curt approval, then turns and starts walking away. They follow, Jessica's now-limp form saddled over Beanpole's slender shoulder.

My shock turns to anger, then to absolute rage. They can't take her like this. I can't let them get away with this. For the first time in my life, I truly understand the phrase *Street Fury*.

The Spankers continue to saunter away in no rush, like they own the place, with not a single look back. Not seeing me in the shadows, not aware of the rage storm that continues to build behind them.

For two long weeks, I've lived my life in constant fear, hiding out and running away from these evil Spanker punks.

Now it's time for me to spank back.

I take a deep breath and embrace the anger, exhaling. My hands are trembling, I feel the wad of bills still in my hand, and I quickly slip the money into my tight jeans pocket. I need these hands to be free right now.

I look down to watch them balling into tight fists, seeing them shake with anger and pressure. These are truly the Fists of the Pissed, now tempered in the ancient crucible of Kicking Ass. Don't think about what that actually means, just go with the feeling, Blaze.

I break out into a dead run, silent except for the quiet gallop of footsteps on the asphalt. They're in my sights. I target the boss man first.

They're all still sauntering along, blissfully unaware of what's coming to them. Four feet away now, I give it everything I've got. I erupt from my dead sprint and leap up to the sky. I extend my leg out in a jump-kick, just like Big Louise taught me.

I'm screaming at the top of my lungs as I fly through the air. *Street Fury* is coming.

Chapter 12

Crash Pad

I'm soaring through the air, propelling forward on pure, righteous vengeance.

I'm the rescuer. The good guy. It feels pretty damn good up here.

Time seems to slow down, and my awareness heightens. I feel the cool breeze from the nearby river, the warm sunshine on my face, the tautness of the denim as my arms lift higher to defend my face. Now the tug of gravity finally pulls me down, my outstretched right leg pointing like an arrow toward the back of the boss's wide head. That head is beginning to turn around, reacting to the sound of my admittedly maniacal scream, but too late for him to do anything about the pain that's coming.

I make contact, though it's not a perfect hit. My right foot glances off the boss's big melon head and slams into his left shoulder blade. But it's still a palpable blow; he staggers forward, stunned. I tuck in and roll to the ground as time snaps back to the shock of the immediate.

I spin upright onto my feet, and wobble a bit, but otherwise, I stick the landing. Hell yeah, my training paid off. Big Louise will be proud. If I can survive what comes next.

I've ended up standing right between the two henchmen. Beanpole is backing away with Jessica still slung over his shoulder, and Paco is standing right in front of me, unmoving except for a series of stunned blinks. I think these guys are used to getting their way. They're about to be in for a rude awakening.

I execute my new one-two combo, punching out a swift left-right to the slowpoke's face. It knocks Paco to the ground. I look up to see Beanpole laying Jessica on the ground to free his hands up for the fight. I make a beeline right for him.

I'm closing the distance, tunnel-visioned, gaining fast, and then I reverse suddenly. I'm flying back where I came from, looking up at the blue sky above.

I hit the pavement, hard. My throat is on fire, and I clutch at it, gasping for breath. I writhe and scramble, feeling the asphalt pebbles digging into my back. After a moment, I'm able to flip over onto my hands and knees, coughing, and look up to see the Many Boss standing to my right, his arm powerfully outstretched.

I piece it together in an instant. He clotheslined me. I literally ran right into the Many Boss's attack. And now he's still standing in that position, showboating like a jerk. How did I not see that coming? I've got to get better at this whole fighting deal. No time like the present.

But Beanpole makes it over to me first. He lifts

me clean off the ground, a skinny guy with surprising strength. He's got me mostly by my treasured denim jacket, I feel the strain in the fabric, hear it beginning to rip.

"Not the jacket, not the jacket!" I cry.

Beanpole grapples with me and I grapple back. I haven't gotten to this point in my training yet, so I'm improvising now. When I see an opening, I quickly grab it and seize his long, skinny neck. He's bent over in a classic headlock under my arm now.

I haven't done this move since I was in the fifth grade and we were play-wrestling behind the school trailers at recess. Our school principal was a big lumbering slob with a combover, but it turned out he could move quick when he needed to, prying us apart and holding us up in opposite arms, both of us dangling in the air in his giant meaty hands. Afterward, we got a stern talking-to about the dangers of fighting and gang life. But no formal punishment. It was enough that all the other kids got to see that the old man was a secret bad-ass.

But this time, there's no giant sweaty school principal to pry us apart. And this time, I'm not play wrestling. Also this time, I'm not a ten-year-old 90s kid, but a forty-year-old man in a twenty-two-year-old body, who's somehow also in the 90s.

So some similarities, some differences here in the two situations. But at heart, still the same primal conflict. One winner, one loser.

In a quick motion, I get out in front of Beanpole, while still maintaining the headlock, so I can raise my knee up into his smug noggin.

"I...just...bought...this...JACKET!" I holler, kneeing my opponent right in the head with each word. Just like *Double Dragon* in the arcade. Cool.

Beanpole staggers back, so I turn around to find Paco, but he's already right here. He has a fist for me. I taste blood as I stumble back. Man, this feels too real. I pick my head up just in time for a matching punch from Beanpole, who seems to have recovered from my attacks just fine.

I'm caught in a loop now, pinging back and forth from side to side like a pinball, as Paco and Beanpole methodically wear me down with a successive series of punches, pounding out a brutal, numbing rhythm on my increasingly glass jaw.

This is bad. This is very bad. The world gets blurry, now I'm seeing stars. I try to focus, all I can clearly make out is my own health bar, floating at the top of my field of vision. The bar is going down, down, down with each blow. I'm getting my ass kicked, and there's nothing I can do about it.

Wait a minute.

I remember the special move that can break the attacks—from the tutorial. I wait for the next punch, and then I make my move, launching more or less gracefully into my unstoppable series of spinning blows, flailing around and around in a tight circle.

The Spanker thugs are not prepared for this onslaught. They get caught right on the kisser with each revolution. Five, six, seven spins. Finally, with the eighth go-round, I slow to a halt. The thugs have been knocked far away by the last blows, both sprawled out on the ground. Beanpole is blinking out of existence. He's done. Paco is clutching himself and moaning. I stalk right to him and execute another staple of the genre.

I jump in the air and land on Paco's prone body.

This is brutal. It feels wrong. Violent and unacceptable behavior in any civilized society. But it also feels very satisfying, I hate to say it. Playing these games in the arcade, I was just pushing buttons like a lab rat, getting a little dopamine fix. Translating that arcade thrill to the feel of my body actually performing the moves, and feeling the visceral impact of each blow, it feels right, in a very deep way.

When you're winning, it feels good. When you're on the right side, it feels good. I revel in this feeling, exult in it, even as it scares the hell out of me.

Moments after I land on him, Paco disappears for good. Now, for...

Suddenly, my head is on fire and I pitch forward. I know it's the boss before I even kiss the pavement.

A moment later, I'm roughly flipped over onto my back, and he's right there on top of me. No evil grin, just a grim, determined expression. Professional. Getting the job done. You don't get to be neighborhood boss without punching your way to the top. You take on all challengers to maintain your position.

That all seems very abstract and animal kingdom-like, until you find yourself on the ground with said boss actually on top of you, slamming you in the face. Twice.

My health is really very low now. Dimly, I remember that I don't get any extra lives here. I don't get to start over. If I get knocked down, I don't get to Chumbawumba. Instead, it's back to my dead-end job in my desert prison home.

Although right now, that doesn't seem so bad.

Instead of punching me a third time to finish me off, like I expect, he instead reaches down with both hands and tightens them around my neck. I struggle wildly, but it's no use. A new bar appears, floating just underneath my health meter. It reads, "Breath."

As you might imagine, the bar started out full but is going down rather quickly.

I focus on my breath indicator plummeting, choosing to focus on that rather than the Many Boss's creepy, impassive face. Red veins start appearing in my peripheral vision, creeping closer to the center. This is an effect I've seen when playing a first-person shooter game, but I must say when it's happening to your actual first person, it's quite a bit more upsetting.

I'm very upset. And almost dead now.

With my remaining breath, I try to engage him.

"M…m…Manny!" the word barely escapes my throat. I use up almost everything I have left just to taunt him. As soon as I say it, pure fire erupts in his eyes. He stares at me and bellows in rage.

"MANY," he screams in a death metal roar, correcting my pronunciation. "I AM THE MANY BOSS."

"Wh…why?" I gasp, confusion overtaking my terror.

Now he clamps down tighter around my neck, and his words echo and circle in my ears. I squeeze my eyes shut, so that his face isn't the last thing I see before I go, but now he's all I see.

His visage is seared onto my brain, and it multiplies in the blackness until there are dozens and then hundreds of Many Bosses, their faces stretching back into forever, an ocean of grimaces distorting into an infinity of funhouse mirror images, reflecting back an endless spiral of madness and rage. My breath bar floats above it all, and I watch as it depletes to nothing.

Then the breath meter stops sliding down. It reverses and expands, my lungs expanding with it. My eyes pop open, and the street sounds come racing back as I gasp for air. No more endless faces of death, only blue sky above now. And a great weight is lifted from my body.

I dart my eyes to the right and see the Many Boss laying on the pavement next to me. There's just one of him now, his cheek is pressed against the asphalt, blood and drool pooling around his big ugly face. Eyes closed. He's peaceful, almost.

I sense motion above me. Jessica! Oh, thank god. She must have snuck up and clocked him on the back of the head. Now that she's closer, right up on me, I can read her stats. Level 4. Good lord, how did she get so much higher than me? And in less time?

I reach out, grateful for her to help me up, but I realize that she's moving too fast for that. It dawns on me that she's really, really pissed.

Instead, she grabs my jean jacket and drags me to a standing position. It rips and strains even further under her hands as I scramble to get my feet under me.

"Not the jacket, not the jacket!" I feebly cry out.

"You *idiot*! You ruined the whole plan!!" she yells into my face.

This is my first up-close view of her. Her poofy hair is askew. One of her high-heeled boots is off and laying on the ground behind her. She's snarling and pointing a finger at me. Behind her, I also catch glimpses of a pile of cash where Beanpole once lay to my left, and the unconscious body of the Many Boss to my right, but my eyes keep pulling back to the sheer anger of the person right in front of my face.

This is definitely not the reaction I was expecting.

"I... I was trying to save you from the Spankers!" I stammer.

She tightens her grip on my jacket. "I was trying to be *captured* by the Spankers!"

I'm shocked. My mouth falls all the way open. "Wait, what?"

She lets go with one hand so she can point an accusatory finger right in my face. "I have been working my *ass* off to get into shape, level up, and get in with these dumb-ass drug runners so I could sabotage their operation inside their base. I bought all these clothes, rented this car, and spent a solid week cultivating my persona, making myself as irresistible a target as possible, and it all worked perfectly. They took the bait, exactly how I wanted them to. And then you waltz in and mess it all up!"

Oh my god. She got in the game, immediately figured out the world, the players, and all the angles, and made a brilliant play to infiltrate the gang to take it all down.

And meanwhile, I've been flipping burgers and punching rats. I thought I was the hero, rescuing a damsel in distress. Instead, I'm a worthless fool. Worse than that. I really screwed this all up.

All this realization must be very visible on my face, because she says, "Yeah, dude, you really screwed this up."

I shake my head in shock and sorrow. "I'm... I'm so sorry. How can I help?"

"How can you—" she begins, shaking her head in disbelief. "BY STAYING AWAY FROM ME." She lets go of my jacket lapels and shoves me roughly away.

And then, something snaps in me. Now I'm righteously pissed off.

"You know what, Jessica, I was just trying to help," I say. "And you're treating me like I'm an idiot. This is exactly why I don't mess around with other people!"

"Why, because you badly misjudge every human interaction you have?" she retorts.

"Well... I'm a little rusty! It's not like I've seen anybody in the last three years. I mean, have *you*? Look, all I know is those guys were hurting you, and I couldn't let that happen!"

We're now both screaming our conversation at each other. It's got to be half-anger, half-adrenaline high from the fight.

"Just get the hell away from me!" she yells. "You've completely blown my cover and now I've got to find a new place to live!"

"Oh, yeah, well, I *am* getting away from you! By the way, how is it living here in this complex?" I change the topic, in a tone of voice that continues to be much too loud.

"It's a real dump! But the price is right!" she yells.

"That's great! How did you sign the lease?!"

"I spoke to the manager! His office is right there!" She angrily points to the corner of the building, where there's a unique door and window next to the last garage door.

"I appreciate that!" I bellow. If anyone was looking down at us from their apartment window, they would have thought we were insane.

"If I see you again, I am drop-kicking you in the face! Stay out of my way..." She looks above my head for the first time and narrows her eyes to read. Clearly, she can see the same info about me that I can about her. "...*Blaze*." She recites my name with much more contempt than I think I deserve, all things considered.

She then flicks a quick glance down at my groin with disgust. "Nice fanny pack."

Suddenly, there's a low moan nearby.

"Oh...my head..."

It's the Many Boss. We turn and see him up on his hands and knees, facing the ground and slowly shaking his head.

I look back to Jessica, my eyes wide, mouth moving but no sounds coming out. She narrows her eyes and points a menacing finger at me. The message is clear. Stay away, you're a loser.

Then she runs back to the garage, hobbling on one high-heeled boot and one bare foot. She jumps into the convertible sports car with a practiced ease, throws it into gear, and squeals out of the driveway, forcing me to scramble out of the way so I'm not run over. The car races past the sidewalk onto the street at high speed, then peels out again as it drifts into a turn, causing traffic to stop and horns to honk. Then she's gone, the motor snarling and fading away into the sounds of the city beyond.

I take one more look down at the Many Boss, see that he's slowly getting up to one knee, still groggy and out of it but getting sharper, and I decide I'm not ready to try my luck again. I run as fast as my legs can carry me over to the manager's office on the corner. It's time to sign a lease.

I sign the lease. That was pretty easy.

After catching my breath and having a few minutes of conversation with the super—he's a nice enough fellow, not very many teeth—I reach into my pocket and plunk down the wad of bills from the pawn shop haul and receive the key to my own furnished apartment, on a month-to-month basis. Or so he says. The contract is a single sentence, not a lot of detail there. Whatever, I'm sure his word is bond, law of the street, or something.

I peek fearfully out of his office window through the blinds, but the Many Boss looks to be long gone. Jessica's boot is missing, but I do see a large box that I didn't notice before sitting in the middle of the driveway. I open the office door and step out, looking both ways carefully.

Nothing. I head over to the box, and as I approach, I now see the handle, and the black mesh circles on either end of it.

The circles are speakers; this is an old-school boombox. This must have been what Paco dropped as he expired, instead of leaving cash behind. I pick it up and examine the exterior. It's a little scuffed up, but it looks otherwise okay.

I've earned this trophy, and I'm taking it. I raise it up and set on my shoulder, like a cool guy from the streets.

I'm about to walk back to the bags that I left against the side of the building when a bright flash catches my eye. It's where the Many Boss was laying on the ground, knocked out cold. I step over to it, bend down—it still feels amazing to bend over without any back pain, haven't quite gotten used to that yet—and discover a shiny golden coin. Or, more accurately, "ONE TOKEN" as it spells out on one side. An embossed image of an arcade machine is on the other side.

"Huh," I exclaim, then shrug and decide to slip it into my fanny pack. Ugh...'fanny pack.' I felt so stupid when Jessica made fun of this thing. It's not my fault the game gave it to me!

I unzip the pouch and wonder aloud, "Is there another name for this thing, other than...fanny pack? Maybe midsection container or...groin papoose? Is that any better? Rump pouch?" The words hang in the air, unresolved.

Disappointed, I pick up my bags, then head across the path to Tower 5, up the stairs to the 4th floor, and down the hall to my new apartment.

I unlock the front door and walk into a single large room, plus a tiny bathroom off to the side. A crummy mattress and box-spring are sitting in one corner. Two bare metal folding chairs and a table are set in the opposite corner. Refrigerator and freezer unit sit in the tiled kitchen area. There's still some food inside the fridge. Everything's expired, and it stinks. I'll have to clean it out later.

In the freezer, there's a pile of meat. I get a clever idea and decide to pull the bag out and onto the kitchen table.

I grab a protein bar out of my groin papoose. No, that really doesn't sound good. I start gulping the bar down, and my health bar begins to creep back up.

I set my new boombox on the rickety corner table and pop open the cassette player.

There's something already inside. It's a mix tape. Scratched in red pen directly onto the plastic is the phrase "Spankers Mix." The R is backwards.

I slap the cassette back in and press play. Then I slowly and painfully sit down and press the bag of iced meat onto my jaw. I can already feel the swelling going down as the first bars of the sweet chiptune music ring out loud and clear.

And that's how I spend my first night in my new place. Nursing my wounds, nibbling on protein bars, listening to cool jams, and thinking of Jessica—the only other real person I've seen here—running around somewhere out there in the big city.

Probably she's thinking about me too. Thinking about how much she hates my guts.

Chapter 13

Pay the Tab

It's been a rough day back at work today.

There were four separate rat incidents—a new record—and those don't ever get any less disgusting. Then, we had an irate customer who threatened to start something with me, which would have been great because I was itching for any excuse to knock a jerk out. But Skip defused the situation with a free fountain soda before I could lunge across the counter and slap the bejeezus out of the whiny punk.

Simply put, I'm still mad as hell. So I'm headed over to the gym.

Yesterday's big fight and my epic screwup with Jessica are still replaying in my mind as I stalk down the avenue. I can't stop seeing every single mistake I made, from the tactical ones of getting surprised and almost killed by the Many Boss, to the bigger, more strategic ones of jumping into a situation I thought I had all figured out. But I didn't. I didn't understand it at all.

I thought this was supposed to be a mindless beat 'em up, but I seem to be using my brain a lot more than my fists here. Or at least, I should be using my brain, but I'm being real stupid. And my brain is reminding me of how stupid my brain is, which I can't tell if that's smart or stupid. Which makes me more mad as hell. Which makes me want to punch something.

I want to punch that newspaper dispenser. I want to punch that mailbox. That light pole looks like it could use a good thrashing. Jeez, what is wrong with me?

A thought comes unbidden to my mind: *to the hammer, everything is a nail*.

Whoa, that's deep, John.

The gym is just around the corner now. Another glance up at my stats shows me I've almost reached Level 3. Maybe the only good thing about that fight yesterday was that it gave me a lot of experience. And tonight, I can take out my frustrations on a speed bag, do some conditioning drills until I'm dead tired, and chances are I'll boost up that level and head home feeling great. Probably get a good night's sleep, too.

I round the corner and see a hand-written sign on the Fun Club gym door. It reads, "Closed due to deep cleaning. Back tomorrow! Sorry!"

In spite of what the sign says, I still try to open the door. I press down on the handle as hard as I can and shove forward, grunting with the exertion. The door is very locked, of course. I try peering in through the windows, but all the shades are drawn, and no lights are on.

Of all the times. Dammit. What am I supposed to do now?

I pace on the sidewalk, clenching and unclenching my fists, the daylight beginning to fade, considering my options. Should I head down an alley and look for some Spankers? Tempting, but possibly suicidal. Who knows how many I'll run into, and how much more powerful they might be. Even after all this training and grinding, I'm still only Level 2. I have no idea how powerful that's supposed to be, but my guess is there's a lot farther I can go.

Go home? I guess I could, but I still don't have a TV. I don't have much food, either. There's really nothing to do there other than sleep. And I'm all keyed up, not ready at all for bed yet.

I stop in my tracks, having walked a little further past the gym, and look up to see a blinking red neon sign.

It reads, "BAR."

I've ignored this sign for a lot of reasons. I've been focusing on my training, to be sure. But also, I've been unconsciously avoiding crowds of people. Especially drunk people. It's been a long time, and for a damn good reason.

But after I think about it for a few moments, closing my eyes and breathing deeply, considering all I've been through lately...

You know what? Screw it, I could use a drink.

✪ ✪ ✪

I open the door and receive quite a surprise. It's not just a bar.

It's an arcade bar.

To my immediate right is the bar top, running all the way over to the far wall, only a few patrons scattered along its length. In the middle, there are a few tables. Most are empty. And then, along the back wall, there's a long row of glorious arcade cabinets and pinball machines, blinking and chirping.

I'm instantly hit by a wave of nostalgia. It's made even more powerful by the familiar smell of booze, with a bit of industrial-strength bleach cleaner blended in. It's intoxicating in more ways than one.

I step right up to the bar and wait to get the bartender's attention. He's a younger guy, pouring some draft beers on the other end for a trio sitting at the stools. I stay on my feet, because my immediate goal is to head right over to the pinball. I had made a quick note of the old-style music as I came in, but now that I'm standing here waiting, presenting myself as patient-but-thirsty, I start listening more closely.

It's that song from the 90s. That reggae song, I remember hearing it on the radio all the time on the way to school, but they wouldn't play this song at dances, because it was supposed to be bad. I always called it "Word 'Em Up" until I finally looked it up a few years ago and realized he's actually saying "Murderer" in the chorus. I had to listen to it again just to make sure. It just didn't seem possible that he wasn't actually saying "Word 'Em Up." I guess that's why they didn't want to play it at my middle school dances.

So, when the chorus kicks in, I start quietly singing along, "Murderer." But something's off. I stop singing and listen carefully.

They *are* singing "Word 'Em Up." I listen for it again the next time. Yeah, I'm sure of it. He's distinctly singing the phrase that almost everyone *thinks* he's singing.

For that matter, the music itself is...off. By just a little bit. I'd guess it's probably on the bleeding edge of copyright infringement. The melody is slightly different, a section is inverted or something. I'm no music expert, but I know something's off when I hear it.

The smooth reggae singer croons the words "Here come the warm creeper / I'm a lyrical sweeper." These can't be the original lyrics. Or the original singer, for that matter, it's got to be an impersonator. And then it hits me.

The game makers went to the trouble of creating the ultimate living, breathing 90s city. And it was critical that they include a legit soundtrack to evoke the nostalgia of the time, but they apparently either didn't or couldn't license the actual song *Here Comes the Hotstepper.*

So they went to the trouble of creating their own terrible rip-off of the song to play in the jukebox instead.

How ramshackle is this operation? For a huge company like Chum, they've got to be operating this game world on a shoestring.

Ini Kamoze. That's the singer's name. Wow, where did that come from? I remember reading his name in the movie trivia book as a kid, but never made the connection to the song. The song became famous after it was used in the 1994 Robert Altman fashion movie *Pret-a-Porter...*

"What are you having, buddy?" a voice calls to me.

And just like that, I'm snapped out of my reverie and into the present moment. The young bartender is in front of me, perched on one foot, ready to leap into making a drink. I scramble, look around wildly, find the chalkboard with the drink list, scan it quickly, then decide.

"...uh... I'll have the One-Two Punch."

The full ingredient list appears to be an urgent pile of whiskey, and a very tiny splash of something fruity. Perfect.

I slip him a few bucks, grab the drink, and now I'm gliding over to the other side of the room, making a beeline for the pinball tables. These are clearly invented machines that don't exist in the real world. They're very simple ones too, but they pretty much nail all the different styles from real pinball. I pick the one that looks like it comes from the late 80s, and it has robots on it. It's called *Danger: Robots.* Great. Good enough for me.

I check the front panel of the machine, remembering that I have that token from yesterday and wondering if that's what it will take to play. But no, the start button is already flashing. Must be free play in here. Nice.

Having raced over here, now I pause, wanting to take it all in for a moment. I'm in a bar, I have a drink in my hand, and I'm about to play a game of pinball. I never thought I'd get to do this again.

I take a sip of the whiskey. It's magnificent. Better than I remembered. I press start and play my first game in over three years. It feels so good.

Speaking of which, a new song is playing on the stereo, and this one is a rip-off of *Feels So Good* by Chuck Mangione. You know, that instrumental horn song? The one that played in every grocery store, back when we had those? Well, this is reasonably close to that.

I'm a little rusty, and this is a table I've never played before. The ball quickly gets caught in a loop between the two kickers above the bottom flippers, pinging back and forth between two angry robot heads. Suddenly, I get an unpleasant flashback to yesterday, when *I* was the pinball pinging back and forth from Beanpole to Paco's punches.

I shudder involuntarily, and the moment I do, the ball flies out of the loop and immediately drains down the side lane. I curse, take a breath to steady myself, and launch the next ball.

After that, it's all over pretty quickly. As the third and final ball drains, I slap the side of the machine lightly in frustration. Then I hear a voice behind me.

"Not bad!"

Great. Another person. What do they want?

"Play you two-player?" the male voice inquires.

I sneak a glance behind me. A fresh-faced kid, looking even younger than me—too young to be at this bar. He's smiling, friendly. I can tell right away that he's like me: a real person.

Player Name: Steel

Level: 1

Steel, like the metal. Or like the 1997 Shaquille O'Neal movie. The movie *Steel*, and not the movie *Kazaam*. And definitely not the movie *Shazaam*, which stars Sinbad and doesn't actually exist, it was just a collective internet hallucination.

Hello, earth to John! You're spiraling out again. Why does my brain do that?

I'm not ready for this.

"Uh... No, that's okay," I mumble as I abandon the pinball machine, slinking off down the row to the arcade cabinets, looking specifically for a 1-player only machine.

There's a maze game, a race car game, and a *Star Wars*-like space fighter game. No beat 'em up machine, though. I guess that would have been a little too on the nose.

I choose the space game, grab the solo flight-stick controls, press the flashing start button, and begin shooting down space warriors with my laser cannon.

Steel is now playing the *Danger: Robots* pinball table, and I keep sneaking glances at him when I can. He's good. After a couple of games, he enters his initials on the machine, High Score #3, then goes to sit down at the end of the bar.

I keep playing and sipping my whiskey.

✪ ✪ ✪

One hour and two generous beverages later, I've sampled all the games, and I'm feeling looser, less freaked out in here. The place is still pretty quiet, and that helps. I guess I was a little rude to Steel earlier. I should probably go talk to him; he's sitting alone at the far end of the bar.

"Hey, man," I say, waving to him as I approach. "Sorry I turned you down earlier. I'm still, you know, getting used to people," I admit.

Steel looks up at me from his beer. His character is similar in build to me. I can't quite place where he's from. He has open features and a kind face, which breaks into an easy smile as he replies.

"Hey, I get it, man. We've all been cooped up at home for years, it's hard to be around people again. At least, it's hard for me. I'm still adjusting myself," he admits.

"Yeah, I hear you," I say.

"I appreciate you coming over." He gestures to the barstool next to him. "Have a seat? Buy you a whiskey?"

I pause for just a moment, gauging my current level of intoxication. It's not bad, but I haven't done this for a long time, and I don't know how it works here in the game world. Maybe I should slow down a bit.

"Uh... Sure, yeah, thanks," I say, sitting next to him. "Maybe... Maybe I'll switch to beer."

"Whatever you like." Somehow, he immediately gets the bartender's attention. He holds up two fingers, says "Two beers," and a moment later, they're in our hands.

"To beat 'em ups!" I toast.

Steel's brow furrows, but he nods and clinks his glass to mine, then joins me in taking a long drink. He gulps it down, then immediately inquires, "I gotta ask you, what is a beat 'em up?"

"You don't know what a beat 'em up is?" I ask, incredulous. "Have you ever been to an arcade?"

"Chuck E. Cheese when I was a kid. I remember skeeball," he admits.

"How old are you? In real life, I mean?"

Steel laughs. "I'm 30, but it's nice to be 22 again now."

"Really? How long have you been here?" I ask, trying to make casual conversation, but I'm really curious. Why would they bring in someone who doesn't know this world?

"Actually, this is my first day in the game," he says. "I just got through the tutorial stage this afternoon, punched a few more barrels until I found a wad of cash, and then I saw this place, decided to come in for a drink."

"Sounds like you're off to a good start, Steel. Or do you have another, non-metal name?" I ask.

He laughs. "Brice. My name is Brice. How about you…" He flicks his eyes above my head to read. "…Blaze?"

Now it's my turn to laugh. "I'm John. John Chambers."

"John," he says to himself. Then, "Yeah, this place is pretty cool. I don't play arcade games, but I am a gamer. I used to have all the consoles, before the Relocation. Now I play on my tablet. I get what they're going for here, I mean with the city and all of this, but it's crazy that it's not, like, a fantasy world. It's just, like, when you would go to the regular bar down the street," he says, indicating our current space.

I feel myself starting to relax again. He's a new kid in town, and suddenly I'm the expert. I know this world a bit now, and I definitely know arcade games. Taking a sip of my beer, I get ready to explain it all. Like Clarissa. Another reference he might be too young to get.

It's time to tell him about the arcades of old.

✪✪✪

"But this game world is different," I explain to Brice, two beers later. "This place doesn't exactly spell it out. It doesn't tell you much of anything, really. Maybe because it's the beta test and they haven't added more tutorials yet, or maybe they just want to see how we all adapt and figure things out. But the basic idea here is that you've got to level up your skills, punch some dudes, and maybe... save the city, I guess. It's hard to know, exactly."

Brice is quiet, reflective, staring down at the bar and nursing his beer.

"And that's about where we are. Welcome to New Arcadia," I conclude, raising my glass to him.

Brice smiles and clinks my glass with his, and we both take a drink. "Thanks, man. Where you are from? I mean, in the real world."

I sigh, considering his question. "Lately I'm out in the desert slinging drones for Chum, not far from the main warehouse. But before that, I was in LA, Silverlake."

Brice smiles, "I was mid-city. Fairfax District. Until the Relocation. We were the first section to move. We got hit pretty hard over there. I got sent to East Asuza. I'm working for Chum now, too. Tech support, I'm a computer guy. I guess that's how they found me for this game."

"Ah," I say, nodding. "That makes sense."

"What did you do? Before, I mean."

I purse my lips and draw them back in a pained smile. "I was a writer."

"Oh, cool!" Brice says. "Anything I would have read?"

"Not unless you're very curious about driving web traffic to your B2B sites. I was a copywriter. Made a decent living. Always wanted to write a screenplay, but never found the time."

Brice chimes in, "I bet you could write one now with

all the stuff you've seen here."

I shake my head. "Yeah, well, I didn't read the non-disclosure agreement word for word, but I'm guessing I won't be able to do that any time soon."

He says nothing. I fill the silence with words that surprise me, words I never thought I'd say out loud.

"I had plenty of time to write these last few years in quarantine, but...I just never wanted to. Nobody I wanted to share anything with. I got sick, you know. The original virus."

"Me, too!" Brice tells me. "Worst I've ever felt for almost two weeks."

"Well, you're younger. For us old-timers, it was harder. I saw the writing on the wall, knew the lockdown was coming, but when my brother Steve invited me and his buddies out for one last night, I went. To a bar, you know? A lot like this one, in fact. Two days later, I was sick. One week later, I was fighting for my life, couldn't take a full breath."

My throat is getting dry. I take a drink from my glass.

"Turns out, Steve had a slight cough, but he went out anyway. All of us got sick that night. But I can't blame him. None of us really knew anything at the time."

I haven't told anybody about this, not the whole thing. I look up at Brice. He says nothing, only listens. I take it as permission to keep talking.

"Steve didn't make it. He passed a few weeks later, just as I was beginning to turn the corner myself."

I take in a breath, but it catches. A sob is lodged in my

chest, and I tremble as I exhale. "I really looked up to him, you know? He was the one who got me into games and movies growing up; they were all his hand-me-downs." I wipe a tear from my eye, then laugh ruefully. "Look at me, some bad-ass street warrior, huh?"

Brice reassures me. "It's okay, man, let it out," he says in a soothing voice. He's here for me. I appreciate it.

"The worst... Sorry." I take another halting breath, get my emotions in check, and continue. "The worst part was that I couldn't even see him. It was...a really hard time. Meanwhile, I was still struggling to get by. I was one of the long-haulers, you know. It lingered for months. I was tired, couldn't do anything. Eventually used up all my leave at work. Doctors couldn't officially find anything wrong with me. I got fired.

"When the other virus came in, the really bad one, I was finally feeling better, but by then, the city was a no-go zone. I took the 'Chum New Associates Assessment Test' online and passed. So I had a choice. I could move to scenic North Fontana right away and be one of their new remote delivery coordinators, working with the drones. Or I could stay in the city and probably die. I guess I made the right choice. But trusting other people got to be really hard. And living alone for a long time made it easier to not have to trust them."

I pause for a long moment. "And that's where I'm at, I guess," I finally say, exhaling a long breath as I stare down at the bar top.

It feels good to get it out. Surprisingly good, like a burden has been lifted. I draw in air as I look around, seeing the place with a new perspective. "It's crazy to be back in a bar again, especially after what happened.

I haven't had a drink in years. It was terrifying stepping in here at first, but now...now I feel better. I think it's... I think it's okay."

"I'm glad, John," Brice tells me.

I empty my glass and set it down with a loud exhale. It's time to go home. But I can't just leave this kid here. It's his first day, and he's got nowhere to go. I know what that's like.

"Call me Blaze!" I say, "It's better for the game immersion. When I was playing *World of Moby*, I tried to pretend I was a nineteenth-century sea captain. I talked all fancy, or I tried to, anyway."

"Yeah, I installed *World of Moby*, but I bounced pretty hard off of it after the first level," Brice says.

"It was a great game! Nobody believes me, not even the people who made it. You know what, I've gotta head home, Steel. I've got work in the morning. But...uh...you're welcome to crash on my couch. It's not much, but it's better than the gutter. Believe me when I tell you that."

His eyes light up. "Really, man? You'd let me stay? I really appreciate it."

"Yeah, no worries! The place is called, and you're not gonna believe this, the 'Ten E. Ments.' Like 'Chuck E. Cheese,' but for slums." I laugh.

Brice laughs, too. "Wow, that's terrible. The game designers must really not be good at this."

I toss a twenty-dollar bill on the bar top. "I've got these last couple of rounds, save your money."

"Thanks, man!" Brice drinks the final sip of his beer

and sets down the glass.

We spill out of the bar and are back on the street. Now it's full dark, and very quiet. As usual, no one is around after hours. I look both ways to get my bearings, then turn right, pointing my finger down the street.

"This way! I'm just a couple of blocks away," I confirm. My hand wobbles a bit as I point, then I stagger slightly as I start to walk again. It's a pleasant sensation; I'm feeling pretty buzzed.

Brice follows behind as I keep talking.

"Man, that place was pretty great. I can't believe it's been over three years. Booze tastes just as good as I remember it, even virtually. Steel, I gotta say, I'm glad I finally got to…"

I hear a loud, sudden smash, but the sound is coming from all around me. I stop dead in my tracks. The back of my head is on fire. I stagger forward, then slowly turn around.

Brice is standing there, his right arm outstretched. In his hand, the top of a bottle of beer.

Below the neck, it's shattered. Because he slammed it on my head.

Brice waggles the broken bottle top in his hand, "Did you know you can use melee weapons in the game, too?" he asks.

I pat the back of my head, then bring my hand forward. It's covered in blood. Brice takes full advantage of my confusion and strides over to me quickly, socking me right in the gut. Hard.

I double over in pain, clutching my midsection. My health bar is almost completely gone; the alcohol intoxication seems to be making the effect of each blow worse.

"I... I trusted you," I cough.

"And I appreciate that this was a big step you took today," Brice says matter-of-factly.

"You...betrayed me." My mind is racing, trying to find a way to escape. Suddenly, I remember. I'm so close to Level 3. If I can get in a few good punches, maybe I can gain a level and regain my health.

Brice shakes his head sadly. "It's true. And right after you opened up to me, and then made a small but very real step to trust another person. I hope you choose to focus on the progress you've made here today. And I'm terribly sorry about all this..." He frowns, then says matter-of-factly, "But this may sting a bit."

I sense what's coming, so I lurch forward to punch him first, but I'm slow and uncertain. Brice blocks my blow easily, then he rears back and pummels me with a savage uppercut. I'm powerless to stop it. I feel the sick thrill of flight as I sail into the air, and make a painful, jarring landing several feet away.

That's it for me. I'm fading away, the red sheen is creeping in fast from my peripheral vision and taking over completely. There's only a blurred outline as I hear footsteps walk up to me slowly, methodically. I feel a tug on my pack, then hear a familiar jingle.

"Tower 5, Room 410." He has to be reading that from my room key. He looms close now. I can see the blurred outline of his face filling my vision. "Thank you, Blaze.

This is where we part ways, I think."

"N-no..." I gasp with what's left of my strength.

Then he begins to walk away.

I can barely see my arm in front of me, sprawled out on the sidewalk. My eyes must be playing tricks on me, because one moment it's there, and the next, it's not. It happens again, and then I realize with sickening certainty: I'm blinking out of existence.

Game over.

"Sleep tight, Blaze," Brice calls back, his footsteps fading away.

And then I do sleep. The red curtain overtakes my vision completely.

✪ ✪ ✪

When I come to, I'm sitting straight up.

I try to stand, but I can't move.

I open my eyes but can only peek them open a bit. They must be swollen. From what I can see, I appear to be sitting in the middle of a large, empty warehouse.

I drop my head down to my chest and see a bandolier of dynamite taped to my torso. My arms are pulled tight behind me—they must be tied to the back of the chair. There are wires running from the sticks of dynamite into an electronic timer secured to the front of the bandolier. The timer is counting down.

10. 9.

Oh no. This is horrifying and ridiculous all at once. I can't believe this is what's actually happening.

I'm inside a continue screen for the game.

Specifically, this scenario I'm stuck in is a riff of the classic Capcom beat 'em up game *Final Fight.* When you lose your life there, the player has ten seconds to insert another coin to stop the timer and get another chance at the game.

If they don't, the dynamite explodes and it's Game Over.

But here in this world, there are no second chances. Dekker said so himself. I blew it. I'm out of the game.

8. 7.

Did he? Did he say that *exactly*?

Thinking back frantically, I remember the token I found from yesterday's boss fight. It wasn't for the games at the bar.

6. 5.

It's for THIS game. The one we're living in.

I have to insert the coin to continue.

4. 3.

I try to grab for my pack, but my arms are held back tight. I can't wiggle free, can't even move. It's not going to work.

2.

I squeeze my eyes shut and visualize the token. Imagine sliding it into a red "Insert Coins" slot.

1.

I peek open one eye. The timer strapped to my chest

is now frozen at "1." A new text prompt appears in front of my face.

PRESS START

In my mind, I do. And everything fades to white.

Chapter 14

Fare Thee Well

I'm still sitting up. That's weird.

I feel brightness and warmth on my face, a cool breeze from my left.

I guess that means I haven't been exploded by a belt of dynamite strapped to my chest in a makes-no-sense-without-a-very-specific-gaming-cultural-context scenario, so I guess I must have used my special arcade token just in time.

It feels nice to just sit here with my eyes closed, the sun pouring down on my face, breathing in the smell of my hot denim jacket. It feels nice to have the time to put all these thoughts together, to be in no particular hurry. Okay, I think it's time to open my eyes now.

There's a car dashboard in front of me. A hole where the steering wheel should be. I'm sitting in the driver's seat.

The windshield is smashed, the rearview mirror is gone, and I can see a plot of weeds and dirt, bordered by tattered wooden fencing, just past the beige-colored hood in front of me. Birds are chirping, and there's a bit of traffic noise, but muted, like the day is just getting started.

My whole body is sore, like the morning after an intense workout. But I seem to be okay.

I look casually to my left. There's no car door there; it looks like it was ripped off. I grunt like a weightlifter and begin to get up out of the driver's seat.

But I can't move. There's pressure on my chest. Uh oh, did something terrible happen to me? Am I drugged? Paralyzed? I try again. Again, I can't move, but this time I notice a thin strap running across my chest. I'm buckled in. Weird.

I fumble for the button and remove the seatbelt, then try to get up again with a groan. My body moves this time, but slowly, like every muscle is cramped. I swing my legs out and start to stand in one continuous motion, but I trip on the uneven ground below me and pitch face forward.

I catch myself on my forearms just in time to avoid a nasty collision, but I get a face full of mud from a filthy puddle I fall into.

Dammit! My beautiful jacket! This sucks.

I do a quick check, and I seem to be okay. Nothing hurt, other than my pride.

I'm about to get back to my feet, but then I catch my reflection in the muddy water below me. My face looks…

alright, although there's a noticeable discoloration around my left eye, the remnant of a fading bruise. I test it, and it's a little painful, but it seems to have healed a lot faster than it naturally would have. Assuming that this is taking place the next morning.

I look around me, see that it's all clear, and slowly stand back up. This appears to be a vacant lot, a small parcel of land between two tall tenements. It's all fenced in, and the space contains only dirt, weeds, scattered trash, and the almost-completely-stripped body of an automobile—the one that I just emerged from.

The car looks like...a Geo Storm, one of those old hatchbacks. Wow, I haven't thought about those in a very long time, I say to myself for what must be the thousandth time. It still hasn't gotten old yet, though. It feels good to be reminded of these things from the past.

I step unsteadily around to the back of the vehicle, noting the rust and the complete lack of tires. It's not a Geo Storm, of course. This car appears to be...an Enviro Flood, whatever the hell made-up brand that is.

Now that I'm up and moving, I'm starting to piece it all together.

I was about to die. I was going to leave this game world permanently. But I saved myself, stopped that from happening with the game token I got from the Many Boss. And I must have...re-spawned in this vacant lot. And for some reason, my bed for the night was an abandoned car that's been stripped for parts.

Why did I spawn in this dump and not inside my own apartment?

Oh, that's right.

Brice. That bastard.

He's going to pay for this.

BAM. BAM. BAM.

First, I tried knocking, but now I'm kicking the front door to my apartment. At least it was my apartment, until Brice almost killed me last night and stole my damned keys.

"Brice! BRICE!"

No answer. No movement. Kicking doesn't work so I try jump-kicking. I don't get anything from that except foot pain.

"Ow!"

"Shut up, dummy!" a muffled voice yells from behind a door across the hallway.

"You shut up, dummy! You're the dummy!" I yell in frustration. "You dumb dummy!"

I stop and lean against the door, breathing heavily. I slam my open palm against it and scream in frustration. If Brice is behind this door: a) I can't hear him and b) he must be really enjoying this. That sick, traitorous freak. Taking advantage of the kindness of strangers. Taking everything I own, everything I worked so hard for. Now I'm back to square one, with only a couple of protein bars in my stupid fanny pack, and the only people I know in this world either wishing I was dead or actively trying to make me dead. That's all I've got left.

My face is now pressed against the door. I'm leaning against the wood with all of my weight. If the door were to open now, I'd fall right in. And that would be fine by me, but of course it doesn't. I'm stuck out here. Defeated.

I notice my stamina meter is low. Warrior needs food, badly. Also, it's time for work.

Damn.

✪✪✪

One hour and one Burger Item breakfast combo later, I'm back to the grind, standing in the back kitchen, flipping patties. Listening to the familiar sizzle from the grill below me, and the ambient bustle of the other employees. Staring blankly at the burgers below, watching them burn. Like the anger that's burning in me.

Ooh, that's a nice metaphor, John. Dare I say, the anger that's...*blazing* in me? Even better.

I'm joking, but it's just to mask the pain. What Brice did was terrible. I felt like I made some good progress last night, and then he just stole it all from me. I trusted him. For the first time in years, I stuck my neck out for someone, and I got my head chopped off. Again.

And now I'm stuck in another dead-end job, with no home, this time in a city that's not even real.

What the hell am I even doing here?

"Skip."

I'm now standing at the open door to the back office. My manager Trevor Pants aka Skip is sitting at his desk, carefully counting out quarters for the cash register. His tongue is thrust out and sticking to the side, brushing up against his wispy boyish mustache. I clear my throat quietly, and he finally looks up.

"Hiya, Blaze!" His smile is quickly replaced by a look of concern. "Oh, what happened to your eye?"

I instinctively touch my left eye. It's still a little sore, but a lot better now. I bet it doesn't look all that great, though. "Uh, slipped and fell. At home, not here. Don't worry, I'm fine. Um, I don't feel too good."

"You just said you were fine," Skip retorts.

This catches me off guard. "Yeah, well, I am and I'm not. You know how that happens sometimes."

He looks at me blankly. The silence is unnerving.

"I… I should probably have called in sick," I stammer. I've just got to get out of here.

Skip brightens again. "No worries, sir! We can cover your shift, just take care of yourself."

"Thanks, Skip. I appreciate it," I call over my shoulder. I'm already heading out.

"All good! Take it easy, sir! Rest up and heal soon!" he calls out as I stride through the kitchen, throw off my apron, and head out the back door.

I'm on the street now. And I'm walking. And I have nowhere to go, but I keep walking. And every step I take, I get angrier.

I walk south down Fuller Avenue, the street numbers getting lower as I pass them. I haven't gone this far before. But it doesn't matter, I don't really care where I'm going. Just so long as it's not here.

Why did I ever agree to all this in the first place? I wanted an experience to escape my regular life. But this is so much *worse* than my regular life. At least at home

I could be by myself. I didn't have to see anyone. I could just keep my head down and play my games and...

"OW!"

I was literally keeping my head down, not looking, and I smacked my forehead right into a wall. I stagger backwards as a fresh bloom of pain erupts, especially on the already-bruised area around my left eye.

"Dammit!"

I look up and squint through the pain to examine my surroundings. There's no wall at all—the nearest building is six feet to my left. There's only a regular intersection ahead of me. It looks like I made it all the way down to 165th Street. I can see the normal traffic going by, people walking on the sidewalks. It's a regular day in the neighborhood. Then why does it feel like I slammed into a brick wall?

I wait for a car to pass, then try to cross the street again.

Another sickening slam, my face and chest smoosh against an invisible barrier.

"OW! What in the hell is going on?"

I bring my palm to my forehead. It's very tender to the touch. I can tell there's going to be a nasty knot there. I still can't see any obstacles in front of me. I curse again, then focus and reach out in front of me with my arm. My hand stops halfway, pressing solidly against what appears to be only air. I push, then push harder, finally press both hands against it now. It doesn't give at all.

A notification window appears in my field of vision.

ATTENTION: YOU HAVE REACHED THE END OF THE NEIGHBORHOOD.

COMPLETE STAGE 1 FOR ACCESS TO THE NEXT NEIGHBORHOOD.

You bastards. I have nothing, and now you've taken away my freedom. I can't even cross the damn street. I can't get out of here.

I scream with all of my strength, shredding my vocal cords, channeling two weeks if not three-plus years of completely repressed fury, and drive my clenched fist into the air in front of me as hard as I can.

"OWWW!" I immediately cry out as my knuckles smash against the unseen barrier. Yelling in frustration, I dance in place as I shake out my hand, which is already swelling.

"Hey there, are you okay, mister?" a voice behind me asks as I feel a hand on my shoulder.

I yell again and swing out wildly with my good fist.

"OW!" the man yells, and crumples to the ground, out cold.

"OWWW!" I echo as I dance and shake out my other hand, both of now injured.

I immediately realize I've done something wrong. Not just stupid and self-destructive, but, like, morally wrong. I punched an innocent man, a Good Samaritan who was only trying to help. He's not real but he feels reel, and that feels wrong.

I stoop over and poke at his prone body on the sidewalk. "Oh, no! I'm... I'm sorry, man. I..." He doesn't move. I think he's okay. He's not blinking out of existence. At least I didn't kill him. Small comfort, that.

I can't take this anymore. I raise my head back and scream to the sky, knowing that they're all listening and watching. I'm sure they're paying very close attention to me.

"This game sucks! I don't want to play anymore! Do you hear me?"

Nothing but the sounds of the city. "DEKKER! GET ME OUT OF HERE. I'M DONE."

But nothing happens. Why aren't they doing anything?

I turn around to face the direction I came from, looking down Fuller Avenue. Traffic is light, but a block away, I see a taxicab barreling down the street toward my intersection. The driver is distracted, talking to his passenger in the back seat, barely paying attention to the road. Perfect.

I walk out into the street and sit down calmly in the middle of the road.

The taxi roars down the avenue toward me. I close my eyes.

If they won't pull me out of here, I'll pull myself out. Screwed-up game physics, do your worst. Shoot me off into oblivion.

I hear the sound of the taxi approaching, it's almost upon me. The horn honks, brakes screech. He must have seen me, but it's too late now. I squeeze my eyes shut tighter, brace for impact.

But even as the brakes slam, a voice screams from the heavens. It's Dekker, all around me.

"GET HIM OUT OF THERE!"

A flash of pure white light suddenly overwhelms me. Even with my eyes closed, I see it clearly.

I embrace the oblivion.

Chapter 15

I Wanna Go Back

Suddenly, I'm gasping for air. I've been holding my breath and I didn't know it.

My body is shivering, I'm cold and slimy, and my armpits hurt. I feel myself being borne up to the heavens. Am I an angel now?

I hear the whirr of a motor as it shifts gears, now I'm moving straight forward, then suddenly down toward the ground, like I'm on an elevator. My feet finally touch solid ground, then my body starts pitching forward while I stand in place. The cold grips under my shoulders now support my chest as I descend. I realize dimly that these must be mechanical arms. Now I'm spitting out a viscous gel, clearing my throat and coughing. My eyes are still squeezed shut.

Is this what being born is like? I'm glad I have no memory of it, because this sucks.

I feel the pressure suddenly release from my chest

and under my arms. The robot limbs have let me go. They leave me on my hands and knees on the ground.

I open my eyes a sliver and see only a blur. With one hand supporting me, I bring the other one up to my face to wipe away a bit of the gooey gel, which reveals the concrete floor of the lab in front of me. I sneak a glance behind me and see my now-empty game chamber. I continue swiping gel off my face, spitting and shivering. I'm a mess.

"What happened in there, John?" A clear voice pierces the mechanical hum of the room. It's Dekker, of course. He sounds confused, angry. "You were doing so well. Why did you try to leave?"

I take a few quick breaths, steadying myself, then push up to a standing position. I look around me. Techs are everywhere. They've all jumped into action, checking levels, cleaning my tank. Dekker is behind me, and I turn to face him slowly.

"Are you serious?" I begin. My throat is parched, and my voice cracks. My muscles ache with the strain, I haven't moved them in days.

"Are you watching the same game as I am?" I continue. "I haven't trusted anyone—*anyone*—for years. And the first time I let my guard down, one little bit, some guy tries to kill me and he steals my apartment. My *crappy* apartment, sure, but it's all that I had."

The techs begin pulling off the electrodes from my chest. I feel hair ripping, but it's distant, I'm not paying attention. I'm pissed, and it's all aimed right at Dekker.

"I work my ass off in this stupid game, literally flipping burgers for weeks, and I'm living worse than I am in my half-broken-down house in the desert. I finally meet two real people in this stupid city, one of them thinks I'm an idiot for trying to save her and the other one took everything I have except for my stupid fanny pack."

"John..." Dekker begins. I cut him off immediately.

"And all I wanted to do when I was there was escape into virtual reality, even though I was literally living in a virtual world already. Because then I wouldn't have to deal with other people, but I couldn't do that because they hadn't even invented virtual reality yet. Or I guess they did, but it's all, like, 90s *Lawnmower Man*-era garbage. So what's the point? Does that even make sense, what I just said?"

Dekker doesn't say anything, he just nods slowly. Good. I've got a lot more to say.

"You said you were going to bring in more people, and on some level, I knew it was coming. But you never said they would be *horrible* people. Jessica hates me, and Steel almost killed me!"

I pause for a moment, considering the name. "*Steel*. Very clever. It's spelled like the metal, but that dude was a damned thief. Why did you let that trash into the game in the first place?"

Dekker doesn't respond. He just keeps looking at me with that maddeningly neutral expression. I decide to give him some more beta-tester feedback, aka a damned piece of my mind.

"Don't get me wrong, Dekker, I love me a good solid beat 'em up. But only for, like, twenty minutes. Punch, punch, jump-kick, special move, lose five bucks worth of quarters, and then you're done, go get an ice cream cone!

How hard is that to get right? You made a whole world that takes us back to before Xboxes, before smartphones, basically before the internet; it should be nostalgia heaven, but instead it *sucks*. Why would anybody want to go play in that trash heap?"

I stare into his face, still impassive. Still unreadable.

"You are very bad at designing games!" I conclude, as clearly as I can. I see a flash of something in his eyes; he can control his face expertly, but not perfectly. He's pissed at me. Good.

Dekker takes a deep, deliberate breath, and says, evenly, "It's been over three years on your own, John. Don't let one bad apple ruin the bunch. You've made incredible progress already. You need to work with all kinds of people if you're going to get along in a society."

"Yeah, no, I don't. I don't need to live with anyone. I can just go back to North Fontana and sit in my little house and never have to see anyone again. Because people suck. They suck very badly. They're not good at not sucking."

I'm on a roll now. An angry roll. And now I get a new thought. "You know who sucks worst of all, Dekker? *You do*. And remember how you asked if I wanted to punch you in the face? And I didn't say anything, I just looked down at the desk? WELL, I'D LIKE TO CHANGE MY GODDAMN ANSWER."

I'm in a fighter's stance. It was automatic, I don't remember doing it. I've been getting louder and angrier, and people are starting to notice. Two of the bigger tech guys race up behind Dekker, ready to jump in, but he raises his hand to wave them away, never breaking eye contact with me.

I'm so pissed off, angrier than maybe I've ever been...and yet I'm also floating a little bit above myself, looking down at my behavior with a dispassionate eye and thinking, "Hey John, this is actually a little much. You're being a wee bit dramatic here." But I don't care. I just want to be angry.

"Do you understand me, Dekker? Or do you need to go look at some more data first?" I challenge him.

Dekker sighs quietly, nods to himself as if making a decision, then looks into my eyes as he speaks. "I understand you, John. I understand you very well. Now I'd like for you to understand me."

This evaporates my anger almost completely. My mouth opens, my brow furrows. I have literally no idea what he's about to tell me.

"This is not just a game. Surely you see that, surely you *feel* that." Dekker indicates the equipment, the rest of the small army of techs still swarming the room and cleaning up the mess. One of them politely indicates that he needs to mop where I'm standing. I keep my focus on Dekker and inch slightly to one side.

"I told you I'm not a programmer, I'm a vision guy," Dekker begins. "Well, would you like to know the vision? I have not received formal training in game design or in programming, although I have been an avid game player since I was a young child. My true areas of expertise are urban design, sociology, and epidemiology."

He looks at me expectantly. I decide to say nothing. Let him keep talking.

"I have dedicated my life to understanding the way societies are constructed and behave, and how they can go wrong. How they're prone to infection—both from physical diseases and diseases of the mind. In some ways, they operate the same way, both corroding from within."

He's on a roll now.

"But it is not enough for me to simply understand these conditions. I must *change* them, engineer the conditions to create a better outcome. I know it seems like things have been bad for a long time, and getting worse by the day, but I truly believe we can make our world a better place if we try." He pauses, considers. "Doesn't sound like a normal background for a corporate executive, does it?"

"I wouldn't know, Dekker. I'm just a drone jockey," I reply.

"Do you want to know why my team and I have slaved over this project for years, John? Why I was able to convince the Chum corporation to set up this lab, to give us all of these resources, and let us build this whole world?"

He's looking at me intensely. He's waiting for a real answer from me. Well, I suppose I would like to know, if I'm being honest.

"Yes," I admit.

"Because we've all been away from each other for too long. And we need to re-learn how to be together again," he says passionately.

I shake my head no. No way I'm going to be around people again. I don't want to get sick again, and I *definitely*

Eric Jason Martin

don't want to get burned again.

"Before I tell you this next part, I'm going to remind you of the NDA you signed."

"I remember, Dekker," I say.

"But I don't think you fully understand the consequences. If you reveal what I'm about to tell you to anyone, anyone at all, you will be returned home, and you will receive an immediate drone shipment. But it will not be groceries, it will be bullets, and they will be delivered directly into your brain. That drone will then scoop you up and drop you in the middle of the desert, and the world will think you're just one more Scummer who left civil society to loot and pillage your community's precious resources."

"That...seems excessive," I offer.

"Not when I tell you this. We have a vaccine, John. A real one."

I blink, try to respond, no words come out.

They've been trying to get a vaccine since this whole thing began. Twice they've rolled out a comprehensive solution, delivered it to every person in the Federation, and twice the virus has come roaring back, stronger than ever.

"Y...yeah. Sure we do," I stammer, scoffing. But still hoping.

"This time is different, John. We had a tablet software update last week. You'll see for yourself. You think it was just 'bug fixes and performance improvements'? No, it installed a program to help guide mass drone distribution remotely for every resident on the continent. Believe me, it's not easy to get a fleet of drones to be accurate enough to insert a needle into a vein, but we figured it out. The first one hundred million doses are sitting in another sealed-off complex, not unlike this one, at the other end of the main warehouse here."

"You all really figured all that out? It's hard enough just getting Salisbury steaks to people," I say. It's something I know all too well as a coordinator. I can't believe they pulled it off, if what he's saying is true.

"However," Dekker continues, "the Federation of Western States and the Chum organization both understand that our citizen-consumers are not yet psychologically ready to leave their homes. Data has consistently shown a clear preference for remaining at home, the forces of fear and habit are now ingrained, and are now very difficult to break. So before we do anything else, we have to solve how to change those habits we once worked so very hard to create. This is for the very survival of our species."

I don't think he's lying to me. At least about all this. He seems very sincere. His eyes have a burning intensity. He's speaking passionately, earnestly. He's too much of a nerd about this stuff to be BSing me, is my guess.

But I can barely comprehend all of what he's saying. I understand the words, but can't quite wrap my mind around the implications. After all this time, could we finally be free again?

"I can see you're struggling with this, John. I understand it's a lot to take in at once," Dekker reassures me.

I'm staring at the ground, putting it all together,

and then I raise my head back up to face him. "So we can knock out this disease, the one that's been keeping us all locked inside for over three years, and we can do it right now. The doses are here, the infrastructure is all in place. It's all ready to go."

Dekker nods.

"But we're not going to do it?" I ask.

He takes great satisfaction in the expression on my face, an expression of slowly dawning realization and shock. This smug white-haired bastard. I should have punched him.

"Which brings me back to why you're here, John. You can't live with other people. You've been alone so long you can't stand to think about living any other way."

He pauses, letting the silence speak volumes. Finally, I can't take it anymore. "Yeah, so what?"

"Well, you're not alone. Far from it. Our world is full of deeply-traumatized people who cannot make a human connection anymore. Those who are not sick with the virus still have diseases of the spirit, of the soul. In some ways, it's a much more pernicious problem to solve."

"I like it just fine the way I am," I state.

"Indeed. John, are you aware of...VRIT?" Dekker asks me, pronouncing each letter.

I don't think I've ever heard of it, but I don't want to sound ignorant. "That...sounds familiar."

"No, it doesn't. You have no idea what I'm talking about. It stands for Virtual Reality Immersion Therapy. It was first used to treat soldiers returning from Iraq and

Afghanistan who were struggling with post traumatic stress disorder."

"Okay, well I have heard of that," I say. "No, really. I just didn't know what it was called. That's all."

Dekker ignores me and continues. "In essence, these soldiers were given primitive VR headsets, the best available technology at the time. They were placed in a three-dimensional rendering of a war zone. A scenario was then played out very similar to the one they were in when they experienced the initial trauma, for example a roadside bomb attack. Under careful guidance from the psychologist, they would safely experience the event multiple times over many sessions, and slowly learn to..."

"...and slowly learn to live with it and decrease the stress response over time," I finish for him. "They also used it on people who had a fear of heights and put them on the roof of a virtual building until they got used to it. I told you, I remember reading the article, Dekker. I'm not stupid."

Dekker pauses and changes tack. "Then you understand why you're here."

I'm about to snap back at him smartly, but then the wheels turn in my head. I'm no longer looking at him, but off in the middle distance beyond him. I feel my jaw slacken as I put the pieces together.

This isn't just a game. It's a kind of therapy.

"We have *all* been traumatized like this, John. You, me, and the whole world. First by the virus, and then by the isolation. And we all need to learn to come back together." Dekker is holding his palm open to me, face up, fingers spread. Now he folds them into a fist. "As a society. You're not just here to play a new game, John. You're really here for a few reasons. Number one, you're damaged and traumatized, quite acutely, I'd say."

"I'm not traumatized," I retort automatically.

"Of course, only perfectly normal people pass out on their kitchen floor," he responds.

"How...how did you know about that?" I ask, shocked.

Dekker doesn't say anything. He just stares at me evenly.

"That was, like...a special occasion," I offer weakly.

He continues. "Number two, you're a skilled game player, in your own stubborn way. You've proven that here. We dropped you right into this all-new world, and you simply barreled ahead and kept chipping away at your goals, often acting first and understanding later. You're exactly the type of person we needed to get this whole thing started."

He pauses again, waiting for a response. It's infuriating the way he's able to control this conversation. I quickly rack my brain and decide I can't find an insult in what he's saying right now. I guess it's a real compliment.

"Thanks," I reply.

"Number three, you're the right age. You have the right experiences. These last few years have gone by quickly, right? I mean, I know sometimes it feels like the days drag by, one into the next, but our late thirties seem to have magically disappeared. I'm thirty-nine years old, John, only six months younger than you."

"Really?" I ask, genuinely surprised. I guess I

couldn't pin an age on him at all. He looks both young and old.

Dekker continues. "It's time for our mid-life crises. I mean, look at me, I literally have a ponytail and a sports car. But more importantly, at our age, we're old enough to remember what it was like to be adults in a society. And we're old enough to remember what came right before this present reality."

"Yeah, things used to be cool. Now they suck," I agree.

"And so I created a whole world from our youth. It's the world of arcades, but also the world of the American city, one before cell phones, before distractions. The game activity couldn't be simpler, just punch the bad guys until they fall down. It's also, as I'm sure you've come to understand, very satisfying on a primal level. But to be successful in this activity, in this game world, you must do something complex, something vital for our species. You must work together in a team."

He looks into my eyes, searching. "John! Twenty-somethings aren't going to grasp this concept in the same way that we can. They've always had the internet and cell phones, and they can live their whole lives with their noses buried in a screen. But that's not real life. That's not human community and companionship."

"Yeah, Brice clearly doesn't get it," I say, anger rising in my voice. "Why is he in there, anyway? He's practically a kid compared to us. What does he know about that world?"

Dekker ignores my question. "You and I remember what it was like to walk around without distractions. To be with people, truly present in the moment. To work together, to use our hands, or fists, as the case may be. I took the game world of the beat 'em up from our youth, but expanded it to create a living urban world, one in which people can work together, live together, thrive together."

He clasps his hands together, leaving his index fingers raised, and presses them up to his lower lip. "We need to relearn how to do that before we can open our doors in the real world. We need to play it before we can live it again. And you're the one I have chosen. You're the one that can start this again for everyone."

I think about all this for a long moment, then look back up at Dekker.

"You're not going to distribute the vaccine until people play this game. Do I understand that right?"

"That's not up to me. That's up to the Federation of Western States and the Chum board of directors. I pitched this idea to them as a way to train everyone to work together again before we do it in the real world. But it's not the only solution on the table. Other beta tests are happening right now, in addition to our own. There are trials happening right now with drug therapy, talk therapy, even horse therapy."

Dekker laughs at this, as though horses could somehow save our society. "But I don't think those paths will be anywhere near as effective and may well fail entirely. I truly believe in the power of games to teach us how to behave. Play unlocks the human spirit. With people like you in the game, John, we can prove that the human spirit is ready to fight back, ready for the next step."

He puts his hands on my shoulders now, calculating that I won't knock him out now. He's right, but only barely. He really wants me to hear what he's going to say next.

"I cannot put this more simply, John. We must come together to succeed in the game, that's how we will learn to succeed together in the real world. That is the true path forward for us. We cannot fail. *You* cannot fail."

He stops now, and he has nothing more to say. I think about what he's told me for a long time. Bodies shuffle all around us, cleaning and testing, but they're just background noise. The important work is happening right here, between one Lucas Dekker and one John Chambers, aka Blaze.

Finally, I speak up. "You seem very sincere, Dekker. But I can't trust you. I don't think I can really trust anyone. You said I could go home. I want to go home."

Dekker lets out a long, sad sigh. "You're right. I did. And so you shall."

I nod. This isn't my fight. I don't want this.

But Dekker doesn't move. He just keeps looking at me, an odd expression on his face.

"Before you go, John Chambers, let me show you something."

He makes a slight nod, turns around, and walks through a sliding door into an adjoining room.

I could just stay right where I am. There's always a choice.

But I don't. I follow him.

The doors stay open for me, and I pass through them

into another room. It's a lot like the one I've been living in, but this one is much larger. There are eight separate stasis chambers here, in two rows of four. Every single tank is filled with a human being, living in the game world. Adult men and women, all about my age, their eyes covered and their mouths and noses connected to breathing tubes. At the far end of the room is another sliding door, and presumably even another chamber beyond this one. And another. Who knows how many players are down here now?

Dekker walks over to a middle tank on my left, staring at the attached video screen. I join him there, allowing my eyes to briefly glance up. I see a female figure in the tank, floating serenely, and then I focus on the video screen at her feet.

I notice the environment first; the screen displays an overhead shot of a large, dilapidated warehouse. People are moving down there, so it's clearly a video image. There are rows of workers stationed at tables. They're all wearing surgical masks that cover most of their faces. Standing on guard behind them are a few people in hazmat suits, overseeing their labor.

But this isn't the present day, the action onscreen seems to be happening inside the game. The analog weight scales, the permed hair and colorful printed T-shirts of the female workers, it's clearly 199X in there. So why are they all wearing face protection?

Oh wait, it's not because of any virus. It's because of the drug. Drug X.

The masked workers are measuring out the telltale green powder on large trays at their tables. Meanwhile, their hazmat overlords are idly holding giant paddles, presumably for beating. Or spanking. This has to be the Spankers' gang hideout. It looks like they've converted it into a lab for manufacturing Drug X.

So, the Spankers are standing watch, but regular people are manning the workstations. Their clothes are dirty, their eyes are downcast.

But wait... Someone looks familiar.

I notice underneath the video screen that there are arcade-like controls. I reach my hands out, and when I don't hear an objection, I grab and then wiggle the joystick, and it toggles the camera in turn. I look up at Dekker next to me, he nods his approval, and I press a button to zoom in. I wonder if these controls can be used for other things in the game. Can the developers here tip the scales inside the world? I bet they can.

But that thought is quickly abandoned as I close in on what I want to see. A female figure, her head is down, wearing not only a mask but also a hoodie pulled low. She really does look familiar, but I can't quite tell why.

I watch her finish working on the tray in front of her, and then she quickly glances up to receive the next batch. The move reveals her eyes for only a flash, but it's enough for me to recognize her.

It's Jessica.

Wow. She's figured it out after all, she's found a way inside the lab. I zoom the camera back out for a wider shot. From this overhead view, she looks like one small cog in a big industrial drug machine.

"Wait," I mutter. I spy a flash of movement, something up on the catwalks.

Using the controls, I pan up and zoom back in. The camera reveals a booted foot standing at the edge of the catwalk, then it continues to pan up to show the rest of the body. My heart drops. It's a dizzying feeling that feels like a faint echo of the virus that once inflamed my chest for months as I realize what I'm now seeing.

It's the Many Boss. He's staring straight down at Jessica, a crooked smile plastered on his ugly face.

He knows.

"Oh, no," I whisper, my eyes widening in panic.

I tear my eyes away from the screen to look up at the actual Jessica, the human figure floating in the tank. She doesn't look exactly like the Jessica I know from the game, but it's close. She's still beautiful, closer to my real age, it seems. I can't see her eyes, can barely see her mouth and nose behind the translucent tube, but she looks calm. At peace.

Because she doesn't know.

Dekker speaks quietly behind me, "Jessica, the REAL Jessica, is thirty-eight years old and is from the former city of Sherman Oaks, California, now residing in Upper Victorville Province. She is participating in this beta test to earn enough money to support her older sister, Tracy, who lives in Oxnard Province, and whom she hasn't seen in years. Tracy contracted the new virus eighteen months ago, and she was fortunate enough to be one of the twenty percent of people who survive it, but she is now in a medically-induced coma."

I try to speak, but there's nothing I can say.

"When we recruited Jessica, it was under the

condition that if she successfully completed the game, Chum would ensure her sister receives an experimental treatment that has shown promise in restoring function to those afflicted with the virus. She is not just fighting for herself, John. She is fighting for someone she loves very much."

My eyes begin to tear up, looking at Jessica floating serenely. I certainly know what it's like to lose someone close to you. I blink the tears away as I look back down at her on the video screen and see her inside the enemy's lair. She's alone in there, a sitting duck.

Dekker continues in his quiet tone. "Jessica is very smart. She quickly figured out a way to level up well beyond what we had believed a normal player would. And she even deduced a new way to infiltrate the Spankers by herself, even in spite of your actions. But she doesn't know that they're on to her. And she was so busy leveling up and focusing on understanding the gang structure and mechanics that she has not yet learned anything at all about the token system."

I look away from the screen to Dekker's eyes, knowing what he means before he says it.

He says, "Meaning she doesn't have any continues. So if she dies in the game world right now, there is no coming back."

I look in panic from Dekker, to the video screen, to the peaceful figure floating above me, then back to Dekker. "Isn't there anything you can do to stop it?"

Dekker shakes his head sadly. "No, John. This is the way it was designed. We need the stakes to be real, otherwise our overseers will not accept the game results."

I raise my fist to my face and bite down on a knuckle in frustration, staring down at the ground.

"You think we're stupid, John. You think the game is dumb and our design decisions are arbitrary and the things we've created are shallow rip-offs of the real world. Perhaps we are not the most clever writers, I will grant you that. But the space that we have created, the feel of contact, from the wind in your hair to a fist in your face, these things are far better than anything you have experienced before, and that is not easy to achieve. You know it's true. This isn't just a game. This is our future."

He's right. I know he is.

Dekker drops his gaze to his fancy ChumWatch. "The next drug shipment leaves the Spankers' hideout in just under 24 hours. Which means that the Spankers need all the labor they have to get the thousands of doses of Drug X processed and out into their channels on the street for sale and distribution. So Jessica is probably safe until then, simply because they need all hands on deck right now. But after that..." He shrugs and holds his hands up, pursing his lips together as if to say, "What can you do?"

I look back to Jessica's face, her real one, floating above me. I was angry and hurt by her, but now I understand what's really motivating her. Why she's doing what she's doing.

And I understand what I have to do now. Not for me. For her.

I turn to Dekker. "I need to go back."

Dekker arches an eyebrow. "Back to the game, John? This is a change of heart."

I make it very clear that I'm not joking. "Let me back in. I can fix this, Dekker. I have to fix this."

Dekker looks down at the floor, considering. Is he actually thinking about whether to let me back in? He has to let me! This smug bastard!

Finally, he looks up and nods. "Of course, John. However, we cannot get you back in right away."

"Why not?" I almost yell, surprising myself with the ferocity of my reaction.

"Please understand, we need to reset your chamber first. It's a bit of a process." He checks his watch again. "We'll need about an hour before you can get back in there."

He's walking quickly back to my room. I'm right on his heels, scrambling to keep up.

"Right this way, John. I'll alert the crew," he calls over his shoulder. "Would you like a robe?"

Chapter 16

Iceman

H ere I am, back in the old conference room.

For twenty minutes, I've been pacing inside the four walls of the large space in my fluffy robe and plastic sandals, practically wearing a hole in the plush carpet. Thinking about Jessica, thinking about the game, thinking about the world.

A wild thought suddenly appears in my head. I stop at the head of the table. A projector screen is behind me on the wall, it's pulled down for the first time I've been in here. I'm just noticing it now. They must have had a new recruiting session.

I clasp my hands together and address the empty room, like I'm a facilitator.

"Welcome, everybody! Please have a seat. We have a short presentation for you today entitled 'How to Punch People to Save Civilization: The Luke Dekker Story.'"

I sweep my eyes slowly across the room, looking deep into the eyes of every imaginary person at every empty seat, really selling it.

"But first, let's all get up and do a fun team exercise where you pick a partner sitting next to you, give them your name and one fun fact about yourself, and then punch them in the face as hard as you can. Remember, this is to save our civilization."

Suddenly, I don't feel funny anymore. I just feel tired. I sigh heavily and walk over to sit in one of the chairs lining the back wall. I pick up a glossy magazine on the end table next to me and start absently leafing through it. I honestly didn't think they printed these things anymore.

This one is an in-house vanity magazine called Chum Living, so there are lots of articles that are basically ads for new products that Chum is more than happy to deliver to your door, like a feature titled "Best Body Pillows with Adjustable Video Heads," for all the lonely hearts out there.

My eyes are glazing over, trying to read a fluff interview piece on a top celebrity gamer, MaddNaddz. He's got a popular channel on ChumNet, I guess. Even just a few years ago, they wouldn't have dared print his logo in a glossy magazine, which is a drawing of a pair of testicles with anger waves emanating from them, hence the "mad nads." That said, the more I look at it, it could be plausibly interpreted as odor waves instead, which makes it both super gross and also really muddled branding. Although, he's 23 years old and has 40 million subscribers, so I guess he's doing just fine.

I can't focus on the words on the page. I'm thinking about getting back in the game, figuring out what I'm going to do. How I'm going to set things right. Less than twenty-four hours to bust in, bust up the drug gang, and save the princess. For real, this time.

Then my eyes scan the paragraph where MaddNaddz talks about the new game he's playing. It's a very familiar one. "Yeah, now I'm streaming this new VR game called *World of Moby*. Nattagame hooked me up with a lot of premium gear and a nice house on the beach. I already killed the whales, so now we're streaming parties from the beach house. It's hella fly."

You son of a bitch. I want that beach house. With nobody in it but me, just peace and quiet. Also, did the phrase "hella fly" somehow come back into the vernacular? I remember the first time it was around. Didn't care for it then, either.

I watch my hand grab hold of this page of the magazine and slowly rip it out of the spine. Then I observe my hands setting the magazine on the chair next to me, bringing the interview page before my eyes, and then tearing little ribbons off it, one after another. The sound that the glossy paper makes as it shreds bit by bit is very satisfying. Soothing.

I hear a noise, and it instantly snaps me out of my reverie. It's the sound of the main entrance door opening, out in the lobby.

My heart starts racing. I gather the shreds of the page that have fallen all around me, hurriedly ball them up, and stuff them into the fluffy front pocket of my robe. Then I pick up the magazine, cross my legs, and arrange my robe so that it looks like I'm just calmly waiting, right in time for the conference room door to open.

Two hazmat dudes walk in, but it's not Tallboy and Short Round. I can tell right away by their figures, these guys are both tall and well-built, almost identical. They do a quick visual inspection of the room, then nod to someone outside the door.

A man walks in. He's wearing street clothes, and I sneak a look up without looking directly over to him. He's an African-American guy, a good-looking dude, maybe a few years older than me. I spot a bit of gray at his temples, though not as much as mine.

One of the Hazmat bros nods towards the med station next to the entrance, and the new recruit dutifully submits to the test. Then the bro broadcasts "MAKE YOURSELF COMFORTABLE," in that weird, amplified voice through his suit, and the bros both leave the room. I watch the new guy react to this out of the corner of my eye as I pretend to read the magazine, something about best indoor camping tents.

"Okay, will I see you fellas later?" the new guy calls after the hazmat bros, but they don't say a word, and the door shuts behind them. Typical.

New Guy looks around the room a bit. He eventually settles on a chair near the entrance. It's a more-than-respectable distance away, but he's still within my peripheral vision. He leans forward on the chair, rests his elbows on his thighs, and clasps his hands together. He seems relaxed, cool.

Long moments pass. I'm reading and re-reading the sentence "Chum anticipates a 150% profit over the next fiscal year due to increased security efforts in the Western states to alleviate product loss from various tribal and outlaw groups..." when the New Guy breaks the silence.

"So, they got any cucumber-infused water here?" New Guy asks.

Confused, I turn and face him directly. He has an open, kind face, although he's smirking slightly. Then he nods down at my clothes. Right, the robe. I must look like I'm at a freakin' day spa, waiting to get a massage.

I freeze for a second. *Don't trust anybody* plays in a loop in my mind. But he's still looking at me and smiling. And I have to admit it was a pretty funny joke.

I nod over to his immediate left, indicating a pitcher of water with glasses on the side table next to him. "Sadly, no cucumbers," I observe. Then, noting the basket next to the pitcher, I offer, "I do recommend the granola bars here. They're pretty good."

"Oh, don't mind if I do." He picks two of them, holds one up. I nod, and he tosses it casually to me, a perfect aim. Man, this guy is pretty cool.

He pours himself a glass of water, offers one to me, I decline. He sits back, takes a bite of granola, sips the water, and rests there. He's hanging back, not pushing it.

I keep trying to read my magazine and ignore him, until I can't stand it anymore. I'm too keyed up to get back in the game. "I'm John," I offer.

"Kevin. Pleased to meet you," New Guy says in a warm, inviting voice. We make an "air" elbow bump to each other from across our 15-foot distance.

"You too," I say. Then, after a moment, "You here to play, Kevin?"

"That's what I signed up for, although I have no idea what it really is, other than they say it's a million times better than staying at home. Although just about anything is these days. How about you, John? You here for the thrills?"

"Well, yeah." I'm struggling here. I want to say nothing, want to protect myself, but I guess I need the human contact a little bit more, especially back here in the real world.

I decide it can't hurt to talk a little. After a moment, I admit, "Actually, I've been playing for a couple of weeks, I'm about to go back in."

A look of surprise overtakes Kevin's features. "No kidding! How is it? What is it? Can you tell me?"

"You know, I actually don't know if I'm supposed to," I admit. "They make you sign a non-disclosure agreement."

"Oh. Okay. That's cool."

There's an uncomfortable pause as I try to figure out what to say next. I don't want to talk about the weather, so instead I choose the second-most-inane topic I can think of. "Where are you from, Kevin? You from around here?"

"Originally from L.A." he says immediately. "But after the Relocation, I'm out in the settlements now, like most people. They've got me in West Diamond Bar, doing telemedicine." He laughs. "I'm no doctor or anything like that, I just confirm people's insurance for ChumHealth. It's not bad. Beats being a Scummer, I suppose. And I like helping people. How about you, John?"

"Same for me. Well, also from L.A., now in North Fontana, right near the warehouse here. I'm a drone coordinator for Chum. Actually, I just started supporting the West Diamond Bar area a couple of months ago, so chances are, I'm probably slinging you your supplies every week," I laugh.

His eyes narrow a bit. "What's your last name, John?"

Uh-oh. I have no idea why he wants to know that, but it probably can't be great. "Uh... Chambers. John Chambers. What about you?"

"Kevin Singleton."

I have to say, the name kind of rings a bell, but I don't remember why.

"That's a pretty common name," he continues. "So maybe it was another John Chambers that lost my weekly shipment to Scummers about a month ago."

Nope. That was me that did that.

"Which is fine," he continues. "That happens, but then this John Chambers fellow apparently misfiled the incident report. I don't know what exactly happened, but I do know I didn't get my replacement shipment, and I had to somehow get by while I waited seven days for my next one." He's looking at me dead-on.

"Oh. Yeah," I say meekly. My face reddens and I stare down at the ground.

Kevin's loss was one of my bad mistakes. It was right when I started playing *World of Moby*, and I was, um, a little distracted at work. You're supposed to file an incident report to generate a replacement when shipments get hijacked, and I did, but I guess I didn't hit the "send" button.

That one went on my record, affected my annual performance review. I was embarrassed about it because I did my job poorly and was punished for it, but all this time, I never actually thought about the person at the other end of the screw-up. The person who didn't get needed toothpaste or ramen or cotton swabs or breakfast cereal for seven full days.

And now, here he is, sitting right across from me. I'm the guy he counted on, the guy who let him down. But mercifully, he doesn't look furious with me, although he certainly has every right to. He's got a wry smile on his face, waiting for me to say something.

"Oh, Kevin, man, I'm so sorry about that," I begin, my eyes still downcast, ashamed to look at him. "It was a whole deal, the paperwork got swallowed up, and as I soon as I realized what had happened, I filed an urgent support ticket and tried to get a replacement in, but I didn't realize it never made it." I look straight into his eyes. "I should have done better."

Kevin, to my great relief, gently laughs it off. "Hey, man, it's cool. I work in administration, I know how hard it is to juggle a whole bunch of people and their needs while you're sitting at home in your pajamas, typing into a tablet screen. Besides, it wasn't too bad, I had some stale bread left, and some 'lightly-expired' jelly. I got by okay."

I'm grateful he's being so nice about it. "I appreciate that, and I'm sorry, Kevin."

"All good. We all make mistakes," He laughs again, this time seeming to remember something. "In fact... Oh man, this is embarrassing. Right around that same time, I wound up forwarding someone a test that said they were pregnant. The man was very surprised, even more so because he lived alone. I was a little…distracted at work, because, and I hate to admit this, I was playing a new virtual reality game."

"*World of Moby*?" I ask, surprised and yet not surprised. He must be another recruit they scouted from the game.

Kevin's eyes go wide, and then he looks down and starts laughing. "Yeah, so I'm guessing you know how addictive it is, too. Well, that all makes a lot of sense." He takes another bite of granola, another sip of water, and makes a satisfied exhalation as he sits back.

"So, John, what am I getting into here? I volunteered for this, but I have no idea what's going on, other than it's supposed to beat *World of Moby* by a landslide."

"Well…since you're about to sign up anyway, I guess I can tell you a bit about it…" I take a deep breath, uncertain of where I want to begin. There's so much to explain, and so little time.

"It is a VR game, yes. But not like any you've ever played before. Not just headsets and finger triggers. It's your whole body. They immerse you in a tank and your mind believes you're inside the game world. You stay there. You live there."

A broad smile slowly spreads across his beaming, open face. He's now perched forward on his chair to listen to my every word, and now he reaches up slightly and pulls down his hand in a fist to exclaim, "Yes! Man, I was hoping that was the deal."

"But it's not like, elves and chainmail and stuff. This is, like, gritty street stuff. They spent all this money and time to create a world that runs like a beat 'em up nineties arcade game."

His face now goes from elation to open-mouthed shock.

"Man, are you serious? Like *Street Fighter*? I was a *Street Fighter II* champion back in the day!"

"Well, no, it's not a one-on-one fighting game like that. It's like a brawler." I clarify. "You know, *Final Fight*, *Double Dragon*, those kind of games. You're beating up a bunch of dudes, only it's all insanely detailed and real."

Now he's back to elation. "Oh man, are you kidding me? That's awesome!" He's seriously happy about this turn of events. "Seriously? A whole game world that's just punching bad guys? Man, I always wanted to learn how to fight for real." He gets a faraway look in his eyes saying this last part.

"Well, actually, it's a little more complicated than that," I explain. "It's like...a whole world. There's all these systems and levels, it's very involved, and I had to get a day job so I could get an apartment and buy some new clothes. Like, I got this really cool jacket..."

Kevin cuts me off. "Wait, so you just, like, live in a city again? With people? Do you have any idea how much cooler this is than telehealth administration?"

I hesitate for a moment, struggling with what I should reveal.

"Yeah, Kevin, but...here's the deal. I'm in trouble. The neighborhood's in trouble."

Kevin quickly gets serious, leans forward ,and locks eyes with me again. He's a chill guy overall, but it looks like he can be focused when he needs to be.

"Tell me more," he says.

✪✪✪

So I tell him. I don't know why; I just feel like I can trust him. Believe me, I'm still very much on guard, and the memory of Brice's betrayal is about as fresh as it can be, but this feels...different. I'm willing to give this a chance. Besides, I need all the help I can get right now.

It all spills out in a mad rush. I tell him about the Satan's Pantry Spankers, the Drug X scourge, Brice and my apartment, Jessica and the twenty-three hours and counting we have to save her from certain death.

I don't tell him about *why* we're doing all this, that it's not just a game for its own sake. I don't say anything at all about the vaccine, about learning to live together again. Dekker specifically told me not to do that, and I don't want to get him mad. Or get myself dumped out in the desert.

When I finally finish, Kevin is silent for a long moment, looking down at his hands, breathing slowly and deeply. Finally, he looks up and says to me, "Well, it sounds like you need a partner."

He catches me off guard. "Uh..." I stammer.

"What's your name? In the game, I mean?"

"Blaze."

He smiles. "Yeah, I can see that. This business has got you on fire. You need an Iceman, and brother, I'm as cool as they come."

"Blaze and Iceman," I say out loud, testing out the names. I like it. I'm wary, keeping my guard up...but I can give this a try.

"You're all Fist of the Pissed. Well, I'm gonna be some of that warrior monk business. Calm and in control. Deep breathing, intense focus and whatnot. But when it comes to battle, I will mess a fool up. That's you and me, Player 1 and Player 2."

I nod, grateful. "You can be Player 1 if you want to, Kevin...er, Iceman."

He smiles, dismisses the gesture. "It doesn't matter. It's more of a metaphor." He turns serious again. "So tell me what I gotta do when I get in there."

✪✪✪

I explain to Kevin all about the unexpected ordeal of the tutorial stage in the alley, and what he can expect going through it himself. Meanwhile, I tell him that I'll be on the streets, gathering intel. Once he's made it out, we can team up and reclaim my apartment first, then get ready to rescue Jessica and take out the Many Boss tomorrow morning.

Suddenly, the red flashing lights in the room spring to life, and the beeping noise indicates the far wall to the elevator is about to slide open. I point it out to Kevin so he can watch it happen.

As the wall panel slides open, a familiar voice can be heard above the beeping. "Paging Iceman and Blaze, Iceman and Blaze, you're wanted on the mean streets of New Arcadia. Please step into the lift to begin your journey."

Kevin looks to me, and I mouth the word, "Dekker." Of course, he was listening. I'm super glad I kept my mouth shut about the thing he asked me to. I stand up, and Kevin follows me into the elevator room.

The wall panel slides shut behind us, and we begin our long descent, standing side by side, facing the opposite wall that will open when we reach the basement level far below.

"How will I know where to find you?" Kevin asks me.

"After an hour, I'll be at the Burger Item on the corner of Fuller and 174th. It should be around the corner from the alley. Just head right over there."

"Is that a real name? You know, John, I believed every word you said up there, but I hear about a food joint called 'Burger Item,' and now I can't trust anything. That is the stupidest name for a restaurant I've ever heard."

I shrug. "They're still in beta." I shrug again. "And also, I don't think they have great writers here. But wailing on dudes, that part is still fun. When it's not horrifically painful."

He nods, considering. Then we stagger a bit, the elevator coming to a stop. The wall panel slides open, revealing the entrance room. This time, no one is here to greet us.

Kevin arches an eyebrow at me. "You remember where we're supposed to be going from here?"

My intense look of confused concentration is answer enough for him.

He sighs. "Alright, player. Let's figure this out together."

He hands me a granola bar from upstairs, and we each take a bite as we exit the lift and try to figure out the correct path to the game rooms.

Chapter 17

Hearts on Fire

I'm back. Back in a New York groove.

Or more accurately, back in a New Arcadia groove. They're very similar grooves.

I've only been gone an hour, and I suppose I left this place under less-than-ideal circumstances, but that's all water under the bridge now. The sun is shining, birds are chirping, car horns are honking. I've beamed back in right to my happy place, at the edge of the corner park. It immediately puts me at ease.

I close my eyes and breathe in that New Arcadia air. A slight tinge of gasoline, a pungent whiff of trash...but also the sweet smell of flowers at my feet. I don't know what kind of flowers they are, or even if they're a real kind or one the game developers made up. I really don't know anything about flowers. But these are purple and white, and they smell nice. It's good to be back.

I look around a bit more to get my bearings. There's

the old Burger Item. Ah, just like the old times. Wait, John, you're nostalgic for a place you just left an hour ago. Well, what can I say? It feels like coming home, somehow.

I've barely taken a step forward when I hear wood shattering and a sustained triumphant yell from far behind me. I know that sound.

I turn to look at the nearby alley entrance from instinct, and of course it's Kevin, spinning like a lunatic onto the sidewalk, fists flailing and pulverized wooden boxes raining down around him. But how did he get through the character select and tutorial stage so quickly?

I start jogging over to him. Kevin stops and hunches over, putting his hands on his knees and catching his breath.

"Iceman!" I call out as I approach. "Iceman! How did you get out here so fast?"

He stands up and lets out a triumphant "Woo!" Then he takes a deep breath and puts his hands on the back of his hips to stretch. Now that I can see his face clearly, he looks as I expected. Very similar to his real face, but younger. It's like an idealized version of his features, the best he can look.

"This is crazy, Iceman, I just got here," I explain. "You couldn't have been more than five minutes ahead of me."

Kevin looks at me, "Well, Mr. Blaze, I appear to be very good at this kind of game."

"Yeah, I guess so!" I agree. "Did Dekker walk you through the tutorial?"

Kevin scrunches up his face. "The dude in charge? Guy we heard in the conference room?"

"Yeah, the white-haired ponytailed dude?" I ask.

Kevin shakes his head slowly. "No, I never saw him. They just dunked me in the tank after I signed the form and then I'm picking my character, and before you know it, I'm punching rats in the face while my trainer was cheering me on."

"Was it Dekker? Did you hear him in your brain?"

Kevin is getting frustrated with me. "Are you hearing *me* in *your* brain? I told you I never saw that dude. No, man, I had this whole experience waiting for me. There was this lady that was my trainer in the alley. She was a lot like Burgess Meredith in *Rocky I* through III, but she was kinda hot? It was very confusing."

"Big Louise!" I cry. "She's my trainer at the gym! Well, that's different. Did you do the hobo fight at the end?"

"Nah, man, it was almost nothing like what we talked about. She had me wail on a giant sack of grain for a while. I'm a southpaw, but the game kept making me lead with my right fist. Then she stuttered for a second like there was something wrong with her, she was like, twitching. And then after that, I was able to punch with my left fist leading!"

"Wow, it's like they were figuring it out as you were playing," I say.

"Yeah, I think that's right. And then there was this giant rat, that part was pretty much like you told me. After that, this punk dude in a ratty old jean jacket busted in and started threatening me and Big Louise."

"Like this jacket?" I ask, pointing to my chest, feeling

hurt.

Kevin's eyes widen when he really notices my outfit, and he quickly scrambles. "Uh... No, man, not like that. Yours is...much cooler. His has sleeves, sleeves are wack. So... Anyway, Big Louise tells me to kick his ass, and I punched him so hard I knocked the denim right off him. He blinks in and out, then disappears like magic. And then I punched through this stack of boxes with my special move, and right now, I'm standing here on the sidewalk and feeling pretty damn good."

He does a few stretches to the sky with each arm, then rolls his shoulders. I don't say anything, I let him burn off the adrenaline a little bit. Pedestrians are smart enough to walk around us in a wide arc. We're too bad-ass to mess with, obviously.

Eventually, Kevin brings his arms down and thinks for a moment before he speaks. "I can see why they changed that fight with the unhoused person. It's pretty problematic from a sensitivity point of view." He looks back at me. "It sounds like they took your player feedback into account."

I consider that for a moment. I guess they did, which is kind of impressive. It's only been about two weeks, and they've already changed the whole beginning of the game. What else have they been able to change? Are they messing with things all around me even now? This whole world could turn around on a single whim from some programmer. My mind is starting to spin out just considering it...

Suddenly, Kevin's fingers are snapping in front of my face. I look up, and Kevin, aka Iceman, is smiling. "Hey, earth to Blaze, earth to Blaze. You were talking about getting a burger first, and I see my health is a little low right now from that special move, but I'm still feeling real good. Wanna go back to your place and kick Brice's ass? Because I'm ready to team up and take him down."

That must have been a cue, because suddenly a text box pops up in front of me.

Team Up with Iceman?

And then two buttons:

Yes / No.

I can tell Kevin sees the same thing in front of him, because his eyes go wide as he focuses on empty air a foot in front of him. "Whoa," he says, waving his arms in front of him, trying to touch the floating box.

I reply, "Yeah, this is how the game system works. It's, like, a translucent prompt that you can see, and I guess nobody else can. But you can't just reach out and touch it. You have to visualize doing it, too, like with intent. You have to, like, *feel* it."

"Alright, well, do you wanna team up, Blaze? Are you *feeling* it?" he asks. That's a clever bit of rhetoric. He's listening and responding to what I'm saying. I like this guy.

"Yeah, man, let's do it." I accept, and I watch Kevin's eyes close and concentrate hard. Definitely way too hard, he looks like he's about to lift Yoda up in the air with his mind. But he's getting used to it, he'll figure it out, probably faster than I did. He opens his eyes, reaches forward with his hand, then smiles. Suddenly, I see a new prompt.

Partners: Blaze and Iceman are now teamed up.

Bonuses: Strength, Endurance, Charisma.

New Item: Pager.

You can now use a pager to communicate with your partner. Check your storage device to equip.

Kevin laughs. "Man, that's awesome! What's the storage device? Does that mean like a folder on a hard drive?" He looks around as if expecting to find it somewhere.

I point down to his groin, then reach down to mine and grab my fanny pack and shake it. "I got your storage device right here," I deadpan.

Kevin's brows furrow in confusion at my pack, then his eyes go wide in understanding. He looks down to discover his own fanny pack. "Man, this IS 199X," he says, laughing. "Look at this nonsense, I haven't worn one of these things since I was a kid."

I open my pack and pull out a gleaming new black pager with a green LED display, like an old calculator. I flip it over and notice it has a very primitive interface—an old phone number pad—with ABC above the number 1, DEF above number 2, etc. Dammit, this sucks. I mean, it's nice to have a way to communicate, but this looks like it's going to be cumbersome, painstakingly typing out each individual letter with multiple button presses. I do not miss this part of the 90s.

I clip the pager onto my belt, and the moment I do, my heads-up display adds the LED screen where the text goes. That's handy. If I can see it in my HUD, maybe I can control it that way, too.

I concentrate and imagine typing a message. I

gingerly tap out "TEST" with my mind, and then press send. Okay, that worked, that's easy enough to do.

Kevin laughs, "Wow! Got it," then focuses on an empty point in front of him. A few moments later, I receive a reply. It's a string of numbers: 55378008.

Confused, I look up at Kevin. "Is this your pager number, Iceman? You've got one extra digit here."

"Do a headstand, Blaze."

"What?" That's totally out of left field.

"You heard me, flip over and get on your head. I'm testing a very important feature of this device."

Eying him warily, I say, "Okay, I think I can do that. I mean, I definitely can't in the real world anymore, but out here, let's see…"

I set my head down on the sidewalk and kick up easily. I hold it there for a couple of seconds to make sure I have my balance, then test moving my legs around. It's shockingly easy. I start kicking back and forth, showboating a bit, and staying in place no problem.

"Do you see it?" he asks me.

I can see his legs standing in front of me, and the sidewalk, but that's about it.

"No, what am I looking for?"

"Just keep looking."

I focus on my heads-up display. Kicking back and forth upside-down like I am, the HUD is struggling to maintain its orientation. It's acting like when you twirl a handheld tablet around and the screen jumps around trying to face upright. Now the pager screen is right side up, 180 degrees from where I currently am. I stare at the LED screen for a moment, hanging carefully in place to keep the upside-down orientation. And then I see it.

"Oh, for god's sake." I exclaim, and immediately kick back out into an upright standing position. Kevin is already doubled over laughing.

"Okay, I saw the word BOOBLESS. I get it. Very mature."

He's still laughing. "Hey, what can I say? It's thirty years ago, I'm a young man." The laughter finally dies down. "Put 'er there, partner."

He's smiling brightly, hand outstretched. I look him in the eye and take his hand. We give it one firm shake. Then he does all this cool extra handshake stuff, and somehow, I don't screw it up. I follow his lead, and we snap fingers and punch hands, and make a cool explosion thing with our fingers, and I guess that's our new handshake now.

"Fire and Ice," he intones.

"Bad-ass brothers," I agree.

Then he asks me very seriously, "Tell me, Blaze, are you a bad enough dude to rescue the president?" He's riffing on the famous line from the 1988 beat 'em up classic *Bad Dudes vs. DragonNinja.*

I laugh. "Well, it's a lady named Jessica, not the president. But first, let's find out if we're bad enough dudes to rescue my dump of a studio apartment."

"Lead the way, kemosabe," he says with a flourish, extending his hand out in invitation.

✪✪✪

My front door smashes open with a vicious crack. It's Blaze and Iceman's first double jump-kick.

We need to work on our timing, but all things considered, we did pretty good. The door gives easily, almost like it wasn't locked at all. It slips right open, and the momentum keeps us sailing inside, barely clearing the door frame and both landing in a crouch, side-by-side, right inside the apartment.

We're immediately up on our feet, ready for anything.

But there's nothing.

Nothing at all, except the bed frame. Everything else is gone, stripped bare. All my stuff: my bags of essentials, the boombox with my killer Spankers mixtape. No more. Looks like Brice took everything he could find and bolted for a place of his own. A good thing, too; I would have knocked him right out the window.

We're both scanning the room, taking it all in, our breathing returning to normal, slowly uncoiling in the absence of danger. Kevin breaks the silence.

"You know, this is actually a little better than my first place in New York," he quips.

I double-check the bathroom. Nobody hiding in the shower. No toothpaste. No toilet paper, even. I trudge back to the main room, sad and frustrated. Kevin is now looking out the window into the alley below, taking in the view.

He says without looking up, "What do you say we head downstairs and beat up those trash cans there until we can find some things to sell in them? Then we head over to the pawn shop and stock this place back up again?"

"Man, I gotta say, Kevin..." I begin.

He turns to face me.

"That's a really great idea," I finish. "On my own, I probably would have just sat here on my ass moping for two days before I figured that out."

He smiles. "That's why it's a good thing you're not on your own."

"But can we make one little change to your plan? There's someplace very important we should go first. I promise you'll dig it."

✪✪✪

"Man, this is a tasty burger!" Kevin exclaims, savoring the bite.

We're sitting at a table inside the Burger Item, full combo meals on our trays. Skip was behind the counter as usual. He was thrilled to see me feeling better, and he already offered Kevin a job. I asked if I could have a few more days off. He was cool with it.

"Mm-mm. The Royale with Cheese..." he begins.

"Alright, man, I get it," I exclaim. "*Pulp Fiction*, we're back in the 90s, Okay, I get what you're doing." I instinctively want to correct him, tell him that he's *technically* enjoying a 'Cheese Royale,' Burger Item's signature sandwich, but I resist the impulse.

He slowly looks up at me, deliberately chews a big bite and swallows it down, then takes an exaggerated slurp of his fountain soda. "Look, you may have been here for a few weeks and got all nice and settled in, got gainfully employed, but I've been in this world for only about ninety minutes and I'm still getting quite a kick out this place."

"I'm sorry, Iceman," I say, staring down at my food.

"I'd like for you to acknowledge that the novelty factor is still high for me right now, and I'd appreciate you not trying to be a mope."

"No, you're right." I sigh. "Honestly, it would have been great to get started here with somebody. So maybe I'm a little jealous. But I guess when I started here, I probably wasn't even ready to hang out with other people. I'm... I'm glad you're here now, though."

He smiles. "Hey man, I'm just messing with you." But I can tell he's touched. Is... Is this what's like to have a friend again?

He shoots a glance behind me and sees something that makes his smile quickly fade. He speaks quietly and urgently to me.

"Hey, who's the gang here in this neighborhood, the Whackoffs?" he inquires.

"The Spankers," I correct him, keeping my voice low and starting to turn around.

"No, no, be cool. Don't let him see you looking. Go get a refill."

"I'm not thirsty."

"Get a refill so you can see the guy, dumbo. Do you know how spy stuff works?"

I sigh and get up, grabbing my drink. As I start filling it up with Ebola Cola (despite the name, it's actually pretty tasty), I nonchalantly glance over my shoulder.

It's a Spanker, all right. He looks just like the one that offered me Drug X in the alley that morning a couple of weeks ago. But that's impossible, that guy's turned to dust, or whatever happens when you kick the bucket in this place. Maybe it's his twin brother, maybe it's a clone. Whoever he is, he's sitting in one of the window booths opposite a nervous young guy that looks like a clean-cut college boy. College Boy nods quickly, and then they both get up and head outside.

Suddenly, a prompt appears in front of me.

Quest: Follow the Spanker and get intel on the gang hideout.

Accept: Yes / No

I glance back at Kevin, and it's clear he's received the same notification. He nods, and I do too, both of us accepting the quest. Once the dealer and College Boy head through the front door and it shuts behind them, I leap into action, and I feel Kevin fall in behind.

"Goodbye, Blaze! Goodbye, Mr. Iceman!" Skip waves as we rush past. I put a finger a to my lips and stare him in the eyes. Skip immediately understands, and makes a zipping motion on his lip.

We head out to the street and keep our distance, but it turns out we don't have far to go: the pair duck into the alley right behind the restaurant. We turn the corner and see them just ahead, standing next to a dumpster parked next to a brick wall. College Boy has a $20 bill in his hand. He looks up first and freezes when he spots us.

The poor kid is sandwiched between the wall and the Spanker, pressed against the dumpster, and now we're bearing down on him from the other side. He has nowhere to go but down, so he immediately curls into a fetal position and presses his back against the dumpster, shielding his face with his hands. I almost feel sorry for him, then I remember how sad he would make poor Nancy Reagan with his behavior, and I don't feel sorry anymore.

Meanwhile, the Spanker stands his ground. Kevin and I stop and face off with him, ten feet away. I check his stats: sure enough, it's Pepper. He palms his little bag of sickly green Drug X back into his pocket.

I flash a menacing grin at him. "Remember me, Pepper? Do you remember that Winners Don't Use Drugs?"

He scrunches his face, confused. "Nah, man. I don't know what you're talking about."

He might be acting, or putting on a front for College Boy, but something tells me he's being sincere. Which means that either Pepper got reincarnated, he got amnesia from one too many blows to the head, or there a bunch of Peppers running around New Arcadia, just like in the original beat 'em ups when they reused enemy types and sent them after you over and over.

When we don't immediately rush him, Pepper senses a possible business opportunity. "Wanna try a sample?" he asks, pulling the baggie back out of his pocket and dangling it in front of him. It's full of green powder and looks like poisoned Pop Rocks. "First one's free."

College Boy's eyes grow wide at the sight of the

drug, and he forgets his fear for a moment. He holds the $20 bill up next to the baggie. "Hey, that's my Drug X, man!"

Pepper doesn't even look down. "SHUT UP, COLLEGE BOY!" Then, back to us, "What do you say, fellas? Wanna fly?"

Kevin and I look at each other. He shrugs, as if to say "Should we?" and I nod as if to say "Yes." And then we fly.

Moving as one, we rush toward the Spanker. He plants his right foot back and steels himself for our arrival. A few feet away, we jump up together and launch into our now-patented double flying kick.

Pepper tries to punch us as we land, but our longer legs have the advantage. In one fluid motion, we crash into his ugly mug, knocking him back and flipping him neatly into the half-full dumpster, screaming all the way. He lands feet-first inside the dumpster, and only stops screaming when the lid swings over and slams down on his head, knocking him down and enclosing him in the trash heap. He's not getting up from that any time soon.

With Pepper out of commission, we turn our focus to the shivering preppie at our feet. College Boy is blond and clean-cut; he probably drove in from the fancy suburbs. He's covering his face with his hands and still holding the twenty dollars between his fingers. I snatch the bill out of his hand, and he yelps a little.

"Hey, College Boy, get the hell out of here," I intone in my best 'DARE to say no to drugs and alcohol' voice. "And stay away from Drug X. That stuff will make you wind up...in the garbage."

I slam the dumpster right next to his head with my

palm for emphasis, making a loud bang and causing him to yelp in terror. He peers up at me from between his trembling hands, fear flashing in his red, teary eyes.

"See what I did there? With the garbage?" I ask him, pointing to the Spanker-filled dumpster behind him. "I put him...in the garbage," I explain, trailing off.

He nods, too scared to speak.

"Get outta here, kid, you're bothering me!" I yell, raising the back of my hand to him.

He gets up shakily and runs off down the alley. I turn back to Kevin. He is not amused.

"Man, you didn't have to take his money," he says.

"Come on, Iceman," I chide. "Consider it a payment for protective services. We just saved this young man from a life of crime."

"I don't know if this game has a morality system, but I feel like you probably just lost some points."

"HEY!" an angry voice cries behind us, and we turn around.

Three more Spankers stand there. Two more Peppers flank a big, hairy leader named, inexplicably, Furbee.

Kevin turns to me, confused. "Pepper's a triplet?" he asks quietly.

I respond quietly, "I think it's like the old games. Either they're paying homage by having repeat enemies, and/or this game world is actually low on working memory."

"Ah." Kevin nods with understanding.

"Hey, that was our sale!" the one called Furbee yells at us from the end of the alley.

"Well," I begin in a friendly tone of voice, "you're in luck, because we are prospective buyers, and we are both interested in acquiring a considerable supply of Drug X. Would you be so kind as to take us back to your retail shop?"

They still look very angry, but now also confused.

I drop the friendly act. "Okay, I'll speak more plainly, Spanks. Take us to your drug lab. We wanna see it."

Furbee is enraged at this. "Watch your mouth! We ain't no Spanks, we're the Spank-ers. And nobody gets into our base."

"Especially not dead men walking!" one of the Peppers exclaims. Furbee promptly smacks him in the shoulder. "Ow!" Pepper is plainly not authorized to speak on behalf of the group.

"Well, you boys are about to become the Spank-ees." Kevin's been awfully quiet so far, but now he pipes in with a solid quip.

"Yeah, because we're going to spank you. With our fists." I back Kevin up, extraneously. "Because you've been very bad boys. We're gonna spank you, even though studies have consistently shown that corporal punishment has no positive effects on—«

"Enough talk," roars Furbee.

"Okay, have it your way," I agree and immediately lunge toward him, closing the distance fast and punching him right in the nose. You'd think he would have seen that coming.

Furbee staggers, but then my hands are yanked behind my back. One of the Peppers has me in his grip. I swing wildly from side to side, trying to shake him, but I can't.

"Iceman!" I yell, and I see him recover from a punch from the other Pepper, then strike right back at him. He sends his Pepper flying down the alley, even as he blinks out of existence. Now Kevin turns to me, sees me struggling with my captor.

"Duck!" he yells.

"What?" I yell back.

Then Iceman punches me in the face. Accidentally, I think.

"Aaaaaa!" I yell, staggering to the side with my Pepper still on my back.

I hear Kevin behind me, "Blaze, I just gained a level with that last punch! All my health is back!"

Okay, a) why did he have to get his level boost by punching me in the face, and b) wow, that's fast. It took him an hour to achieve what it took me almost two weeks to grind out. I guess teamwork really does give you an advantage in the game.

"Gggaahh...that's...GREAT!" I scream the last word as I hunker over and fling my Pepper forward. The sudden move catches him off guard. He flies right over me and lands flat on the ground. I squat down and smack him right in the kisser. He's down for the count.

Suddenly, I feel that familiar dopamine rush, notice the warm glow surrounding my body, and watch my health meter top off like I just got a fountain soda refill.

Congratulations! You have reached Level 3.

Sweet. Kevin and I both gained a level, and I'm still one ahead of him.

"I'm ahead of you again, bro! Level 3 now!" I call out.

I turn to look for Kevin, and he's got Furbee in a full nelson move, standing behind him with his arms latched around the back of his head, trapping the big man's shoulders behind him painfully. Furbee's health is way down. Not far enough for my taste, though. I step over and smack him right in the face.

"OWWW!" Furbee cries. He's so hairy that I have to pick the hairs out from between my knuckles. His health is almost gone, but he's not gone yet. Good, because we need him for information. I grab hold of his hirsute face.

"Where's your gang hideout, Spanky?" I demand.

He turns his eyes away from me. "Aw, man, you know. We just hang out. There's an alley off Fuller and 174th that's like our home base."

I hear Kevin's incredulous voice behind me. "The tutorial stage? Really?"

I shake Furbee by his collar. "The only guy that's in there now is a hobo drinking coffee from a hubcap!"

Kevin chimes in, "Actually now it's just a lady named Big Louise with a punching bag!"

"Yeah!" I shake the lying Spanker by the collar a few more times, but he clamps up tight and won't look me in the eyes.

I get a sudden idea, then reach into the inside pocket of his denim jacket. I pick a telltale baggie out and hold it up to his face.

"You talk to us right now, or you're getting high on your own supply!" I threaten.

His eyes widen and he immediately stops struggling. Wow, this Drug X must be pretty bad news if he's reacting this way. I mean, he would know. He wastes no time telling us what's really up.

"Okay, okay, fine! We relocated, man. We're moving up in the world. Got a whole building all to ourselves now to manufacture the stuff! It's all the way on the other side of the hood, in an abandoned warehouse down at Fuller and 150th. Corner building. Red double-doors out front. I swear, man!"

I consider for a moment, look at Kevin. He nods.

"Okay, thanks!" I punch him one last time. Kevin gasps, and Furbee starts to blink out of existence. It really shouldn't feel so satisfying to do that, but I'm afraid it does.

I turn to look back at Kevin, who's still wincing from witnessing the blow. "Aw, don't worry about him, I'm sure we'll run into a dozen more Furbees before this is over." But Kevin just shakes his head.

Then, we both get a notification.

Quest Complete: Follow the Spanker and get intel on the gang hideout.

Cool. Looks like we're officially on the right track. We acknowledge our pop-ups and take a look for any loot the Spankers left behind.

On the ground are now two shiny objects where

Furbee was just standing. They're coins. I bend down to pick them up.

"Hey, Iceman, I think these are the free life tokens I was telling you about." I'm turning them over in my hands, but they don't look familiar, and they're silver, not gold. I begin reading the coins, "New Arcadia... Metro..." I look up at Kevin, surprised. "These are subway tokens."

Kevin smiles and claps his hands together. "Well, there we go. That's how we'll get all the way down to their base, Blaze. You said yourself we can't walk there, we'll hit the invisible barrier on the street in only a few blocks."

"Yeah... I guess..." I hedge, feeling my face flush and wanting to change the subject.

I walk away from Kevin and pick up the haul left behind by the dearly-departed Pepper brothers. One item is a soda can that neither of us need right now for energy, but the other one is a new mix cassette tape. Perfect.

"What, are you not a subway fan, John?" Kevin asks, a teasing note in his voice.

"Please, Iceman, it's Blaze out on the streets," I correct him.

Kevin holds up his hands, "Whoa, my apologies, Mr. Blaze. Didn't mean to get you all hot under the collar."

I look up from the cassette tape at him and sigh deeply. It's time to level with him.

"I just... I'm from L.A. I know you grew up in New York, but I...I guess it's been a while since I've been in an enclosed space with a lot of people."

Kevin has had a bemused smile on his face, but now he gets it. He understands why I don't want to go down there. We've spent a long time avoiding other people, and it's a very hard habit to break. Getting into a tight space and breathing the same air as a bunch of other city dwellers, even if it's not real, it sure feels real, and that's hard.

"Hey, I hear you, man," Kevin reassures me. "Tell you what, let's sleep on it. We've still got time. Let's stick with the plan. Do some errands today, fix up the apartment. Plus, we need to get stronger for the final fight. We can get in some training, build up our stats. Then we'll be ready in the morning."

I nod slowly, taking it all in, and what I say next is quiet, yet very determined and extremely bad-ass.

"Alright, Iceman. Let's do this. Let's go shopping."

✪✪✪

Back home in the apartment now. We stopped over at Pawn Shop Pete's first, and she hooked us up, big-time. We set up another mattress and box spring for Kevin, and I got a replacement mattress too. We filled the fridge with snacks, and finally set down a brand-new boombox and put in our new Spankers mix cassette tape.

"Are you sure you don't want to go down to the Fun Club to see Big Louise and start your training?" I ask.

"Not tonight. Time is short, and we've got to save Jessica in the morning. Just teach me what you know right here, right now."

I sigh, nod, and press the 'play' button on the boombox. Once we get some killer tunes going, we start with fifty pushups. Kevin counts us off. After a few reps, he switches it up to one-handed pushups. I can't do those at all.

This music is fantastic. I'm feeling better than I have in a long time. This is the perfect soundtrack to a training montage. I just wish we could dissolve to the end of the scene, but nope. We've got to get through this, one pushup at a time.

"Seven...eight...nine...ten..."

Chapter 18

Subway

We haven't even gone through the turnstiles, and I'm already shaking.

The station is packed. Countless bodies pour down from the street and clash with more surging up from the trains. I've pretty much lived in my sweatpants for the last three years, but even now in my upgraded denim street threads, I still stand out in a sea of business suits and power dresses. It makes me even more self-conscious, and that increases my anxiety even more for being down here.

I check my pager: it's just past nine o'clock, which means it's rush hour, so that accounts for the crowd. It doesn't make me feel any better knowing the reason, though.

We have less than two hours to rescue Jessica and stop the shipment of Drug X.

I'm pressing myself against a white tile wall, trying

to stay as far away from the human swarm as possible. *VRIT*, I whisper the letters to myself between shallow, halting breaths. *Virtual Reality Immersion Therapy,* that's what Dekker called it.

I'm no soldier, far from it, but I still think I've got some version of shellshock. Post-traumatic stress from years of thinking all other people on the planet are the enemy, that their very breath could kill me. And now, down here in a tight space with hundreds of them crammed up against me, it's too much. It's just too much.

Kevin is standing right across from me, looking much more relaxed and in his element, studying a subway map on the wall with a practiced eye. Meanwhile, I'm studying a garbage can a few feet away, wondering if I'll have enough time to reach it in case I barf.

"Hey, Blaze, check this out, man," Kevin says, tapping me on the shoulder.

"Uh... Okay," I say queasily.

I flip around and inch back a little from the wall I've been clinging to, carefully, like I might slip and fall off a building, then focus on the giant image before me.

At the top of the poster, near the ceiling, there's a big black horizontal bar that reads *New Arcadia Subway Map*. The city below it appears at a glance to be a long, thin island. I'd say it's just on this side of being a straight-up rip-off of Manhattan. The island contains an impossible tangle of many different subway lines. The scale and density of the system overwhelms me when I'm in New York, and it freaks me out ten times as much here in New Arcadia.

Fuller Avenue runs down from the very top and

continues all the way downtown to the bottom of the skinny island. Our location is well uptown, a couple of miles south of the north tip, where the street numbers stop at 210.

To the east of our stop at 172nd Street, there's another, bigger land mass across the river, I guess it's like Brooklyn and Queens. There are only two rail lines that go over to this place, but they both say "Closed for Repair" on the map. Probably those boroughs are off limits until a future game expansion.

I scan quickly over the jumbles of lines and curves, trying to absorb it all at once. It's too overwhelming, so instead I shake my head and look away. "I don't know, maybe we should just take a cab or something," I plead.

Kevin puts his hand on my shoulder; it calms me a bit. "Blaze, we just spent almost all our money on groceries and supplies, and we've got these shiny subway tokens right here in our hands."

I look at the silver coin he holds up. It fails to convince me.

"I promise, it's easy as pie. We're gonna get on the A train here and take it five stops to 152nd, then walk right down to the Spanker base on 150th." He points at the A line on the map. It heads south to 152nd, then veers due east and across the river out of the island. Or it would, if the line weren't closed for 'repair.'

"I don't know about this," I mumble.

"I *do* know about this. New York is my city, and this place is its weird little twin brother. I can find my way around. Just follow me and we'll be just fine."

He strides to the entrance turnstile, confident in his decision. I've got a sinking feeling in my stomach, but I move forward anyway. We just don't have much time left. I must not be walking fast enough, because a man in a suit pushes right past me.

"H-hey, watch it!" I cry feebly. Not like a bad-ass street warrior at all.

Business Guy barely looks back at me, and all I see is an expression of contempt on his face. Out on the streets, I'm gleefully punching rows of Spankers in the face, but stuck down here, I'm losing my edge...badly.

Kevin calls back over his shoulder, "Be cool, just follow me, man."

It takes me a couple of tries, but I eventually get the subway token in the slot and slide through the turnstile, all while trying not to touch anything. I hear an impatient "Come on!" behind me from two different voices, and what feels like a tidal wave of people are surging around me to the turnstiles on my left and right. I'm holding things up here, and it's frankly not making my anxiety any better. So I focus, swallowing hard. I push firmly, and then I'm through, running after Kevin to keep up with him.

I follow him down the stairs and through a maze of people going every which way, sometimes holding on to his shoulder for support. There's a dull roar of conversation, echoing footfalls, and live music. We pass by break-dancers with boomboxes and buskers playing violins and guitars. One guy is sitting against the wall and slamming like crazy on an overturned bucket, and that's frankly a little too loud and jarring for my current temperament.

After crossing over to a couple of different landings, and heading down a couple of staircases, we eventually find our destination. At least, I think we do, because Kevin breaks into a run, heading for the train that has just pulled up. I run too, chasing after him.

He slips in through the open subway doors easily, but I stop at the threshold on the platform. This car looks pretty full; there are too many damn people packed inside.

"Come on, man! Get on!" Kevin calls to me.

The gates begin to close. I'm still frozen at the entrance, people brushing past me. Kevin shoots out an arm to hold the doors open. I suck in a huge breath and step over the gap. I'm in. Kevin's arm folds in to pat me on the shoulder as I enter, then continues the motion and pushes me farther in to the subway car. The doors slam shut quickly behind us.

Well, here we are, no going back now. I look around warily. There are no seats, it's too full, but there's still a decent amount of room to stand. The car lurches into motion, and it catches me completely off guard. I fall forward, past the other riders and right onto my face. Man, I forgot that that happens on these things.

Kevin starts laughing. He has an arm locked around a pole, and he leans over slightly to extend his free hand. I grimace and take it as I get back to my feet, grabbing hold of the lower end of the same pole. This time, I lock my legs in a slight crouch and press my feet into the floor, probably way more than is strictly necessary, but I don't want to fall again. I still lurch like an idiot when we bank our first corner, but I stay upright this time, at least.

Kevin's mouth is admirably free of expression, but I can still see the smile in his eyes. "Ever been on the subway, man?"

"Yes, Iceman, yes, I have been on the subway," I reply, a little too sharply. "It's just... It's been a little while."

He doesn't say anything.

"Shut up."

He purses his lips and opens his eyes wide as if to say, "Who, me?"

I settle in a bit as we continue forward, just a bit, and begin to look around the subway car. People are mostly focused on their feet, or on their newspapers, although the person sitting right next to me has a handheld game system. He's a nebbishy guy with a combover, wearing a brown tweed vest and a bowtie.

I peer at Bowtie's handheld more closely, the logo stamped under the screen reads "Game Friend." He's playing a block puzzle game on it, furiously clearing the lines piling up at the bottom of the screen, and this whole scenario looks a copyright lawsuit just waiting to happen.

The far door of the subway car slides open with a loud bang, which makes me look up. Three punks push in from the next car over. It has an immediate effect on the nearby passengers—I can see ripples in the crowd as these timid commuters move away from them. They want no part of these guys. The punks press forward a little closer, and once they come into clearer view, I can see they're Spankers. Great.

The smallest punk appears to be the leader of the three. He's short, skinny, bald, wild-eyed, and his stats tell me that his name is Maynard. I wonder if he screams the lyrics to ten-minute prog metal epics in his spare time. His backup consists of a tall skinny tweaker named Jackboot and a beefy lunkhead named Paste. Jackboot wears a blue jumpsuit and looks like he eats his enemies for lunch. Paste wears a complementary orange jumpsuit, and he looks like he eats, well, paste.

They're menacing a few of the passengers, but it's perfunctory. They're basically just saying a quick 'boo' and moving on. They're prowling forward, like they're on a mission. It looks like it's a mission to the front of the train.

I brace for a confrontation as they approach me, feel my fists clenching and unclenching. But Maynard and Paste brush right past us, while Jackboot suddenly stops to snatch the Game Friend out of Bowtie's hands. Bowtie looks up, startled, and in a high, upset voice, says, "Hey, that's my Game Friend!"

The Spanker mockingly repeats "Ohhhh that's my Game Friend!" and then immediately holds the device in front of him and starts pressing buttons. "Beep boop beep boop you're my fwiend I wuv you widdle game you're my only friend in the whole wide world!"

I'm about to deck the jackass, but he suddenly tosses it back to Bowtie. "Games are for babies," he says with a scowl.

Bowtie catches his Game Friend and begins caressing the little machine and murmuring to it soothingly. Jackboot sneers and laughs, then hightails it to join his two friends, who are already pushing forward to the front car.

Kevin and I exchange a meaningful look. In our unspoken way, we share what we both know that something's gonna go down. Something gang-related. Which can't be good because gangs are bad. All of this we communicate in a single look. I guess we're developing a rapport.

We give it a long moment, letting some space get between us and the Spankers. Once they exit the car on the other end, we press forward. We make it to the far door and step out onto the open space between the two cars. It's dark and loud; I can feel the wind rushing past as we careen down the subway tracks. Iceman and I peer through the windowpane of the front subway car. It's jam-packed. We can barely see to the other end, but I can see waves of people moving in the middle of the car. Surely the Spankers are pushing past the jammed commuters right there.

Kevin pushes open the door, and we both squeeze ourselves into the car. I should be really freaking out right now about all these bodies pressed together, but magically, I'm not. Instead, I'm entirely focused on knocking these Spankers out.

I can see the far door to the conductor's cab open from over the tops of the commuters' heads. Kevin and I are pushing past people as fast as we can, while still being polite.

"Excuse me, excuse, me, pardon me, I beg your pardon," I repeat like a mantra.

"Well, I never!" an old woman cries, clutching her purse tightly as we squeeze past.

People are pissed off—first the Spankers and now

us trying to push past them. We apologize and try to keep things cool, while still keeping one eye on the door.

I hear a scream at the end of the car. It's audible even over the din of the other passengers and the train car, and I look up in time to see the conductor's door slam shut. A moment later, the P.A. system crackles to life. It's muddy and distorted but it's plenty loud, and we can all hear what it's saying.

"Welcome to the Spanker Express. Our next stop is the end of the line, and it's the bottom of the South East River!" This was followed by a maniacal burst of laughter.

Great. That's got to be Maynard, and now I can take an educated guess as to why they all seem so twitchy and on edge. They're probably hopped up on that Drug X, and now they've got a death wish to run this train car to the end of the line and smash us all to pieces.

The crowd starts panicking. No screams, not yet, but a disturbed murmur spreads quickly through the car. Seated riders start to get up, while those on their feet are already pressing toward the door.

"Iceman..." I begin in a warning tone.

"I know, Blaze," he calls back.

Kevin is clearing the way, pushing commuters aside, laser focused on reaching the front of the subway car. I follow in his wake and prepare myself for the fight. Soon enough, we make a final push through the parting crowd, and then Iceman leaps into a flying punch. I push past the last of the crowd to see Jackboot and Paste standing guard at the conductor's door, then watch Paste stagger from the impact of Iceman's hit.

The blow seems to have a limited effect, because Paste immediately shakes it off and starts grappling with Iceman. I'm about to help my partner, but then I'm grabbed by Jackboot. He promptly gets me in a headlock and starts slapping the back of my head.

"Beep boop! Beep boop! I'm playing a video game!!" he screams as he treats my noggin like a giant controller. I'm about to revoke his game privileges and send him to a time-out, permanently, but first I have to break his steel-like grip on my neck.

I struggle and flail to escape his grip, but he's much fiercer than I expected. It must be the power of all that Drug X coursing through his veins. Now he's punching me in the face while his other arm keeps me in the headlock. All I see is the ground, his fist, the ground, his fist, while around me there's chaos. People are screaming and shouting to move back, to hightail it out of the subway car. The space around me finally opens up and I can move around a bit, but I'm still caught in this damned headlock and losing health fast.

Suddenly, I hear a sickening crunch, and the pressure around my neck immediately slackens. Gasping, I straighten up, about to high-five Kevin. But he's still grappling with Paste. Confused, I whip my head around.

Bowtie stands behind me with his fist raised high in the air. Jackboot wobbles, then falls limp to the ground and blinks out of existence. I hear another sickening punch as Kevin sends his buddy Paste to the glue factory. I rub my sore neck and gasp for air.

Bowtie glares at the blinking body of Jackboot and snarls through gritted teeth, "Don't you dare mess with my friend."

"Thanks... Thanks, man." I'm genuinely touched by the gesture.

But then Bowtie pulls something out of his pocket. He gently strokes and cuddles his handheld game system, kissing it even, saying, "Oh, my sweet Game Friend. There, there, now, the bad man has gone bye-bye. He won't bother you anymore."

Oh. He was not, in fact, referring to me. I'm actually kind of hurt by this. But whatever, we've got bigger problems right now. Namely, we've got to save this train before it slams into a wall.

"Hey!" I search for the stats floating above Bowtie's head, "Uh... Chester! You like playing block games, right, Chester?"

He looks up at me, surprised, "How did you know my name?"

"No time for that. We're all in danger. Your *friend* is in danger. Your *friend* might die!"

Now I've really got his attention.

"Listen to me, Chester. Here's your chance to be a hero. You've got to play the block game, but this time in real life, okay? You've got to move all the pieces, meaning all these people, to fit at the back of the subway. You've got to go through and help everybody get to the last car. And tell everyone to hang on tight. Can you do that, Chester?"

He looks at me, down at his handheld, then back at me. "I've always wanted to be the hero in real life and not just in the game," he tells me in a quiet voice, full of emotion.

"Well, here's your big chance. Now go save the day!"

I tell him.

He suddenly scrambles away, shooing the last few looky-loos out of this car with him, literally bellowing "Yah! Yah!" like a rancher. It's quite a transformation.

I look over to Kevin, who's regarding me with an arched eyebrow. "I didn't realize you had any people skills."

"I don't know, man, I didn't make this game. I'm just playing it."

"Well, how do you want to play this next part?" he asks, shooting a glance toward the closed conductor's door.

I start to answer, but then we're thrown to the side of the train as it rounds a corner at high speed. I worry that we're going to crash right through the window, but thankfully, it holds. We've got to be rounding the curve past 152nd Street that we saw on the subway map. We're almost to the river. We don't have much time.

We push off the wall and straighten, and I tell Kevin, "I think we're gonna smash right into the construction wall at the tunnel. We've got to get inside this door and take Maynard out, fast."

"Yeah, I figured that out," Kevin explains. "But what's our strategy? How are we gonna get in there and take him down?"

I consider for a second. "Do our double jump-kick thing and then punch him a lot in the face?"

Kevin nods. "Very straightforward, but it's worked so far."

"Alright, then," I say, nodding.

We both take a couple of big steps back. Now it's like a routine, we're getting good at this. We spring forward and leap into the air as one, executing a perfect arc and aiming right at the locked door with our outstretched legs.

The moment our legs extend, time slides into slow motion.

I've been experiencing a couple of these big game moments in a state of heightened awareness, and a bit of a feeling like time slows down, but this is the real deal. It's like *The Matrix*.

We're moving now at an interminable pace, still rising off the ground but feeling gravity's pull more acutely. Kevin and I start to look toward each other as we jump, which of course takes us a little while to execute. When we finally lock our gazes, both of us are goggle-eyed with shock at the slowness of time.

Then we hear the unmistakable sound of a lock unlatching, even though it's three octaves lower than we would normally hear it. Somehow, our eyes go even wider with shock, and we start to look back toward the door we're jump-kicking at.

After a beat, we're facing the door again, which is now beginning to open. Maynard stands before us, wearing a stolen conductor's cap. He must be checking to see what all the ruckus outside was. Drug X has got to be speeding up his reflexes because he immediately marks us flying towards him, feet beginning to descend from the air right toward his unprotected jaw. He keeps opening the door while hardly missing a beat, and now he hides behind it as he goes.

He's out of our reach. And we're already committed to this damn jump-kick. We can only watch in slow-motion horror as we agonizingly finish what we started.

We've sailed past the threshold of the door, and my foot is pointing toward the center console in the front of the cramped compartment. I watch in horror as my kick slams into a giant lever on the train controls, which follows my forward momentum and shifts up toward the windshield. Then I spring back from the impact and crash to the ground, knocking my head on the rubber matting.

At the moment of impact, everything snaps back into normal motion again. I get what the developers were going for with the high-impact slo-mo flourish, but it really just served to highlight what an idiot decision I just made, and I truly don't appreciate the feature at the moment.

Speaking of the present moment, it involves me crumpling up on the ground in pain, while Kevin's kick has smashed him into a pole and he's now curled up around it to my right. Meanwhile, our mad hijacker Maynard stands staring at the track ahead, cackling with sickening glee, overjoyed because my errant kick somehow shifted the train into overdrive.

Now we're barreling down the track even faster than before.

I'm still dazed and struggling to find my feet. Finally, Maynard breaks from his joyful reverie when he notices me laying on the ground and bends over to pick me up and hoist me in the air with all of his drug-enhanced strength.

My legs are dangling behind me as he pulls my face up to his, and he's laughing like a madman. I have to say his breath is unsurprisingly poor. It's a very well-observed design detail, however I don't appreciate it one bit.

Maynard screams at me as the steel columns along the track whoosh past the car at maximum speed, "I LOVE THIS!!"

I'm still blinking and trying to find my bearings. That fall really knocked it out of me.

Maynard's eyes go wide as he pulls me close to his face, and I feel like I'm staring into the very maw of madness. You could go crazy staring into these eyes. He holds my jacket tight as he screams, "CHOO CHOOOOOOO..."

My vision is filled with his screaming face and the walls of the track zooming past us at a sickening speed. Everything is loud and insane and on drugs. We're all going to die on the subway car.

All I can think is, this is *exactly* why I don't get close to people. It's just going to lead to more pain. Literally, in this case.

Suddenly, a giant foot replaces his face in front of me, and everything slips into slow motion one more time. I track Maynard's motion as he flies to my left from Iceman's high kick. His eyes glass over, drool flies out of his mouth in an arc, and he sails gracefully backward through the air, tipping upside-down in a beautiful swan dive, smashing through the large front windshield. It shatters beautifully in a million pieces.

I'm too transfixed to move. Instead I can only watch

as Maynard continues to sail out of the window and out into the tunnel in beautiful slow motion.

He flips back upright as he begins his descent back to the earth, now outside the car entirely. There's just enough time for me to see him clearly mouth the word "Why?" as he stares plaintively into my eyes. Then he smacks into the grill of our car as it hurtles along the track at maximum speed.

The sickening impact slams us right back into regular-speed time, and I jolt forward and brace myself on the conductor chair, jumping slightly as the train runs over the body of its most recent driver. RIP Maynard.

I catch my breath for a moment, leaning on the conductor chair as the columns of the track whip past us impossibly fast, then look back at Kevin, who's frozen in a very high kick behind me. He slowly brings his leg down in a controlled martial arts way. He's glowing with energy.

Kevin smiles. "I just gained another level, Blaze! Now we're both Level 3."

How can he be thinking about that at a time like this? We're still barreling down the track. Also, that's a little irritating that he's the same level as me already.

"Congratulations, but we've gotta stop this thing. Right now," I tell him.

But rather than roll into action, I can see that Kevin's got that glazed look in his eyes, like he's checking his stats in his HUD. Meanwhile, we're still barreling ahead, and I'm starting to see orange cones and construction signs fly past us.

"End of the Line," the signs all read. That can't be good.

"Iceman, now is not the time! How are we gonna stop this thing?! KEVIN! Help me!"

I move to the conductor's console, which is smoking and sparking. I don't know how to run this thing, even in the best of circumstances. I try to pull back the lever I smacked into earlier, and I yank hard, but it's completely stuck. No matter how hard I try, I can't budge it. But I keep trying anyway.

"GggggggGGGGHHHAAAAAHHHH," I exclaim as I give it all I've got.

Then I feel a tap on my shoulder.

"Not now!" I scream. "I've almost got it!" I do not almost have it.

It's almost a relief when I feel Kevin's hands prying me from the console's lever. I stagger back against the other wall of the cramped compartment. Kevin is standing perfectly still and facing me, and then he nonchalantly-but-savagely kicks his right leg out to the side, directly into the center console. The whole console explodes, and I instinctively shut my eyes and cover my face.

But I feel that we're actually beginning to slow down. Iceman stopped the acceleration. It's not enough, though. We're still moving too damn fast.

I lower my hands from my face and peer out the broken windshield. Maybe 100 yards ahead, the tracks end abruptly at a solid wall. A huge sign on the wall reads, "Danger! End of the Line." It's coming up on us way too fast. In that moment, I notice that one of my hands had instinctively grabbed onto a pipe for support. I look down now to see what it is.

It's not a pipe. It's a handbrake. How did I not notice this before?

Immediately, I yank on the lever and lean back into it with all my might. Tires begin squealing underneath us, and the ungodly noise grows louder and louder. I'd cover my ears, but I can't let go under any circumstance.

Smoke is now pouring in from under the car through the broken windshield. We're still going too fast. I yank down harder, still harder, screaming all the way. Kevin is sitting in the conductor's chair, head between his knees and bracing for impact.

Only when we're five feet away do I begin to realize that we might survive this. By the time we reach the wall, it's only a gentle little tap that knocks us forward a bit. But we stay on our feet.

Kevin slowly lifts his head to look over at me. We're both breathing hard. I'm still holding the handbrake, but sagging against the side wall now.

"See?" he says breathlessly. "Told you...the subway... was a great way...to travel."

We stay where we are for a long minute, letting our breathing get back to normal.

Then I hear a familiar, but quite unexpected, voice coming from every side.

"Blaze. Iceman."

It's Dekker. I look up at Iceman and he can hear it too. He looks around and sees nothing, it's like the man is right inside our heads. I mouth the word "Dekker," and Kevin nods.

"Nice work on the subway," Dekker booms. "You appear to have overshot your destination by a couple of stops."

I say, "Well, we ran into a bit of trouble."

"Understandable," he says. "The station you've stopped at is closed for construction and does not have a path back up to the street. I ask that you give the dev team a few minutes, and then we'll have you walk back through the subway tracks to the 152nd Street Station. It will be perfectly safe; no trains will be coming your way. The line has been shut down due to the accident."

Iceman and I look at each other, puzzled.

I let Iceman take the lead in replying. "Okay, thanks for letting us know. Dekker, is it?"

A pause. "Yes, hello, Mr. Singleton, I'm sorry we did not get the chance to meet. Things were moving rather quickly."

"Well, now things have finally slowed down a little bit," Kevin replies. "I gotta say, Mr. Dekker, the slow motion is a pretty neat touch."

I say nothing. I'm not a fan of it.

"Sorry, don't have the time right now to chat any further," Dekker says, sounding distracted. "You'll hear from me in just a few minutes when it's safe to head out. In the meantime, please grab a seat and wait for the all-clear. Dekker out."

Iceman looks at me, then says very quietly, "I don't

think this was supposed to happen."

I nod. They did not plan for this. What's going on here?

Chapter 19

Lair

I take the last flight of stairs three at a time, bounding back up to the street at last.

Kevin, aka Iceman, is right on my tail as we both emerge from the bowels of the earth, aka the subway station at Fuller and 152nd.

I stop right up at the top, forcing other commuters to walk around me, but I can't wait another moment to stop and smell that fresh city air. It's a mixture of garbage and some kind of meat cooking nearby, but it's awesome. We were only underground for thirty minutes, tops, but most of that time, I wasn't sure if we'd ever make it back up.

Kevin's already past me and down the street a bit, he's raring to go. He turns back and motions impatiently. "Come on, man. It's this way!"

Instead, I shoot a glance over next to me and identify the source of the cooking smell. It's a hot dog cart.

Kevin stops. "We've got exactly forty-seven minutes to get inside and rescue Jessica!"

"Hey," I begin, turning around to face him. "I know we're a little pressed for time, but... Could I get a soft pretzel real quick?"

Kevin's arms, which are both reaching out to indicate our destination down the street, now drop to his sides as he processes my request. He spots the vendor cart next to me and checks his pager again for the time. "Well... I suppose we could take a minute. Been too long since I had one of those."

He jogs back over to me, and we order our pretzels from the cart.

"Oh, you're getting a side of cheese, too?" he asks as the vendor starts punching the keys of his register. "I thought we were gonna, like, walk and eat."

I shrug, then nod over to a small park across the street, not unlike the one in our neighborhood.

He sighs and then says to the vendor, "Okay, I'll have the cheese, too. And this guy's paying." He jerks a thumb at me.

I smile and pay for both pretzel and cheese combos, plus two large cups of Ebola Cola. Kevin's pretzel is otherwise plain, while mine has a truly life-ending amount of salt dumped on top. We cross the street, me trailing little white crumbs like I'm lost in the woods, and sit down at an open park bench.

We eat in silence for a few moments, taking in the mass of people and traffic passing by. Kevin seems to be getting his bearings quickly; he's much better at this city stuff than I am.

Kevin points to an old building a couple of blocks down.

"Do you see that? Next to that old Irish pub? Two red double-doors. That's gotta be the spot."

"Yeah, I see it," I tell him. I don't see it.

More silent munching. Finally, there's quiet and space enough for me to say what's on my mind.

"That was weird back there in the subway," I tell Kevin. "It's like...when we went into slow motion, it broke the game. I mean, you go into slow motion and then the rest of the game world does...what? Does it slow down, too? Or are you in a little slow-motion bubble while the rest of the world moves in regular speed?"

Kevin laughs. "I have no idea. We're basically glorified bug testers in here. Think about how many testers there are for a regular video game, playing it all day just to figure out what's wrong. Now imagine you've created an entire living, breathing city, and nobody's ever done this before, and we're the first people in and we're just screwing around and improvising, and well, weird stuff happens."

"Yeah, I guess so. I bet they cut the slow motion with the next game patch," I say, and take another bite of my pretzel and sip of Ebola Cola. God, this is good. I got an especially salty piece. My favorite.

"Also, uh..." I begin, after I swallow the soda. "I noticed something else down there. When we were walking back here through the tunnels after we derailed, I took a quick glance down a side path, and it was, like, empty. I mean, it was supposed to be dark in there, but this was like, blackness. Emptiness. I looked away and turned back to it after a second, and that time, it was all filled in, but like...not right. It was cookie cutter assets, I guess. Like suddenly Random Tunnel Pattern #1 was snuck in there when I was turned away for a second. I didn't say anything at the time because I wasn't sure if I was imagining it."

Kevin considers this for a moment as he sips from his straw. "Sounds like we were supposed to follow a more-or-less guided path to the end of this first stage, but we kind of skipped the groove, which knocked things out of whack in the programming. We weren't meant to walk through that subway tunnel. So because we were improvising, the developers were improvising, too."

I'm lost in thought for a long moment, ignoring my pretzel. Finally, I reply, "That's kinda cool and kinda horrifying."

Kevin thinks about it too and then nods. "Yeah, you're kinda right." He takes another look around at this new neighborhood, taking in the people, the buildings. He starts to say something but is drowned out by the sounds of motorcycles. A whole gang of them—guys in black leather with black helmets, some with ladies holding on to them—rumble down the block.

"Man, this is some *Streets of Fire* business going on in this town," he mumbles to himself.

"1984. Directed by Walter Hill," I chime in.

He turns quickly back to me with a smile. "Hell, yes! I loved that movie growing up! Used to watch it all the time."

"I never saw it," I admit.

"You never saw it? That's crazy! Well, why do you know so much about it?" he asks.

"The Roger Ebert movie review bible," I explain. "We had it growing up. It was basically an encyclopedia of all the movies of the eighties with his reviews. We would read it all the time, over and over again. I got pretty conversant with it, but my older brother Steve practically memorized it. I basically experience life through the lens of the Roger Ebert review book to this day. Even though I haven't seen most of the actual movies. I've caught up a lot in my twenties and early thirties, but I still have some big gaps."

"That makes sense," Kevin agrees. "You know, I never saw *Citizen Kane*."

"Oh, it's great!" I say.

"Well, man, *Streets of Fire* is like the *Citizen Kane* of beat 'em ups. Did you know that?"

I did not know that. "What do you mean?"

Kevin takes a quick drink of his soda and begins explaining. He's excited to tell me, and I'm excited to hear. "So, *Streets of Fire* was like this street-fighting movie of the mid-eighties, and it was supposed to be this big deal, and was supposed to be a trilogy and all that. It came out and it had a hit song, but the actual movie was a flop."

"But," he continues, "it did live on in a very unusual way. It directly influenced the beat 'em up game genre. Remember in *Final Fight*, one of the player characters is named Cody?"

I try to remember the game. It's the blond guy, I

think. "Yeah, I think so."

"Well, he's named after the main guy Tom Cody, played by Michael Paré in the *Streets of Fire* movie. In fact, the whole plot of the game is basically the plot of the movie. The dude's girlfriend gets captured, and he's got to rescue her from the gang."

"Huh." My mind immediately goes to Jessica and the Spankers, and how I thought that's what was happening. But Jessica's not my girlfriend, and also, she *wanted* to get kidnapped so she could take their whole operation down.

I thought that scenario was only in the *Double Dragon* game, but now Kevin's reminding me it's in *Final Fight*, too. And it turns out that both these games ripped it off from this movie. Oh, and then there's the *Streets of Rage* series on the Sega Genesis. That's got to be connected, too.

"Yeah," Kevin continues. "So this movie basically babysat me when I was a little kid, and then later on, I started playing these games and seeing the connections, and it got me all fired up. I was like, I want to be a street-fighting master. I want to learn martial arts!"

"Well, did you?" I ask. "You've really taken to it here, you jumped up two levels right away. You're a natural."

Kevin looks down at his soda cup, not meeting my eyes, suddenly sad. "Nahh, I started to take lessons, but... I don't know, I guess I got scared. Found some other hobbies." He brightens again. "I'm here kicking ass now, though." He considers for a moment, sucking down the last drop of soda. "How about you? Did you and your brother start writing film reviews, like Siskel and Ebert?"

I laugh. "No. Actually... My brother didn't make it. He...passed a few years ago. When this all started."

I don't have to say why. It's assumed.

"I'm sorry, man," Kevin says gently.

"We did a lot together, and I've really missed him. I guess, uh, I guess I haven't watched any movies since then," I say, wiping my eyes with my napkin. "But, uh... I gotta say, Iceman. It's good to have someone to hang out with again. Been a long time."

He smiles and clasps my shoulder, "Well, when we make it out of here, if you want to, we'll watch *Streets of Fire* and you can see what I'm talking about first-hand."

"Sounds like a plan," I say, smiling.

He pats my shoulder, then gives me a quick bro hug. The human contact feels good. I went from avoiding people straight to punching them, and this simple gesture of friendship really helps. I pat his shoulders a couple of times, sniffle a bit, and then let go and stand up.

"Thanks," I say quietly, wiping off the pretzel salt from my pants, which makes a sound like a small rainstorm on the sidewalk.

Kevin effortlessly wads up the pretzel wrapper, napkin, and paper cheese cup, then tosses it into the nearby trash can. "Shall we?"

"Hell, yes," I say, and do the same, but my wrapper does not make it in. Instead, it bounces off the side of the trash bin and onto the sidewalk. I lurch forward, pick it up, and make a successful rebound from about two inches away from the lid. "Swish," I mumble.

✪✪✪

"Are you seeing what I'm seeing?" Kevin asks. He and I are both wearing dark sunglasses now, standing in the shadows across the street from the main building. We're trying to blend in, to look incognito while we scope out the drug lair.

Stage 1

Boss Lair

A prompt has appeared in front of me with this text. There's also a button underneath that says *Info*.

"You know it, partner. Let's see some more info, I guess."

The button depresses, and the text box expands.

Quest: Infiltrate the drug lair and take down the Boss of the Spankers Gang.

Critical Warning: Three party members are very strongly recommended.

Kevin lets out a low whistle. "Wow, so Jessica must have seen this info, too. And she decided to go in solo anyway."

I nod slowly. "Yeah, I get it. Until a couple of days ago, I would have, too."

Kevin looks at me expectantly. "There's still only two of us, though, you know."

I return his gaze. "Then we'll just have to get Jessica to join us inside, won't we."

He scoffs. "Yeah, sounds like she's already a real big fan of yours. I'm sure that'll go over great."

"She'll join us. It's the only way forward," I say quietly. Then, to Kevin, "You ready?"

"You know I am."

I purse my lips and nod grimly, then take a deep breath and focus on the prompt.

We accept the quest.

Slowly, two objects appear in our field of vision. Well, they're not exactly objects, more like beams of light, faintly overlaid on the street in front of us. After a moment, I realize they're two illuminated paths, very light and translucent. One beam leads in a trail to the front door, while the other leads around the side of the building to the rear.

"Huh, that's weird," I say.

"Ohhhh, I get it," Kevin says, nodding with understanding.

"What?"

"The game is helping us. We have a choice. We either smash or bluff our way through the front door or try to sneak in around the back."

I scoff. "No choice at all. Let's head for the front door, talk our way in, fight if we have to." I crack my neck to either side and jump up and down, psyching myself up.

Kevin puts an arm on my shoulder. "Hey, man. That path might work for Jessica, with her feminine wiles, but I don't think that's gonna work for us. Look at us, we look like a couple of jerks."

I look down at my incredibly stylin' denim outfit and fanny pack. "I think we look...pretty good. We're just two regular guys, trying to make a living in the big city. Why wouldn't we be hired immediately off the street to sit in a drug lab and count out coca leaves or whatever."

Kevin looks at me like I'm an idiot. I try to look like I'm not.

I exhale and try a different approach. "Iceman, look, there's no way I'm gonna go in through the back! And it's for one simple reason. Stealth missions in games absolutely suck! You've gotta wait for dudes to do patrols, and they walk really slow, and you've gotta hide, and it's all just stupid. No way! They gave us a choice, and I'm gonna pick the non-stupid choice."

Kevin points at me and yells, "We go in through the front door, we're gonna get our asses kicked!"

I point at him and yell, "We go in there, we're gonna kick so much ass and it's gonna be great!"

An old hippie-type walks past us on the sidewalk and exclaims as he passes, "Chill out, man!"

It stops us cold. Wow, we're really fighting hard about this. This isn't about making a dumb game choice. This is about our partnership. And right now, it's fraying.

Kevin smiles. "Yeah, chill out, man."

I mumble, "*You* chill out." But I'm smiling now, too.

"I guess we were making a scene. I'm glad that hippie was walking by."

I nod in agreement. "Thank you, good citizens of New Arcadia. Man, I hope we didn't just blow our cover."

Kevin pops the collar of his leather jacket and ducks his head a little lower. "I'm gonna go around back and check it out."

I snap, "You're crazy."

"Watch me," he says, and he smoothly slips into the street through the traffic and makes it to the other side. Walking nonchalantly, he suddenly slips into the alley when he sees the coast is clear.

I don't move. I'm frozen there. What do I do? I wait, and then wait a little more. I don't need him; I can do this myself. No sneaking, just punching. I mean, it always works in the arcade.

"Forget this," I mumble. "It's time for El Solo Lobo."

I cross the street and approach the front door. It's quiet, nobody's around. I try to reach for the door, but I can't get my hand to move just yet. I start to psyche myself up. I can do this.

Eye of the Tiger. The Burning Heart.

Hm... What other hit singles are there from the band Survivor? Uhh... *High on You. The Search is Over.* Eh, those are more like ballads, much less relevant to my present state.

Back to *Eye of the Tiger.* But now I'm just humming Weird Al's parody of it, *The Rye or the Kaiser* (Theme to *Rocky XIII*). Ha, thirteen Rocky movies, that was pretty funny, back in the day. Although, I guess they've actually made it up to eight Rocky movies, if you count the two Creed films...

Jeez, I'm stalling. What am I so afraid of? Forget it, I'm going in. I raise my hand to knock on the door.

And then I feel a sudden buzz in my body.

What is this? Am I going crazy? Having a seizure?

There it is again. Wait, it's really just around my groin. Have I been shot? It buzzes again, and then I place it.

It's my pager. It's Kevin.

"Found a way in," the primitive LED text reads in my HUD.

I let out a long sigh. No El Solo Lobo. No, sir, it's time for some Fire and Ice.

I trot back down the stoop, look both ways to make sure nobody's watching, and then duck around the back alley to meet up with Kevin.

Chapter 20

This Is a Sneaking Mission

"You know what?" I whisper. "This isn't so bad."

"Oh yeah?" Kevin asks, also in a hushed whisper.

"Yeah, it's much worse."

I'm wearing a large cardboard box. The top is open, and the edge is perched on my forehead like a giant hat. Kevin is wearing his own box the same way.

We're deep inside the Spankers' lair, hovering just outside an open door that leads into a long hallway. Kevin squats to a crawling position, letting the box cover him completely.

"This is the stupidest thing I've ever done," I sigh, my own box covering me as I get down.

"You look great," Kevin encourages me.

"How can you even see me?" I ask. I can barely see what's in front of me, squinting through a tiny open slit in the box where your hand would normally carry it.

"I just know you look great. This is really going to work," he says.

"What?" I ask. Our voices are both muffled now because of the boxes.

"This is really gonna work!" he repeats, daring to speak a little louder, his enthusiasm sounding a little more forced.

How did we get to this sad place, down here on the floor, dressed in our finest sneaking mission apparel?

Well, literally speaking, we came in through the fire escape.

First, Kevin found a path around the back of the Spankers' drug lab. The rear door was bolted tight, but with a little teamwork, I boosted him up to reach a dangling fire escape ladder, and then he pulled me up to join him. From there, we clambered up to the rooftop, where we found a window that was slightly ajar. And now Iceman and yours truly have spent the last twenty minutes slowly creeping around the top floor of this building like a couple of jerks.

We're trying to find a path down to the ground level, but we've got quite a gauntlet to get through first. The hallway in front of us is long and narrow. There are several doors on either side, most of them closed, but a couple are ajar. At the far end of the hallway, another open door reveals a glimpse of a massive room beyond. We can see the ceiling above from our angle, but no bottom, only an open-air lift and a catwalk stretching beyond.

That has to be our destination: the drug lab. But the

path to get there is full of danger. We may be hiding in boxes like in the *Metal Gear* games, but what this hallway really reminds me of is *Elevator Action*. It's an old arcade game where you rappel into a tall building and try to make your way down to the ground floor, but doors could open and bad guys could spill out at any moment. I liked that game a lot. Now I'm rethinking my opinion.

One false move from us could bring out an army of Spankers from any one of these rooms, so our brilliant strategy is to scooch along the hallway floor in these ridiculous boxes all the way to the other side, hoping that we'll…blend in somehow?

I start shuffling forward underneath the box, crawling on my hands and knees, inch by inch. It's very uncomfortable, and I'm very impatient, so I start pushing the pace, breaking out ahead of Kevin, making a little more noise as the box scrapes along the floor.

I hear Kevin's muffled warning behind me, "Slow and steady, Blaze."

What a sight we must have been to anybody who could see us. Would these ridiculous disguises fool anybody? Why are we not punching our way through this? It's stupid to be using our brains!

We've been shuffling forward in this hallway now for maybe two hours. Possibly closer to twenty seconds.

Finally, I inch past the first door on our left. I can barely see where I'm going, so I have to rely more on my ears. I'm hyper-alert, listening intently for the slightest hint of activity. I'm not sure if I can hear murmuring from behind some of the doors, or if it's just my heart racing in my chest. And the sounds of whirring machinery coming from the far door to the lab are getting a little louder and more distinct.

"Ow!" Suddenly, I bump my head and can't move forward anymore. And then Kevin stops when he bumps into the back of my box.

"You okay?" Kevin whispers.

"Yeah, I think I just walked into the door," I reply quietly, backing up an inch and only seeing peeling beige paint. Yeah, it's a door.

Then, I hear a muffled voice behind said door. "What was that?"

Oh, great. We don't have much time. I skitter on my hands and knees over to the right of the door, and Kevin does the same on the left. My heart is pounding in my chest, and yet I still have to stay stock-still under this stupid box.

I hear a sound inside the room like a chair pulling back. Someone's getting up. Now steps. Getting closer. The door opens, and I can see a pair of blue jeans standing right in front of me through the slit in the box. I feel completely exposed, like he can see right through this lame disguise. I steel myself for a fight, albeit one starting from an extremely disadvantageous position on the floor.

Instead, the figure abruptly turns away from me and calls back into the room, "Shipment's here!"

Another voice, from inside, replies, "They processed it early!"

The first Spanker absently kicks the cardboard in front of my face, flooding me with adrenaline. But it's a gentle kick, like he's idly checking the contents. Again, I'm convinced the game is up, and again, we escape detection.

"And they didn't stack the boxes!" the Spanker calls back. "Just left em here. Only two of them, though. Gimme a hand!"

"One second," the other voice sighs.

Blue Jeans Man leans down right in front of my face, sizing up the box. I can see the bottom of his face and the top of his chest as the door automatically swings shut behind him. He's wearing a puffy parka that reads "New Arcadia Devils," which has to be a sports team of some kind.

Then, he twists his body to look at the other box, where Kevin is. His legs are still in front of me, squatting down. Now's my chance. I gingerly push up a bit from my crouch, enough to create a small opening near the floor. I reach underneath the box and push my arms through gently, then quickly grab his ankles, yanking them as hard as I can. He spills right onto his ass. Perfect.

He makes a surprised "Ow" sound, but it's faint. He's landed so that his head is right next to Kevin's box, and the Iceman leaps into action. His box raises up like a ghost and flops down to smother the Spanker's head, obscuring it from what's about to happen next. Namely, Kevin smacking him in the head and knocking him out. One down, one to go.

There's no time to plan our next move, because I can hear more footsteps from inside the room, coming closer. Spanker #2 cracks the door open a moment later.

"Germ?" he calls out. "Where did you go, Germ?"

The Spanker opens the door all the way, staring down at the two boxes in front of him. But we're not in them this time.

The moment he steps out into the hallway, I shoot forward from behind the door, standing where he can't see me, and take him out quickly with a blow to the back of the head.

"Guh," he exhales as he crashes to the ground, flattening my now-empty box in front of him.

"Shoot," I whisper. I was hoping he wouldn't fall like that, but of course he did. I look at his stats. His name is Tito, and he is officially unconscious. "Dammit, Tito."

Kevin leaps into action, holding the door open with his foot and pulling Tito's prone body into the room, the flattened cardboard box dragging underneath.

Once Kevin clears the hallway, I step forward to grab the other box, pulling it up to expose the first Spanker laying underneath. I toss the box inside the room, then drag him in, too. I catch a glimpse of another door down the hallway opening, right as the door to our room is swinging shut, and I hurry to shove the body in and close the door behind me.

I immediately put my finger to my lips, signaling to Kevin that we may have been spotted. It's deathly quiet for a long moment, and then:

"Tito!" a muffled voice bellows from the hallway.

Kevin and I look at each other, panic making our eyes wide.

"Jermaine!" the gravelly voice repeats. "Are you guys okay in there?"

I check the other Spanker's stats. Oh. Germ was short for Jermaine, and he's officially out cold, too. I pause for a moment, and then yell back in a very deep voice, "Yeah!"

I nod quickly to Kevin, who also mimics a deep voice to agree. "Yeah!" he also chimes in.

There's another very pregnant pause. Finally, the voice yells, "Okay!"

And then it's quiet. Kevin and I let out a long collective exhale, even as we start looking around to see what fresh hell we've stumbled into.

It appears to be a supply room for the lab. On one wall is a rack of hazmat-style suits, surely for the gang members working in the drug lab downstairs. Which gives me a possibly-brilliant idea. I grab the intact cardboard box and slip it back on top of Tito.

"Iceman," I call to Kevin, who's busy rummaging through a desk in the corner. "Help me build this other box back up, we're gonna cover Jermaine up too, leave them here to sleep it off. We've got a new plan."

✪✪✪

Four minutes to go. We're walking back down the hallway now, this time wearing the latest in drug lab fashion: i.e. full hazmat suits covering our heads to our toes.

We're getting closer to the end of the long hallway. I can see more of the catwalks behind the door, hear the whirring machinery in the lab getting louder as we approach.

But then the final door to our right opens wide, and my heart immediately sinks into my stomach. Three massive Spanker thugs pile out right in front of us.

They're the biggest enemies we've seen so far. They're all the same size and shape, tall, wide, and muscular; one is white and the other two are black. They look completely the same, except the white guy has a tall blond mane, like Guile from the *Street Fighter* games, and the black guys have afros. The blond guy's name is Ashley, and the black dudes are both named Mr. Pickles.

God, I hope I survive this. Just so I can have some more time to think about how stupid these names are.

"What are you doing here?" Ashley asks us in a big, booming voice.

His eyes narrow as he stares down at us. They're all Level 3 like us, but they look very, very tough. I think it's pretty unlikely we could take these guys on and win. Not to mention there are probably a dozen other dudes just like them behind all these other doors in the hallway. And the Spankers in the drug lab. We'd probably be dead before any of them could make it up the stairs to us.

I start stammering, unable to form the words. "Uh, we...uh..."

Iceman slides in for the save, cool as ice. "What's up, Ashley." He nods to the other two. "Mr. Pickleses. So, we've just brought up a sample of primo stuff for testing, and now we're heading back down to pack up the rest."

Ashley's eyes peer suspiciously from me back to Kevin. I don't think they can really read our faces behind the reflections of the face shields. I'm pretty sure they can't see the flop sweat pouring down my face. I hope.

Kevin continues, smooth as butter, "Yeah, we're right

on schedule. Shipment's almost ready. In fact, they're waiting for you guys downstairs to help with the pallets."

Ashley looks over to me, staring me down, eyes boring right through me. What do I say? Come on, John!

"Yeah, the drugs go on pallets," I rasp in my best Clint Eastwood impression, which is not great, either in form or content.

Ashley's eyes narrow to the tiniest slits staring at me, then he suddenly shifts his gaze over to Iceman and growls, "Alright, boys, you heard the man. We're wanted downstairs. Let's hop to it."

And without a further word, they turn around as one and walk through the door into the main drug lab.

I look at Kevin, and we exchange bug-eyed looks that say, "Can you believe we got away with that?" and "No way, bro, that was crazy!" but without words.

We hang back for a moment, but only a moment, because a look at my pager shows we've only got two minutes left.

We jog the last few steps to the end of the hall and poke our heads through the open door. I can't see much from here, but it sure looks like a giant drug lab, alright. We're on the top level of a giant room, three stories tall, and a maze of catwalks is laid out before us. I can spot a glimpse of the floor far below; there are a couple of tables visible, all manned by workers in protective gear, big trays of familiar green powder in front of them.

Drug X. Bingo.

Just inside the room next to our door is an open-air elevator lift, one of those industrial deals with a railing around the four sides, so you can bring big shipments up and down. Ashley and the Pickleses are already riding it down to the lab floor, I can see their heads disappearing as they sink below the catwalk in front of us. When they disappear completely, we straighten up from our position, then take our first steps into the lab.

It's time to take a bite out of crime. Like a giant dog in a trench coat.

Chapter 21

Neutralize

Jessica

I don't have a lot of time. Two more minutes until the deadline.

Come on, Jessica, keep your head in the game. Focus.

The Spanker guard approaches my station. He's moving awkwardly because of his bulky hazmat suit, and also the paddle he's holding under his armpit. He's using both of his hands to set down an open tray of Drug X.

It's all I can do to stop myself from reaching up and smacking him in the face. But I can't blow my cover. Not yet.

It's time for me to process this one last batch of poison.

I've been in here for two straight days and nights, working almost 18 hours a day with the other women. I'm dressed head to toe in protective gear: a plastic smock with attached hoodie, surgical mask, gloves, and plastic booties. The only parts of my body that are visible here in the lab are my eyes and the bridge of my nose.

I was hired with a group of other young women, all of them immigrants from Asia and Eastern Europe. I disguised myself in rags, pretended I didn't speak much English. They liked that. They put me to work right away, manufacturing this week's precious shipment of Drug X for the Spankers, making enough poison for them to sell it all over their turf in Satan's Pantry.

But they don't know why I'm really here.

I'm here to sabotage this whole batch, and then take all of these monsters down. And I must succeed. Lives are at stake.

Especially my sister's life, in the real world. If I can beat this damn game, there's a chance for her to jump the line, be the first for an experimental treatment. She's given me so much in my life, I have to give her a fighting chance.

This time, I have to be strong for us both.

The Spanker sets the tray down and steps away. I make a move to adjust my protective smock and brush against my bra, checking for the telltale bump. I feel the outline of a small tube under the layers of nylon and fabric. It's still right there. Good.

So far, my plan seems to be going off without a hitch. I don't think anyone suspects me. I'm a good, quiet, diligent worker. They check our pockets when we go back to our living quarters, looking to make sure we don't smuggle any of the stuff out for our own personal use.

But they don't search everywhere, and they don't know about the neutralizing agent I'm carrying. The antidote. One dose of this is enough to destroy an entire week's supply of Drug X. Fancy that.

My first ill-fated attempt to infiltrate the Spanker gang was bold, crazy even. With a little perspective, I'm now not so sure it would have worked. For my first week in this new game world, I quickly learned the lay of the land, and then made a decisive move to spend all my time and resources building up an image of myself.

I wasn't just Jessica, fresh-faced young street fighter, like the game wanted me to be. I was Jessica, cosmopolitan international supplier of the hottest new street narcotic, Drug X. I made myself appear indispensable, the perfect bait.

I lift the tray of raw white powder off the table and shake it gently to even it out. Then I sprinkle in the green flakes, like a chef seasons an entree. The special stuff. The secret ingredient that gives Drug X its hallucinogenic, often-deadly kick.

And of course, the Spankers tried to take the bait by capturing me, because they thought they needed my expertise. As far as they could tell, I was direct off the plane from Hong Kong, and I was the person that could help them make Drug X even more potent, more addictive.

I heard whispers about a mysterious Dr. X at the top of the whole drug trade, somewhere downtown, but the game wouldn't let me go there. I kept bumping against invisible walls. I guess I have to get in on the ground floor, start at the neighborhood level. Fine by me, I'm flexible.

Take a sample, check the levels, not bad. I almost

got it on the first try. It needs 25 more ppm. One more tiny tap of these sickly green flakes into the tray.

So I started going to the bars and nightclubs, kept my ears open. Made discreet inquiries. Seeded a reputation through influence and suggestion. All the while, I was training my body and mind, and learning what I could about our neighborhood, and about Drug X. It's amazing what I was able to find out just from the library. The local branch is boarded up, but I kept searching and found a branch of the New Arcadia College Library eight blocks uptown from my place.

Pull my face shield up to adjust my mask. Make sure it's airtight for the next step.

The day of the attack at the Ten E. Ments, I let slip to a Spanker contact that I would be heading out to meet my supplier from Hong Kong. So, I dolled up as best I could. I must have looked totally out of place. In a pencil skirt, heels, and full makeup, I was the perfect picture of luxury and elegance, but I was stepping out of a tenement apartment. It was all I could afford, but I tried to play it like that was how I stayed under the radar, and it seemed to work. I was the perfect bait. I knew the Spankers would be waiting for me. And then that idiot Blaze jumped in and undid all of my meticulous planning.

Set the face shield back down. Stir the materials together. A fine powder begins to plume, but I'm protected from its effects. Drug X can't get me, but if anybody else walked by right now unmasked, they'd probably turn into a gibbering psychopath.

I can't believe this has taken over the streets of New Arcadia so completely, so quickly. One dose of this could easily end your life, or make you wish it did. It's synthetic poison. I know this world is all just technically ones and zeros in my mind, a shared digital dream, but it still feels very real.

The batch is mixed. Tap the spoon gently against the edge of the tray to free the stuck powder.

I'm feeling real fear, real danger here. But I'm also feeling anger, absolute fury at these Spankers for destroying my city with their garbage. That fury has kept me awake nights, fueled my efforts to craft this Drug X antidote. It's taken almost everything I have. Thankfully, the adrenaline is running through me now, otherwise I'd be falling asleep right here at the table.

Measure again, check the levels. It's perfect. The last batch. Moments to go before the bell rings and the packaging operation begins at the main tank. These guys may be low-level punks, but they keep a tight schedule. Even from afar, the Many Boss keeps them in line, ruling with an iron fist.

Ugh, the last time I actually saw the Many Boss was when that idiot called Blaze tried to 'rescue' me in my driveway. He screwed up my entire plan, but maybe forcing me to take this other path was the right way to go after all. It would have been hard to control what they would have done to me after they had captured me. I was betting on talking my way out of it, negotiating a position here on the drug lab floor as a supervisor. But maybe they would have seen through my cover story and kept me off the lab floor. Maybe they would have kept me locked up here with no way to escape. Maybe they would have done much worse.

Secure this batch for transport, attach the protective lid. Look around, make sure no one's watching. Check the clock. 30 seconds left. Look over to the mixing tank. The packaging operation is ready to go on the other side of the tank; the distribution vans are parked and idling behind the large metal roll-up garage doors along the far wall. They're all waiting for us.

I had driven to my other safehouse after the screwup at the apartments and made a new plan. I removed the makeup, ditched the heels. Became one of the tired, poor, huddled masses. Went down to the train station, blended right in with a group of folks fresh off the boat, and got spotted by a Spanker recruiter.

Which brings me to the current situation.

I make sure nobody's watching, then lean far over to grab the tray. I squeeze my chest with my arms in a well-practiced motion. The neutralizing agent pops free and slips out of the top of my smock. I catch it with my left hand, hide it underneath the edge of the tray, and turn to cross the room to the main Drug X tank.

This mask and hoodie are always constricting, but now they feel like a slowly-tightening vise with every step I take. Only twenty paces away now, but each one feels like an eternity. I feel the weight of everyone's eyes on me. Surely that's just my imagination. Everybody's focused on finishing the job.

Fifteen seconds to go. I approach the main tank, now full of all the Drug X we've been manufacturing at our workstations. There has to be fifty pounds of the stuff in here, worth over one million dollars on the street. And that's in 199X money! If I can wipe this all out, it's gonna set these criminals back a long way.

The antidote vial is still sitting hidden between the

palm of my hand and the tray. With a single, practiced motion, I can pop off the top with my thumb and pour it all right into the main mixing vat. And if all goes well, the chemicals will instantly mix, and these guys will basically be selling powdered soap on the street instead. No one will know the difference until customers start sniffing it.

Fifteen paces to go. Ten. I'm almost there. A warning bell sounds throughout the lab: ten seconds to go.

I raise my tray higher in my hands, the antidote right underneath it. This is it.

Suddenly, something black fills my vision. There's a loud smack as it hits the concrete floor in front of me, just in front of the mixer.

I freeze. I look down to see what it is.

It's a boot. Long, black, high-heeled.

It's *my* boot. The one I left behind at the apartment complex.

"SABOTEUR!" a terrifying voice rings out.

It's coming from very high above. I look toward the ceiling.

I can hardly see up there because my face shield is fogging up. All I can make out is a hazy silhouette of a huge and menacing figure that looks like a demon. I flip open the shield, and now I can see the person staring down from the high catwalk, pointing at me.

It's the Many Boss.

His chest is heaving with rage, and I can see the evil intent in his eyes, and also...understanding. He knows. He must have known all along. I wasn't fooling him.

And now I've walked right into his trap.

"STOP HER!" he screams.

The Spankers quickly run over from their stations around the room, while the other frightened workers duck under their tables. Soon, all twelve guards encircle me in a tight ring. I know this number because I've been watching them, marking them.

I'm surrounded. There's nowhere to run. I try to keep them all in my field of vision as they stalk forward, but they're everywhere, and my mask only lets me see what's right in front of me.

One shot. I throw my tray of drugs into the Spankers as a distraction. I don't wait to see who it hits, no time. I turn towards the mixer, flick my thumb to pop the cork of the antidote...

But it's smacked out of my hand before I can open it. I don't know where because I'm pushed violently away from the mixer, and then I get a kick to the midsection.

I stumble backward, try to get my bearings, but I'm caught in an armlock by an unseen guard behind me. I manage to hurl myself forward, and he bowls right over into a guard closing in on me from the front, and they both go down in a heap.

Where is the antidote?

I turn to the right but the only thing I see is a fist. Thankfully, my face shield absorbs most of the blow. It flipped back down when I pitched over to hurl the Spanker off my back. I steady myself and wind up a punch in reply, but my fist is suddenly grabbed tight as I pull it back.

"Got her!"

Another Spanker spins me around to face him. I take a step back but get a kick to the back of the knees. It buckles me, and I fall back. The Spanker holding me takes advantage of this, spinning me round and pressing me against my workstation, then roughly ripping off my face shield and pulling down my half-mask.

"Wait, it's her!" the Spanker cries up to the catwalks to his boss. "It's Jessica, the dealer! She's in disguise!"

I struggle but I can't escape. He laughs and pins me harder against the table, looming over me. My feet are now completely off the ground.

"Where do you think you're going?" The Spanker leans in closer. "There ain't no getting out of here. Not alive, anyway."

It's too much. I don't want the last thing I see of this world to be a hazmat-suited Level 3 scuzzball named Dillweed. So I squeeze my eyes shut, and the picture that comes to my mind's eye instead is my sister, Tracy.

I'm so sorry, Tracy. I let you down.

"...yyyyaaaAAAAAA..."

Wait a minute. That's some kind of crazed scream. From high above, but it's getting closer. Like it's a scream of rage, but also, kind of crazy and out of control. It's moving fast. It's already almost here.

I peek one eye open to see something I did not expect.

It's Blaze. Not wearing that stupid denim jacket of his, but wearing a hazmat suit like the other Spankers, only his helmet is off. He's jump-kicked off the top-level catwalk and now he's screaming as he falls onto my head.

Hold on. He's not trying to kick me. He's trying to save me. Again.

There's almost no time. I act. With all my strength, I move this Dillweed latched onto me into position. Dillweed's head moves right into the path of Blaze's boot, and I turn my head to the side to avoid the impact.

Blaze's scream fills my brain as he slams to the ground.

Chapter 22

Beat 'Em Up

John

I truly have no idea if I'll survive this fall. But at least I'm going to go out fighting.

Jessica was super-pissed at me the last time I tried to rescue her, but this time, she really needs my help. We all need to help each other if we're going to make it.

But again, first things first. I have to survive jump-kicking a guy from a thirty-foot drop, and also avoid landing on Jessica. Whoa, now he's only like ten feet below me, that was quick.

On the plus side, I've been training for over two weeks, and I'm Level 3, so that's probably really good. On the minus side, I really have no idea what I'm doing.

Am I screaming? It sounds so distant to my ears. Wow, almost on the ground, no slow motion this time.

Here we go.

"YaaaaaAAAA-OW!" I cry, until the breath gets knocked out of me by the impact.

The first thing I realize is I'm laying down on the table. Ah, this feels nice, to take a little rest like this. I've been working so hard lately.

I'm also laying on top of the Spanker. Somehow, I landed with my foot right in his face. And now I'm flat on my back, on top of the rest of his body, my head between his feet. I look beyond his shoes and see the ground next to me. Looks like the table collapsed upon impact.

After a beat, I hear a muffled "Ow!" below me, then I start to feel myself swaying back and forth a bit. It's Jessica, and it sounds like she's on the very bottom of this Spanker sandwich, struggling to get free.

"Jessica!" I gasp, then gulp down another breath. "Are you okay?"

I hear Jessica's voice underneath me, muffled, pissed off beyond belief, but strong. "I'll live. *You* on the other hand..."

Suddenly, the Spanker between us blinks out of existence. With him suddenly gone, I fall another few inches and land directly on top of Jessica.

"OW!" she cries in anger.

I think I maybe accidentally kicked her face a little bit just now.

"Sorry! Sorry," I say.

She grabs my ankles and violently pushes me to the side. Now I'm lying on my back next to Jessica, in pain, breathing hard. I probably kind of deserved that.

    From my vantage point, laying next to the broken table, I'm staring up at the high ceiling and catwalks above. *I just dropped down from way up there, on purpose*, I think. I notice for the first time that there's a staircase right next to the elevator lift. *Oh, I guess I could have just walked down*, I think absently for a moment. Then I notice Kevin high above on the top of the stairs, grappling with two of the big Spankers from earlier, Ashley and one Mr. Pickles, near the catwalk. He seems to be holding his own, for the moment. Good.

    "Jessica! We're here to rescue you!" I tell her once I catch my breath. I can only see her feet when I look to my right.

    "Who's we?" she asks, confused.

    Suddenly, I'm yanked from the floor and roughly pulled to my feet. Now, I'm face to face with another Spanker guard, this one also in a hazmat suit. I barely have time to notice that the headpiece is almost a foot taller than it should be, and in the shape of what surely must be his mohawk, before I pop him right in the face shield a few times. He quickly goes down for the count, defeated, but probably still with great hair.

    I plant my feet and hold my hand out to Jessica on the ground below me. "Come on, we gotta get outta here fast!"

    But she turns away from my hand, instead madly searching the ground around her. "I have to find the neutralizing agent! I have to destroy the Drug X!"

    "DON'T MOVE!" a muffled voice nearby cries. Jessica and I turn toward the sound.

The other Spanker hazmat guards have all teamed up and are now only ten feet away, swarmed around the next table over. They're mean and yellow and they're ready to pounce.

Before I can do anything, Jessica pulls out a tiny pipe with a fuse, lights it using an open flame that fell off the table, then tosses it expertly behind her head. Even laying down and not looking, her aim is perfect. It lands inside the drug tray on the table next to the Spankers and immediately catches fire like creme brûlée.

The Spankers are distracted, impressed by the throw, curious about the flame. They peer down at the quickly crisping Drug X tray, and then it suddenly explodes. I'm knocked back, but stay upright, but those Spanker guards are all down for the count. Just like that.

I reach out again to hoist her up, "Good lord, that was awesome," I exhale, seriously impressed.

Jessica looks at me, hard. "I can take care of myself, Blaze." She starts to stand on her own, and I awkwardly withdraw my hand.

"BADOGOS!" comes a sudden cry from high above.

It's the Many Boss, calling out from on high. It sounds like a cry for assistance, for reinforcements. But what the hell are Badogos?

Suddenly, a piece of the brick wall to our left explodes! It's a little ways away from us, but the impact is big enough that it blows me to the ground. I roll past Jessica, who staggers to one knee but remains upright, and I look up in time to see the brick pieces landing on the ground around us.

A ridiculously-huge dude emerges from this new opening in the wall. He's got to be eight feet tall, with, like, muscles upon muscles. No shirt, no hair on his body, except for a long, thin mustache. An overall appearance I would describe in a word as nightmarish.

And I find myself wondering, is this like a Mentos-type situation, while a single Mentos is called Mentos? Is there only one 'Badogos'? Maybe? Hopefully?

And then another section of wall explodes outward, this time at the far end of the big room, and an identical figure emerges out of the dust and debris. Nope. There are multiple Badogos. Great, how many more are there?

A rain of bricks suddenly erupts right in front of my face. One of the shards clips me, knocking me right back down to take a knee. A third Badogo emerges directly above us, he'd be towering over us even if we weren't knocked down.

He looks down impassively at us, watching us stagger. But I'm playing possum, only pretending I'm getting my bearings. Suddenly I spring up to a standing position with a punch to his gut, as hard as I can given the angle, but it's like hitting a brick wall. He doesn't move, and the only one hurt appears to be me. Ow.

He doesn't move at all, so I rear back and punch him again, as hard as I can this time. It's another body blow because I don't think I can even reach his face. This one hurts me worse. Ow.

He looks down at my fist, I look down at my fist, then I slowly pull it back from his abs like I'm trying to recall an angry email I shouldn't have sent. He looks into my eyes; his expression is terrifyingly blank. Something tells me I'm not done hurting just yet.

SMACK.

I fly across the room. Like, literally across the room. Like I have enough time to mentally hear the chorus to *I'm Like a Bird* by Nelly Furtado. I'm just playing that automatically in my head as I sail through the air in slow motion. I'd really rather not have that song playing in my head, ironically commenting on my current predicament, but here we are.

Mercifully, I land in a somewhat supported way, crashing onto another drug station. The table helps break my fall, but I still lose half of my life bar. And I appear to have been knocked entirely across this giant room, which I can't say I've enjoyed.

From my vantage point on the broken table, I can see Jessica's faraway figure making another run for the giant Drug X mixer. I don't think she has the neutralizing agent, but maybe she can tip the mixer over, scatter the drugs on the floor, do something to throw a wrench in the works. But the Badogo is too fast. He scoops her up easily in a headlock with his long arms. Before I can do anything to help, I get scooped up, too.

Dammit, it's another Badogo. He's lifting me ten feet into the air by my neck. I struggle and pull at the giant meaty hand around my gullet, but it's no use, I'm like a toy doll to him. I'm scrambling to find purchase on his fat hand and lessen some of the pressure on my throat.

I steal a glance across the room to see Jessica struggling in the grip of her Badogo. She's now in the same position as me. Next to them, Badogo #3 is fighting it out with Kevin at the bottom of the stairs. Kevin is in full health and throws a great punch, but the Badogo dodges and deftly grabs Iceman's neck, hoisting him into the air, too.

Now we've all been caught in the vise. This is it. The pressure increases on my neck, and blackness begins to creep in around the edges of my vision. This grimy drug lab and this 'roided-up baldy are going to be the last things I see. The last things any of us see.

Wait. I have a crazy idea, and it just...might...work.

I focus intensely and direct all my mental energy into one final Hail Mary play.

Team-Up Request: Join Blaze and Iceman's gang.

I send my in-game text message prompt to Jessica. But she's struggling hard, eyes closed, so I can't tell if she notices at all. I hope she does. I hope she doesn't reject me again. This is our last chance.

I call out, "J-Jessica!" My air is fading fast.

Her eyes suddenly pop wide open. Now she recognizes the prompt in front of her.

"J-join us!" I croak.

Instead, she keeps struggling against her captor's squeezing hands. Good god, she really, really wants to go this alone. *Please, Jessica, this is the only way.*

"P-please!" I choke out to her as loud as I can, then... "ACK!"

The Badogo squeezes tighter on my neck, cutting off what little breath I had left. I can't say any more.

Every last ounce of my focus is trained on her. My eyes are dimming, and I can see her start to slacken, too.

She has no fight left. Oh no.

But then her eyes pop open again. She's calm. She's made her choice.

Team-Up Request Accepted.

The world explodes.

Our bodies fill with sudden light and energy, and the energy fills the room in a flash. It knocks all the Badogos back. My Badogo releases his death grip on my neck, and I collapse to the ground.

The blackness that's been creeping across my vision is immediately replaced with pure white light. Somehow, though, I can still see everything around me, as darker outlines still frame the room and the people and things inside of it. A new prompt pops up before me.

TEAM UP COMPLETE

Your gang is now a trio.

Quest conditions met.

Bonus: energy, strength, stamina.

The bright white light fades back to normal. My Badogo is now laying on the ground before my feet, stunned. I look up across the room, and it's the same for Jessica and Kevin's Badogos. Both of their stats are now visible to me, even from here. They look enhanced, more bad-ass. It's hard to describe. I must look that way to them too.

"Let's get 'em!" I cry out.

Then I turn my attention to my nemesis, who's now slowly getting up from the ground.

It's hard to believe I had any qualms about punching someone even just a couple of weeks ago, because now it feels like the most natural thing in the world. So satisfying. Where my attack earlier basically just bounced off his abs, now I'm having a real impact. It's not like I'm knocking him clear across the room with one punch, like he did to me, but now the playing field is a little more level, thanks to our team bonuses.

My Badogo manages to get to one knee, making him roughly the same height as me, and he gets in a couple of slugs to my jaw. They sure do smart, but I'm more powerful now, plus I've got the momentum. I grab a giant glass beaker from a nearby table and break it over his head. He staggers but doesn't fall over, so I lift the whole table up.

"Badogo...party of one..."

He looks up at me, his impassive face finally changing its expression. To fear.

"Your table is now ready."

I smash the table down on his fat head.

That did the trick. A few blinks, and he's gone. I toss the table to the side.

With the immediate threat removed and my wits beginning to return, I focus my attention back on my gang. They're taking on their own Badogos, turning the tables and knocking them both out, also literally with tables they've picked up. In a few more moments, we're the only ones left standing down here.

We barely have a moment to catch our collective breath before the Many Boss yells again from his protected perch on high.

"BELINDAS!"

Good lord. We took out the guards, then we took out the giants, now we have to deal with yet another wave of bad guys? Or, I guess, bad gals?

I find out the answer to that soon enough when a far door bursts open and a team of six tall, lean, leather-bound ladies runs in with military precision. They stop in a single line, facing us. They're identical in appearance and their names are all Belinda. Teased hair, heavy makeup, high-waisted leather pants, and matching jewel-studded bikini tops.

They maintain their formation and stare us down menacingly, which gives our trio time to meet up in the middle and form a line of our own opposite them, albeit in a more sloppy, ramshackle formation.

In their hands, the Belindas appear to be carrying... pipe bombs? Retracted sticks? I can't tell.

Jessica breaks the silence, calling out with contempt, "You call that armor, ladies? You're basically wearing leather bikinis! This is so objectifying!"

I support her, "Yeah, put on some clothes! It's embarrassing!" Then, after a moment, "I mean, you all look great, don't get me wrong, but it's very impractical. OW!"

That last bit was Jessica punching me on the shoulder. Pretty hard, too.

Kevin doesn't want to be left out of the pre-battle repartee. "Red Rover, Red Rover, send...Belinda on over!"

Eric Jason Martin

"That's a pretty good line, Iceman!" I yell. He gives me a thumbs-up. Man, he's cool.

The lead Belinda responds by screaming as loud as she can. That's apparently a cue for the other Belindas to attack. As one, they lash out with the sticks in their hands. We flinch, sure that they're going to be projectiles, but the sticks stay in their hands. Instead, six long strings race toward us at once, and then all crack at the ground right in front of our feet.

Oh, great, they're bullwhips. We're supposed to punch out a bullwhip leather lady posse. Was there *ever* a time when this was considered a socially acceptable objective, even on an arcade screen thirty years ago?

They advance as a single unit and lash out with their whips again. Iceman and I get stung pretty bad, but Jessica figures out how to grab one of the whips right in the air. Once we learn that trick, it makes everything go much smoother. We kick their asses in pretty short order, although I still don't feel right smacking a lady, even a digital one.

As the last Belinda falls, the Many Boss roars again.

"LAST STAND!"

But there's only quiet. Then, from the far door where the Belindas emerged, a timid male voice replies, "W-who do you want now, boss?"

We all look up at the Many Boss. He's trembling with rage.

"EVVVVVERYONE!!"

Whoa. He just went full Gary Oldman. As in, *The Professional* aka Leon. 1994, Director Luc Besson. Nice pull, game devs.

More importantly, we see our first crack in the Many Boss's armor. He's down to his last wave of support. We've got a shot at this.

Now the final enemies begin to pour in from the open door. Some of this stage's greatest hits are back, like Crowbar Craigs, a few Peppers, even a couple of the lab-coated drug scientists have gotten brave and grabbed two by fours. All told, nine bad guys face off on the other side of the lab. Three for each of us.

They don't attack, but instead try to intimidate us first, assuming power poses, making their stances wide, rolling their fists in front of their faces slowly as they flex their arms, or deliberately smack their melee weapon into their other hand, letting the sound reverberate through the large, brick room.

"Alright. Are you ready, Iceman?" I call to my left.

"Ready, Blaze," Kevin replies with steely determination.

"And you, Jessica?" I ask to my right.

She says nothing.

"By the way..." I begin, still speaking to Jessica, trying to fill the awkward silence. "Do you want another name for your character, like a street name? I mean, we've got Blaze, and Iceman, maybe you could be, like, a third element?"

Silence from Jessica. Probably the bad kind. I glance over to Iceman. He normally has my back, but he's staying out of this one.

"Maybe...Thundara?" I ask.

"No."

She doesn't even look at me, just keeps her angry, determined stare on our enemies. One of them coughs quietly, but it still echoes in the large space. I don't know if it's possible for a room's energy to be more awkward than at this exact moment.

Time to change the dynamic. A scream bursts from my mouth, *Braveheart* style. This time, Iceman and Jessica back me up, chiming in with battle-yells of their own. The battle is on.

The moment we make contact with our enemies, I slip into a flow state. I'm going through the motions, just like Big Louise taught me. Just like Billy Blanks showed me on those Tae Bo VHS tapes when I was a kid. Just like mashing buttons in *Street Fury* in the Safeway, all those years ago.

I'm fully present in my body but floating above it at the same time. I can see the impact of each punch, each kick I throw out, but I can also see the big picture, how Iceman and Jessica are filling in the gaps, how we complement each other. I imagine a 360-degree tracking shot circling around the three of us as nine enemies take turns jumping into our circle and getting promptly knocked back out.

The next thing you know, there's nobody left. The final Crowbar Craig falls to the ground, his namesake weapon clattering loudly on the concrete floor. We kicked all their asses.

Except for one. And now he's clapping slowly, high above us, mocking us with sarcastic applause. Each sharp slap of his hands ricochets through the large room, sending a sharp jolt to my central nervous system.

The three of us look to each other, fear returning to our eyes. Jessica is the first to respond.

"I've got to destroy those drugs," she tells us, nodding toward the giant mixer.

The mixer is only about twenty feet away, still sitting untouched on the main floor near the staircase. Exposed inside the giant bowl are millions of dollars' worth of newly-made Drug X. Jessica takes a single step toward it, then the Many Boss leaps from the catwalk and lands right in front of us, the floor shaking from the impact. He's halfway between us and our goal.

The Many Boss has landed in a crouching position with one fist pressed against the ground. Are those little cracks in the concrete where his fist impacted? I can't tell if my eyes are playing tricks on me. Is he really that powerful? Big, if true.

Now he smoothly rolls up to his full height. I have to admit, I'm a little jealous, because I basically landed on my ass when I tried that same move, and he looks really cool when he does it.

"My, my, my, you've made quite a mess here," the Many Boss sneers in his terrifying voice. "You think you've made a big dent in our operations, don't you? Defeated your enemies. Saved the neighborhood."

Jessica retorts, "No one's left to save you. Get out of our way or we'll drop you where you stand."

He barks a short laugh. "Even if you could beat me, which, let's face it, is not happening, even then,

344 🖫 Eric Jason Martin

what do you think you would achieve? This is only one neighborhood in a very big city. And Drug X is going to take over *every* neighborhood. It's already happening."

Kevin and I look at each other uncomfortably. His confidence is shaking us.

"Are you going to take out *all* of the gangs? Even if you did, others will rise up to replace them. Have you heard of a term called vertical integration? It's the business buzzword of the nineties! And the people who make this stuff mean business. They're organized at the highest levels. This goes straight up to the top, my little babies. All the way up to the highest penthouse on Broadway."

Jessica says, "Oh, you mean the lair of Dr. X?"

The Many Boss stops in his tracks, then frowns. "How do you know that name?"

Jessica replies, "I've heard whispers on the streets. Thought it was a rumor. Thanks for confirming."

His frown deepens, then he starts slapping his own face, hard. "Bad job, Many Boss! Stupid, stupid, stupid!"

He's really doing some self-harm with each cry of "stupid." It's not as awkward and uncomfortable as when I asked Jessica to change her street name, but it's close. All of us look at the ground. I quietly kick some debris away, then examine the scuffs in my boot.

Finally, he stops, composes himself, and offers us a grotesque smile. "It doesn't matter, you're not going to make it out of this room to do anything about it. You're all going to get a very...bad...spanking."

Jessica is quick with her reply, "There's three of us

and only one of you. This is going to be easy."

"Yeah!" I yell in support. "You're easy like Sunday morning!"

Kevin chimes in, "Yeah! Lionel Richie! Love that guy!"

Our team patter isn't the best, frankly. But we're still kind of feeling out the group dynamic, and frankly, the adrenaline and exhaustion from the previous battle is sort of preventing us from sounding our very best right now.

We turn to each other, and in subtle acknowledgment, our body language communicates an entire silent conversation: yes, that wasn't great taunting. No, it doesn't really matter. So, let's go kick his ass.

We advance as one, striding forward purposefully, in full ass-kicking mode. The Many Boss stands his ground for a moment, then begins to back up slowly. Ha. He's scared. We move forward, closing the gap.

We're right up on him, about to launch into our first attack. His back heels stop against the side of the massive drug mixer. He's trapped between us and the mixer, there's nowhere to go from here.

But then he looks up at us, and he's not scared at all anymore. It was a ruse. He flashes an evil grin, then launches into a sudden spin, bringing his open palm up and skimming it across the top of the mixer as he passes, grabbing a massive fistful of Drug X.

Oh no.

"HA!" he bellows, flicking his arm forward and releasing his fist.

Before we can do anything at all, we're covered in Drug X.

We all stagger back, coughing. The air around us is choked with drug dust. In our shock and surprise, we inadvertently gasp and bring the Drug X deep into our lungs. I sink to my knees, hacking violently; Iceman and Jessica do the same.

The Many Boss's shadowy form looms over us, laughing cruelly. My vision begins to blur. His silhouette appears to fracture and replicate exponentially behind him, and his voice warps and choruses.

"FIRST ONE'S FREE! HAHAHA!"

Chapter 23

The Gauntlet

Kevin

Everything is green.

I'm swimming in an ocean of green. It's like I got slimed. You know, by Slimer, from *Ghostbusters*. That's my favorite movie.

But I don't like this green around me now. It's thick and it's melted and it feels like soup. It's swirling all around me. I don't feel good at all.

And then, slowly, the world comes back. And I'm outside. And I'm walking. And I'm short. And I'm *wearing* shorts. And it's a school I'm walking through.

Whoa. I'm back in summer school. Weird.

"It's a cruel...cruel summer," I'm singing to myself as I walk along. This song is from *The Karate Kid*. That movie that replaced *Streets of Fire* in our VHS player, and I watch it every day now: both *The Karate Kid* and *Ghostbusters*.

It's the summer of 1986. I recognize these old beige trailers. This is Glen Parkman Middle School. Wow, how did I remember that name? This was the middle school across town. I didn't go here, but this was the one that had the summer school program. My mom signed me up, because she got a job, and I couldn't sit at home all day anymore.

I'm walking down the hallway and approaching the quad now, the open space between the main buildings. Actually, I'm not technically walking down the hallway, because it's all outside. It's California, man, they don't have hallways in schools here.

That was one of the weird things about moving here from New York, not having hallways.

I also don't have any of my friends here. And I don't have my dad, either. He didn't come out with Mom and me to California.

The school building and doors to the classrooms are on my left, the empty quad courtyard is to my right, and there's a sheet metal awning protecting from the elements overhead. Nobody's outside with me because everybody's in class.

I should be in class, too. It's first period, I should be in my martial arts class. But I'm not.

Now I really, really wanted to learn karate, and be just like Daniel LaRusso in *The Karate Kid*. I was all excited for it. But on day one, I walk in the door, and everybody already knows what they're doing. Everybody's had karate training, and they're punching and kicking and I didn't know what to do. I got scared. So I left.

The next day, my mom dropped me off, I waved good-bye, and then I just…hung out in the parking lot. Until my second class began.

I mean, it was kind of nice. I just spent an hour walking around, thinking my thoughts, being cool, figuring it was no big deal. But after a couple of days, it turns out the summer school people noticed that I wasn't going to my first class but was showing up to all the other ones, so they called my folks, and then they came to an agreement.

Instead of going to martial arts class, I would become a teacher's assistant. This meant for first period, I could work on my computer programming by myself in the lab, making little video games. But when there was a message to be delivered from one teacher to another, I would be the courier that brought that message between the classrooms. And that's what I was doing now.

I look down at my hand, and I'm holding one of those legal-size brown envelopes that's been tied shut with a little string at the top, so it can be used over and over. Somehow, I know that there's a message inside the envelope, and it's supposed to go to Mrs. Artucci in Room 103A.

I look up ahead, and there's Room 103A, just to my left. I pause, take a breath, and slowly enter the room.

It's dark inside. I can't see because the lights are all off. There's a male voice talking; it's not Mrs. Artucci at all. I stand there at the door, quietly, letting it shut behind me as my eyes adjust from the bright morning sun outside.

All the chairs in the classroom are huddled in the middle. They're all facing a glowing box. That's where the male voice is coming from—they're watching a video. That's cool.

I see Mrs. Artucci's desk on the far side of the room. I walk over to it, going behind the chairs so I don't disturb the other kids. I try to be very good at my job. As I pass, I notice a few of the kids closest to me turn around and watch me walk by. They're big kids, I recognize them from the first day of class. They're the advanced martial arts students. They did a demonstration for us at our first class. It was cool, but scary.

I make it over to Mrs. Artucci at her desk at the back of the classroom.

"Hi, Mrs. Artucci, I have a message from Mr. Stanz."

She's a nice older lady, very sweet. She thanks me and takes the envelope, unwinds the string, and reads the paper inside.

"Thank you, Kevin," she tells me quietly, so as not to disturb the video. "I have to write a reply to Mr. Stanz. Will you wait a few minutes? You're welcome to sit and watch the video while you wait."

"Okay," I say, and then I turn around.

Something's different in here. It's hard to see with all the lights turned off, but I can still tell that something is wrong. There are big grownup bodies sitting in all the little kid chairs, hunched over and almost spilling out of their little seats. I stare at them for a moment, trying to understand what happened.

Each one of the kids watching the video, all thirty of them, are the Many Boss.

"Kevin," a voice calls out behind me. But it's a deep

male voice.

I spin back to the desk, and the Many Boss is there, too. But this one is wearing Mrs. Artucci's clothes, he's wearing her bifocals, and her gray hair is pulled back tight in a bun. He's sitting behind the desk, pen poised above the paper and looking at me expectantly.

"You can go sit with the other children. It's okay."

I nod, because I can't speak, and slowly creep around behind the other Many Bosses. They don't pay attention to me, they're all just watching this video about science experiments. It looks like it's *Mr. Wizard*, the old Nickelodeon show. Wow. He's scolding some poor kid for messing up a baking soda volcano, just really laying into her on the TV. Was he always a jerk and I just didn't notice?

I walk all the way around to the other side of the Many Bosses, halfway between them and the door, wanting desperately to sneak out. I have a terrible feeling about all this. I remember something bad happened here, but I don't remember what. But it's very familiar and it's very scary.

I'm just about to leave the envelope and everything else behind and walk out the door, when a voice whispers, "Hey."

I look over to the sound. It's one the Many Bosses, perched on a little chair on the edge of the group. He and his three Many Boss friends are all waving me over.

"Hey, have a seat with us, watch the show!" one of them whispers once I walk over to them.

"Oh, thanks, I can stand," I reply, also in a whisper.

Another Many Boss says, "I'll get you a chair!" He gets up and grabs a chair from the back of the room. The other three Many Bosses scoot their chairs to make room in the middle.

I hear the chair slide in behind me, the metal legs squeaking as they slide across the tile. They're all very friendly and encouraging, inviting me right into the center of their tight little circle.

"Have a seat, Kevin!"

So I do. As I'm sitting down, I hear the sudden squeak of the chair legs again behind me. And I just keep sitting, falling until my tailbone slams down, hard.

They pulled the chair away from me.

I feel pain like I've never felt before. God, it's agony. It starts at my bottom and goes all the way up to my brain. I shut my eyes tight and collapse to the side. I feel tears streaming down my face and onto the cold tile floor.

Now I feel hot breath in my ear. It's one of the Many Bosses, and he's whispering to me.

"You're a wuss. You're too afraid to learn how to fight. You'll be weak for the rest of your life."

The other Many Bosses are laughing all around him. Where's Mrs. Artucci? Can't she see me?

This really happened to me, in real life. I mean, I don't quite remember all these big drug lord dudes in the original memory, but the basic event is real. Back in '86, I went to the principal's office to report it, and my mom came and picked me up, but I don't think the kids ever got in trouble. What *did* happen was that I put the thought of doing martial arts ever again out of my mind completely.

If I was scared before, I was terrified after this. The only fighting I did was with a game controller after that.

I gave up my dream, and I hadn't thought about it again in thirty years.

The sounds are changing now. I don't hear Mr. Wizard anymore, just the echoes of faraway footsteps.

I open my eyes, and the Many Boss figure is still in front of me, but he's warping and shifting. His body is farther away, and we're back in the warehouse now. I'm still on the ground, shivering and crying. I cough, and green powder flies out of my mouth. It's the Drug X. I'm fighting it, but I'm losing.

Then, right in front of my face, I see a vial filled with red liquid on the ground.

This has to be the antidote. The neutralizing agent.

I don't know if it will work on me, but I do know it will destroy all the stuff in that big mixer over there. And that's what we need to do.

But I can't get up, no matter how hard I try. My legs don't work, and my head is the only thing that still moves. I turn it and see Blaze on my left. He's getting to his knees, very slowly.

With my last bit of strength, I push the antidote over to him with my forehead. I watch the red vial roll along the ground, and then I see green. I get slimed again.

John

I'm on my knees. I can't get up.

The Many Boss is standing before me. Even on my knees, I'm forming a fist, trying to throw a punch, trying to win.

Then everything turns green, and I'm swimming in the thick of it. It's a very familiar kind of green, and it takes me a moment to place it. It's Ecto Cooler, the Slimer-themed Hi-C drink from when I was a kid. Based on the *Ghostbusters*. Wow, it's a been a long time since I had a healthy vitamin-packed strawful of Ecto Cooler Hi-C. Now, I'm practically drowning in it.

The sounds change. I hear punches, kicks, men screaming in pain. It sounds a lot like the fight we just had, but this time, it all sounds tinny, distant.

I open my eyes. I'm back at home. Not my home now, but my childhood home. I'm in my brother Steve's bedroom, sitting in front of his TV. I'm playing the home console version of the beat 'em up arcade smash hit *Street Fury*. I look to my right, and Steve is here with me. He's 14. I'm 8.

We're playing two-player co-op, facing off against the Stage 1 Boss, Mr. Teeth. He has an evil smile. I'm still not very good, but Steve is carrying it for both of us. We're whacking away at this guy. We've played it a hundred times before in the arcade, but this is the first time we've had it at home. Steve just got it for his birthday.

We're not supposed to be playing it until the weekend. We're supposed to be doing our homework.

"Steeeeve! Jooooohn!!" a woman's voice screams. Shoot, it's Mom. Calling from the other room.

Steve and I freeze, look at each other, pause the game.

"Yeah, Mom?" Steve calls.

"Are you helping John with his homework?"

We look at each other in terror. We know we shouldn't be doing this right now.

Finally, Steve replies. "Yeah!"

Silence. For a moment, the only sound we hear is the sound of our breathing. Eventually, he shrugs and says quietly, "Okay, I think we're good." We start playing again.

I'm down to my final sliver of health in the game. I'm grimacing and sucking in air, slamming on the buttons. Mr. Teeth has me in his sights, I'm done for. But then Steve jump-kicks from the other side of the screen and knocks the boss right in the chops. The moment he makes contact, the action breaks down into slow motion, the sound deepens and echoes, and Mr. Teeth's snappers fly out of his mouth with the punch as he crashes to the ground. His gums gnash against each other as his eyes turn into Xs. He's defeated.

We both scream "Yes!" and raise our fists in the air.

Then Steve's bedroom door explodes.

The blast knocks us forward off our beanbag chairs and showers us with splinters. Coughing, we push ourselves up to our hands and turn to look behind us.

Standing inside the blown-out door is a large figure wearing a house dress and curlers in her hair. It's Mom.

But it's not Mom. It's the Many Boss.

"Why aren't you doing your homework?" the Many Boss asks, full of snarling menace.

"Steve... Steve..." I begin.

"STEVE CAN'T HELP YOU NOW," Mom / Boss roars. She / he unsheathes a sword from his back.

No, wait. Not a sword.

A giant wooden spoon.

"IT'S TIME FOR YOUR PUNISHMENT."

"No!" I cry. My heart begins to race. My mouth dries up, and my hands start to tingle. I'm terrified of punishment.

The Mom / Boss begins to advance.

"Corporal punishment is bad!" I yell, hoping I can stop what I know is coming. "Violence is never the answer!"

But my words have no effect. Steve is frozen like me, kneeling on the floor, mouth open wide. He can't save me. Only I can save me. The menacing figure looms high above me and begins to raise the giant spoon.

Suddenly, I feel a reassuring hand on my shoulder. I turn. It's Steve. He looks into my eyes.

"You can do this, bro."

"Steve, I—" I begin.

"I believe in you. And I'm sorry," he says. And then he's gone.

I turn back to look at the Many Boss, hovering menacingly above me. He's pulling the massive spoon back for a giant swing.

"Bend over, you've been a very bad boy!" the Mommy Boss snarls.

I shake my head, grit my teeth, and lunge forward with all my strength, throwing everything I have into one punch.

"AAAAAAAAAAH!" I cry out, punching through the air, hitting nothing. Suddenly, there's only green mist.

The force of the swing almost makes me fall over. Instead, I steady myself with my other hand. I'm on my knees, looking at a concrete floor. Everything's hazy, but I think I'm back in the Spankers' hideout.

A red vial rolls over to me on the ground and stops at my knees. I look to my right. Kevin is laying there, dazed, clawing at the ground in front of him weakly.

I look in front of me. Jessica is there. She's getting up slowly, shaking her head, standing right next to the giant Drug X mixer. The Many Boss, the real one, looms just behind it.

We have one chance.

"JESSICA!" I cry. Her head snaps towards my direction. Her eyes are glassy, unseeing. She's fighting this, too.

And then, I see her eyes focus. They focus on me. It's only for an instant, but it's enough for me to try.

I grab the red vial and throw it toward her with all the strength I have left.

Jessica

Everything is green around me. It's such a familiar shade. What do I know this color from?

Oh my god, it's the color of Slimer pops, my favorite ice cream when I was a kid. For years, I never knew that the cartoon was based on a movie. And they had to call it *The Real Ghostbusters*, because there was already a weird old cartoon called the *Ghostbusters* on TV.

I loved getting my Slimer pop from the ice cream man.

But I *don't* like this green mist. It's thick and scary, and it's hard to breathe. Then the mist fades, and now everything is a deep blue.

I'm outside. The sky is clear. The sun is high, and it's warm on my face. I'm wearing too many layers, but my Mom dressed me all special, so I'm afraid to take any of them off.

I hitch up my huge backpack, which sits too low on me, and try to get it back up into place. Then I take a deep breath and walk through the rusty metal turnstile, set in a gap in the fence. This is the back entrance to the school.

I've just finished my first day of 6th grade. Our house is only a few blocks away. I start walking home.

I have to pass the cool kids. I remember passing them this morning, and they're already back here, even though the bell rang only a couple of minutes ago. Were they playing hooky? They're all smoking cigarettes, sitting in the front yard of the house next to the fence.

I start moving past them, staying away by walking down the middle of the narrow residential street. I'm not bothering them, and I'm really hoping they won't bother me. Maybe they won't notice that I'm a scared little nerd. That this huge backpack is stuffed with my anatomy textbooks as well as my regular schoolbooks. Because I know I already want to be a doctor.

Success! I pass them and nobody says a word.

"Nice backpack, JESSICA," a girl's voice calls out behind me.

Oh no. How does she know my name? I'm brand new here!

I stop in my tracks, and then it hits me. She's reading my new backpack. The backpack that my mom had embroidered with my name. In very large letters. In cursive. She thought it would be a great present for my first day of school. That it would set me up for success. After all, I'd always know where my backpack was. What could go wrong?

I turn around, watching the cool blonde girl get up from her friends and walk over to me.

"So, Jessica," she begins, staring at me. "Are you a good student? You wear glasses, you look pretty smart."

"Uhm..." I unconsciously push up my glasses on my nose and hitch up my backpack again. I don't know what to say. My mouth goes dry, and I can't find the words. "I... I'm trying to be."

"Huh. That's cool," the girl says, and then she nods at her friends. The guys stay sitting—apparently, I'm not worth it—but the two other girls come over and surround me. They're not menacing me outright, not quite, but I feel a tension in the air. I'm scared now.

One of the other girls, a brunette, says, "Yeah, we're

bad students."

The third, a redhead, starts laughing. "The worst!" she agrees.

Feeling trapped, I look back toward the school, to see if I can make it back to the turnstile. A few kids are crossing the field, but they're far away.

And then I see Tracy.

I remember when this happened, for real. These girls kicked my ass until my sister Tracy ran over. She was in the eighth grade when I was in the sixth. Tracy was a dancer, and one of the popular kids, but she was also a mean fighter. She taught me how to fight back.

She always had my back. And now she's in a hospital bed, fighting for her life. When she needed me most, I couldn't be there for her.

"Want a cigarette?" a voice brings me back to the present moment. But it's not one of the girls, it's a scary man's voice.

I turn back to the girls. But it's not the girls.

Instead, there are three Many Bosses towering above me. One is a blonde, one is a brunette, and one a redhead. They're wearing his full street gear and gold chains, but their hair is still long. They look ridiculous.

"First one's free, kid," the blond Many Boss says.

"Come hang out with us," the brunette says.

"Yeah!" the redhead agrees.

Then, they all move as one, and they grab me by my arms!

"Jessica!" I hear a faint voice call out from afar. It's my sis. She sees me.

"TRACY!" I yell back, terrified.

I'm struggling with the Girl Bosses, but I can't break free. Meanwhile, Tracy leaps over the school's back turnstile, and she throws something to me as she's running over.

I watch it come toward me in the air. It's a small red cylinder, and I try to grab it, but my arms are held tight.

With only a moment left, I close my eyes, and now everything is green again. I square my stance and hunch forward with all of my strength.

"YAAAAAAAAGH!"

I feel the weight slacken, and the Girl Bosses roll forward, following my momentum, letting go of me as they tumble.

I open my eyes and the Slimer pop green is gone. Now I'm inside a big room. Brick walls, concrete floor.

That jerk Blaze is over there. His arm is outstretched towards me. Something small and red is flying toward my face. It's almost here.

It's my antidote. To destroy the drugs.

I grab it perfectly from the air and pop off the cap even as it lands in my hand. I keep swinging my arm forward, turning as I go.

"NOOOOOO!" a voice cries.

It's the Many Boss. The real one. He knows what's coming. He knows it's too late.

I spin until the giant mixer is standing before me. All the Drug X that me and the other workers have been churning out for the last three days is right here. Over a million dollars' worth of poison.

I dump the vial into the mixer, and I destroy it all.

I did not expect it to explode, but it does.

It knocks me off my feet. Then all I see is green again.

John

"Jessica!" I scream, watching her get knocked back from the explosion. A giant plume of smoke explodes from the top of the mixer, great gouts of flame instantly destroying the deadly payload inside.

The Many Boss is hit by the blast, too. He staggers backward, though he stays on his feet. He's dazed now and trying to will himself back to his senses. I'm not going to give him a chance.

I run forward and slug him in the face as hard as I can. His head snaps back.

Then I do it again. This time, he staggers to the side. I track his movement and watch him stumble right over to Kevin, who's also back up on his feet.

Kevin smacks him as hard as he can, too.

The Many Boss ping-pongs back and forth between us, we bash him left and right, slowly, methodically, savagely working him over.

To this point, the fighting in the game has felt like a bloodless romp—kind of fun, even—but this encounter feels different. Brutal. This guy really messed with our minds, and now we're fighting back with everything we have. And all he can do is stand there and take it.

We've been slowly backing him up to the staircase with our blows, and now Kevin rears back and slugs him with a monster punch, which finally knocks him over. The Many Boss falls back into the open elevator lift, slamming against the control panel on the far side of it. He staggers back to the edge closest to us and collapses to the floor. The gate closes, and the lift begins moving. He's going up with it.

We watch him ascend. He's lying flat, his face smooshed up against the edge of the open lift. His eyes are glassy, and drool spills over the side and onto the ground next to us. Kevin and I step back to avoid getting hit, and then we keep walking backward to track his movement as he continues to rise.

Suddenly, Kevin and I are both knocked away from each other. We stumble but keep our balance, then look to see who clipped us.

It's Jessica. She's back on her feet, shoving past us toward the lift. She doesn't say a word.

Kevin and I watch as Jessica reaches the stairs next to the lift and begins climbing, keeping pace with the open elevator as it slowly goes up, staring daggers at the prone Many Boss as she matches his ascent.

The Many Boss starts to get to his hands and knees. He looks down, twenty feet off the ground now, and sees us.

"Y-you..." he spits out in a low growl. "We are not defeated. We are Legion. We are many."

Kevin and I say nothing. This moment is taking an agonizingly long time. The lift is twenty-five feet in the air now.

"You are not strong enough to face what's coming." The Many Boss is up on one knee now, gaining a little strength back, pointing at us menacingly.

Thirty feet in the air, and the lift finally stops at the catwalk level. The lift gate begins to open. Jessica enters just as the Many Boss rises fully to his feet.

"This is for Tracy," Jessica says. Then she punches him as hard as she can.

The Many Boss spins over the waist-high railing and falls screaming all the way to the floor, landing with a sickening crack right between us.

The last thing we see of him are his eyes, goggling up at us from the ground, in perfect and total surprise.

His body quietly blinks in and out of existence. In and out, in and out. And then he's gone.

Quest Complete: Infiltrate the drug lair and take down the Boss of the Spankers Gang.

Chapter 24

Loot

The sound of the elevator lift starting again snaps us out of our spell. Kevin and I tear our gaze from the limp form of the Many Boss below us and look back up toward the ceiling. The lift is coming back down, this time with Jessica riding it. She stands in the center of the platform, staring straight ahead, lips shut tight, not moving.

I sneak a glance over at Kevin, who's also looking up in fear and wonder at Jessica. I murmur, "That Drug X stuff was...genuinely messed up. Like, psychologically disturbing."

Kevin nods. "Yeah." He starts to say something, then stops himself. After a moment, he decides to say it. "You know, Blaze, I...faced some weird childhood stuff just now. Things I had been avoiding for a long time. It was painful, and really weird, but... I kinda feel better."

I think about that for a moment. "Yeah, now that you mention it, it feels helpful to actually...kind of deal with some of that stuff. I might have just figured some things out that prevented me from being...like, a good team player?"

Kevin looks at me sideways. "Well, I hope so. You were a little stubborn about trying to get in here through the front door."

I nod. "Yeah, I've been kind of stuck in my ways, I guess."

The lift stops, and the gate slides open. Kevin and I watch Jessica get out and stalk calmly toward us, still not saying a word.

I try to break the ice. "Jessica! How's, uh... How's it going?"

She comes to a stop a few feet away, looking at us calmly and evenly. Our figures form a perfect tiny triangle in the center of the large industrial lab space.

"I'm fine," she says. "It's done. So that's good enough for me."

"Is it done, though?" I ask. "I mean, shouldn't there be some kind of reward or something? Like, I don't know, a cutscene or a bonus screen, maybe? Everything feels kind of the same as it did before."

"Well, maybe we need to pick up that loot!" Kevin says, pointing to the ground.

A few feet away from us, at the spot where the Many Boss fell and blinked out his last bits of existence, sits a small pile of treasure. All his belongings, ready for us to take, like the greedy ghouls that we are. Hey, those are the rules. I didn't design the game, I'm just playing it.

Jessica strides over, bends down, and picks up three

gold coins from the pile. "What are these?" she asks, turning them over in her hand.

"A second chance," I confirm. "Extra tokens so we can come back if we lose a life."

She looks up at me, her eyes narrowed. I swear she hesitates for a split-second before tossing one to me, and then one to Kevin. Okay, we're all for one and one for all here, glad to see that.

"Thanks," Kevin and I mutter, and now it's my turn to bend down and pick up an item, like it's Christmas morning and we're handing out gifts from under the tree. Except this time, the tree is the disappeared corpse of a drug lord.

I choose the leather vambraces the Many Boss wore. They don't look medieval, more street-style. I pull the top of my hazmat suit down, exposing my arms and chest. I hold a vambrace up to my forearm and flex, testing out the aesthetics.

Kevin nods approvingly. "Looks cool."

"Should be good armor for blocking. Does it look good with the jacket? It's got to look good with the jacket," I insist. Kevin nods, and Jessica rolls her eyes.

As I start to slip on the vambraces, Kevin's eyes light up, and he picks up a small box from the pile.

"What's that?" I ask.

He searches along the edges of the box, then taps a little circle on one side, which pops out of the box to reveal a tiny cylinder. He takes the cylinder in his hand like a pen and presses the tip to the top of the box. Suddenly it lights up, revealing a loading screen. The cylinder is

368 🖫 Eric Jason Martin

a stylus, and the box is a little handheld computer! You know, from the olden times.

"It's a PDA!" he exclaims, holding it up and smiling.

"I mean, if you want a hug, bro, just say so," I joke.

"No, not public display of affection," he says. "Personal Digital Assistant! This was like a smartphone before smartphones. I can take notes for us. And I could probably get on the internet, too, find out more about the city."

He taps the screen again with his stylus, and suddenly we hear a familiar noise shooting out of the device. The sound of a dial-up modem.

"Just give it a minute," he explains.

Kevin's machine sputters and beeps as Jessica focuses back on the loot before us. She leans down to grab the one remaining item.

It's the Many Boss's gold chain. Jessica holds it up to the light. As it twinkles and reflects the rays of sun now peeking in from the high windows near the catwalks, I can make out a silhouette on the coin-shaped pendant. It's the same silhouette of the Many Boss that I saw in the newspaper my first night here in New Arcadia. Underneath this bust of the Many Boss is a phrase curling around the bottom edge of the coin. But instead of saying "E Pluribus Unum," or something like that, it reads, "Drugs Are Cool." Not the fashion choice I would make, but I guess it's pretty on-brand for the guy.

She holds it up to her neck, as if sizing up the way she would wear it, then looks up at us suspiciously. "What? I'm going to sell it," she explains.

"Hey, no worries, you can do whatever you want with it," I assure her, holding my hands up. Then, the loot pile exhausted, I take a long, searching look at the giant lab around us. All the furniture is broken, the equipment shattered. We really did a number on this place. "But, uh, is this it? I kind of thought there'd be a little more to it. It feels kind of, I don't know..."

"Anti-climactic," Kevin finishes.

Jessica frowns. "Well, let's get the hell out of here."

✪✪✪

We're in the main hallway now, walking to the front door of the building, as far as I can tell. There's trash and broken furniture everywhere, and graffiti all over the walls. Jessica is leading the way, and Kevin and I are hustling to keep up with her. It's a long hallway, so we've got a ways to walk. I attempt to lighten the mood with a little small talk. I have a feeling it won't go well, but I try it anyway.

"It's good to see you again, Jessica," I say. "Glad we could reconnect. Uh, I'm Blaze, as you know, and my real name is John. John Chambers."

She says nothing.

"...and this is Iceman, aka Kevin Singleton."

Kevin smiles and says, "Pleasure to meet you, Jessica. You've got a lot of courage coming in here alone like that."

She throws a terse glance behind her and says, "Nice to meet you, Kevin."

"We're really glad you decided to join our gang." I

continue. "Have you given any thought to what our team name could be? You mentioned you weren't particularly keen on the themed elemental approach, but maybe we can..."

Jessica stops in her tracks and turns to face me, eyes blazing. This makes me stop, which makes Kevin stop.

"I mean, we're absolutely open to suggestions," I offer weakly.

She narrows her eyes at me. "I work alone."

"Well, it got you real far, didn't it? Right into a death trap. They would have killed you if we hadn't teamed up. Look, this place is designed for people to work together. You can't make it on your own, none of us can! We need each other to survive."

Her jaw twitches.

"I hate to admit it myself! But it's true," I finish.

Jessica opens her mouth and looks like she's going to cut me down with her next sentence, or maybe she's just going to cut me down, period. But then, underneath us, we hear a low but clear groan.

Surprised, we all look at our feet. Hidden behind a broken, upside-down couch is one of the scientists, a mousy little dweeb in a lab-coat with just a sliver of health left. He's lying on the ground, clutching his arm, and moaning. I don't know how he made it all the way out here. Maybe he escaped us in the lab, but a group of the drug workers ganged up on him before he could escape, turning on their overlords.

I lift him up roughly and prop him up to a sitting position against the upside-down end of the couch behind him.

"Ow, my back!" he cries. According to his stats, his name is Dr. Goodfeel.

"Alright, doc, where do the drugs come from?" I ask, holding on to his jacket lapels.

He laughs weakly and says, "You can't stop it. Plenty more where this came from. Much more."

Jessica interjects, "How much more? Who controls the shipments?"

The scientist says, "I can't tell you that."

"Is it Dr. X?" she asks.

His eyes widen in shock.

"Yeah, your boss gave that up to us before we took him out. Now, where can we get this guy?" she asks in a low, menacing growl.

"I don't know, I swear! You have to believe me. I've never seen him. All I've heard is that he lives downtown. Some big penthouse somewhere. Please."

I flinch, expecting Jessica to reach forward and slap the guy into next week, but now she's looking away, focusing on something in the distance, something in her own mind. I take the chance to continue my line of questioning and snatch the doc's coat again, shaking him so that he turns his attention back to me.

"Hey. You refine the drugs here, I get that part," I begin. "But where do you get your raw materials?"

"I can't tell you that! No way..."

"Okay, smart guy, I'm giving you a new name. Your

new name is Dr. *Bad*feel."

I lift him off the ground in a bear hug. He yowls in pain.

Kevin calls out to me over the man's sobbing cries, "Come on, man, that's not cool."

I yell, "You know what's not cool, Kevin? Drug X! Drug X is very not cool!" He has nothing to say to that. We're both still pretty messed up from that bad trip. Jessica too, probably, but she's doing her best to hide it.

I turn back to the mewling scientist, grabbing onto his lapels and shaking him. His legs are dragging below him, so I'm holding him up in place and yelling in his face. "Oh no, I think I'm having flashbacks, Dr. Badfeel! What are you gonna do about that? What are you gonna do? Do you have a prescription for me?"

"Owowow!" he yells.

"Are you gonna tell me where this stuff comes from, or are we gonna dance the Cha-cha?" I yell, faking being pushed to my limit and going full-on psycho, but frankly maybe not faking it a little bit, too.

"Okay! Okay! Put me down! Put me down!" he cries.

I do, setting him down, not overly roughly, back to a sitting position against the broken couch. He takes fast, pained, shallow breaths.

"We get shipments...every Friday night at the docks. Pier 38, east side. That's where you'll find it. More than you've...ever...imagined."

Suddenly, he begins blinking away. He screams weakly, then he's gone entirely.

And then the guitars squeal.

The sound is all around us, like we're wearing headphones but we're not. It's guitar overkill, a completely unnecessary amount of electric guitar noise. I can see that Kevin and Jessica hear it too. It's loud, but not so loud that we have to cover our ears, although I begin to.

A large text box appears in my vision.

STAGE 1 COMPLETE

Level 4 Achieved.

And level up I do, feeling that same rush and burst of light and power.

Apparently, Kevin leveled up with me, too. "All right, there it is! Level 4! Congratulations, gang!"

"Sweet!" I say.

"I'm Level 6," Jessica says flatly.

"Whoa, really?" Kevin asks. "That's crazy."

"Okay, guys," I say. "Let's get out of here and back to our place. We can figure out skills and power ups and next steps and all that..."

Suddenly, the ground shakes. We all shoot our hands out to steady ourselves. It's over with fast, but that was a really rough shake.

"What was that?" Jessica asks.

Kevin shrugs. "I don't know, earthquake?"

This feels very wrong. At this moment, a new prompt appears:

STAGE 2: THE DOCKS

BEGIN STAGE?

YES / NO

"You guys see this, too? What do you say, shall we start the next stage?" I ask.

But then the shaking returns, much harder this time, and it doesn't stop. The floor slams back and forth, the building groans and buckles, and it seems like the whole thing might just come down around us. I've been through a few big earthquakes in California, and at first it feels like a lot like those. But then things start to...glitch.

Suddenly, a section of the hallway next to us disappears, and we can see the neighborhood outside. The wall flickers in and out rapidly as the sound of metal scraping on metal assaults our ears. Then another, larger section of wall goes away.

We can hear the street sounds outside, and then those noises warp and stretch. Day turns into night in a moment, then back into day. The earth is still shaking, but that feels like the least of our worries. Even the Stage 2 text box in front of us is glitching in and out, like we're getting bad reception on an old TV.

I lunge toward the flickering text box and accept the quest as the world violently shakes and blinks in and out of existence around us.

It's the last thing I do before everything fades to white.

Chapter 25

Take Me Home Country Roads

Suddenly I'm gasping for air again, like I've been holding my breath and didn't know it. I've been here before. My eyes are shut tight, and I feel myself being lifted and pushed forward as I gasp and choke out gel. Then I'm half-laid down, half-dropped onto the ground, shuddering.

Right away, I start wiping the gel from my eyes. I hear a familiar voice over the sounds of my gasping for air. It's Dekker.

"I'm sorry, gang, we are having...technical difficulties with the game right now," he says.

I open my eyes, blinking away the gunk, and look up, expecting to see him standing before me. But he's not actually there. Instead, his face is on a video screen on the wall in front of me. He's not talking into his watch this time, but he looks to be in an office, sitting at a desk, facing a desktop webcam.

"We have had to remove all of you beta testers from your chambers," he continues. "I'm sorry I can't be there with you all in person, but there are too many now for me to make the rounds individually."

I've pushed myself up onto my knees. I'm still pretty out of it, feeling sluggish and confused, not quite ready to stand yet. There are a few scientists working in here— they're all intensely focused, but not panicked, which is a relief. I feel kind of special being in here, knowing that I've got the place to myself while the other rooms down the hall are all packed with many other players. I'm still the number one beta tester. It's petty, I know, but the status makes me feel better.

Dekker continues, "We think we can get the world back up and running relatively quickly, so we're asking for your patience. Please wipe off the gel solution with the provided towels at your stations and sit tight where you are. A team member will be around shortly to provide refreshments. We hope to get the technical issue resolved and get you back to the fight ASAP. Thanks, gang."

Wow. So it really was a problem with the game. Maybe a bug. Or maybe it was some kind of sabotage? Anything's possible, I suppose. I grunt and strain as I get to my feet. Ah, there's the old back pain, I've missed you. I stretch tentatively, feel the tightness. Yeah, that's not going away any time soon.

I look around and find a towel on a heated rack nearby. I start toweling off. The warm cloth after the cold gel and floor helps a lot. The scientists in here, all four of them, are clustered around the control panel of my chamber now, running diagnostics. Their dialogue is all gibberish to me. It's clearly English, but it's all computer stuff, and I have no idea what they're talking about.

I take care to fold the towel and set it back on the warming rack, feeling a bit more civilized as a result. As I do, the far door slides open, and a thin man in a hazmat suit strides in. It's Tallboy, it's got to be. He's holding a fluffy white robe.

"Tallboy, I presume." I stand there calmly in my undies, regarding him.

"FOLLOW ME, PLEASE," he commands through his amplified talk-box.

I start to move automatically, then reconsider.

"Dekker just said for us to wait here," I say, suspicion clear in my voice.

"I KNOW WHAT HE SAID. FOLLOW ME, PLEASE," he says, throwing the robe to me.

I catch it with one hand, then swing it around my back to slide it on. Tallboy is already moving, so I step into my nearby sandals on the ground and they slip on as I walk forward, tying the robe's belt as I rush to catch up.

✪✪✪

I'm back in the conference room. Drinking ice water, eating granola bars from the basket. It's nice.

I've been up here for eleven minutes, all alone. Tallboy instructed me to get inside the big elevator room to get upstairs, then he walked right back to the game rooms. I arrived at the conference room and was all keyed up at first, partly from our big battle in the game, partly from the confusion and excitement of not knowing what was happening here in the real world. But now the

378 Eric Jason Martin

waiting is starting to wear me down.

I'm examining the granola bar, looking at it more closely for the first time. This one is a cherry vanilla Chum-Num, and a brief story on the wrapper tells me about the natural ingredients the good people at Chum have harvested from the earth, which is a very nice thing for them to do.

Then the familiar red lights begin circling in the corners of the room, the beeping triggers, and a moment later, the far wall begins to slide open.

"Hey, man, save some granola bars for me!" It's Kevin, smiling broadly.

The door slides open farther to reveal a woman standing across from him. I realize right away that it's Jessica, I'd recognize that stoic expression anywhere. They're both dressed in the same fluffy white robes I'm wearing.

"Kevin! And...Jessica, I presume! How are you?" I smile, standing up in greeting as they enter the conference room.

Jessica says nothing, Kevin laughs and replies, "Reborn! I feel like a new man. Like I was literally just given birth to. You know, confused and disgusted."

I laugh ruefully. "Yeah, I've gone through the extraction one more time than you have. It hasn't gotten any easier yet."

"Can you, uh...toss me one of those?" Kevin asks, indicating the basket next to me.

"Sure," I say, obliging by tossing a bar to him in a smooth lob. He catches it with ease.

"Can I have one?" Jessica asks, surprising me. She sounds the same as she does in the game. Cold. Focused. Possibly slightly annoyed.

I clear my throat nervously. "Of course," I reply, tossing her another granola bar. But I completely whiff it. I don't know how this is possible, but the bar shoots out of my hand as I start the throw and flies straight to my right, soaring across the large table and landing on the ground, ten feet away from all of us.

"Sorry! Sorry," I apologize, standing up, picking up the entire basket, and walking over to present it to her. I hold my arm out as far as I can, so that I don't get too close, out of consideration. And maybe out of a little fear that she'll smack me.

She sifts through the assortment in the basket, considering.

"The…uh…mixed fruit and nut ones are the best, I think," I say, clearing my throat and not looking her in the eye. I notice that she picks out two apple cinnamon instead. A message to me? Maybe she genuinely prefers apple cinnamon? I shouldn't read too much into it, and then I promptly ignore my own advice, reading too much into it. She must hate me.

"May I?" Kevin asks, grabbing another one—a mixed fruit and nut. Thanks, buddy.

"Have a seat, guys," I say, indicating the broad table behind me. I walk back to my seat and set the basket down. Kevin and Jessica take chairs of their own, each of us a few seats apart.

"Well, uh…" I begin, looking for some way to break the ice. "Congratulations, everybody. We beat Stage 1."

"Go team," Kevin says warmly.

Jessica snorts. "Yeah, and apparently, we broke the game doing it."

"No, you didn't." A new voice. Dekker.

He's here in person, having entered through the sliding door that leads into the complex on the main floor. Which means he wasn't way down in the game rooms with us. He looks tired, haggard. He always seems to have this burning all-consuming energy, and now it looks like it's turned inward to consume him. What has he been dealing with?

There's silence. We're waiting for him to say more. He eventually does, but it's not what I'm expecting.

"Toss me a granola bar, will you?" Dekker asks.

Kevin's a little closer to the basket now, and he obliges. Dekker catches the bar, then slumps down into a chair across the table from us. The chair rolls back a bit as he lands, then he stops himself, concerned. He reaches down and picks up another granola bar, the one I had tossed over to Jessica and whiffed badly. It's been halfway run over by his chair. I feel my face redden in embarrassment. He shrugs and tosses the bar on the table in front of him.

"Thanks, I'm starving. Haven't had a minute to eat," Dekker says.

He rips the first bar open and starts chewing. We all sit there waiting, uncomfortable, churning over all the questions in our minds while he wolfs down his first bar, and then he unwraps and eats the smooshed second bar.

"These Chum-Num bars are great, Dekker, my

compliments to the chef," I say as he finishes the last bite, in a lame attempt to start the conversation. Jessica huffs. It makes me feel lame and self-conscious.

Dekker smiles tightly, swallows a drink of bottled water, and then says, "You three did very well. You are the first gang to advance to the next stage. Mind you, our second round of beta testers have only been in the game for a few days, but still. It's an impressive achievement. My congratulations to you."

I suppose I should feel grateful for the compliment, but I don't feel gratitude. I feel angry.

"Hey, Dekker, what was up with that Drug X stuff? I get that it's supposed to be bad for you, but does it have to be, like, legitimate nightmare fuel? I'm no psychologist, but it feels like that crap burrows right into your brain and finds your deepest childhood fears. So that you have to, like, face them and stuff."

"Yeah, that's a hard agree from me. That was real messed up," Kevin chimes in from his seat.

Jessica says nothing, but meticulously crushes her empty plastic bottle into a tiny pancake. It speaks louder than any words could.

Dekker looks at each of us with a genuine smile. "I cannot tell you how pleased I am to hear you say that."

"Well, I'm *not* pleased," I retort. "I'm pissed off. If that's what you're going for with this thing on purpose, then that's all kinds of messed up."

Kevin backs me up. "Yeah, man, I'm, like, traumatized. I mean, I'll live, but that was a real tonal shift in the game."

"It's like..." I begin, trying to put my thoughts

together. "You called the gang the Spankers, and then I have a Drug X hallucination that involves childhood corporal punishment. Did you...design the experience knowing that a large percentage of kids of our generation were, like, messed up by that? Or was that a unique experience just for me?"

Kevin immediately becomes interested in the blank wall across the room. Jessica stares down at the table in front of her. Dekker says nothing. Instead, he drums his fingers on the conference table.

"Just me, then?"

Jessica speaks up for the first time, in a quiet, threatening voice, "I'm beginning to reconsider whether I'll be going back in."

Dekker considers for a moment, his fingers drumming faster and faster on the table. Then he abruptly stops and says, "You're not going back in. Nobody is."

"What?" Jessica asks, her voice suddenly rising with anger as she leaps to her feet, leaning over the table, staring him down and seething with hatred. Whoa. I guess that was a bluff.

"For now!" Dekker says, placatingly, raising his hands and gesturing in a 'simmer down' motion. "Just for now. There is a...legitimate technical issue, and now that we've had a little more time to review, it's clear we are not going to be able to solve it today. Perhaps not for a few days."

He pauses, letting it sink in. Jessica, Kevin, and I all share uneasy glances.

"So we're taking you home, all of you. Our teams are

preparing the other players downstairs, and our drivers are preparing the van fleet outside. I promise you, once we get the issue solved, we'll bring you all back here and back into the game. You three will be sharing the first van out. I wanted to tell you in person."

There was a time when all I wanted to do was go back home. Now, I'm surprised to feel disappointed... and sad. Even with the struggle for survival, the constant threat of fighting and pain, even with my fast food job, I'm going to miss being in that world. I'm going to miss having the freedom to move around again.

I'm going to miss my gang.

"Can we keep in touch?" I blurt out. "I mean, Kevin and Jessica and me? While we wait to come back?"

Dekker looks at me, and I think I see a little smirk on his face. He turns to Kevin, waiting.

Kevin says, "Yeah, it'd be good to stay connected." He looks to Jessica pointedly. "You know, so we can strategize, keep our heads in the game."

Dekker then turns to Jessica. Her lips are tightly pursed, but finally, she says, "Yeah, that would be... helpful."

Dekker sweeps his gaze over all of us now. "Yes, now that I have your permission, we can arrange for you all to connect online back at home."

The far door, the door to the main warehouse, now opens. Tallboy is back, this time with his little buddy Short Round, their plastic suits squeaking as they enter the room.

"Time to go," Dekker tells us. "Very sorry about the

timing of all of this. I am hopeful that we'll get everything patched up overnight. Safe travels."

✪✪✪

Back in the van.

Kevin and I are sitting on the second-to-last bench. Jessica has the back row to herself. Tallboy is driving, and Short Round is riding shotgun. We're past the gates of the main complex and driving back on the main desert road to my house.

The only sounds are the dull roar of the van's engine and air conditioning, the ground racing past underneath us, and the steady respiration from the hazmat suits up front. Tallboy and Short Round's breaths are calm and even, but they have different rhythms. I'm lulling myself to sleep listening to them breathe opposite each other; they slowly sync up, then drift apart again. My eyes are beginning to close looking out the window, watching the sameness of the desert scenery passing by. I might fall asleep right here.

"I'm guessing they're gonna drop me off first," I say to Kevin and Jessica, shaking my head in an effort to stay awake. "I'm just another few minutes away, right up here in North Fontana."

Kevin says, "And I'm probably next. It's about forty minutes to West Diamond Bar from there."

"How about you, Jessica? How's the drive out to you? Not too long, I hope," I try to engage Jessica behind us, but she's not taking the bait.

There's awkward silence for a long moment, and there's not much I can do about it. Thankfully, Kevin finally speaks up.

"Man, it feels so crazy to be back here in the world. And I was only in there a couple of days. I can't imagine what it must feel like for you two," he says, touching his face. "Wow, it feels weird to have wrinkles again," he says, laughing.

I laugh along with him, then unconsciously touch my own face. "Yeah, this is very weird. I feel like we're coming home from camp. We've been practicing for the talent show all week, and now we're going home before we get to perform our skit."

Kevin laughs, but he sounds odd. "Yeah, I know what you mean. I've been to summer camp. But it was…a day camp, more like summer school. We… We never did a talent show." He gets quiet and withdrawn. I know him well enough now not to push it.

After a moment of listening to the sounds of the road and the respirators, I start in again. "We've made it so far, guys. We've done really well together. We've got to keep up the momentum. Let's be in touch at home, I'm serious about that. We can plan our next steps on Amigo."

Amigo is Chum's proprietary messaging app. I use it for work when I have to, but you can use it with friends, too. Until now, I never had a need to.

Jessica says nothing, but Kevin agrees, "Absolutely, I'll message you both once I get settled at home." He notices a sign coming up out his window and reads it aloud as we pass. "Now Entering North Fontana. This is you, John."

The scenery outside my window shifts from bare desert to a familiar row of suburban houses. Or rather, skeletons of houses first, concrete foundations and wooden slats, falling apart.

I peer ahead through the front windshield, then point.

"Home sweet home. My house is just ahead, see it? It's the white one on the…"

There's a deafening pop underneath us, and the world spins until everything is black.

✪✪✪

I open my eyes. I'm still in the van. It feels like all the blood has rushed to my head. I feel top-heavy, weak and woozy. My arms are swaying above my head. That's weird.

I focus on the sounds. The a/c is off, and the engine is sputtering, clanking. Something's wrong with it.

I hear one loud smack on the roof, then another. I look forward, and Tallboy and Short Round are crawling upside-down on the ceiling!

I look to my right. Kevin is asleep, but his hands are swaying above his head, too. Is this a game glitch in the real world?

I look past Kevin out into the street. We're next to a house. The house is upside-down. The sky is on the floor.

Wait a minute.

The van flipped over.

Far in front of us, I hear several screams in the distance. Other humans. They sound like war cries.

"SCUMMERS!" Tallboy shouts through his suit's talk-box.

"WE'VE GOT TO MOVE!" Short Round calls out. He's working on his passenger door, but it seems to be stuck.

Oh my god, it really happened. The Scummers laid a trap for us. Maybe they think we're a shipment of peanut butter pretzels and rice cakes. And maybe when they find out what we really are, they'll eat us anyway.

"Ow!" I hear Jessica behind me unlatch her seatbelt and drop to the ground, or rather the roof. She's already scrabbling past Kevin and me, making her way toward the big sliding door in the middle.

Kevin's beginning to stir now. "Wha— What..."

I shake him gently. More screams and yells outside, they sound like they're getting a little closer. We're both still upside-down. He blinks heavily, and then focuses on my eyes.

"Kevin, we've got to move. Can you make it?" I say, holding onto his shoulder firmly.

"I... I think so."

Suddenly, there's a dull boom at the front of the van that echoes powerfully back to us. Short Round can't open the door, but he's found another way: firing a gun at the windshield. No, not a gun, it's some kind of energy weapon, I can literally see the shockwaves in the air. The windshield shatters outward.

"OW!" I've been fumbling with my seatbelt, and the backlash from this blast causes me to press the button, releasing me so that I drop right to the ground. Even though I had one arm up to protect me, that was pretty much head-first. I shake my head, then reach over to help Kevin, cradling his head and controlling his fall so that he doesn't have to go through the same thing I just did.

Tallboy and Short Round have scrabbled out of the van and onto the street. Meanwhile, Jessica—stubborn Jessica—is still pulling at the big sliding door on the side with all of her strength. I scramble forward on my hands and knees, grabbing her shoulder to stop her.

"Follow me!" I yell, crawling forward and not stopping to look behind me. I make my way to the front of the van to follow the hazmat bros out, watching them take kneeling positions on either side of our overturned van. They're ready to protect their cargo—namely, us.

Jessica and Kevin are crawling right behind me. I pull myself out of the van and try to get my bearings while the other two join me outside.

It looks like our van flipped over its front and landed upside-down. We're turned backward, facing where we came from. There's a giant divot in the road where we flipped, and the space around the hole is scorched and blackened. There must have been a grenade, or some kind of landmine. Whatever it was, we drove right into the Scummers' ambush.

Suddenly, my hair flies around—something just whistled past me. I turn and see a large rock skitter to a halt on the asphalt. The Scummers are throwing stuff at us and judging from what I know about them and supply drones, they're damn good shots. That was too close.

"GET DOWN," Short Round commands, and we oblige, squatting behind the van with them, using it as a shield. Tallboy fires two dull booms from his own energy weapon, trying to keep the angry horde back.

I can't see anything, I only hear their shouts, still

far away but getting closer. I've never really seen the Scummers in person before, and I'm not about to now. Kevin, Jessica, and I are pressed against the grill of the van as it lays upside-down. I look down the street and find my house. It's about a hundred yards away. Home sweet home.

"Guys! There's my house," I explain, pointing down the street. "Can you both run?"

Kevin and Jessica both nod at me.

"We can make it if we're fast. Let's go!"

I start sprinting as fast as I can. I hear the two of them follow close behind.

"Hazmat Bros! Come on!" I yell out without looking back.

"GO! WE'LL COVER YOU!" one of them yells. The Scummers are getting closer, rushing down the street, screaming inhuman sounds. Some are reacting in pain to the booms of the energy weapon. I don't dare look behind me.

I sprint over to the front yards—to get us out of the middle of the street. I dash across the lawns, jump the low hedges. There are no cars to get in our way in the driveways, those are all long gone. If we do have to make a stand out here, it will have to be behind one of these houses. That's our only cover.

But we won't have to do that. We're gonna make it. Five more houses.

I hear more sickening, muted blasts far behind us. The sound is like someone punching holes in the air itself. More screams from the Scummers. They sound

Eric Jason Martin

really, really pissed.

Four houses. Three. Boy, I never thought I'd get a chance to take a stroll in my neighborhood, this is really delightful. Nothing like racing for my damn life.

"We're almost there!" I yell, chancing a quick glance behind me.

All I see are Kevin and Jessica, they're right behind. Kevin waves his hand violently forward as he sprints, shooing me to pay attention. "Go! Go!" he yells.

One more house. I jump the hedge separating us. Skid to a halt at my front door, feel Kevin and Jessica scramble to a halt right behind me. More blasts are firing, the sounds farther away.

"Open it!" Kevin yells.

I try the door. It's locked, of course.

"Use your key!" Jessica yells.

"I don't have one!" I yell, jiggling the handle.

"Why not?" she yells.

"WHEN DO I EVER GO OUTSIDE?" I scream.

"Try the…" Kevin begins, but then is cut off by a scream of agony from afar. An amplified, unnatural scream. Then another. Then silence.

I turn around. We can't see anything in the street because of the hedge in my front yard. Jessica, Kevin, and I stare at each other without a word. We know what this means. They got Tallboy. They got Short Round.

Now we hear the Scummer cries again, but this time, it's a chorus of triumph. I shudder at the sound.

They're coming for us now.

Panicked, I start ringing my doorbell. Jessica starts kicking the door. Kevin joins her. My mind is racing, desperately searching for a solution. I start thinking about the back of the house. Maybe between the three of us we can kick down the back door. But how do we keep the Scummers out then?

I stop ringing the doorbell and put my hands on Kevin and Jessica's shoulders, signaling my new plan, or last-ditch impulse, whatever it is. Then I face the doorbell, hoping the camera recognizes my face.

But Jessica breaks free from me and rears back for a massive, desperate kick.

The front door quietly clicks, then slowly opens inward with a sickening creak.

Jessica's already committed to her flying kick, though, and is about to go sailing right through the door and onto her ass. She's really going to hurt herself. I grab her right before she runs past and jumps into the air. She screams in frustration at being restrained like this, but then she sees the door opening before her and stops herself.

With the hordes just around the corner, and the screams signaling the Scummer war party's imminent attack, we pile in through the front door. Kevin and Jessica run all the way into the living room, going as far back as they can go. I slam the door shut and lock both locks, backing up fast. As I do, I trip over my own feet, fall on my ass, then scramble back crab-walk style until all three of us are pressed against the far wall, just as fists begin to slam on the now-locked door.

The Scummers pound and pound. It sounds like a dozen hands and feet all smashing at the door. The three of us look at each other in terror. How far away are we from them? Not thirty feet, that's for sure. Is it far enough away to not be breathing their air? I hope so. I have to take comfort that we're sealed inside. But will it hold?

The brutal hammering continues, but the door stands. There's one more giant, angry slam, and then, silence.

We sit against the wall for a long time, staring at the door, letting our racing hearts slowly come down from the red zone.

Long moments later, I'm back to breathing more or less normally, and I carefully stand up. The Scummers have got to be gone now. We made it.

"Uh... Welcome to my place, guys. Can I get anyone anything?"

Chapter 26

Hackers

" **A**re you all okay?"

It's Dekker, calling on my tablet screen. His face is haggard, worried.

Kevin, Jessica, and I are now standing around the kitchen table, crowded in behind me to frame all our faces in my tablet's camera. I scrambled in here to pick it up when I heard it ringing. It's been maybe two minutes since the war cries of the Scummers stopped, and we're still on edge. Still getting our breathing back.

"I remember," I say by way of answering, between labored breaths, "at one point...you said you could guarantee my safety...in the real world."

Kevin calls over my shoulder, "We're fine, Dekker. But they got our drivers! I don't know what happened, but...I don't think they made it."

"I am aware. This is all...quite unexpected," Dekker

says, and from the pale expression on his face, I believe him. "The Scummers have gotten bolder. The increased van traffic must have alerted them that something new is happening at our facility."

He's speaking to us through his ChumWatch, back down in the game lab, but now he's checking his own tablet in his other hand, his face intense, his eyes scanning rapidly across the screen in front of him.

"A containment team should be there to secure your neighborhood within ten minutes. You'll be safe, but I'd recommend staying away from the windows and doors until you hear them drive up. And you will hear them drive up."

Jessica pushes forward and points at the screen. "When can I go home, Dekker?"

"You're not going home. We'll keep you and Kevin at John's house until we can figure out how to bring you all back here safely."

Jessica huffs and stalks away out of the kitchen. She's done with this conversation.

"Make yourself comfortable!" I call after her. I'm a little hurt that she's not a fan of my hospitality. Okay, maybe a lot hurt.

I make a little room for Kevin so that we can stand side-by-side and face the screen together.

"What about all the other players over there at the base? Are they still going home, too?" Kevin asks.

"Well, it's an interesting dilemma," Dekker admits. "It's clearly not safe to send people out of here. We are very concerned about certain proprietary information about our operation, and we are not ready to reveal it. Also, of course, there is the safety of all our players," he adds.

"Yeah, that guaranteed safety you like to talk about," I remind him.

"We can accommodate thousands of players in the game world here at this facility. What we have not planned for is storing them *outside* of their chambers," he admits.

"Well, you are inside a giant supply warehouse," I offer. "Maybe order a few thousand blankets and pillows on the Chum app and have them delivered to the conference room."

He smiles tightly. "We're working on that now, thank you."

"And add some delicious Salisbury steak frozen entrees," I add, rubbing it in. "If you need a drone coordinator to help with all the logistics, let me know, and I'll jump into action over here. Just put in a good word with my boss, will you?"

"That's very kind of you, John. I'll certainly reach out if we need you. We just may," he says mysteriously.

Loud engines suddenly roar down my street outside, and my heart skips a beat. Kevin jumps too, and Jessica runs right back into the kitchen with us.

"What's that?" she asks, on edge.

Dekker, however, is unfazed by the noise. "That must be the advance team. The other vehicles will arrive soon to secure the neighborhood. You're safe. In the meantime, North Fontana is in complete lockdown, both ground and air. I'm afraid Chum won't be able to make any deliveries there until tomorrow at the earliest. You'll have to make do with what supplies you have."

"That's okay," I say. "I should still have enough from my last shipment to last us all for a couple of days."

"Great," Dekker says. "Then my strong suggestion to you all is to hunker down and try to get some rest. The attack on our game infrastructure is stronger than we thought at first look. To be frank, we're having some difficulty overcoming it at the moment. But we have a great team, and we're reasonably confident we'll be able to get things back up and running in the next few days. I hope to see you all then. Dekker out."

The connection ends, and the tablet blinks back to the home screen. I set it on the table.

"Alright, gang, it looks like we've got some time to kill," I tell Kevin and Jessica. "Please make yourself at home here. Kevin, do you mind crashing on the couches out here in the living room with me?"

He nods.

"Jessica, you're welcome to take the bedroom."

"Thanks," she says evenly, and walks away.

Kevin and I exchange a glance. What's up with her?

"Up the stairs, second door on your right!" I call out. "Ignore the mess!"

I hear the stairs creaking. She's walking up.

"You're welcome to use the VR gear! I highly recommend *World of Moby*. You can start a free trial..."

The bedroom door slams shut. Even downstairs, we

can feel it as well as hear it.

Kevin and I look at each other. He holds up a cloth bag and pulls it open. Inside, there are a bunch of granola bars from the conference room.

"Movie night?" he asks, tossing me a Chum-Num. "I know it's not buttered popcorn, but it's close enough."

"Wow, Streets of Fire is...weird," I exclaim as the credits roll.

We watched the whole movie on my couch, setting up the tablet on the coffee table. I didn't have any spare credits, but Kevin logged into his own Chum account to rent it. We ate our granola bars on the couch and tried to ignore the frequent flashing lights and vehicle sounds out in the neighborhood. I peeked out my window at one point and saw giant armored tank-like vehicles with massive tire treads. They were rolling down the street slowly, definitely making their presence known. It really did make me feel safer.

"Yeah, see what I mean, man?" Kevin pushes. "It's this weird fifties and eighties mashup of music and style. The guy's got a shotgun, but he just uses it to shoot the motorcycles. It's pretty much all punching."

"I didn't realize that's where that Dan Hartman song, *I Can Dream About You*, came from," I offer. "Also, it's crazy all the things that beat 'em up games basically ripped right off from this movie." I shake my head. It's weird, finding some old media that rewrites what you thought you knew about your childhood. Puts it in a new perspective.

"This was one of our favorite movies in the Singleton household growing up," Kevin says. "Haven't seen it in years. It sorta holds up. Kinda."

Kevin moves over to the other couch across from me. He's taller, so he gets the longer one. He's already lying down and grabbing his blanket. It's early, maybe 9pm, but we've had a long day. That's a bit of an understatement. I'm exhausted, too.

"I, uh...haven't seen any movies in years. At all," I offer when Kevin settles in. My voice is quiet in the darkness. "Not since my brother died. I've just sort of stayed away from them. Never watched anything, never read anything but the news, just spent my free time playing the stupidest time-wasting games I could find. I kind of... I guess I kind of just shut it all down, on the inside."

Kevin turns over on the couch, making himself comfortable. With the tablet off and the room lights out, only the outside streetlight offers any illumination.

"I'm sorry, John. And I get it. Stories can get you in touch with your emotions, and that can be really hard to deal with. So you think if you turn off the stories, you can turn off your emotions. And you can. At least for a little while."

"Yeah," I agree. "You can only fool yourself for a while. Kevin, I'm... I'm grateful to have you as a partner, and as a friend."

"Me too, John."

A spinning light from a passing patrol car outside the window briefly illuminates Kevin's face. He's lying on his back, arms above him and hands criss-crossed under his pillow.

"In the morning," I say, stopping to yawn, "...we'll start planning our next moves when we get back in the game. You know, I always did want to write my own screenplays. Now, we get something even better. The chance to create our own adventure, and live it, too."

Kevin yawns as well. "Yeah," he agrees. "Not a bad way to make a living."

"Yeah," I mumble. The moment I finish saying the word, I'm asleep.

✪✪✪

I'm up. What's that noise? Ringing. It's a ringing sound.

My eyes peek open. It's my tablet. It's still pitch-black outside. I try to focus, and after a moment, I see that the tablet's screen reads 3:37am.

Kevin begins to rouse, too. The ringing noise is still blasting away. "Wha—" he mumbles thickly.

"Got a call," I mumble as I pull myself off the couch, spilling to the floor. I reach forward and swipe the tablet screen open to see who's calling at this ungodly hour. I assume Jessica is still asleep upstairs; I don't want to wake her. God knows how she'd react if I did.

The caller ID reads, "Unknown." I answer it, deciding not to turn the room lights on.

A video image pops up. I see a person's head and shoulders facing me, but the face is obscured. There's a filter that smudges out the features.

Then the voice speaks, "John. John, are you there?" It sounds all distorted, someone disguising their voice.

I pause for a moment, unsure. Finally, I ask, "What is this, *Dateline NBC*?"

The voice doesn't say anything, forcing me to cover the awkward silence by explaining my joke. "Because you're disguising your face and voice, like they do on the old newsmagazine show *Dateline*," I offer.

"It's still on the air," Kevin whispers from his couch.

"Is it really? Wait…" I say, shaking my head and turning away from Kevin to face the camera again. "Never mind. Who are you?"

"An ally. Although you don't think of me that way."

"I don't think I know you at all, buddy," I say, injecting a toughness into my words that I don't feel. Kevin is now behind me, hovering just over my shoulder, out of view.

"Are Kevin and Jessica with you right now?" the voice asks in its inhuman rumble.

"I don't know what the hell you're talking about," I reply.

Suddenly, a switch flips, and my living room is flooded with light. I'm clearly visible on the video screen.

"What the hell is going on?" It's Jessica, her voice thick with sleep, standing at the light switch across the room.

I sigh angrily. "Nice," I mutter under my breath.

"Jessica, Kevin, get over here, you'll want to see this, too," the voice says.

"What are you watching?" Jessica asks, suddenly wide awake now and walking over to us.

"What do you want?" I challenge the mystery voice as Kevin comes around to sit next to me.

"To get you back in the game," the voice says. "But we need your help to do it."

Jessica is now standing over Kevin and I, leaning over the couch behind us to look at the screen, while Kevin and I are both sitting on the floor between the couch and coffee table.

"We have no idea what you're talking about," Kevin says. Nice one, bro. Thanks for backing me up.

Suddenly, the perspective shifts on the screen. The faceless man—maybe it's a woman?—picks up the tablet and points it to their right. The image is handheld, but it stabilizes long enough for us to clearly see that it's a game chamber. My chamber. Scientists in white coats are working feverishly. Their faces are blurred out, too. The image swivels back to our mystery caller, who sits back down on a desk inside the lab. Whoever this is, they're all up in our business.

"Our fearless leader authorized me to reach out to you," the voice explains in its weird timbre. "We've identified the technical issue. The issue is that we were hacked, and the game grid was shut down with a computer virus."

"Oh, great, just what we need, another virus," I quip.

"What's more, this hack originated from inside our warehouse," the voice explains.

Kevin considers, "So you've got, like, an internal sabotage-type situation going on over there?"

The head on the screen nods. "Most likely. There

are powerful forces within the organization that want to see our entire enterprise fail. Furthermore, we have discovered that we are completely unable to remove this virus from our computers. It has effectively shut us out."

Jessica chimes in, "When can you fix it?"

The head shifts focus, seeming to look up at her. "We can't."

I'm worried that Jessica is going to slam this entire couch down onto our heads, but then the voice continues.

"But *you* can," the voice explains.

I look to Kevin, then up at Jessica. They're not saying anything. I look back to the screen. "What does that mean?" I ask.

"We can't hack back into our own system—we're locked out—but I've created a backdoor so that you can enter the system and neutralize the virus remotely."

I can't hear anything of what the voice actually sounds like, but there's something about it, maybe it's the speech pattern. I'm convinced that I know this person, I just don't know from where.

"We're not hackers!" I reply. "I'm a freaking drone coordinator. Kevin works in telemedicine! And Jessica is... Actually, I have no idea. What do you do for a living, Jessica?" I ask, turning around.

Jessica is silent for a moment, grinding her jaw, then she admits quietly, "I'm a doctor."

Kevin nods in respect. "Wow, congratulations."

I turn back to the screen. "So how are we supposed to hack into the system?"

The figure doesn't reply directly. Instead, the screen shifts. The lab environment disappears entirely, replaced by a black screen, then a wire-frame image of a grid draws into the frame. A very familiar grid.

It looks like my drone delivery screen. From work.

The weird computerized voice talks over this image. "You can hack in by doing something you already know how to do."

The icon of the main warehouse at the bottom of the screen begins blinking. This is where all my shipments start from and end at. It still looks like it normally does in my work interface, but now it's named, 'ANTIDOTE.'

A bunch of houses pop up on all the line intersections on the grid, dozens of residences populating the screen in the space of a few moments. But instead of displaying addresses, like it normally would, these houses are named 'TERMINAL 1,' 'TERMINAL 2,' etc. At a glance, I see that the numbers go as high as 128.

Finally, pirate flag icons begin to populate the lines of the grid, roving slowly between the houses, or terminals. Normally, this would be the way we knew that Scummer patrols were in the area, and we would do all we could to avoid them. Usually, there would be three or four at a time. But now, they continue to populate the screen until there are at least two dozen of them. Instead of 'HOSTILES,' the program is calling them 'VIRUS.'

"What the hell is this?" Jessica asks.

"John knows," the voice replies. "This is what he does every day for a living, coordinating drone delivery of supplies to the New Los Angeles settlements."

"What does that mean?" she presses.

"It means that we've created an interface where John can use his skills to avoid the virus and deliver the electronic antidote to our computer terminals in the server room. From your remote location, you can use your tablet to repair our game grid and get us back online."

I close my eyes and exhale deeply. This feels like a nightmare.

"It's okay, man, you got this," Kevin encourages quietly.

"What's the matter?" Jessica asks.

"I'm...kind of on a performance plan at work right now."

"He lost my shipment a few weeks ago," Kevin offers.

"OH, HELL NO!" Jessica grabs a giant cushion from the couch below her and throws it across the room. It slams into an end table lamp and shatters on the floor. Half the lights go out in the room.

"Jessica, please, we're guests in the man's house," Kevin exclaims.

"I'm sorry," she says, meaning it.

"Hey, I'm sorry, too!" I offer. "I was distracted. Unmotivated. But I'm definitely not either of those things now."

"You've got us now, too," Kevin encourages.

"Yes, you do, John, and you'll need them," the voice says. "This is too difficult for any one drone coordinator, even the very best. And you're far from the best."

"Hey!" I retort. "I'm pretty damn good when I want to be!"

The voice continues, ignoring me. "You'll need both Kevin and Jessica to spot you and guide your path. Do you have your VR hand controllers? Are they still paired with your tablet?"

"Uh...yes," I say, trying to remember where I left them. "Why?"

"Have Jessica and Kevin each grab one. They can use the controllers with the program to erect temporary barriers to the virus, while you focus on using the touchscreen and keypad to deliver the antidote."

"Okay..." My mind is racing now, thinking about strategy, thinking about the controllers, thinking about all of this and more at a hundred miles a minute. I force my mind to focus for a second, to remember where my hand controllers are.

"Jessica," I begin. "Can you go up to the bedroom and grab the hand controllers and bring them down? They're on my nightstand, next to the VR helmet."

She huffs and says, "I'm not your servant." But she's moving, fast, taking the steps three at a time.

"You're the one sleeping up there, jeez!" I yell after her, then I focus back on the screen, taking it all in, mapping possible pathways in my mind.

"This setup is like...asynchronous couch co-op multiplayer," I say, piecing together terms I've heard from the gaming podcasts I listen to.

"Something like that," the voice agrees. "We thought this would be the easiest and fastest way to succeed.

If we don't get this back up tonight, we run the risk of getting shut down permanently. Next thing you know, every single citizen in the Federation of Western States is getting six months of horse therapy instead. We know that we have the right path forward. Now, we have to prove it."

Jessica is back with the controllers, and she throws one to Kevin, the left one. That's very nice, she must remember that he's a southpaw, like Rocky Balboa. Or maybe she paid no attention at all, is just a selfish person, and wanted to keep the right one for herself. I have no idea. It's not like she'll say more than five words to me anyway.

The voice returns, noticing Jessica retake her place behind the couch. "Welcome back, Jessica. Alright, all of you, work together and support each other. I can only give you thirty minutes on our end to keep the channel open to finish your work. Good luck."

A timer appears in the lower left corner of the screen. Thirty minutes, zero seconds. It starts counting down immediately.

"Dateline? Hey, Dateline? Are you there?" I call, but there's no answer.

I look at my team. "Alright, guys, we can do this. Gather around and watch me make the delivery to this first terminal, and I'll teach you what to look for as we go."

✪✪✪

"Dammit!" I yell. My drone explodes in a digitized ball of light on the screen.

Jessica screams in frustration; she was a fraction of a second too late trying to intercept the virus with her controller.

Our first three runs have been a mess. I'm trying to teach as I go, moving the 'drones' from the 'antidote' stockpile to the 'terminals.'

But the 'virus' is proving to be a very slippery customer.

In real life, this job is much easier, because the roving Scummer gangs are much less frequent. They're much slower, too; it takes time to walk from real-life neighborhood to real-life neighborhood. But here in this game version, the patterns are much faster and more random.

"Jesus, John, your job feels like a damn video game," Jessica growls. It's not a compliment.

"I know!" I reply. "That's what I always say. It's, like, a commentary on society or whatever. Okay, let's try again. Get ready."

Kevin is on my left, Jessica is on my right, each of them watching their half of the screen like a hawk, waiting to see if any of the viruses get close, or somehow double-back to threaten a shipment.

"Here we go!" I cry, pushing the next drone forward. I move it steadily from node to node, moving up the grid to the first available terminal.

Suddenly, a virus strand on my right that had been squiggling around in a tight circle breaks free and makes a beeline directly toward my ship.

Jessica yells in surprise and lashes out with her

motion controller. This time, her timing is perfect. There's a flash of light on the screen, and the virus zags away to the far corner just as I land my drone on the terminal.

"We did it!" Kevin yells, laughing.

I allow myself to be happy for a moment. "Nice job, Jessica. Okay, let's do the next one."

✪✪✪

One minute left. One terminal left.

It's the one that's farthest away on the map, of course—all the way at the top of the screen—but we should have enough time to get there. If just about everything goes right, we'll have this in the bag.

But if we screw this up, it's Game Over. There'll be no going back to New Arcadia.

I really want to go back. And I know Kevin and Jessica want that, too. Hell, Jessica *needs* to get back, to try to save her sister with that experimental treatment. The stakes can't get clearer than that. I think we're all fighting for her now.

"On your left!" Kevin cries, but it's too late. The virus is just too fast. My drone explodes.

"Dammit!" Jessica yells.

"It's okay!" I tell her, quickly wiping my sweaty palms on my pajamas, then returning my fingers to the touchscreen. "We still have one more ship online."

"Then we'll just have to make it count. Pretend you're back in West Diamond Bar," Kevin says.

"In my mind, I'm always in West Diamond Bar," I quip. "It's, like, a state of mind, man."

"Just picture me sitting there in my little house. Papa needs his tube socks and reduced-fat Triscuits."

"I got you buddy," I reply.

"You guys are dorks," Jessica says as she swipes at an incoming virus with her controller like a pro. The well-placed shield sends it skittering away toward the periphery. She's come a long way in this last half-hour. Kevin has, too.

"Thank you, Doctor. Time check?" I ask, not daring to risk even a glance down at the timer while I deftly snake in and out of the incoming virus storm.

"Forty seconds left," Jessica calls out, tension in her voice.

"Gah!" I yell, narrowly missing a virus that suddenly goes crazy and zigzags toward me.

I straighten the ship again, try to fly it dead on to the final target at the top of the screen.

"*Use the Force, Luke,*" Kevin says quietly, in a vaguely robotic voice.

"Jesus, you guys are *real* dorks," Jessica says as she smacks away another virus. She's right, because I know from Kevin's telltale delivery that he's not just referencing *the movie Star Wars*, and Obi-Wan Kenobi's classic intonation to Luke Skywalker, he's referencing the 1983 *arcade game* version of the *Star Wars* trench run, featuring an early primitive synthesized voice sample.

But it works. It calms me down. I remember to take a deep breath, centering myself for the final run.

I know how to do this. This is my job, and I'm good

at my job. Use the damned Force.

Seconds to go. Is it enough to simply make the last delivery, or am I supposed to make it all the way back to the warehouse before the timer is up? If this were real life, I'd need to get back to the warehouse before I could clock out, but now I think all that matters is that I release the payload.

Suddenly, a robotic voice chimes in. It's not Kevin playing around again, it's coming from the tablet, counting down, "Five...four..."

I'm on the final approach. Kevin and Jessica are battling viruses on both flanks. Then a new virus suddenly zags straight toward me from above.

It's actually *two* virus strands, because they start snaking in and out of each other as they bear down. The little pirate flag icons are both right between my ship and the final terminal.

I should veer away, but there's no time. I shoot straight up instead, staying on target. At the last moment, the two virus strands break apart.

"Three...two..."

I steer the ship home between them and release the payload.

"One. OBJECTIVE COMPLETE," the robot voice intones.

"YES!" I scream.

Kevin and Jessica scream too, raising their arms in triumph. Kevin high-fives me. Jessica lets me high-five her. It's thrilling.

We're still laughing, patting each other on the back. After a few moments, the screen changes.

It's Dekker. He's smiling. A real smile, I've never seen that before.

"Great job, gang," he tells us.

He appears to be in his office, talking to us through a webcam on his desk.

"Thanks!" Kevin and I both say, more or less at the same time.

"Did we fix it?" Jessica asks, going right to business.

"Yes, you most certainly did fix it. We have full access again, and all appears to be well. There are still a few hours of diagnostics and tests to run, but we should be able to get you back inside the game in the morning."

He looks up, past the webcam, at somebody out of frame, probably at his door.

"Ten AM," a voice says quietly.

Dekker nods and looks back to us. "I don't know if you heard that, but we can open for business at ten AM. We'll pick you up at nine. Right now, it's..." He swipes at the screen, briefly obscuring our view with his finger.

"Oh god, it's four in the morning," he says, rubbing his forehead with his other hand. In that moment, he looks truly exhausted. "Well, get some sleep, if you can, and please take showers before we pick you up. If all goes well, you'll be back in the game world for a rather long time."

Chapter 27

The Center

Back again.

Fuller Avenue and 174th Street, Satan's Pantry, New Arcadia. The sun is shining, and people are out. It's another beautiful day in the city.

To my left, Kevin fades in. It looks like when people get beamed down on *Star Trek*, but sounds instead like an electric guitar riffing on a single distorted note. Huh. So that's what happens when you come into the game world. I don't see or hear any of that when I beam in myself.

Then Jessica fades in the same way on my right. Kevin and I are both still wearing our hazmat suits. Jessica is still dressed in her Drug X lab uniform from the warehouse. We've got to change out of these clothes quick.

"Fancy meeting you both here," I say in greeting.

"Been a while," Kevin kids.

I look around a bit. The neighborhood basically appears the same at a glance, but still, something feels off.

"That building is gone," Jessica says, pointing ahead of us.

Sure enough, the building two doors down from the Burger Item is just...gone. I don't remember what it looked like before. It had blended right in, so it was probably another three-story walkup with a shop on the ground floor. But now, it's just a big hole between two buildings, with a hastily constructed fence out front on the sidewalk.

Looking around, a few other buildings have boarded-up windows. One has scaffolding set up around a damaged brick wall. All the streetlights are blinking, like the power just came back on.

"What the hell happened here?" Kevin breathes out, confused.

I look down and see a newspaper vending machine at my waist. I lean back and give it a sharp, easy kick. The door snaps open. I swipe the top paper off the rack and hold it up.

"New Arcadia Struck By 6.0 Earthquake," the headline blares in bold type.

"Uh, guys," I begin, but they've already seen it. Jessica snatches the paper from my hands.

"Hey!" I yell, surprised.

She reads aloud, "Yesterday afternoon, New Arcadia was struck by a six-point-oh magnitude earthquake. Although many windows were shattered, and store shelves knocked down, the greater metropolitan area largely escaped intact, with only a dozen buildings reportedly suffering structural damage."

Kevin whistles and mutters, "Could have been worse."

Jessica continues reading, "Mayor M. Buffalo has authorized use of emergency resources for citizens affected by the damage, while saying that this does not pause efforts to get control over the scourge of the Drug X invasion for the city." She scans it for a bit longer silently, then lets the paper drop into a trashcan below her.

"Hey," I complain. "I was gonna read that."

"Help yourself," she says.

But I'm already turning, looking across the street to spot the familiar neighborhood park. This is the image I had in my mind late last night. Imagining I was back over there calmed me down, let me finally get back to sleep for a bit. The park looks exactly the same, nothing seems to be damaged. In fact, it looks better than ever.

In a trance, I start walking over slowly. Kevin eventually jogs up alongside me. I'm not sure if Jessica is following, but I'm not going far.

"Hey, Blaze, shouldn't we start working on our characters?" Kevin offers.

"Yeah, that's just what I was thinking," I agree, then sit on my favorite park bench to do just that. Jessica sits on the other side, and Kevin hunkers down on the grass.

"This feels nice," he says, running his fingers through the green grass.

"What are we doing?" Jessica asks.

"You know, checking our character stats," I explain. "Dorky stuff."

✪✪✪

I flick the switch. The sound echoes through the cavernous space.

A long moment later, ceiling lights flash on across a large brick room. They buzz, flicker, and finally stay lit.

The three of us stand dead center, taking it all in. We're all back in our street fighter clothes. I'm wearing my cool new arm vambraces, Kevin's wearing his tank top, and Jessica's wearing a leather jacket and a leopard-print leotard.

The big room is mostly empty, but some equipment is still here, and a few exercise mats are scattered about.

"This place sucks," Jessica says.

"It's a fixer-upper," Kevin hedges.

I say, "We've got a bit of work to do, but we can build this up." I raise my voice, so it carries to the far corner of the gym. "Hey, Big Louise, what do you think?"

A tiny head pops out from the far door. "Once we punch these huge rats, this place will be in pretty good shape!" A hand pops in below her head in the door frame. It's giving an enthusiastic thumbs-up.

"Okay, save some for us to punch, thanks!" I call out.

"No problemo, I'm just gonna clear a path to the little girls' room," she calls out, then ducks her head back behind the door. We hear a series of progressively fading "HA" sounds, followed immediately by loud smacks and the distressed squealing of rodents.

Jessica steps forward, running her finger along a nearby weight set, covered in dust. She examines her finger and flicks the dust away, frowning. "So let me see if I've got this right. We pool all the money we have, and then we buy the deed to this gym. It becomes our home base, but also a base for other fighters like us."

Kevin chimes in, "And for the neighborhood at large. Like a community center. For punching."

I add, "For us to fight against the Drug X menace, and to build bodies and minds for the future. We've got to track down specialized trainers for us, too. Fist of the Pissed for me, Zen Crusher for Iceman, and you need... uh..." I have no idea what her fighting style is.

She declines to answer. "This will be a place to bring the city together," she summarizes instead. Keeping her air of mystery, I guess. Well, lah-dee-dah.

Jessica crosses over to a dirty folding table near one wall, and a prompt appears above the table. It's only in front of her, not us, but we can see this one too, so we walk over to join her.

COMMUNITY CENTER / HOME BASE.

DO YOU WANT TO PURCHASE? YES / NO.

$700 MONTHLY

We all reach into our fanny packs and pull out bills. Jessica collects them and consolidates them into one big wad of dough. We encourage her, and she looks back toward the prompt.

YES

The text box turns into a congratulatory screen.

BASE UNLOCKED

Invisible guitars squeal all around us. The sound is more than a little dated, but it's still pretty bad-ass.

"Congratulations, everybody!" I say, grinning.

Kevin slaps his hands together and laughs. "Break out the champagne!"

"Oh, shoot, I didn't think to get any!" I say.

Jessica walks over to a nearby punching bag. "Well, we can still christen this place."

Kevin and I nod and take up our places in a perfect triangle around the bag.

"You know, our work is just beginning here," I say. "We've got a lot of enemies—more street gangs, and even other players, like that Brice joker. I owe that guy a big knuckle sandwich, and I intend to serve it up piping hot."

"And don't forget the bigger picture. We've got to get down to the docks for tomorrow night's Drug X shipment," Kevin says. "That's where Stage 2 begins."

"We will," Jessica says, gently spinning the bag and considering. "And we'll kick their asses."

We smile, then rear back in unison, fists drawn back.

"To the Elementals!" I intone.

"To the Elementals!" Kevin agrees.

"I am not changing my name to Thundara, and we are not naming our gang The Elementals, and we still need to talk about all of this," Jessica argues.

The punching bag before us squeaks gently as it slowly spins to a stop, the only sound in the large room.

"Whatever!" I finally exclaim.

"Whatever!" Kevin agrees.

Jessica looks at us both and smiles crookedly, but she's genuinely amused. I can tell. "To whatever may come."

This is it, our big chance. We can do this, and we can do it by working together.

We stand in our perfect triangle, here in our new home base, and aim our fists dead center at the bag.

POW.

Epilogue

From the Journal of Lucas Dekker
Thursday, May 11ᵗʰ

The game is back on. Although its return came at a considerable cost.

We don't have specific proof, but all signs point to the shipping division shutting us down—also known as the drone department.

Our operation is sealed tight, but somehow, they got through our defenses. Maybe they breached the company intranet, maybe they got in through a janitor, I don't know. But we'll find out.

It was beyond infuriating to have to present this update to the board. I had to stand there in front of all the other division VPs and announce that while our game has made great progress—incredible progress, really—unfortunately our servers had been disabled, and we were completely offline.

And what's worse, our drivers Johnson and Stevens

were apprehended by itinerant rebels transporting our beta test subjects back to their homes. That is to say, the Scummers kidnapped our drivers and were holding them for ransom. They advised us that they wanted a piece of whatever was going on with our operation or the hostages would be terminated.

Well, you can imagine how all of this news was received by the Chum top brass. They were ready to pull the plug on us. No more of this Project X. It's too expensive. Too dangerous. How could this possibly save our society. All of that nonsense.

The thing that galled me the most was when my counterpart, Arlo Masterson from shipping, spoke up. He suggested that if we were somehow able to repair the server damage, we should incorporate the Scummers into our game world. That it would be the ultimate test to see if my vision for a restored society could be realized.

It was then that I knew that he was behind the server sabotage. Possibly even behind the Scummer attack, as well. Perhaps he's even feeding them information.

Regardless, the Chum board leapt at his idea, and they quickly agreed on a new course of action. To save Johnson and Stevens, we would offer ten spots to the Scummers in our next onboarding session for the game— pending restoration of the game world, of course.

Thank god John Chambers and the others were able to pull together and help us from home. Now we need them to perform in the game world as well.

To be forced to bring in Scummers from the outside could destabilize and ruin all that we've worked for. They want to bring down our whole system, so their presence in the game world could destroy the fragile cooperation among the fragile society that is beginning to form there.

I was very clear about all of this, and yet the board has overruled me, and they have definitively decided: Scummers are going into New Arcadia to play our game.

But I can make sure that they won't be alone in there. It's high time for the mayor to initiate a city-wide crackdown.

They are preparing my chamber right now.

Tomorrow morning, I'm going in.

Acknowledgments

I wrote this book, but I didn't do it alone.

My name may be on the cover, and I may have typed all of these words, but I sure had a lot of help along the way.

Like the world of New Arcadia itself, crafting the story and delivering it to the world takes a community, all working together.

Only with much less punching, in this case.

This project began development at Audible in 2018, in a very different form. My thanks to Morgan Jones, who helped us develop the project there. Huge thanks also to my writing partner Justin Michael. Together we were able to work out the rules and realities of living in a beat 'em up world; and although the book eventually spun out into an entirely new story, it was invaluable to have laid a foundation well before I started typing Chapter 1.

In March of 2020, I had set aside a week to travel to a cabin in Big Sur and begin writing the first draft of the novel. I never made it, because two days before the trip I got sick with a mystery viral illness. Many weeks later, I was finally feeling well enough to start writing again, and as soon as I could, I wasted no time in setting words to the page. My thanks to the team at LivingWriter, the online platform I used to craft the novel.

Even though we may be physically apart in these times, I'm so grateful that many of my dear friends and colleagues were able to work with me online to tell this story.

I want to thank my alpha readers. They read early chapters of the book in the summer of 2020, and provided invaluable feedback. Cindy Koepp zeroed in on the details, and hugely improved my writing as a result. Author S.L. Rowland was a giant help as I got started. He's a great author, and I'm proud to narrate his series Sentenced to Troll. In addition to reading and giving feedback, he helped a great deal in terms of how I should approach publishing, and how to get the book off the ground. Finally, my dear friend Kelly Campbell was an early cheerleader of the project, and it was a big help when I was finishing the first draft, knowing that someone was very invested in how the story would end. Hearing positive feedback from all of them gave me the encouragement to keep moving.

The book was written between June and September 2020, and then it was off to the beta readers. Thanks to their feedback, they helped me understand the story better, make adjustments where needed, and let me know when I was on the right track. My huge thanks and gratitude to Tara Sands, Suzanne Elise Freeman, Melissa Wotkyns, Jordan Morris, Mike Sacks, Neil Hellegers, D.C. Pierson, Justin Michael, Liana Allday, and Seth Allen. During this time, Camilla Ochlan also gave great advice on publishing and storytelling.

The book was revised in October and November 2020, and I want to thank Mia at LKJ Books for doing an incredible job with the edit. She worked fast, knowing that we were going into the audiobook record at the beginning of December, and her work is excellent.

Our cover artist is the great Danielle Deschenes. I had previously worked with her for the audiobook versions of Stinker Lets Loose! and Passable in Pink, and she did incredible work bringing the world of New Arcadia to life. I didn't even know that I wanted a neon 90s future-scape instead of a realistic representation of the Mojave Desert, but it turns out I really, really did.

I have narrated nearly 300 audiobooks, but this is the first time I've ever actually written one. I want to thank the authors of all the books I've performed over the last eight years, because in working with their texts so closely and completely, I've learned invaluable lessons about how to communicate a story through the written word.

In December 2020, we began recording the audiobook. I'm an audiobook narrator myself, so I knew I was writing a main character that I could play. I was also writing in first-person, so that the listener experience would be immediate - like you're inside their head, seeing what they see, feeling what they feel.

But I knew I needed help. And as a producer and director of many multi-cast audio projects, I wanted to bring some of my favorite people into the mix as well.

I wrote all of the roles in the book with a performer in mind. It made the writing easier, and I think it improved it as well, simply because I could imagine them working with the material and bringing their myriad talents to it. I'm so grateful to have them all agree to be a part of this.

My huge thanks to our incredible audiobook cast: Matthew Mercer, Dave Fennoy, Erika Ishii, Sam Riegel, Betsy Sodaro, Dana Snyder, Andy Merrill, Justin Michael, Marin Ireland, D.C. Pierson, Tara Sands, Suzanne Elise Freeman, Scott Brick, P.J. Ochlan, Johnny Heller, Neil Hellegers, Ron Butler, and John DiMaggio.

Many thanks also to Tom Lawless at Vox, Inc., Sax Carr at Bohemia Group, and Richard Larkin at SAG-AFTRA.

On the post-production side, it was my great fortune to be able to partner with the great team at Mumble Media. They did all post and sound design for the audiobook. I've worked with them on several Audible Originals, and it was a true delight to team up again for this one. My thanks and gratitude to Mumble Media's Jake Young, Jaymeson Catsouphes, and Renée Vargas.

Lloyd Cole is one of my very favorite musical artists of all time. I've enjoyed his songwriting for years, going back to his work with Lloyd Cole and the Commotions in the 1980s. In recent years, he's expanded into electronic music, and his work was a big inspiration as I wrote the book. It was a true honor to have Lloyd compose and perform the main theme for New Arcadia. Please check out his work at www.lloydcole.com. My thanks to Lloyd, and to his manager David Whitehead at Maine Road Management.

Casey Trela is an incredible composer. I've previously worked with him on our all-improvised audiobook, Bad Reception. He's an accomplished chiptune artist, so I knew he would be perfect to bring the blips and bleeps of the arcade into the world of New Arcadia. Casey's soundtrack is the perfect accompaniment to the gritty

16-bit nights in New Arcadia.

Jeff Cappleman created a fantastic trailer for the Sentenced to Troll audiobooks, and I knew I wanted to work with him on this book. He's created two awesome video trailers that suck you into the world of New Arcadia. My huge thanks to him, as well!

I also want to give huge thanks to my mom and dad. They're incredible people, and they've been so supportive of me and my creative work since I was very small. Growing up in the 80s and 90s, they made sure our household was stocked with great movies and cool video games for us to play...after we did our homework, of course. Thanks also to my brother Ryan, whose devotion to the giant Roger Ebert movie book as a kid inspired a big part of this story. It's been great to stay in touch with them via phone during this time, but I hope we can all see each other again in person soon.

A huge thank you to Tara Sands. She's been with me through the whole project, patiently listening, and helping with very smart suggestions and advice. She's been a reader, a cast member, a sounding board and a cheerleader throughout the project, and I'm so very grateful and appreciative. Thank you, love.

Finally, big thanks and gratitude to YOU for reading and/or listening! Stage One is now complete, and there's more to come in the world of New Arcadia.

Eric Jason Martin
January 15th, 2021

About the Author

Eric Jason Martin is a producer, director, and voice performer based in Los Angeles. He is the AudioFile Earphones and Audie Award–winning narrator of over 250 audiobooks, including works by Kurt Vonnegut, David Foster Wallace, Karin Slaughter, and Lee Child. He has also narrated over 350 feature articles for the New York Times and Audm, including Michael Chabon's stories for the New Yorker, as well as stories for Wired, The Atlantic, and Rolling Stone.

Eric has produced and directed a number of original audio productions. In 2016, he produced a documentary of Tenacious D for Stitcher Premium, featuring Jack Black and Kyle Gass. Later that year, he and Justin Michael co-wrote and co-directed the original scripted audio series Hoot Gibson: Vegas Cowboy, starring Andy Daly, and featuring Weird Al Yankovic, Rachel Bloom, and Paul F. Tompkins. In 2018, he re-teamed with Justin Michael to create the fully-improvised Audible Original Bad Reception, also starring D'Arcy Carden, Kyle Mooney, Lauren Lapkus, Nicole Byer, and many more.

In 2018, Eric produced, directed, and narrated the Audible Original Stinker Lets Loose!, written by Mike Sacks. The audiobook was a New York Times Monthly Bestseller, starring Jon Hamm, Rhea Seehorn, and Philip

Baker Hall. For the release, the show's cast reunited in San Francisco to perform a sold-out live performance at the Castro Theater for SF Sketchfest. Eric then re-teamed with Sacks for the Audible Original Passable in Pink in 2019, starring Gillian Jacobs, Adam Scott, Bobby Moynihan, and Bob Odenkirk.

He directed and co-starred in the musical comedy series Heads Will Roll for Broadway Video and Audible, created by and starring Kate McKinnon and Emily Lynne, also starring Meryl Streep and Peter Dinklage. Eric also directed and co-starred in Maximum Fun's scripted fiction podcast Bubble, written by Jordan Morris, featuring John Hodgman, Judy Greer, and original songs from Jonathan Coulton and Lisa Loeb. The show received the Best of the Year award from Apple, and is now in development as an animated feature film with Seth Rogen and Evan Goldberg's Point Grey Pictures.

Eric is a lifelong arcade and pinball enthusiast, and he started podcasting about video games in 2005. New Arcadia: Stage One is his first novel.